The Pirate Wore White

The Laced Ladies of Black Point Series:

Book #1

Best Selling & Award Winning Author

Lisa A. Olech

The Pirate Wore White
The Laced Ladies of Black Point Series, Book #1

COPYRIGHT © 2021 by Lisa A. Olech
ASIN: B09KG4XCV1
ISBN: 979-8-9851921-0-0

Contact Information: lisa@lisaolech.com

Cover by Olech Designs

About The Pirate Wore White

AS THE DAUGHTER OF A PIRATE, THE SEA WAS HER DESTINY. BUT WILL IT TAKE A BATTLE AGAINST THE MAN SHE LOVES TO LAY CLAIM TO HER FUTURE?

ALICIA STEELE is the daughter of a pirate. Adventure is what she craves. It's in her blood. Escaping a loveless marriage and eager to claim her destiny, she travels across the wide ocean to the elegant coastal village of North Carolina known as Black Point, where, by pure grit and determination, Alicia claims her heritage as a captain.

RICHARD DUNBAR is adrift. After the ship he was charged to protect was stolen and he unceremoniously tied naked to the dock by those doing the stealing, his disgrace and dismissal from the British Navy was guaranteed. It's only because of his father's money he wasn't cast aside by society, as well. Too rich to ignore, too poor to matter, Richard finds his only solace at the bottom of a cut-crystal bottle of the finest brandy. And now he's forced by social protocol to watch his best friend's sister, the "forbidden" girl who's stolen his heart, walk down the aisle to marry some prig. It's more than one man should have to bear.

But when Alicia vanishes, it's Richard who sets out to find her with a promise to her family he will bring her back and stay sober until he does. Traveling clear across an entire ocean, he finds her… at least she looks the same and answers to Alicia, but what he finds is a once-pampered society woman hell-bent on following some foolish notion of becoming a pirate come hell or high water… or in her case, both.

Dedication

To the dreamers and the doers, and those who support them.

And to my beautiful family—my safe harbor and my fair seas.

I love you so much.

Chapter 1

Weatherington, England - 1721

"Aren't you supposed to be strangling flowers walking down an aisle?"

Alicia Steele let out a gasp. "Bloody hell!" She glared at him. "Ducky. You arse. Dammit, you scared the shite out of me." She shot a nervous glance over one shoulder.

"Still cursing like a cuckolded sailor, I see. Is that any language for a proper lady?" He cranked an eyebrow.

"It is when I'm talking to *you*." Alicia clutched a hand to her stomach to catch her breath in a corset laced so brutally, her breasts were in danger of reaching her chin. Hadn't she been poked and prodded enough for one day? Wasn't it enough that she was going through with this ridiculous wedding? She stifled a scream. "Leave me alone." Alicia jerked the heavy fabric of her skirts a bit higher and took another step. Her mother had threatened her life should she dirty the blasted hems.

The last few weeks of endless planning had turned Alicia into a short-tempered shrew. The weight of impending doom clutched at her like this bloody gown. She'd been battling against bouts of panic for days. With the minutes ticking by, she was losing her grip. Of course, Ducky would be the one to witness her unhinging. Alicia shot him a scathing look.

Richard "Ducky" Dunbar leaned a broad shoulder against the trunk of a large elm. One booted foot crossed over the other. The picture of an uncompromising rake. Unless you knew him, and Alicia did. And unless you didn't notice the near empty bottle of brandy dangling from his fingertips.

"Why are you still loitering about out here? Aren't you afraid you'll miss the grand coronation?" Sarcasm soured in her mouth.

Richard turned his gaze back toward the great manor house before taking another pull off his bottle. "Couldn't breathe in there. Did your blessed mother leave a single bloody flower unarranged in all of England?"

Shaking her head, Alicia followed his gaze. "I know…" She drew another constricted breath. "What did you expect?" Alicia held her arms wide. The gown seemed to drag her closer to the ground. She jerked it off the garden stones once more. It was a hideous creation. With so much froth and ruffles of shimmering white satin, she looked like a huge dollop of meringue. The only concession to the outfit was the stunning Chantilly lace veil sent to her from the colonies by her friend Jocelyn Robbins. The delicate weave was exquisite. Alicia had never worn anything so beautiful. As for the rest… "Only daughter hooked a Duke."

"Every mother's dream." Richard raised his bottle in a mocking salute. "Bravo."

"Mother's been beside herself with joy since Frederick asked for my hand. It's all she's ever wanted. She's been planning this elaborate fiasco for better than six months."

"The proper storybook ending. Each perfect detail. Your

mother's outdone herself."

"It's the wedding she never had. Remember? She and father were married by a one-legged cook in the belly of a pirate ship."

"Ah yes, the *Scarlet Night*." Richard curled his lip and spit the words. "Seems that wretched ship continues to curse us all one way or another."

Alicia grimaced. The *Scarlet Night* had been her father's ship. Captain Jaxon Steele was a successful privateer more than thirty years ago. Later, her brother James, also a Captain but for the British Navy, was ordered to round up errant pirates fleeing the King's command to surrender their ships and crews to the crown. To James' horror, the *Scarlet Night* was among those seized. And to Richard's horror, it was that exact ship, which was stolen back under the nose of the British Navy by those very same errant pirates. Mere mention of her ruby decks sent Richard into a temper.

Alicia's impassioned defense of Richard's role hadn't changed the outcome. The ship was gone, and his naval career was over.

"It wasn't fair to place all the blame on you."

"I was Senior Officer on Duty. Your sainted brother was off marrying Samantha. He left me in charge." Richard pushed away from the tree and tipped the bottle to his lips. "I don't even blame the bastards for stealing back their cursed ship, but did they have to tie me to the blasted docks with me bollocks catching the breeze?"

The mental image of him lashed to a pier, in nothing but a blindfold and his hat, had Alicia biting the inside of her lip. It wasn't comical, but oh, to have seen the sight. She pressed her lips together and adopted a proper somber tone. "You landed on your feet after your discharge. Dishonorable or not, you're now living a life of ease."

Richard gave a bitter laugh. "Ah yes, thanks to father's money. Too rich to ignore, too poor to notice." Richard pointed the neck of his bottle back toward the church. "Not like your Duke Freddy Big Nob."

"*Bi-neau*, Frederick Bineau."

"A thousand pardons." He sneered before bending into a shaky bow.

Insufferable man. "I wouldn't throw around nicknames so casually, *Richard*."

Capturing her with an impertinent gaze, he stepped closer. "Oh, I beg you…call me 'Ducky' once more, for old time's sake?"

Alicia notched her chin as a wave of emotion washed over her. It was a stupid name from his time at Eton. A leftover of days long past. But it brought back all the memories of her ridiculous crush. Losing her heart in foolish daydreams of running away with him only to have him cast her aside.

"I only call you "Ducky" now to irk you."

"You could never irk me." A low rasp to his voice raised gooseflesh on her skin as his gaze raked over her. "Beguile me, perhaps, but never irk me." His eyes held hers for a heartbeat too long.

The little air in her lungs left in a gasp. Heat rushed to her cheeks, but she refused to look away. "Don't speak to me like that," she whispered. Old feelings welled in her. The striking image of him flashed in her memory. Emerging from a carriage like a prince. His golden hair capturing the glint of the sun had caused her breath to still in her throat. Handsome, crisp uniform, tall polished boots, pristine white neck stock.

And then he smiled, and for a brief moment, the rest of the world simply stopped. Was it any wonder she'd lost her heart?

Richard was unlike any man she'd known. Full of daring and adventure. He carried the swagger of easy confidence. A helpless philanderer. A rogue. Fawned over her mother, completely enamored, and wouldn't have noticed Alicia back then if she'd been set aflame at his feet.

Except for that one kiss.

"Why not?" His words snapped her back to the present. Why was he toying with her emotions today, of all days? His closeness laid siege to her resolve as the memory of that single kiss rushed more warmth to her cheeks.

Alicia pressed a hand against the stiff bodice of her gown and fought to pull a decent breath. "You're my brother's friend, for one. And, two." She cast a glance back toward the house. "There are three hundred people stuffed into a chapel, waiting to watch me drag myself up the aisle."

Richard turned away and took another drink. "Two hundred, ninety-nine," he muttered.

"What?"

"Two hundred, ninety-nine." He tipped the bottle in her direction. "I won't be watching you."

The churning of her emotions swelled and crested to anger. Why should she care? She didn't, damn him. He could drink his way straight to hell.

The shrew was back.

"Good," she snapped. "I didn't want you there to begin with. I don't know why we wasted an invitation. If you think I care a wit about some…some…" Alicia wagged a finger toward him.

"Drunken sot?" he offered.

She turned her back on him in disgust, "Your words." Alicia closed her eyes at the growing ache in her chest and the dull pain gathering at the base of her skull. "Why can't you just leave me alone?" She fingered the fragile edge of her veil.

Silence hung behind her. *Had he left?* Thoughts warred in her, confusing her even more, but she refused to look back. *Let him go.* She'd given up caring about Richard Dunbar a long time ag—

"Don't I at least get to kiss the bride?"

Alicia spun as far as her iron-anchor of a dress would allow. He was dangerously close. "You're drunk."

"Not nearly enough," he murmured. He held her gaze before dropping his to her mouth, her throat, the rapid rise and fall of her breasts. Another step closed the space between them. "It's considered lucky, am I right?"

He focused on her lips while her heart tried its best to break through a prison of corset stays. Alicia opened her mouth to object, but no sound came out.

"Nothing to say?" he taunted. "No blistering remarks? No cursing? Has true love for your Duke claimed all your passion?" Richard reached out and caught her chin with his finger and tipped her mouth toward his. She could smell the brandy on his breath. Feel the heat of him. See the flecks of silver in his eyes. "Perhaps you'll make a proper wife, after all."

The veiled insult skittered over her skin. He was far too close to have his words penetrate her brain. *Stop talking, damn you, and kiss me.* Alicia closed her eyes and laid a hand on the silk of his cravat.

When he tipped her chin down and brushed her forehead with his lips, a shroud of ice encircled her heart.

"Best wishes, little Alicia. May you have a fine, rich life with the man of your dreams." He murmured against her brow before stepping back and walking away.

Little Alicia? Little Alicia! Anger shoved aside the ache in her chest. Tears belied the fury that blazed through her. She scrubbed the patronizing kiss from her forehead with the heel of her hand.

"Damn you!" And damn her foolish heart for blinding her, once more. "Keep your '*best wishes*,'" she railed at his retreating back. "What would you know of my wishes or my dreams? Yours are floating face down at the bottom of a bottle. The only rich life you'll ever have is with your drunken arse roped to a bloody pier!"

Alicia tried to storm off in the opposite direction, but her gown had rooted itself to the ground. She pressed a hand to her rib cage as a sob escaped her throat. "Damn you, *Ducky* Dunbar, and damn this blasted, bloody dress."

She covered her eyes and fought the flood of hot tears that would surely drown her if she let them breach the crumbling wall of her control. Her anger at Richard fueled another bout of panic. She couldn't breathe as his parting words swirled like a storm through her mind.

Rich, full life? Man of her dreams? Richard knew nothing. Not about her life or her dreams. How dare he presume to know what she wanted?

Frederick Bineau *was* a good man. A Duke. Handsome. Gentile and reserved. Society's ideal. He'd been nothing but patient, understanding, and sensitive. He was everything her mother wanted for her. Everything any other young woman would kill for. Respectability. Social standing. Security. She'd want for nothing. Well, almost nothing.

He wasn't the most…attentive man. They had barely held hands. Today's kiss would be their first. Frederick felt it would be best to wait until they were married to explore their physical relationship. He'd been almost relieved when Alicia confessed before accepting his proposal to her unfortunate decision to give her innocence to the wrong man years before. *"Deflowering virgins is such a distasteful task."* What might have precluded a union with most men, was a blessing it seemed to Frederick.

Alicia couldn't foresee a life with Frederick overflowing with passion. If her limited experience was any indication, she wouldn't be missing a great deal. But love? Love was something else again.

Her thoughts returned to Richard. She'd been so in love with him and wanted that feeling again. This time, of course, with a man who would love her in return. She prayed it would come in time with Frederick. Her mother told her this was often the way of things. Couples' affection could bloom and grow into something quite acceptable after they were wed. In the meantime, she and Frederick held each other in fond regard. That was enough for now…wasn't it?

The nagging doubt she'd battled for weeks crept in again.

Alicia lifted her chin and stood tall. *I can do this.* She could do anything when she set her mind to it. Look beyond the physical. Be a proper wife. A refined lady. Curbing her tongue, quieting her temper. How difficult could it be? She could be docile. Tamed. Meek. Properly restrained… Her breath caught on her ribs. *Properly boring.*

Alicia tried to bend at the waist and fought to draw a proper breath. Panic wrapped her chest tighter than her corset. Looking down at wide hems of pure white satin pushed her over the edge. *What was wrong with me? I can't marry Frederick. A bloody Duke?* When had she ever been able to hold her tongue? *I'm not meek. I am the very opposite of meek!* Father called her stubborn, opinionated, and headstrong. Brash. Impetuous. She was a Steele.

Father loved her fire, but she'd lay bet that Frederick wouldn't appreciate those qualities in a wife. If love and desire did come, Frederick would never truly love her. Not the real her. How long could she pretend to be someone she wasn't?

Their marriage was doomed to wreck upon the rocks before they even said their "I do's." This wasn't what she wanted, and it wasn't as if she could walk into that chapel and say, "I don't." in front of all those people? It would kill her mother, and Frederick deserved better. *She* deserved better.

Aye, better. More. New experiences. Excitement. Passion. Seeing the world beyond the safe, sheltered village of Weatherington. How could she have convinced herself that she could live a life of quiet tea parties during the endless hours of the day, followed by long nights lying next to a man she didn't love? Who didn't touch her? That was just the kind of rich, full restrained life that would kill her.

"I can't do this." Alicia gathered up the length of her veil. The garden, the gown, her life, and her future all at once became claustrophobic. She yanked at a sleeve. "Get me out of this dress!" It had taken three maids and her mother close to an hour to get her into the damn thing, but even if it took her father's cutlass, she'd get herself out.

Out of all of it.

Dampness of the grass seeped through her silk slippers as she fought her way back to the manor. Her mind rushing far faster than her feet. How would she ever explain this to mother? *I need time…and distance.* Looking over her shoulder toward the direction Richard had gone tugged at her heart. Yes, distance was truly needed. From everything. She couldn't stay here under the stares of everyone, including him, silently condemning her.

Alicia yanked the veil from her head. She wasn't rushing off to holiday with a mountain of trunks and chaperones and endless details to debate. She'd be on her own in this. Most of her belongings had already been sent on ahead to Frederick's household. There really wasn't much left in her rooms to pack. She would take only the barest necessities. Enough to make a quick escape. But escape to where?

I know where I've longed to go. To see. Protecting the yards of lace, Alicia clutched her veil to her chest. *Now, that would be an adventure.* Alicia gave herself a mental shake. *Impossible.* She stopped. *'Nothing is impossible if you're determined enough.'* Hadn't Father always said that? *'Don't go off halfcocked.'* Father said that as well. The temptation of throwing caution to the wind and striking out on her own gave her a thrilling rush.

Why not? I've got a bit of savings.

The surge of excitement was doused by a sudden tidal wave of uncertainty. *Dammit!* Either she was strong and independent, or she wasn't. This was her moment. If she was going to strike out on her own, she'd best do it. She may not get another chance. *Make up your bloody mind, Alicia!* Weeks of playing the submissive ninny had turned her into an indecisive fool. Where was her spine? Richard's words echoed in her mind, *"Has true love claimed all your passion?"*

With each determined step, a plan swelled to life, and Alicia's confidence once again took flight. *Hell yes, I can do this!* A tenacious wind filled her sails and blew away any lingering doubts.

Hugging her veil, she buried a wicked smile in its froth.

Impossible, my arse!

Chapter 2

Richard Dunbar stumbled through the cluster of fine carriages parked along the side drive of the Steele's grand alley. The wedding festivities were due to last into the next day or two. He tugged at the resting hitch as if he could move his ornate barouche alone.

"Where the hell is my groom? He's stolen my horse…and my driver." Pitching to the side of the carriage, he caught himself before dropping into the dust like some common drunkard.

He tipped his bottle to his lips and came away dry. Who was he kidding? He *was* a common drunkard. Richard scrubbed a hand over his eyes. A bloody sot, and still all the brandy in the world wouldn't erase the smell of her perfume.

"Dammit, Alicia." Even in a mountain of satin flounce, she was coarse, petulant…beautiful. Too beautiful. "Well done avoiding her," he muttered. Now, he would forever recall their final scene like a maddening one-act play, performing over and over in the place of his mind where regrets took root and grew in tangled thickets. A constant recollection of her eyes mirroring each expression, every fiery emotion she possessed. "When had they gotten so damned blue?" Richard raised the empty bottle to his lips once more before flinging it in resignation into the tall grass.

He glanced toward the chapel, imagining Alicia on the arm of her father walking toward her groom. Perhaps the deed is done.

Have the chapel bells rung? Had Alicia already looked lovingly at that insipid Freddy Big Nob and promised herself to him until death?

Richard's shoulders rounded as the thought brought a deep ache to his chest. *Dammit all, it should be me. Alicia should be marrying me!*

They should be the ones gazing lovingly into each other's eyes, saying "I do," making promises, talking about *their* future, *their* life together.

In classic style, he'd ruined everything. He had his chance and blown it clear out of the water. Utter fool. He'd looked into the depths of those obstinate, determined, loving blue eyes more than a year ago and killed any feelings she might have had for him. The memory pricked at his heart.

It had been the day he received the missive from His Majesty's Navy confirming his ultimate failure. A dishonorable discharge from a career of service. He'd been drunk then, too. A dangerous combination of humiliation, shame, and anger raged in him. He remembered pacing his father's study, after the man had skillfully eviscerated him and left him to wallow in his disgrace. That was where Alicia found him.

"Ducky?"

"Great. One more to witness my plunge into the icy depths. What the hell do you want?"

He'd shown her his back. The last thing he needed was the sympathy of his best friend's sister. She was a child. Well, not a child. Not anymore. She'd become her own woman. Strong. Confident. He reminded himself even though she carried herself with a certain amount of daring, she was still young, innocent. Naïve.

She'd lived a loving, yet sheltered, existence regardless of her audacity. He wasn't about to be the one to explain the prejudicial realities of life. Not then, and certainly not now.

"Go home, Alicia."

"I shouldn't have come, but I was worried about you. When I saw you the other evening at the Elliot's ball, I barely recognized you. I thought for sure you were ill, but James said—"

He spun on her. "James said. James said. I don't give a damn what James said!"

Startled indignation flashed in her eyes. "Don't you dare shout at me. You have every right to be angry, but I'm worried for you. We are *all* concerned. James, Mother, Father."

It was rumored that Alicia's parents were part of the small group of pirates that stole back the *Scarlet Night*, but he had no proof. The thieves blindfolded him before they left him airing his balls. He couldn't recall if there were six or eight. It was a dark, moonless night even without the blindfold. And cold as a witch's tit…

Richard finished his drink. "I don't want your concern." He turned back and splashed more brandy into his glass. "Or your pity."

She moved to his side and took the brandy from his hand. "I'm not here to offer you pity. I want to help. We'll fight together to clear your name."

"Our James already tried fighting for me." He held up the missive and crushed it in a fist. "He failed. Your father attempted to intercede. Still nothing. I'm finished." He snatched the glass back from her.

"So, we keep fighting. Eventually they'll come to realize—"

"Enough," he snapped. "They *have* realized. I'm not fit to serve. I failed at my commission. Lost a ship, allowed prisoners to escape, ended up stripped naked and strapped to a damn pier! There is no fighting the truth. It's bloody over." He tossed the crumpled parchment to the floor and drained his glass.

Alicia was still for a moment. The air in his father's study hung heavy with his anger and humiliation.

And then she moved closer. She again pulled the glass from his fist and set it aside. "Then perhaps it's the perfect *bloody* time for a new beginning." She straightened the ties on his neck stock before lifting her eyes to his. "If they can't see your innocence or your sacrifice, they can all be damned. You don't need them. You're a man of adventure. Daring. Brave. Loyal." Her hands brushed his shoulders. The warm smell of her perfume stirred his senses. "Perhaps this is your chance to carve a new life. A fresh start. For both of us." She stroked a smoothing hand down his lapel. "I could go with you. We'll leave before first light. I've not much to pack. No one knows I'm here. They won't miss me for hours. We'll ride straight through, get to London, and book passage on the first ship we find." She laced her fingers with his and held his gaze. "Let's sail away together. Tonight. To Spain. France. Wherever you want to go."

He watched her mouth as she spoke, and before he could stop himself, he kissed her. It was only supposed to be a quick kiss of appreciation for her faith in him—even if he didn't deserve it— gratefulness for her innocent attempt to help him escape his ruination. But as soon as his lips brushed hers, some small part of the universe tipped.

She tasted like a new day. Sunshine and hope when he'd been

immersed in darkness for months. For one single bright moment, he forgot all the rest and greedily took his fill of her.

In one flawless breath, his world lightened. Uncertainty, stress and strain faded away, and there was only her. Her mouth. The slight trembling of tender lips. A rising pace of their breathing. The pressure of her body against his. Warm. Soft. How perfectly she fit, nesting each bend and curve as if she'd been made just for him. Desire flared into an insatiable hunger.

Slipping a hand into the softness of her hair, he deepened the kiss. Her mouth opened beneath his in a gasp. His free hand caught Alicia at the waist and pulled her tight against him as his tongue slid into her sweet mouth.

He bit her lip, tightening his hold, and tugging her roughly to him, grabbing fistfuls of skirt to hold her against the growing heat of his arousal. She released a small sigh before whispering his name against his mouth. *"Oh, Ducky...."*

The childish nickname fired a warning shot across his bow. As if scalded by the growing heat between them, he shoved her away. Shock and confusion shown in her eyes as a war of emotions waged in his mind, his body, and his heart.

What the hell were they doing? This couldn't happen. He couldn't betray the respect he had for Alicia and the family by sweeping her into his arms and carrying her to his bed. He wouldn't ruin her.

Dammit! He'd let the alcohol disguise the weakness of his own failings. What was he thinking? He had no right to prey upon Alicia's affections. Abuse her trust. She was the one with the fresh new future. What was *she* thinking? Sailing off? With *him*? Last thing she needed was the burden of a life with a bloody albatross. A sot. A drunken fool who'd just crossed a line that should never have been crossed.

Had he simply said those words aloud, explained why they couldn't run away that night or any other. How they could never be together because she deserved someone worthy of her strength and loyalty. If only he'd formed those words, perhaps he wouldn't be sitting in a sea of carriages waiting for church bells to ring the final death knell to his heart.

No, idiot that he was, he'd looked into her beautiful, confused face that night and said, *"Get. Out."*

Richard closed his eyes to the sharp ache in his chest. "I need a bloody drink."

The sound of footfall had him lifting his gaze. Alicia's brother, Captain James Steele headed toward him in all his wedding finery. Habit made Richard jump to his feet and snap to attention. His brain sloshed in his skull as the world swirled. He focused his vision and caught himself before he attempted to salute his friend and former superior.

"Where the hell is the groom?"

Richard gave a small jerk of surprise. "You, too? They've taken all the horses, as well. How's a man supposed to bugger off without a blasted horse and driver?" He made a wild sweep of his arm toward the sea of carriages.

James bent and plucked Richard's empty bottle from the grass. "You're pissed. Dammit man, it's barely past noon."

Richard held his arms wide. He would have bowed had he not

feared toppling over. "Would it help if I told you I began this current binge last night? Or was it two nights ago? Hard to know. My days are so full, you know."

James looked about. "I've no time to play drunken guessing games with you. I'm looking for Bineau."

Richard frowned. "Oh, *that* groom. Haven't seen him." He flipped a hand and moved to sit once more as James' words slowly pierced his brandied brain. "A bit soon after the ceremony for the groom to disappear, isn't it?"

"No, the guests are still waiting for the wedding to begin. The groom's nowhere to be found. The bride is missing, as well. Mother is searching for her now."

Richard stood and looked over his shoulder. "Alicia was in the gardens not long ago. Perhaps the two snuck off for a bit of…" he tried to wiggle his eyebrows, without success, "…early honeymooning." The thought of Alicia and that man together in some lover's tryst made Richard queasy. He rubbed at his stomach.

James held up a note in his fist. "Not likely. According to this, Bineau has made the ill-advised decision to leave my sister at the altar."

"What? He left her? Bloody hell!" A jolt of anger sobered him. "He should be flogged! Damn fool. Walking out on Alicia? The man's an idiot. What reason could he possibly give?"

"Some prattle about living a lie. Being in love with another." James unfurled the note and read. "It says, 'I need to follow my heart along an unholy path and cannot pull you into my inequity.' Whatever the hell *that* means?"

Richard snorted. "Means he's bloody run off with his valet."

James grimaced with a look of disgust, "You might be right, but either way, when I find him, I'm going to ring his skinny starched neck." James planted his hands on his hips and continued to scan the area. "Mother was pressuring Alicia to make this union, but I never thought she'd agree to marry such a prig. Any fool could see they weren't suited, but she insisted he was what she wanted."

He held up the note. "Do you know what the gossips will make of this? The humiliation will ruin her. Suppose my sister found his note before I did?" James looked over his shoulder. "I'll check the gardens again."

Richard knew a thing or two about humiliation, and he wasn't about to let Bineau's betrayal spill over onto Alicia. She was resilient, but something like this, with all of society's elite looking on, judging, the aftermath could tarnish her forever. "I'll help you search." Richard straightened his jacket and ran a hand through his disheveled hair. "Then we'll both track down Bineau, the bastard."

"I don't think so." James shot Richard an impatient look—a look laced with the mistrust he'd seen far too often. "You're in no condition."

"I'm pink. Truly." Richard spread his arms wide, and even did a little jig to prove his point. "Quite sober now. I want to help."

James gave him a long stare before shaking his head in frustrated resignation. "Fine. Come along."

Chapter 3

Richard and James arrived in Alicia's rooms after a fast search of the grounds hadn't found either the bride, the groom…or his valet. James moved to join his wife, Samantha. She held their young daughter, Amelia, on her hip and was already heavy and swollen with baby number two.

"I'll kill the scurvied son of a whore. Fetch my pistols." Alicia's father, Jaxon Steele was a former privateer, fierce fighter, and currently a very protective father of the bride. "I told you he wasn't fit to shine her boots. I don't care if he's a bloody Duke. The man should be keelhauled and strung up by his royal jewels."

Jaxon paced the room while James took his daughter from Samantha. "If we ever find him, I'll help you rig the rope." The sleepy child curled contently into her father's shoulder as James stroked a wide hand over her tiny back. A familiar shaft of sharp green envy pierced Richard's chest at the sight.

Alicia's mother, Annalise, stood with her arms overflowing with wedding dress. "I'm the one who should be keelhauled. This is all my fault. I pushed her to accept him. I only wanted the best for her. A good match, so she wouldn't have to live with the small-minded people of this town looking down their noses at her." Annalise pointed a finger toward the chapel before giving Jaxon a tearful look. "Like they've done to us all these years."

"Privileged, pretentious, blue-blooded bastards, the whole lot of them. I've known better pirates," Jaxon growled. "Why do you give a shite about what they think?"

"I never have. Not where you and I are concerned." Annalise chewed at her lip and lifted a hand toward James and his daughter before placing it on her heart. "She's my child. I was trying to shield her."

"Alicia doesn't need shielding. She's a grown woman and has more backbone than half the men out there," Jaxon's voice raised. "At least she did until that fop started nosing around." The baby started to cry. Jaxon stopped his rant and laid a gentle hand on his granddaughter's head, quieting her. He lowered his voice and continued pacing. "Got to be I barely recognized my own daughter when he came calling. Waving a damn fan." He flipped his hand back and forth, "holding her tongue, batting her eyelashes. Bloody hell."

"She was trying to be gentile," insisted Annalise. "The man is gentry. There's a certain protocol when a man…a Duke comes calling. If you'd had your way, Jaxon, she'd win a husband in a duel."

"At least she'd have landed one that wouldn't pale at the sight of blood." Jaxon turned to Richard. "Rare roast beef at dinner nearly did him in."

Annalise rubbed at her forehead. "We can stand here and argue all afternoon, but the fact is the man is gone, our daughter's future is in tatters, and she's vanished like smoke. We need to find her. And in the meantime, what am I supposed to do with three hundred guests still sitting in a chapel?"

"Two hundred, ninety-nine," muttered Richard.

Annalise shot him a glare, which he deflected with a sheepish shrug of one shoulder.

"Tell them to go eat the month's wages worth of ridiculous food waiting for them in the ballroom. Stuffed virgin quail with glazed yam balls in a cold cumquat sauce…" Jaxon shook his head. "If you served them roasted bilge rat, gave it a fancy French name, and doused it in cold cumquat sauce, they wouldn't know the bloody difference."

"Please, Jaxon, I can't think. This is a disaster." Annalise scanned the room as if looking for clues. "Where could she be?"

Samantha stepped forward. "I'm sure she hasn't gone far. We'll find her." She stroked the swell of her belly. "Why don't I take Amelia and go back to the chapel? We'll lead everyone into the ballroom."

"What will you tell them?" asked Annalise.

Samantha smiled at her mother-in-law and patted her arm. "I'll start them all on the wine and wait 'til they're good and drunk, then I'll make something up." She continued to smile but shot a worried glance back at James.

"Thank you, my dear."

"Perhaps my delicate condition will be of use, after all."

Annalise spread her daughter's gown on the bed and moved to find comfort in Jaxon's arms while James passed a sleeping Amelia back to his wife and walked them to the door.

Concern continued to gnaw as Richard's gaze scanned the room.

Perhaps Alicia had only taken a walk in the woods surrounding the estate, or could be she was tucked into a quiet corner of the stables, feeding her favorite mare apples?

But what if she wasn't? There was something odd about her demeanor in the garden. He struggled to make sense of it all. If only he could wipe away the brandy-colored haze fogging his memory and get past the uneasy feeling in his gut.

The voices of the others faded into the background as Richard examined a small pile of books on Alicia's night table. Poetry. A study of constellations. A sailing log titled, *Coryat's Crudities?* There was so much he didn't know about her, but a few moments here in this room painted a far different Alicia than he'd imagined. Beyond the frill of the wedding gown, the room was subtle, rich in wood with leathered chairs. No ruffles, pastels, or lace.

Lace. Richard paused in front of a standing mirror and tried to imagine Alicia preparing for the day in her gown and delicate veil, but only his own image stared back at him.

I looked like shite. He raked fingers through his hair. *Rewarmed shite. Bloody hell.* Red-rimmed eyes sunk behind deep shadows. Hair still askew. Skin the color of paste. Richard ran a hand over the gaunt hollow beneath his cheek bone. He barely recognized himself. Catching his own gaze, he held it steady, silently berating the man he'd become even while wishing he had another drink.

Turning away from his image in disgust, he plucked a small crystal bottle from Alicia's vanity and waved it beneath his nose. Clean citrus with a gentle touch of spice. Her. He'd recognize her scent anywhere. It had burned itself into his memory. Richard closed his eyes at the sudden sense of intimacy. The smell of her perfume brought him right back to his father's study the night they kissed.

And even in the garden earlier, the warmth of that spice lingering across her skin as he pretended to wish her well. It would haunt him. The subtle blush to her cheeks. Her beautiful face framed in lace. *Where the hell is she?*

Richard slid aside the remains of a large parcel to drop into a side chair. A leaf of Lavender tissue fluttered to the floor and caught on his leg. With a snatch of his fingertips, he plucked up the tissue and shot a look back at Alicia's gown laid out upon the bed. "Where's the veil?"

Annalise shot him a worried glance before looking behind her. "I don't know, but Alicia treasured that veil. It was a gift from JoBo," she spoke to Jaxon.

Richard knew the name, and unlike Alicia's perfume, it did not conjure up lovely memories. "JoBo *Robbins*?" His gut tightened at the memory. "Beautiful woman. Dark hair. Slight build. French. Wed to a pirate?"

"Yes, that's her. It's Jocelyn, actually. No one calls her JoBo anymore. She's a lace merchant now. Her husband Ric left piracy years ago."

Richard fingered the twine used to secure the package. His thumb brushed the blunt end where it had been cut. No doubt the knot had proved too difficult to untie. JoBo, Jocelyn, or whatever name she went by now was an expert at tying knots. With twine…and rope. Especially rope securing a certain naked Lieutenant to a certain familiar pier.

"If she's a legitimate lace merchant, I'm a blue-faced gull." Jaxon scoffed. "Ric may not be firing a swivel gun anymore, but he's been running stolen cargo in the profiteering game since leaving the *Scarlet Night*."

Annalise turned back to Richard. "Jocelyn and Alicia correspond quite often. She told Alicia she and Ric ran the shop together. It's called…something 'Laced.' They've settled in the northern Carolinas. America."

"Doesn't matter what it's called. The shop is a ruse," Jaxon insisted.

"Well the veil is real, and now it's gone, along with our daughter."

"Mistress." A servant rushed into the room and bobbed. "The chambermaid found this in your quarters." She handed her a note.

Annalise tore it open and read it before passing it to Jaxon. She covered her eyes with a shaky hand. "It's from Alicia."

"What does it say?" Richard was on his feet.

The muscle in Jaxon's jaw pulsed. "All it says is, 'I'm sorry. I'm not a Duchess. It's time I behaved like a Steele.'"

Richard's gut tightened. "What the hell does that mean?" James took the note from his father and read.

"It means she's gone." Annalise crossed to Alicia's secretary and began rummaging through her things.

"Where would she go?" Richard's stomach dipped.

"I have a guess." She closed the lid of a carved wooden box with a snap. "The letters are gone. Jocelyn's letters." Annalise whipped open another drawer. Its small brass key still in its lock. "So are her savings. I think she's headed to America."

"Impossible," added James. "Alicia has never been further than London."

"All the more reason." Jaxon moved to Annalise's side and laid a hand on her panicked face before he kissed her. "Our daughter heading off on an adventure isn't the worst thing. It's good for her to spread her wings. See a bit of the world. Get her away from all this." His hand swept the room. "Better an escape with dignity than to be shackled to that Frederick arse-hole."

"But she's alone." Annalise's eyes glittered with threatening tears. "It's not safe, Jaxon. You know the dangers of a young woman traveling by herself. And an ocean crossing?" Her tears spilled over and ran down her cheeks.

"She can't have gone far," Jaxon murmured, soothing Annalise, wiping at her tears. "We'll catch up with her, and send her on a proper trip, with a hull full of baggage and a seasick spinster as a companion."

Richard dropped into a chair. *America? That's half a world away. What if I never see her again?* Just the thought caused all the blood to leave his head. He braced both hands on his knees and reigned in his anxiety. No, Jaxon was right. Alicia hadn't been gone more than an hour. She couldn't have covered much ground. They would split up, take the fastest horses. They'd find her in no time at al—

"Pardon me, Captain, Missus…" Richard turned to find one of the liveries standing by the door. "One of the delivery wagons has gone missing."

Chapter 4

For the thousandth time, Alicia shot a glance over her shoulder. The wagon rattled like a cantankerous old man. Surely its owner chased after her. She flicked the reigns across the flanks of the huge quarter horse pulling the crate of a cart and urged him to go faster. Furry ears laid back in annoyance. It was obvious the horse was moving as quickly as he cared to regardless of her leathered insistence.

The animal's irritation was contagious. "Stubborn beast, move!" Alicia pulled her cloak tighter about her shoulders and adjusted the long gentle curve of the beautiful cloak brooch her father had given her on her last birthday. Only a few weeks past, it seemed like a lifetime ago. Running her fingertips over the cool metal calmed her somehow.

"A feather? Father, it's lovely. Is it pewter?"

"No, had the blacksmith craft it out of steel. Polished and waxed like a fine suit of armor."

He'd pinned it to her shoulder and ran a gentle finger along its spine. "Soon you'll sail off to live the rest of your life and give up the Steele name. I wanted you to carry a wee bit to remind ye who you be."

"I could never forget. Not if I married twenty men."

"One is more than enough for me." Her father softened his gaze. "Are ye happy, lass?"

"Of course. It's my birthday, I love my pin, and I love you."

"But do ye love him?"

Alicia made a feeble attempt to laugh off his concern. "Of course." The lie lodged in her throat, and she was quick to embrace her father so he wouldn't see the truth in her eyes. "Foolish man. You worry too much."

Her father tightened his arms around her and held her as he had done as long as she could remember. "Yer my blood, my child, my daughter. I'd fight a fleet to protect ya and see ye happy."

"I'm fine. Truly." She pulled back enough to kiss his cheek and wipe away the tears that threatened to undo her if he persisted. "There's no fleet to fight, Captain Steele," she teased.

"Nay, just a man who's not near good enough for ye."

"You don't need to fight him either."

"Good thing for him. One sniff of me comin', guns a-blazin', he'd raise the white sooner than he'd shite his satin breeches."

"Father. Please. All will be well. I promise."

"I promise," Alicia repeated the vow out loud as she shifted the cloak about her shoulders and straightened the graceful pin. The horse's ear pivoted once more. "If anyone will understand, it's Father." Alicia looked back over her shoulder once more. "He will explain it to Mother. Perhaps, one day…" she gave the reins a sharp flick, "…they'll both forgive me."

Close to town, she passed a young lad heading back the way she had come. "Boy? How would you like to earn six shillings?"

His face lit. Given the state of his clothing, six shillings was more than a half a year's wage. "Who do I have to kill?"

"No killing. Just riding." She set the brake on the cart and leapt down. Clouds began to close in as weather started to build from the north. She pulled a scrap of paper from her bag and quickly jotted down the address and scribbled a note, then pulled some coins from her purse. "I want you to take this cart back to the Marquise's estate at Weatherington. Do you know it?"

"Aye." When she dropped a few coins into his outstretched hand, he narrowed his eyes and shoved it back. "You said six. There be only three. Do ye think I can't count?"

"Call it insurance. When you get to Weatherington, give them this note. You will receive the rest of your money. And a full belly. If you can get this beast to hurry." She shrugged a shoulder as a rumble of thunder threatened. "You might find yourself a dry bed for the night as well."

By the time Alicia walked the last few miles into Liverpool and made it to the docks, she would have bargained another six shillings for a full belly and a dry bed, yet the ticket to sail had all but emptied her purse. When she boarded the *Albatross* with a small group of travelers some hours later, her nerves were frayed, her clothing was soaked, and any bed would do.

Alicia tucked herself amongst the other passengers as the crew prepared the ship for departure. Traveling alone was risky, and she had already caught notice of several questioning stares. One crew member in particular, a barrel chested, bearded fellow seemed to be overly curious. She'd noticed him watching her a few times. Perhaps if she could appear to be part of another party, she wouldn't stand out.

A small family was traveling with two children. A young girl, perhaps four years of age, held tight to her father's hand. The mother cradled a swaddled infant. Their companion was a dour woman, dressed bonnet to hem in black. A governess perhaps? Maid servant? While the group shared a look of eagerness and excitement as the ship moved away from its berth, their companion paled to a sickly green almost at once. Before the *Albatross* hit open water, the woman was at the rail losing the contents of her stomach.

Alicia approached the family. "Oh, dear, is she ill? Or does the sea make her so? My own cousin, who was due to travel with me, came down with an awful sickness two night's past. I hated leaving her, but she insisted I continue our journey. She promised to join me when she's able." Alicia covered her nose and mouth with a handkerchief as she formed the lie. "I hope your friend isn't contagious."

The man passed the older child into his wife's charge and moved to the retching woman. "Tis my mother-in-law," the wife confessed. "She warned us something like this would happen. Loathes ships. We'd hoped she was just being contrary. She lives to be contrary." The woman sighed and readjusted the hold she had on the baby while the other child tugged at her to be released. "Rupert insisted she'd be fine. For goodness sake, we can still see land."

"My own mother had terrible problems with seasickness, but I've heard in time it usually passes. Father calls it getting your sea legs. Another day or two, she'll be fine. I'm sure."

"Not the way she tells it. Her last crossing had her flat on her back being spooned broth the entire trip by my sainted father-in-law. Now, my dear, sweet Rupert will be her over-burdened nursemaid. With me looking after the lot of them. This trip is a disaster before it has begun."

"I am sorry."

"Lillian, please." She jerked the child back to her side. The babe began to cry. The wife looked as if she, too, wanted to bawl.

"I'd be happy to help, if you'd allow it."

She tipped her head toward her retching mother-in-law. "Could you push her over the rail?"

The woman's dark wit caught Alicia off guard. She liked her immediately. "Well…no. Too many witnesses. Perhaps after dark?"

The baby began to screech. Lillian fussed and tried to pry her mother's fingers from her wrist.

"Why don't Lillian and I take a quick tour of the deck? You can settle the baby, reclaim your husband, and find your mother-in-law a lovely bucket while we wait for a better opportunity to toss her over."

The wife sniffed and hid the hint of a smile. "I don't even know your name."

"Alicia."

"I'm Margaret."

"Good day to you, Margaret." She turned her attention to the child flailing at the end of her mother's arm. "Mistress Lillian, would you care to see this fine ship?"

Together, Alicia and the child made several passes from stem to stern and back again. Lillian was clever. They counted the belaying pins lined up along the gunwales. Lillian delighted in pointing out the gulls chasing them out of the harbor. There was even a lively discussion as to whether the man in the crow's nest was sitting on any eggs.

"Do you think we'll find pirates?" Lillian looked up at her with wide brown eyes.

"Pirates? How do you know about pirates, little miss?"

"Father says they're ugly and mean. They don't take their baths or say their prayers."

Alicia crouched down to look into the child's face. She brushed hair from the girl's cheek. "Some pirates are very handsome and kind."

Lillian frowned. "No, they aren't."

"Aye, a few are. I know one, myself," Alicia confided in a whisper. The striking image of her father's face came to mind. "He's handsome and tall as this mast." The child's eyes grew round. "He is very kind, and very clean. He takes all his baths," Alicia continued and gave a small frown, "but I think you're right, he doesn't say his prayers."

"If he doesn't say his prayers, he won't have lovely dreams," Lillian insisted.

"I'll be sure to tell him that the very next time I see him." Alicia stood and looked back toward the stern of the ship. Only a thin line of land could be seen on the horizon. *...the very next time I see him... I pray he forgives me.*

Her heart gave a small lurch. She couldn't be missing her home, not yet. Alicia took Lillian's hand and they walked to the furthest point in the bow. As the ship made her way through the water, Alicia adjusted her stance. Would she ever get used to the deck swaying beneath her feet?

Lifting her face to the breeze, she eased the slight queasiness of her stomach with great gulps of fresh sea air. It smelled like nothing she'd ever smelled before. Crisp. Cold. She could taste its salt upon her lips. With the sun dipping beneath the sodden clouds to give the tips of the waves a final bright orange kiss before it melted into the water, it was more beautiful than Alicia had imagined.

All her father's stories about his time at sea had failed to mention just how glorious the ocean looked. It stretched on forever. Glancing back once more, Alicia could no longer see land. All around them was nothing but fathoms and fathoms of water. The thought was exhilarating and humbling, as if their ship was nothing but a tiny, single star in a vast open sky.

She held tight to Lillian's hand. With the other she held tighter to the ropes holding the sails or masts, in the tangle of lines, she couldn't tell which. It hummed beneath her touch. At the same time the wood of the ship creaked and moaned. Father often said ships were living breathing beings. She hadn't believed him until just this moment. It was all so wonderful.

It was just after four bells when Alicia returned Lillian to her grateful parents.

In hindsight, booking passage on a ship called *Albatross* may have been unwise, but Alicia had been in such a rush to escape England she'd jumped on the first vessel scheduled to leave the dock. Ironic. The *Albatross* was a tub of a merchant ship, loaded to the gunwales with all manner of things for the new world. Leaving from Liverpool, Alicia was thankful its cargo did not include slaves, but according to those who knew such things, the great hulking ship moved like a fat garden slug through the water.

It was due to be six long weeks of travel for them all. Twelve if their initial speed was any indication. Alicia didn't mind. She was falling in love. The journey could last forever if it pleased. There was so much to see and learn.

She was glad for the company of Margaret and her children, however, and could easily join their party to quell the scandal of being an unchaperoned young woman, even if there were still some curious about her situation.

For one member of the crew, curiosity took a dark turn more than a week into their voyage. It was late. Dinner had been served and eaten and most of the other passengers were settling in for the night. Alicia had just left her adopted family and gone topside to breathe in the sweetness of the air and bask in the beauty of the night sky. The waves and the winds had calmed with the setting sun and the light of a million stars reflected all around them. It was as if they were cradled in a sparkling jeweled box.

As the night air got chill, Alicia wrapped her cloak tighter and made her way below to her tiny quarters. It was a lucky thing her imaginary traveling companion had come down with sickness, two women sharing her closet-sized cabin would have made the crossing a cramped uncomfortable venture.

Below deck, the darkness was broken only by the odd lantern. She lifted one from its hanger. The air was humid and stale, and it smelled of water-soaked wood, tar, and bilge. Moving about was a tight fit for most, and as Alicia tried to skirt that curious, bearded crewman in the corridor things got uncomfortable in quite another manner.

"Are ye lost?"

She could smell the rum on his breath. "Certainly, not."

He blocked her way. "Perhaps I should walk ye to yer cabin, ye being alone, like ye be. Wouldn't want some swabber making any untoward advances te ya."

"I'm quite capable of making it to my own quarters, thank you." Alicia attempted to move past.

"A bonny lass like yerself be keen 'bout lots of things, I'm thinkin.'" He moved closer, blocking her way once more.

The tiny hairs of the back of Alicia's neck prickled. "Indeed. I'm able to scream louder than a dozen women in a room full of mice, should I need to. Now, let me pass."

The man's eyes narrowed. "Ye got me all wrong. All I want is a little fun. I see the way ye've been lookin' at me these past days." He ran a wide thumb down the front of her throat. Alicia swallowed the fear that rose at his touch. "And I know just how te keep a lass quiet, should *I* need te." He applied just enough pressure to assure his meaning as he jerked the lantern from her hand and cast them both into darkness. "Ye know ye want a bit of a tumble. I ken tell. I ken always tell." He took her hand and forced it against his crotch. "See what we got fer ya?"

Alicia began to tremble. The man outweighed her by a good six stone. He smelled of rum and fish and unwashed male. If she made a single sound the hand on her throat would no doubt silence her, perhaps forever. Her mind raced for a way out.

"You want to have me here? Against the wall?"

"Ken ye not feel how ready I be?" He pressed his erection into her hand as his free hand yanked her cloak to one side and grabbed fistfuls of skirts.

Her cloak pin sprung from its clasp. If she could only reach it. "Wouldn't you prefer a more comfortable bed?"

"And give ye a chance to slip away? Nay." Rough fingers scrapped at her thigh. "Got all we be needin' right here." His beard scratched at her cheek as he tried to kiss her. Alicia turned away in disgust, but it didn't stop him from planting a line of slobber down her neck and pawing at her breasts.

Alicia's hand closed around the feather pin as he unbuttoned the front of his breeches and pushed her other hand inside. She nearly vomited at the feel of his swollen flesh. Instead, she grasped his stump of a penis in a tight hold. In response, he grunted like a rutting boar against and pushed his hips forward.

"Ah, that's it…Give us a stroke…" He pulled back slightly and pressed forward against her hand.

"You're so…big and…and hard. I…I need two hands…to hold all of you."

He shifted his weight to give her full access while he kicked her legs wider and let his breeches fall to his knees. "Yer a hot bit of cunny, ye are. Ye want it all, eh? I be givin' it to ye. Every rock 'ard inch."

Alicia moved her second hand to join her first. Instead of stabbing through the man's genitals with her cloak pin, she pressed the cold steel edge firmly under the man's testicles.

The man gasped and froze. She increased the pressure of what was sure to feel like a knife in the dark. "You're going to take your filthy hands off me, or I swear I'll cut your balls off and feed them to the sharks."

When he didn't immediately release her, she gave a sharp tug with one hand and tipped the point of the feather brooch into his flesh. His hands flew away from her. Alicia shoved him off and covered herself. "Touch me again, and I'll be running your tiny cock up the flagpole as well." With her legs threatening to give way, she raced away toward her quarters.

"Teasin' bitch!" he barked at her back but didn't come after her.

Alicia reached her cabin and secured the door before rushing to throw up in her chamber pot. Shaking from fear, anger, and shock, she moved everything in the entire room that could be moved against the door. Splashing cold water from the pitcher, she scrubbed at her hands and her neck, and even the flesh of her thigh to rid herself of the man's vile touch before sliding to the floor and bursting into tears.

For the remaining weeks of the voyage, Alicia made sure she was never alone, and never without a knife. One she stole from the galley—it could barely cut bread, but she soon traded it for a thin-bladed dirk she found during one of her times on deck. It had been stuck in the lid of a barrel. Careful not to cut herself, she fashioned a sheath and carried it securely lashed to her calf. And she was careful, too, not to find herself within arm's reach of a certain vulgar, bearded, barrel chested, small-penised, crewman.

The day they anchored offshore of the northern coast of the Carolinas, Alicia embraced Margaret and Lillian and promised to keep in touch. After boarding the lowering skiff taking passengers to shore through the thick mist of rain that had followed them for most of the trip, did that certain crewman notice the steel feather pinned to her cloak. She watched as his gaze took in the brooch before shooting upward to glare at her. She gave the curved bit of steel a loving touch while holding his glower with a defiant stare of her own.

Chapter 5

A small amount of light coming from the shop illuminated Alicia's reflection in the glass window of the door. She pushed the sodden mess of hair away from her pale face. Her coif now resembled something her mother's cat would throw up on the carpet. The sad feather clinging bravely to her ruined traveling bonnet limped in defeat about her chin. Her dress and cloak hung heavy on her shoulders and smelled like bilge, and if the squishing sounds coming from her shoes were any indication, they were a total loss. But she'd made it and praise be, she was well away from the *Albatross* and all who sailed upon her.

In the street a man moved from lamp to lamp struggling to keep the spill flame lit as he blazed each protected candle lighting his way through the growing darkness. The sign in the window of Jocelyn Robbins' lace shop read "Closed," but Alicia recalled Jocelyn once remarking in one of her letters about the convenience of living above their shop. The rain spattered her face as she lifted her gaze to the darkened second story windows.

She rapped on the door and waited. There was no movement in the store, but Alicia could see a bit of candlelight coming from a back room. Someone must be there. She knocked harder. Still, no one came.

Alicia shivered and looked over her shoulder toward the quaint town square of Black Point. The shine of the street's lamps wavered in their reflections on the muddy street. A lone horse and cart carved puddled tracks in the muck. She'd passed an inn down near the dock, but she wasn't sure she could pay for her dinner, let alone lodging for the night. For the millionth time since she set off on her own, in what some would call an "ill-conceived" adventure, Alicia questioned her sanity.

She sneezed.

"Jocelyn?" Alicia pounded on the door once more in earnest. "Ric? Anyone?" Shifting her bag to her left hand, she tried the door and nearly sang with joy when she found it unlocked. "Jocelyn?" Alicia poked her head into the shadowed shop. "Hello?"

Angry voices greeted her from somewhere deep in the building as she slipped in. Was that her and Ric arguing? It sounded like French. She couldn't understand what was being said, but for a moment she considered ducking back out into the rain.

"Hello, Jocelyn?" She called out once more.

The argument ended abruptly. Silence followed. A moment later, a door slammed.

Jocelyn Robbins emerged through a lace-curtained doorway carrying a glass chimney oil lamp. Alicia recognized the slight woman at once, graceful and poised. Dark curls piled high in perfect array. Only a gentle kiss of gray at her temples spoke of her age. She wore a stunning gown of deep violet to set off her dark coloring. Its cuffs and collar adorned in beautiful webs of the finest lace.

"We are closed. The candles have been snuffed, the sign hangs in the window, no?" She pressed the back of her hand to bright cheeks before flipping her hand at Alicia. "*Allez-vous en.* Go away"

"I'm so sorry to arrive unannounced."

"Unannounced and uninvited. Get out." Jocelyn pointed to the door and spun her skirts as she turned to leave.

"No. Wait. But I am invited. You…" Alicia dug through her bag and pulled out a small bundle of letters written on distinctive lavender dyed paper. "You wished for me to visit many times." At Jocelyn's frown, Alicia pushed the hair away from her face and straightened. "It's me. Alicia. Alicia Steele."

Jocelyn laughed, "*Menteur*. You lie." With another flick of her hand, she dismissed Alicia. "My writing paper is not unique, and Alicia Steele is at this moment enjoying the attention of a new husband. I designed the veil she wore at her wedding myself. Whoever you truly are, you must leave." Jocelyn turned her by the shoulders and pushed her back toward the door. "I have my own problems. I have not time to listen to yours."

"Wait. Please." Alice opened her bag and pulled the treasured lace from its protected wrapping of cotton and oilcloth. "Does this prove who I am? My veil was stunning."

Jocelyn narrowed her eyes and stepped closer to examine the pure white of the lace before peering into Alicia's face. "*Sacré bleu*—It is you… How?" She pulled her into a quick embrace then held her at arm's length. "You were sent to bring me news? *Oui?*"

"News? No…no one sent me—"

"You look a fright. Why are you not in England? Who is with you?" Jocelyn looked past her to the door. "Where is your husband?"

Alicia shook her head. "There is no husband. There was no wedding."

Jocelyn gasped. "*Connard.* That bastard Bineau called it off?"

"No...I...he didn't call it off. I never arrived."

"What?" Jocelyn gave a quick shake of her head before looking at her as if she were mad.

"I couldn't go through with it. I was ready to walk into the chapel, wearing your beautiful gift." Alicia stepped away and tried to rub some warmth into her arms. She looked back at a confused Jocelyn. "All at once I couldn't breathe. It was a huge mistake. I should have talked to Frederick before I left, I know. That part was cowardly. But all I could think was that I had to get as far away from the chapel as I could—from a life...a future...without color...without passion."

Alicia removed her ruined hat and tucked her disheveled hair behind one ear. She gave Jocelyn a resigned shrug. Somehow saying it out loud made everything sound even more impulsive, but time and distance had only proved to her that she was right in her decision. "The marriage was a lie. If I stayed, my mother would've talked me into going through with it. So, I found the first ship heading here."

Jocelyn held up her hands in surrender. "But I thought you cared for this man? *Oui?* That's what you told me in your letters."

"When I wrote you, I truly believed I could grow to care for him. I hoped I would. But the closer the wedding came, the more I realized how wrong it all was. If I married Frederick, I would be living the wrong life."

"I cannot believe your parents agreed to your coming here. I would think I would be the last person they would send you to." Jocelyn put a hand to her forehead. "What could they have been thinking? And without a chaperone—"

"Coming here was my decision. My parents only know that I left."

"—If I had only known you were coming…" She gathered Alicia's bag before dropping it and spinning on her. "They do not know you are here?"

"No."

"But surely, you told someone where—"

"No." Alice gave a quick shake of her head. "I know how impetuous it all sounds."

"Impetuous? Is that what you call it?" The brightness in Jocelyn's cheeks rose again. "I would call it bloody reckless. All this way without anyone knowing your plans? A young woman traveling alone? Did you ever once think how dangerous? Think about the risks? Not only to your reputation, but to your safety? And you simply left?" Jocelyn's voice rose in volume and pitch.

Alicia had no excuse that didn't sound trite. She should have expected Jocelyn's reaction, but it wasn't as if she'd stowed away aboard a pirate ship to escape England like her mother. Of course, Mother had been running for her life all those years ago, but then, in a way, so was she.

"Believe me, my reputation is already in tatters. And it is obvious I arrived safely. I can take care of myself." Alicia had no intention of mentioning the harrowing aspects of her trip. No point adding black powder to this fire.

"Oh, yes. Independent! Because you have had so much experience?" Jocelyn threw her arms wide.

"Why are you shouting?"

"Because you are a fool! Why am I surrounded these days with nothing but headstrong ninnies and fools?"

"I hardly think—"

"Well, that's the first intelligent thing I have heard from you since you arrived." Jocelyn grabbed Alicia's hat from her fingers and threw it into a nearby bin. "Come with me." Storming past her, she pointed with a sharp finger. "Don't forget your bag."

"Jocelyn, the last thing I wanted was to make you angry. I thought you'd be happy to see me."

"Happy? Happy that at this moment your poor parents are probably beside themselves with worry? Have you no notion of a parent's fear for their child? Of course, you do not, you foolish girl. Not knowing, imagining all of life's horrors. Earning a few more gray hairs." She turned and tugged at the graying hair decorating her temples. She tossed an exasperated hand in the air before she gathered her light and continued to lead Alicia toward the back of the shop.

Alicia could just make out stacks of crates and trunks in the darkened storeroom. She slowed her step to let her eyes adjust to the lack of light. It didn't carry the same floral scent as the shop. It almost smelled like the belly of the Albatross. Tar and bilge and spice? "What is all this?"

Jocelyn yanked at her arm. "Never you mind. Keep moving."

Alicia's shoes sloshed as she followed the ranting Jocelyn.

"No, you have no consideration for the sleepless hours they are spending. The constant ache in their chest." Joselyn turned and pressed a fist to her waist. "Worry gnawing at their bellies as each day passes into the next without a single word that you are safe. Or alive."

Jocelyn continued to sputter as she climbed a narrow set of stairs. Was she still talking about Alicia's parents? Or was she referring to herself? Hadn't she written that her son, Beau, was traveling abroad? Was he one of the headstrong ninnies she spoke of? She remembered Jocelyn's initial question. *"You were sent to bring me news?"* Was that at the root of her distress? Alicia didn't dare ask. At least Jocelyn stopped shouting. Now she simply muttered to herself. In French.

At the top of the stairs, through a blue door, was a well-turned-out apartment. It was as tastefully decorated as Alicia had always imagined it would be. Soft golden colors, floral prints, elegant furnishings. Jocelyn raised the flame on the closest lamps and added wood to the stove before sliding a copper kettle over the heat.

She turned and pointed to a delicate gilt-edged writing desk and chair. "Sit."

When Alicia did as commanded, Jocelyn reached past her, pulled a sheet of lavender paper from a drawer, thrust a quill into Alicia's hand and flipped a delicate pewter lid off the inkwell.

"Write. Now. This minute."

"What?"

Jocelyn jabbed a finger at the paper. "A letter to your sainted parents. Start with 'I am alive' followed by 'I am sorry.' There is a mail ship leaving day after tomorrow for England, and that letter and possibly *you* will be on it."

Alicia gritted her teeth and flipped the lid closed on the inkwell. "I have every intention of writing my parents once I'm settled. You can shout at me if you must, but I've come too far to turn around now." Glare met glare. "I didn't just vanish. I told them I was leaving." *In not so many words.* "Perhaps my biggest mistake was to come here. I thought you of all people would understand my need to make my own way in this life. Didn't you tell me you were led around by the will of your father until fate intervened for you?"

"You have no idea about life," Jocelyn fired back.

"I'm a grown woman. It's time I found out, don't you think?" Alicia pushed the paper away and stood shoving her sodden cloak back into place. "I'm sorry to have caused you such distress, Mademoiselle Robbins," she snapped. "It may be better if I found lodging at the inn." Grabbing her bag, Alicia headed for the door, mentally counting the meager coins in her purse. "I fully accept the consequences of my actions, and what you may see as reckless—" She raised a hand to stop a further tirade from Jocelyn. "I, however, see my coming here as daring. What I did took fortitude. Courage." Alicia notched her chin. "I won't apologize to you, or anyone, for taking charge of my own future."

Jocelyn took a deep breath and released it slowly. "Put down your bag, Alicia. I will not cast you out into the night." She crossed her arms over her chest and shook her head. "You and I are too alike, no? Our passions and tempers are quick to flare. Come the light of day, when cooler heads prevail, we will have a long talk about just how you imagine your *daring* future to be." Jocelyn pointed a sharp finger back at the desk. "And you will send word to your mother and father that you are well. I insist, *oui*?"

Relief as deep as the ocean she had just crossed washed over

Alicia. She unclasped the feather holding her cloak together and let it drop to a sodden heap at her feet. "*Oui.*"

Chapter 6

Alicia swung her legs off the side of the narrow bed and sat on the edge. The long dark hours of the night stretched out before her, and as tired as she was, sleep continued to elude her. Worry gnawed at her mind. Perhaps it had been a mistake to come here.

She pulled the quilt around her shoulders and shivered. More from unease than cold now. It was perfectly within Jocelyn's right to ask her to leave come morning. She hadn't agreed to any of this. But if Alicia couldn't stay here, where would she go? There were larger cities to the north, but how to get there? How would she pay for passage? She could work, of course. She was strong and able. But what on earth was she qualified to do?

"Jocelyn is right." Alicia dropped her forehead into her hand. "I'm a bloody fool."

She took a deep breath and pulled the quilt tighter as she stood and paced the small room. The quilt dragged behind her like the robes of some pauper queen. "Daring. Adventurous. Remember? I made it here, didn't I? I'm headstrong, but I'm resourceful. I…I…" she threw off the quilt and peered at her reflection in a tall looking glass. "I'm a Steele. I can do anything I set my mind to do. I'm my father's daughter. The captain of my own ship. No turning back. No white flags." The chill in the room had her reaching for the quilt once more. "I'll leave before first light." Her gaze settled on her meager possessions. "It's not like I have much to pack."

The words stopped her. A memory hit her like a wave. She said something similar in the past. The night she'd promised to run away with Richard. Just before he kissed her and her young tender heart fell hopelessly in love, and then shattered into a million pieces mere moments later.

She'd been a fool then, too. Even more so in the days that followed when Alicia had done everything possible to push her feelings aside. Erase him from her heart and her mind. Wipe the taste of his lips away. It hadn't worked. Only time, and it seems, an entire ocean could do that.

There was a bit of comfort in the thought that she'd never see him again. Never be reminded of what wasn't to be. Ache joined that comfort, however. Never was such a frightfully long time. At least if she ever crossed paths with Richard Dunbar again, she'd be older, wiser, secure in her future. Alicia sighed and nudged at her ruined shoes with a toe. Or perhaps never wasn't long enough.

In the quiet of the room, Alicia startled when she heard an odd bump coming from somewhere beyond her door. A low murmur of voices. Had Ric returned? Alicia hadn't seen him in ages. Given Jocelyn's anger, what would he say about all this? He knew her parents probably better than she did. He'd been a member of the crew of the *Scarlet Night* during her father's days of pirating. Ric also sailed with Alicia's namesake, Captain Alice "Tupper" Quinn. Alice was larger than life in Alicia's imagination. She could listen to those pirate stories all night.

Alicia heard another soft thud from below. The door creaked as she peered into the dim hallway. The living area stood empty. Creeping out, she looked toward Jocelyn's open door. Perhaps

Jocelyn and Ric were working? What time was it?

Snatching Jocelyn's shawl from the back of a chair, Alicia eased open the door leading downstairs, a weak shaft of shifting light filtered over the skirts of her shift. Muted conversation met her ear. Instructions. "Slide it against the wall." "No, over there." "Stack those here." She slipped like smoke down a few stairs to peek.

Men, rugged, filthy, six that she could see, carrying various things from an open door in the back corner of the storeroom. None looked to be Ric. Trunks, casks, barrels. The storage room appeared much larger than before. Was Jocelyn getting a shipment in the middle of the night? Since when did lace come in barrels?

The rain still fell beyond the doorway, and the men's wet clothes clung to massive shoulders and muscular arms that spoke of hard, heavy labor. Alicia stayed in the shadows and pulled the woolen shawl tighter. A shiver rode up her spine. She was hardly dressed for company, especially given the dangerous look of said company. She'd left her knife in her room. Her cloak lay drying by the fire, but these men didn't look like they'd be fooled by a feathered brooch. Soft grunts and grumbles accompanied the work, but within minutes, the job was seemingly done. The men filed out.

The flare of a taper lit from a passing lantern caught Alicia's attention as the sweet smell of pipe tobacco wafted up the stairs to mix with the pungent aroma of unwashed bodies, and wet wool.

She inched down another stair.

It was then Alicia spotted Jocelyn, deep in conversation with the owner of the pipe. They kept their voices low, but Alicia watched as Jocelyn's elegant hands accentuated her obvious distress.

With the bit of the long clay stem clamped in his teeth, the pipe smoldered in the dangerous nest of a beard. The man's hands were still. His arms folded over the width of a brawny chest. Finer dressed than the others he still carried a fierce edge about him with a pistol lashed to one thigh and a sword on his hip. His back against the wall, he shifted his gaze between the door and Jocelyn.

When Jocelyn pulled a substantial amount of cash out of her pocket, Alicia's foot slipped off the edge of the stair, and she tumbled down the rest.

"What the bloody hell goes on here?" bellowed the man. His pistol was pulled and cocked before Alicia could right herself. Three men rushed back in, and before she or Jocelyn could answer, two of them had grabbed hold of Alicia's arms and nearly wrenched them from her shoulders.

"Let go of me!" She bucked and kicked back to connect with a shin. The man huffed a pained curse before giving her arm another brutal twist.

"Who the hell is this? One of your spies?"

"I have no spies." Jocelyn stepped between Alicia and the pistol and hissed. "Have you gone mad? Let her go. She's nothing. *Rien.* Knows nothing. An idiot girl who dropped at my doorstep tonight. She is *supposed* to be asleep, not sticking her nose into my business."

"It's *my* business she shouldn't be stickin' her nose into. Not if she don't want it shot off." He raised the gun.

Jocelyn raised her hands in surrender and shook her head. "She is no one. I promise you. I give you my word."

"I don't take the word of a woman." His eyes narrowed. "A

French woman, even less."

Jocelyn lowered her chin. "Ric has dealt with you honestly for years, and now you insult his wife?"

"Don't you mean his widow?"

"Ric is *alive*." Jocelyn bit out the words. She planted her hands on her hips. "Fine, call back your men. Take your goods. Give me back my money and find yourself another dealer. If you are too fine a thief to lower yourself to deal with me in Ric's absence, I do not need you or your bloody business." Jocelyn held out her hand.

The man lowered his gun and signaled his men to release Alicia. She let out a cry of relief and rubbed at her shoulder as she backed herself away from the standoff. The man sucked loudly at his pipe. The glow from the bowl cast an orange ruddiness to his cheeks. He jerked his head and his men filed out into the rainy night once more as he folded the cash with his thumb and stuffed it into his vest. "You better hope your husband turns up soon." He uncocked the pistol and shoved it back into the leathered sheath at his hip.

Jocelyn notched her chin. "And you better hope he never learns of your insults."

The man just laughed around the stem of his pipe and left.

Jocelyn followed him and closed the door behind him with a slam. She shoved the bolt of the lock into place before leaning her forehead against it.

Alicia pushed away from the wall and rushed to her. "Who the hell was that? What was he saying about Ric? Jocelyn, what is going on?"

Jocelyn spun on her. "What the hell is going on? I will tell you!

You have lost your mind! What were you thinking coming down here? You could have gotten us both killed, or worse." She pulled a lace-trimmed handkerchief from her sleeve and covered her mouth with a shaking hand. "Do not I have enough troubles of my own, you need to heap more upon my head?"

"I'm sorry. I heard voices. I don't understand."

Jocelyn began tugging large tarps into place over the items the men had stowed. "There is nothing for you to understand. This is none of your business."

Alicia's heart raced as fast as her mind. She tried to put the pieces together, but with so many questions unanswered, it all kept circling around in her brain.

She reached out and grabbed Jocelyn's hand. "Why did that man think you were Ric's widow? Where is he?"

Anger, panic, and despair passed over Jocelyn's eyes as she held Alicia's stare. "*Je ne sais pas.*" She gave a shake of her head and bit at her lip. "I do not know. Ric has disappeared. He has been gone more than twelve weeks now without a word."

"That's why when I arrived here tonight, you thought I was bringing news."

Jocelyn nodded and sniffed. "*Oui.* I have been desperate for word from him, or Beau. I am near frantic with worry."

"I thought Beau was traveling through France?"

"He was. But there was trouble." Jocelyn waved a hand through the air. "The last we heard they were holding him in Paris. At the Bastille."

Alicia's stomach dropped. The Bastille was rumored to be a brutal prison. "What kind of trouble?"

"They say he is involved in misdealing with land here in America. The facts are unclear. The whole notion is ridiculous. Beau cannot be part of what they are accusing him of doing. Which is why Ric rushed off to help him."

"Then I'm sure that is exactly where Ric is."

"Are you not listening? He has disappeared." Jocelyn drew a shaky breath. "The ship Ric was on arrived in Brest more than a month ago. He was not aboard."

"That makes no sense."

"Of course, it makes no sense. Why do you think I have spent the last month using every resource I can imagine for information? Some sliver of explanation."

"Maybe if you follow his path? Book passage. I could go with you."

"Impossible. Ric took most of our money with him. To free Beau. I have just used the last of it to hire Captain Bradford to make inquiries when he reaches France. It would take me a full year to collect enough for my own passage, and then what? I could spend another year chasing shadows through France if that is even where Ric is. And what of my dearest, Beau? Every day he spends in that…that horrible place." She pressed her handkerchief to her mouth and shook her head. "I am at my wit's end."

Alicia touched Jocelyn's shoulder in comfort. "I haven't much, but you're welcome to what coin I have left."

"That's sweet of you, but I need thousands."

"There has to be a way to raise what you need." Alicia's hand swept the stacks around her. "Surely, if we sell off—"

"Naïve, girl. None of this belongs to me."

"But the shop must do well."

"How much lace do you think I sell? The shop is an illusion. A front. A pretty face on an ugly woman." Jocelyn scanned the storeroom. "After Ric left pirating on the *Scarlet Night*, we became profiteers. For years we did well, but the Watch is making it increasingly difficult to move the more lucrative items, and Ric was always the one to handle that side of things. Without him, I am merely a stop along the way. You heard Bradford. I cannot negotiate the exchanges like Ric. The type of men he dealt with will not do business with a woman."

It all started to make sense to Alicia. Of course. Pirates don't quit being pirates, after all. It was in their blood. Her father may have been the exception, but that was only because he'd promised her mother a life of civility. No matter how many years he'd been away from the sea, it didn't stop him from being cunning and shrewd in all his business dealings. Like Ric, he was a pirate through and through, and still a great proponent of a loaded pistol. The bigger the better. Knives were good for defense, but a gun carried power and authority.

If not for Mother's cooler head, a well-oiled, primed pistol would be Father's answer to most problems. He said many times all he had to do was place a gun on a negotiation table, and suddenly no more negotiations were necessary. Truths were revealed. Heated discussions ended. Obstacles vanished.

Alicia looked about the storeroom. Now she understood the

smirk Father wore each time she talked about Jocelyn's lace shop. He'd known all along what Ric's business dealings were like. Dammit, there was no room for such naivety. She was smarter than this.

Reaching out she stroked Jocelyn's arm. "We'll think of something. I'm here to help."

Jocelyn wiped at her nose and shook her head slowly, still scanning the room as if the answer lay within one of these crates. "And what can you do?"

Alicia slipped an arm around Jocelyn's shoulders. "I don't have the slightest notion."

A snort of laughter escaped Jocelyn. "At least you are honest."

"And, I'm told, stubborn and bull headed."

"Barnacles are less stubborn."

Alicia followed Jocelyn upstairs. "I wish you'd told me about all this in your letters."

"What would you have had me do? Stitched a note to your veil? 'Oh, I forgot to mention, *mon amie*, my husband is missing, my son is in prison, have a nice wedding?'" Jocelyn flipped a hand.

"Not in those words, of course, but Father might have been able to help." Alicia had a quick pang of regret. "I wish he were here. He'd know exactly what to do."

Jocelyn shook her head as a sadness washed over her eyes. "You are lucky to have such a champion, no? Ric was that for our Beau."

"Father always had a fondness for Ric. Mother as well. They

would want to know he's in trouble."

"What could I tell them when I have nothing to tell myself?"

"True." Alicia worried her lip. "It would be hard to ask them for help when we don't know which direction to head ourselves."

Jocelyn sniffed, dabbed at her nose, and tucked her handkerchief away. "I must hope Captain Bradford will bring me the information I so dearly paid for tonight. For now, it is late, and I am *épuisé*. Exhausted." She pushed Alicia toward the stairs. "Tomorrow, we go to tea."

Alicia stopped and gave her head a quick shake before looking back. Had she missed something? "Tea?"

"*Oui.*" Jocelyn gave her another nudge to continue climbing. "You will come with me to the governor's house. And while you sip English tea with his boring wife and her tedious friends, *I* will work my charms on Governor Wilson. He is one of Ric's best clients with the deepest purse. If I can get him to do business with *me*, there may just be a chance I can raise the money I need."

Chapter 7

The sun finally agreed to show up. Richard stood at the bow of the ship and pulled in his first dry breath in days. If the wind held, and the captain made use of all his canvas, they'd sight land in a few days.

He gripped the tarred rigging and felt the hum of the rope. His gaze ran up the mast to the bowed white sail set against the brilliant blue of the sky. A grin tugged at the corner of his mouth as he recalled those almost human qualities of a fine ship.

There was life to each of these wooden beasts that those who had never sailed could hardly imagine. A ship breathed. On a clear calm day such as this, it danced beneath your feet in a slow rise and fall. Rigging sang. Sails sighed and snapped and filled like great lungs. Ribs creaked. Bellies rolled and swayed.

As the last of the sails were set and caught the breeze, the ship leapt through the tips of the waves. Richard smiled, adjusted his stance, and gripped the rigging tighter. Aye, sometimes she even flew.

Son of a bitch, he missed this life. He'd almost forgotten the clean tang of the ocean. The taste of salt upon his lips. The constant pitch beneath his feet. The vastness of the ocean where it reached out and met the sky. He even loved watching its power when a storm would stir the dark water to boiling and waves taller than trees would threaten to swallow a ship whole. When only by the grace of God would you live to see another day. It made a man feel triumphant. More alive than he's ever felt before.

Richard shook his head at the poetic nonsense of his musings. "Nothing worse than a seaman set to rot in dry dock." *Damn*, he wished he hadn't said dry. And he wished more than anything that he hadn't made that promise to "Saint" James about staying sober.

The afternoon of Alicia's would-be wedding turned into Richard's own day of vows and promises. He'd known where she was headed before the rest. The return of the merchant's cart along with her final note confirmed what he'd already guessed. There was only one reason anyone could think of why Alicia was on the road to Liverpool. She was on her way across the ocean to the Carolinas. Black Point to be exact, and Jobo, excuse me…*Jocelyn* Robbins.

Richard prayed he'd find Alicia safely waiting for passage at the docks of Liverpool and he'd never have to lay eyes on Black Point, or any other point in America. The last thing he wanted to do was cross paths with the good Mistress Robbins or her husband Ric ever again.

James had been insistent that he himself follow his sister and return her safely home. But with his wife, Samantha so close to her time, and given the difficult birth of their first child, Richard could see the worry etched on his friend's face. He had been with James through those brutal hours of Amelia's birth. Long agonizing days of not knowing if Samantha or the babe would even survive.

James pushed his fingers through his hair. "The boy says she was on the road to Liverpool. I can leave at dawn, but if she's already found passage, it may take me months to return with her."

"I'll go," Richard volunteered.

Annalise put a reassuring hand on James' arm. "Samantha and Amelia can stay with us. We'll take good care of them. The doctor is close by. You mustn't worry."

Richard's impatience flared. Had they not heard him? They were wasting valuable time. "I said, I would go." He spread his hands wide. "I know the roads. If I leave now, I can be there in a few hours."

They all turned, startled, as if they'd suddenly remembered he was still in the room. Annalise had given him a tiny smile before looking like she'd eaten something rotten. James replayed the pitying look he'd given Richard out by the carriages. "I don't think that's a good idea."

"Don't be an arse, James. You're needed here. No one will even miss me. Let me do this. I promise you, I'll find her."

James' hesitation cut him. There was a time not too far in the past where James had trusted Richard with his very life. How far he had fallen from grace.

Richard raised his hands in surrender and continued. "I don't blame you for not trusting me. Hell, under the same circumstance, I wouldn't either, but do it anyway. I won't let you down. I give you my word." He placed a hand over his heart for good measure.

James exchanged glances with his parents.

It was then Richard threw in his final bargaining chip—idiot that he was... "I won't drink another sip of alcohol until she's returned home safe and sound." As soon as the words hit air, he regretted them, but he was a man of his word if nothing else and finding Alicia was worth more than a few hours of sobriety. He stood tall, pushed back his shoulders, tugged down his hems, and raised his right hand. "Trust me, James. I swear an oath on our friendship. I'll find her. Should I fail, you can blacken my name from your memory."

"And no drink?" James pinned him with an intense gaze.

"Not a single solitary drop."

The first few days without his favorite brandy had been brutal. Hell, those first hours had all but broken him. Richard had missed Alicia's departure by less than an hour. It was another full day before he could secure passage himself. By then, the cannonball sized headache and sweats had begun in earnest. Anxiously pacing nearly drove him to the brink. But he kept his word. Nothing stronger than tea passed his lips since he swore his oath to James. Thankfully, the shaking in his hands had subsided.

Richard drew in a deep clean breath of sea air. There was still the pull of blind cravings for the dusky amber liquid, but through it all, his anchor, his life's tether, the reason he was on this blasted ship heading for a place he didn't want to go to see people he didn't want to see, had been the image seared into his mind. Alicia in white.

Had he ever seen a more headstrong, infuriating, beautiful woman? Through the pacing, through the long nights, the sweating and the shakes, he had but one thought. *Please, let her be safe.*

Regardless, how long it took, he would find her. And not so he could fulfill his drunkard's promise to James and rush off to pickle himself in brandy again. No, he needed to find Alicia so he could sweep her into his arms and tell her once and for all how he loved her and wanted to spend the rest of his days with her. Then he would beg her forgiveness for being the biggest horse's arse that had ever sailed the sea.

Richard drew another deep pull of salt air into his lungs. Bracing his arms against the polished rails, he gazed out over the deep blue green of the waves and made a practiced sweep along the horizon, looking for any sign of land. They should be close now. Where the hell was the land?

Patience was not one of his virtues. Neither was idleness. It was enough to drive a man... to drink...*Bugger!*

* * * * *

Two days and a hide and seek sail up the coast of the Carolinas finally had them docking in Black Point. The ship's navigator had overestimated the strong currents working off the coast and they had arrived further south than expected.

Then came the threat of landing squarely in the known territory of the pirate Lucifer. With half a dozen ships and a crew of more than a thousand men, Captain Leathan Dhu became known to all as Lucifer after he and his crew laid a bloody swath across the waters off the coast of what was known as the Outer Banks. No ship to cross his path was immune from the devil himself. His brutality was legendary. Some said he was mad, but then would any sane man roast a prisoner and feed him to his crew?

One glimpse of Dhu's ship, *The Devil's Breath*, would cause seasoned men to leap into the waves rather than face the known atrocities that an encounter with Lucifer and his crew guaranteed.

Fortunately, the captain commanding the ship on which Richard traveled knew this coast well. He'd faced the threat before and could find hidden coves and island blinds to creep along the narrows of the sound due west of the Outer Banks. It was well past midday by the time they finally made port at Black Point.

Under the Crown's appointment, Black Point was becoming a thriving town. After the prior wars with the indigenous tribes, the settlement around this busy harbor had flourished. The English influence and wealth were obvious along its merchant's row, the main street, and in the grand homes being built along the waterfront.

A quick query of two matronly, well-appointed women, had Richard stowing his travel bags at a local public house for safekeeping and arriving at the front door of the Laced Ladies shop in short order.

Upon entering, the cloying smell of lavender assaulted his senses. As if dropped into a woman's dressing room, he was surrounded by frills of every description. There was a time and a place for a fine lace cuff, but this was too much froth, even for him.

A tall, beautifully dressed woman behind a wide marble counter lifted her gaze from her work as he entered. Hair blacker than a raven's feather gave her a striking appearance. High, strong cheekbones and dark eyes made her quite lovely. Foreign was the word that immediately came to mind. Intense. Tamed. The sharpness of those dark eyes spoke of an innate suspicion and deep mistrust. Richard was thankful only ribbons of lace filled her elegant fingers.

He ran a smoothing hand over his hair and fell easily into his most disarming and charming self.

"Good day, my dear woman. Would you believe I've traveled clear across the ocean with the sole purpose of visiting this fine establishment?" He reached out and fingered a wide ruffle of lace-edged ribbon.

The only response was an icy lift of an ebony winged brow.

Richard continued, "I'm searching for a young woman."

Deep, almost black eyes made a slow, pointed appraisal of him from the top of his head to the toes of his boots and back again before she met his gaze. "I'm sorry. The shop is closed. I cannot help you."

Her accent was not English but spoke of some breeding and education. He tried to place her. Glancing at the door before resuming her work, she thought to dismiss him. He'd travel much too far to be so easily put off.

"Let me be more specific," Richard insisted. "I'm looking for a woman named Alicia. Alicia Steele. She would have just arrived from England. Fair hair, blu—"

"I'm sorry, sir. I cannot help you."

"Then, if you please, I wish to speak to your proprietor. Jobo, rather Madam Jocelyn Robbins, or is Mister Robbins about?"

"I'm sorry, sir."

Frustration welled. Part of him was tempted to push past this stony sentry and search the premises himself, but he had never manhandled a woman before, and he wasn't about to start today. Undaunted, he used his most powerful weapon when it came to the opposite sex. He flashed a smoldering smile before running his fingers through his hair and giving a quick huff of amusement.

"Let's try this from a different angle." He kept smiling as he pulled out his leather wallet. Placing a small stack of coins upon the counter, he adopted a casual stance crossing one booted foot over the other, leaning on the edge of the counter. "I'd like to purchase a length of your finest lace."

She didn't even lift her eyes. "I'm sorry—"

Richard's hand slipped off the edge. His control snapped, and he slapped the counter, upsetting the coins. "I swear if you say, 'I'm sorry, sir,' one more time."

With a quick bend, the woman produced a thin-bladed dirk from beneath her hems. She rasped the sharp tip across the stone countertop as she met his furious gaze with her own chilled, impertinent stare. There was no doubt as to her threat, her disdain, or her infuriating commitment to being one of the most uncooperative individuals he'd ever had the misfortune to encounter. He'd dealt with hardened prisoners more accommodating.

"I'm sorry, *sir.*" She lifted the blade almost casually, as if she held out a cup of tea, but there was little doubt as to the serious threat attached. If she lunged, the knife wouldn't necessarily kill him, but he wasn't about to test that theory.

By instinct, Richard reached for the pistol he no longer carried. The corner of her mouth flickered into a smirk as she caught the movement, and he tried unsuccessfully to conceal it by placing a hand over his heart.

"You have me at a disadvantage, mistress. I never dreamed I'd need a weapon when shopping for lace." Richard raised his hands in surrender. "And, as it would be most ungentlemanly of me to bleed all over your shop. I'll save us both the trouble and be on my way."

When he reached for the coins he'd laid on the counter, the insolent wench covered them with her delicate fingers and swept them into one of her pockets. Still holding the knife pointed toward his heart, the dark-haired witch notched her chin and stared him down as if daring him to challenge her over the money.

Richard bit back a curse, but a torrent of blue expletives rushed through his mind. Of all the cheek! Turning to leave, he plucked two snowy lace handkerchiefs and a pair of black gloves from a small vignette and, smiling back at her, pushed them into his breast pocket. "It's been a pleasure doing business with you. I'll be sure to tell all my acquaintances what fine service they can expect here."

He slammed the door behind him and was relieved she hadn't planted that blade in his spine on the way out. Richard looked up and down the street and back toward the building. There wasn't so much as a flutter from the curtains in the upper windows. He ran an irritated hand through his hair and headed east before circling around to the back of the building. The first floor had no windows on this side. Twin steel straps reinforced the door. A bit secure for lace, don't you think?

What had Alicia gotten herself into? Presuming she was here at all. Was there a chance he was wrong? Could she have gone elsewhere? He scanned the second-floor windows once more. No, she was here. He would bet his life on it. It might take that to get past their stunning guard, but he was getting into this building one way or another.

Chapter 8

Alicia smoothed the bodice of her borrowed, rose-pink gown. Jocelyn had seen fit to burn the two gowns she'd traveled in, insisting she knew from experience that they would never get the vile odor of bilge from the fabric. This gown belonged to her assistant, Raine, who was taller and a good deal smaller through the bust than Alicia. Jocelyn had done her best to de-scandalize her décolletage with trim from the shop, but an ill-timed, deep breath would surely cause her breasts to break out of their lace-trimmed prison.

The governor's drawing room was a true taste of home. It resembled every well-appointed English drawing room Alicia had ever visited. The fact it had traveled piece by piece across thousands of miles of ocean should have impressed her. It certainly impressed their hostess.

Gladys Wilson was nearly as round as she was tall. Steel gray curls hung stiffly at each ear, which dragged lower than prudent by the weight of large blue topaz earrings. Her low neckline cradled a matching necklace with an impressive center drop threatening to be lost forever within the deep, crepe-lined dip of the woman's cleavage.

"I'm heartsick over it, truly. How am I ever to host a proper dinner party with only service for twenty? I warned Emmett something like this would happen. It's not bad enough we have to deal with those savage natives still lurking about the woods. Now, the pirate trade along the coast has gotten out of hand. Nothing is safe. I heard they stole Elaine Riddle's great-grandmother's silver, every bit of it. They melt it down, you know. But what they would do with my precious Staffordshire, I have no idea. Emmett tells me they strip the gold mounts and..." she paused and gave a tiny sob for effect, placing the back of her ringed fingers to her forehead. "...simply smashed the rest. They're heathens, I tell you. All of them." Gladys popped a small, glazed cake into her mouth and shook her head as she chewed. Her curls never moved.

Alicia sipped at her tea and quietly observed the other women filling the settees around her. She'd lost track of Jocelyn shortly after they'd arrived. Once the introductions were done, and Mistress Wilson and her companions had surrounded her like fresh meat at a banquet, Jocelyn and the spindly Governor Wilson had engaged in their own hushed conversation. Sometime during the women's inquisition of her, Alicia had misplaced them.

The high society ladies of Black Point descended upon her begging for news from their beloved London, what did she know of Paris fashions for the season, or the latest society gossip. They fawned over her dress, making her execute a slow agonizing turn. But as soon as Alicia explained that she wasn't an authority on fashion, Parisian or otherwise, her dress was borrowed, and she hadn't traveled to London since she was a child, they quickly abandoned her to her tea. She couldn't decide whether she was profoundly insulted, or secretly relieved.

Relief won, and she smiled into her cup. Out of the women's spotlight, Alicia was free to wander about the room and be grateful. Had it not been for her sprint away from the alter this was the life that awaited her as Mistress Bineau. A Duchess. Tea parties, uncomfortable gowns, and insipid conversation about trivial things. Utter heartbreak over a few stolen dishes?

What a tiny world to live in. How could these women have braved all they had to accompany their husbands and families to this new land only to bring their suffocating little lives with them? They were like elegantly dressed garden snails dragging their shells—their protected, safe, boring, Staffordshire-lined shells—along with them. Didn't they want to experience something beyond their narrowed view of the world? Why embark on such an adventure to waste it on tea parties?

Alicia glanced back at them. Perhaps she was being unfair. Ungrateful. She'd had this life and thrown it away. Many didn't have a choice. Still others would kill for the chance to live a life of ease. Just because she couldn't envision herself in this scene didn't mean it was wrong. But, thank goodness it wasn't the life for her.

Strolling around the room, Alicia paused to admire a painting of a fine three-mast sloop. Now that she'd made her first crossing, she could smell the sea air. Feel the movement of the deck beneath her feet. It was a beautiful ship. Father's ship the *Scarlet Night* was a sloop like this. He used to tell her how at full sail she would dance over the tops of the waves. It must have been magnificent to stand in her bow and feel that power. Alicia remembered begging her father to tell her his stories and wanting to know the difference between a sloop and a frigate, and a galleon versus a brigantine. He was the expert, after all, her father the pirate. Regret continued to snag at her heart whenever she thought of him. She missed him, but somehow the more she experienced, the more she fell in love with the sights and sounds and smells of the sea and ships, the closer she felt to him.

Looking at the artist's depiction of the ship at full sail cutting through the white tips of the waves, she could imagine her father standing strong at her helm. He never hid his passion for ships and the sea. He'd led a life of extraordinary journeys and adventures. Now more than ever, she wondered how a fierce pirate captain could have left all of it behind to sit behind a desk in a dark, dusty study merely to engage in land negotiations and the running of a grand estate?

The answer was easily summed up in one powerful word…

Love.

He'd been so in love with her mother, he'd traded everything to be with her. Given up pirating and traveling to exotic points around the world to live out his days far away from the sea in the rolling hills of Weatherington. All so he could live a life full of love. Her parents didn't talk about those early days often, but when they did, the affection they had for one another was woven through every story.

Alicia couldn't fathom such a romance. Perhaps that was the real reason she hadn't married Frederick. Having grown up within such a love story, she couldn't settle for less in her own life.

Certainly, her history on that subject was far from stellar. She thought she was in love with Richard, of course. He'd been so handsome and charming. Having lost her head as well as her heart, she'd spent weeks arranging "accidental" meetings just to be near him. Chasing him like a new pup starving for one bit of notice. In the end, she'd handed him her heart only to have him crush it and hand it back to her. He'd never know how that doomed night had set up a tidal wave of recklessness. Alicia was lucky to emerge unscathed. Relatively.

Seeing Richard in the garden the morning of the wedding day had stirred it all anew. Anger, frustration, shame, heartbreak. A life with Frederick wasn't the only mistake she'd escaped from that afternoon. It was good she left the past an entire ocean away.

Guilt threatened when she thought about leaving her family behind, but a deep sadness still flooded her heart when she realized she'd never see Richard again. Even after all they'd been through. Even after the way he'd rejected her. The heart remembers more than the head can forget.

"Oh...I beg you...call me 'Ducky' once more, for old time's sake?" Alicia gave herself a mental shove. *Forget him. Leave the past in the past. He's probably still floating at the bottom of some brandy bottle.*

Jocelyn interrupted her musings, *"J'ai terminé.* I am done. We need to leave."

Alicia swallowed her last mouthful of cold tea. "I was done before I began." She tipped her chin in the direction of the cluster of other women. "I didn't make the best first impression on the fine society of Black Point."

Jocelyn glanced back at Governor Wilson and smoothed the bodice of her gown. "Seems neither of us was very successful. Insufferable, pompous, chauvinistic, egotistical...," she muttered as she looped her arm through Alicia's and led her back to their hostess. "...arse." She took Alicia's cup and handed it to a waiting servant and adopted a brilliant smile. "Gladys, ladies, it has been a delight..."

Moments later they were on the street heading back toward The Laced Ladies.

"The man is playing both sides against the middle," fumed Jocelyn. "*Les porc.*"

"I don't understand." Alicia lifted her hems and hurried to keep up.

"Swine. The man has his own suppliers. It all makes sense now." She tapped her forehead with her fingertips. "Why did I not realize it sooner?"

Evidently, Jocelyn's hands were not the only thing that moved at high speed when she was agitated. Alicia struggled to keep pace. "Please, Jocelyn, slow down and tell me what you're talking about," panted Alicia.

Jocelyn turned back. Her color was up, which could have been due to her growing anger or the fact that she'd just sprinted from the Wilson's front door. "Emmett Wilson is one of this town's dignitaries. The governor. A founding father. He may not look the part, but he is an extremely powerful man." She leaned close. "It was not until Gladys was going on and on about her precious china that I realized it. He hates huge dinner parties. Loathes them. Too many cross purposes in the room. If you are playing more than one angle, having them all in your ballroom makes for a very tense evening, no?"

Alicia struggled to catch her breath. "Jocelyn, you're talking in riddles."

"Who do you think stole Gladys's china?" A hand flew in the direction of the Wilson's estate. "Him. The pig himself. He has his own crews. His own ships. *Les pirates.*" She jabbed at the air. "He pays off key officers in the British Navy to look the other way, so he pays no tax. He gets a double share of the bounty for his protection, of course. His private stock in the trading company insures heavily against these types of attacks, so he loses nothing. Then he turns around and makes a fortune selling the stolen items *back* to the fools who lost them in the first place."

"But Gladys never got her china."

"That is because he sold all that lovely Staffordshire up north for twice what he paid for it to begin with. Add that to the insurance payout and his share. *Pour l'amour de Dieu*, the man could have bought enough plates for eight parties!" Jocelyn pressed the backs of her fingers to pinked cheeks. "And we are not just talking about china. Do you have any idea how lucrative the spice trade is these days? The slave market? Everyone is making a profit, and our crafty Governor Wilson is dipping his hand into every pocket he meets."

"He's not going to help you." Alicia shook her head and frowned.

Jocelyn huffed. "Why would he?" She opened and adjusted the elegant lace parasol she carried to keep the sun from her face. "He made it very clear. There is no profit in helping me. I am barely a threat to his operation. Still his competition, but as he so kindly reminded me not ten minutes ago, now with Ric gone, Jocelyn Robbins is hardly worth his notice. Arrogant pig. *Les porc*!"

"Could he have something to do with Ric's disappearance?"

Jocelyn gave a quick shake of her head. "I do not believe so." She began walking again. "He seemed genuinely concerned when we spoke of Ric. Not surprised, just concerned. I think he has suspicions, *oui*, but he did not voice them. It is all so damn frustrating. I needed his help. I do not know where else to turn."

After several quick yet quiet steps, a thought began to bloom in

Alicia's mind. "Perhaps, in a way, he's helped you after all."

"In what way?"

Alicia gestured back toward the estate. "The secret to his success. Without realizing it, he's given you the answer as to how to raise the money you need."

Jocelyn stopped and frowned. "Now it is my turn not to understand."

"All you need is your own pirate."

"Of course. I will just order one, shall I? Summon him out of thin air, no?" Jocelyn fluttered her fingers as if to conjure one.

Alicia shrugged as the idea bloomed. "Perhaps you already did."

"Oh? How so?" Jocelyn's well-shaped eyebrows reached for her bonnet.

"Me." Alicia held her arms wide. "I'm here to find my true path. I *am* the daughter of one of the fiercest pirates to have sailed. I have seawater in my veins. You practically begged me to come visit. How serendipitous that I arrive at your door at this very moment?"

Jocelyn rolled her eyes, flipped a hand at Alicia's gown, and kept walking. "Oh, *oui*, my pretty pink pirate. Very amusing."

"I'm not making a joke." Alicia fell into step with her and dropped her voice. "Think about it. No one would suspect a woman. Surely not me. I could play the proper lady during the day in my skirts and corsets and lace. By night I could don men's clothing, dress all in black, white, pink, it matters not, and slip out to plunder the unaware. All under the cover of night. We could work the same angles as Governor Wilson, but through his wife. All the wives. The women are the ones with all the money. Most brought their family's fortune into the marriages. They all have healthy household accounts and monthly allowances. Their husbands may control the purse strings, but it was their wives' purse to begin with.

"We'd not deal with spices or, *horrors*, slaves." Alicia shivered and continued. "We could deal in what *they* most covet. Fine furnishings, china, silk gowns from Paris, perfumes. Why melt down the silver, when they would pay twice the amount for a lovely tea set with matching candlesticks and sugar shells?" The rush of ideas raced through Alicia's brain as she hurried after Jocelyn. "There's just one problem."

"Just one?" Jocelyn's dubious tone didn't faze her.

"I'd need a proper ship."

Jocelyn laughed and flipped a hand, "Oh, I have a ship. The *Ruby Mist*. I do not know that I would call it proper, but it floats…in a manner of speaking."

"You do?" Alicia tugged her to a stop. "What kind of ship?"

"Well, it is not mine exactly." Jocelyn sighed as if she regretted encouraging such foolishness and bringing up the subject. "The *Ruby Mist* is Ric's. He had always said you cannot land lock a pirate without a ship." A flip of her hand dismissed the idea. "It has spent more time decomposing at the dock than it ever did at sea."

Alicia was quick to keep her from walking away. "Why didn't you say so before? We could be off following Ric's trail by now."

"We are not talking about your father's *Scarlet Night*," Jocelyn snapped. Lowering her voice, she leaned closer to Alicia. "Ric would have taken it himself if it were seaworthy. It is a leaky, old bit of driftwood with a cracked mast and a seepy hull. I certainly do not have the money to repair it. Even if I was crazy enough to go along with this foolish notion, we would be lucky to get halfway to the outer banks before the *Mist* decided to cease floating."

Undeterred, Alicia thought for a moment. "So, long sea voyages are out. But I'll bet we can make it safe for short hauls. We can steal what we need to repair the ship. Call it part of my training. Even with minor leaks in the chinking, it might work. I wouldn't need to stray too far from the coast to begin with. It would be suitable for that, don't you think?"

Jocelyn broke out of Alicia's grasp. "*La démence.* You are mad."

Perhaps she was, but the momentum of her building determination wouldn't be stilled. "We have a ship." She began to tick off the items she'd require on her fingers. "I'd need proper clothing. A weapon, of course. Something mightier than a dirk. Supplies…" She reached her pinkie and stopped. "Crew. Who do you know who would be willing to sign on to crew? Perhaps the men from last night know some available sailors looking for work?"

Jocelyn raised her eyes to the heavens before shaking her head and turning back to Alicia. "Stop." She held her hand in front of Alicia. "You are talking nonsense. A rotting ship, a crew of castoffs, and a captain who does not know the business end of a pistol or the first thing about sailing or pirating. It is a prelude to disaster, not a solution to my problems."

Alicia smiled at her. Determination filling her sails. "*But* a ship can be repaired. A crew can be trained, and *I* can learn everything I need to know."

"I do not think you realize all there is to *being* a pirate. You are romanticizing this. There is nothing glamorous to that life. It is dangerous, and violent. And deadly." She gently brushed at Alicia's sleeve.

"I understand what's involved. It's going to take a lot of work, and courage. I have no illusions about it being easy."

"Easy?" Jocelyn hissed, her patience obviously at an end, "Have you ever seen a man shot before? Had his throat slit? A body after it has been dragged across the keel of a ship? Tried to walk across a rolling deck that is slippery with blood? Do you know it takes six men to properly load a cannon? Or that a pistol kicks like an angry mule when you pull the trigger?" Jocelyn peered back over her shoulder and lowered her voice. "Let us not even get into the fact that you are a woman. Do you have any idea what men like this *do* to women? And even if they are not thinking about tossing your skirts over your head and rutting between your thighs, any seaman who has ever sailed will think being on a ship with you is bad luck. Most will not set foot on deck if there is a woman aboard. And a woman captain? *Oui*, there are rare cases when women have led crews, but that is *not* the reality."

Alicia crossed her arms over her chest and stood her ground. "I'm named for one of the best women captains out there."

Jocelyn threw up her hands with impatience. "Oh, *oui*, I know. The *great* Alice Tupper Quinn, but sharing a name is not the same as sharing a life. Do you even know the truth about your namesake? She became a pirate because she had to. She killed a man. A bloody Duke. She is an outlaw. A murderer. Pirating and living forever far out at sea is how she keeps her neck out of a noose…barely. I was there, too, the night we kept her from hanging at Newgate and helped her escape. It was not as if she had a lot of choices in this life. You do. Why would you want to fight and claw your way through the remainder of your days never knowing when a storm or an enemy or a cannonball will end it all?"

Alicia struggled to find the words to explain. She was quiet for several pounding beats of her heart before pulling in a steadying breath. "Have you ever worn someone else's shoes?"

"We are talking about shoes now?" Jocelyn looked incredulous.

"Yes, shoes. Someone else's shoes. They're a size too small, pinch at the toes and blister the heels. Every single step is a reminder that these are not your shoes." She clenched her jaw. "It starts slowly, enduring those first uncomfortable strides, but soon it's unbearable. Excruciating. Each step you try to take forward becomes so painful that soon you stop trying to walk at all." Alicia met Jocelyn's dark gaze. "I love my family, my home, my friends, but it has felt as if I've been wearing someone else's shoes my whole life. Can you possibly understand?"

"*Mon cher…*" Jocelyn gave her a pitying look.

Alicia pointed back toward the harbor. "I left everything and everyone I knew to come here and find out what my life is supposed to be. Discover *my* purpose. I believe I've finally found it. The longer I think about it, the less crazy it sounds, and the more it feels right. It goes beyond my wanting to help you find Ric and Beau. Don't you see? It's about finding me. My true course. Discovering who I'm meant to be." Alicia laid a hand over her heart. "I'm not blind to the life I'm suggesting. I've heard the stories my father tells when he thinks I'm not listening. I've read the horrific battle accounts in the books in his library. I may be inexperienced in some things, but I can learn. I need to try, if not for your sake, then for my own."

The more Alicia spoke the deeper her conviction became. She had to make Jocelyn understand. "Have you ever known something is right before you even know it? It's a sense deep in your belly. I may not have the right words to explain it, but I must do this. And more importantly, I'm certain I can."

Alicia planted her hands on her hips and continued. "And whether you help me make it so, and allow me to help you in return, or whether I hack off my hair, bind my chest, disguise myself as a lad, and live the rest of my life as a man, I *will* follow my destiny. Somehow, some way, I will be a pirate."

Chapter 9

"You are serious." Jocelyn tipped her head and gave her a hard stare.

Alicia notched her chin and realized she'd never been more serious about anything before. "I am."

"I'm beginning to believe you." A vertical line creased between Jocelyn's brows. "I still do not think you realize how difficult a life you are craving. It is a brutal, barbaric *man's* life."

"Not all pirates are barbarians." Alicia argued. "Some, I hear, are quite gentlemanly, and many of the finest pirates are women."

"*Oui, oui…*" Jocelyn raised a hand in surrender. "But Tupper is the exception to the rule."

Alicia placed a hand to her chest and gave Jocelyn a coy smile. "But who better to follow her example, than I?"

Looking off toward the center of the town, Jocelyn tapped her lower lip with the gloved tip of her finger. "I have not laid eyes on the *Ruby Mist* in more than a year."

A bubble of excitement burst in Alicia's chest. "What kind is it? A sloop? Like the *Scarlet Night*?"

Jocelyn gave a small shake to her head. "I have no idea."

An image of a sleek, beautiful ship flashed in Alicia's mind. The gleam of the scrubbed deck, brass fittings, and polished rails. Its tall masts reaching high to brush the clouds waiting impatiently for the sails to unfurl and take her on a dance across the waves. Her own hands guiding the wheel. "When can I see her?" Eagerness laced her words.

"Let us not get ahead of ourselves." Jocelyn shook her head.

Was she changing her mind? Alicia reined in her enthusiasm. She brushed an invisible bit of lint off her sleeve. "You're considering my suggestion then?"

Jocelyn turned and swept her gaze the full length of her. Alicia held her breath and gave her a small smile. Jocelyn tossed a hand before slipping it into the crook of Alicia's arm. "I must be as mad as you, to even entertain this idea." She continued moving them toward the shop.

"We'd be helping each other." Alicia prodded.

"Enough of your hawker's pitch," insisted Jocelyn. "Give me a moment to think."

Alicia tightened her hold on Jocelyn's arm. She watched the play of sunlight through the patterned lace of Jocelyn's parasol and concentrated on their path across the still soft ground.

A smile spread across Alicia's lips. Part of her wanted to swing Jocelyn into an excited spin. It's a heady business when you discover your life's desire lying dormant within your soul. Once brought into the brilliant light of realization, it can never truly go back into the shadows.

She was destined. By circumstance? By blood? She'd come

from two parents who had straddled society throughout their entire lives and shown her both sides. Rich, poor, right, wrong, lawful citizen, thief. Daughter of a Marquise, son of a whore. Perhaps because of that, it was easier to see herself living the dual life she envisioned. Finery and grace by day, danger and debauchery by night.

Alicia tucked her chin and stifled a wicked smile.

Whenever will I sleep?

They soon reached the Laced Ladies. Entering the shop, Alicia was once again taken aback by the dark beauty of Jocelyn's clerk, the very serious Raine. Alicia had yet to see the woman so much as grin. Still, she was stunning. Alicia felt pale as chalk in her presence and couldn't help but wonder about where she was from. Presently, she was helping a woman choose between a beautiful pair of lace lengths. One the color of rich raw cream, the other a deeper shade of ecru.

"Good afternoon, Mademoiselle Gardener. I see you are in good hands with Raine. Those are lovely pieces. We just received them last week."

"I need to speak with you, Mistress Robbins. It is important." Raine cast a pointed glance at Alicia.

"Have I had word from my adventurous men?" Jocelyn tried to hide the anxiousness in her voice with a wooden smile directed toward her customer. Raine shook her head. Jocelyn drew a forced breath and broadened her smile. "Then whatever it is cannot be more important than helping Mistress Gardener with her purchase, no? I need to see to something upstairs." Jocelyn gave Alicia a small nudge toward the back curtain. "I will be back down shortly. Be sure to show our guest that stunning pair of gloves we just acquired from Italy."

At Mademoiselle Gardener's delighted gasp, they made their escape.

Upstairs, Jocelyn tossed her parasol onto a waiting chair and pointed to a seat at the table. Alicia removed her hat and smoothed her hair as Jocelyn produced a bottle and two short glasses. She poured a small measure into each and recorked the bottle. Pushing one glass across the table toward Alicia, she lifted hers and drained it in one swallow. She uncorked the bottle and splashed more into her glass.

"*Prendre*. Drink."

"What is it?" Alicia lifted the glass and took a sniff. The warm smell of sweet spice tickled her nose.

"Jamaican rum. Ric's favorite. I figure if you are going to live the life, you should learn the first lesson, no?"

"How to drink rum?"

"That, and the old saying that it is a bad day when the rum runs dry. A dangerous crew is a sober one."

"Wouldn't having the crew drunk all the time be counterproductive?"

"You want them to follow you blindly into battle, do you not? Fight like savages?"

"I suppose…" Alicia lifted the glass and tossed the liquid into her mouth like Jocelyn had done.

Instant fire ignited in her throat and stole her ability to breath as it burned a fiery path all the way into her belly. Her eyes watered as the heat bloomed in her chest and rushed to flush her face. "Oh, bugger!" she wheezed. "What the hell?" She clutched at her neck.

"*Encore?*"

Alicia was quick to put her hand over the top of her glass and shake her head.

Jocelyn shrugged and helped herself to more. "I remember my first bit of rum. It was in the galley of the *Scarlet Night*. A beast of a man in a filthy kilt. Name was MacTavish. He told me after the third swallow, I would not notice the burn. I did not. Hell, I did not remember noticing much after that…save Ric, of course. We spent that night sleeping on the deck in each other's arms."

Finishing her drink, Jocelyn was quiet for a moment. She traced the top of her glass as she spoke. "You know, you and I are not so different. I, too, longed for the freedom to live my life as I chose. Those first days at sea with Ric were surreal. I had never known such a life even existed. My father sheltered me away in a convent for most of my life, and I wanted nothing more than to break free. So, I do understand your desire to find your own path more than you believe." She dropped her chin and shook her head. "I must be mad, or desperate, but in truth." Jocelyn lifted her gaze and captured Alicia's. "I can help you. And if you are determined one way or another to live the life of a pirate—"

"I am." The rum added a huskiness to Alicia's voice.

"Then we agree to help one another?"

"Yes, absolutely."

"You will need assistance. Training. I may know the right men who might be trusted... for a price."

"Of course." A well of exhilaration began to swell in her belly. "A percentage of the take." Alicia nodded.

"The *Ruby Mist* may be the hair in the stew, however. I don't know its condition. We'll look tomorrow. If it does not leak like a codger's hat, we might be in business." Jocelyn rose and rummaged through a drawer in a long buffet. She pulled out a tight roll of parchment and a narrow wooden box. Sitting again, she unrolled the parchment showing Alicia a simple map of the coastline. "You would have to stick to these waters *north* of Black Point. Only north. There are plenty of small ships moving goods up and down the coast, and plenty of coves for you to hide in wait." She ran a finger back and forth along a section of map. "Never venture south of this point. That is Lucifer's lair. Unless you want to be roasted like a bilge rat, you will stay away from this area. I am sure there are more detailed maps we can look at, but before you raise one inch of anchor rope, you will study them until you know each and every inch of this coast like you know your own mother's face."

Alicia nodded as she studied the map. "I will." She tapped the area along the south that Jocelyn had indicated. "Who is Lucifer?"

"Not anyone you ever want to meet. He's a pirate. As vicious and vile as they come, but I have never heard of him venturing further north. His ship, the *Devil's Breath,* attacks the larger, heavy-laden merchant ships coming from the African continent. His favorites are the Spanish. He is looking for gold but will sell anything he can lay his hands on." Jocelyn pointed a finger at Alicia. "Including fair young women who get in his way—unless he decides to keep you for his own *amusement* first. Or kill you."

If Jocelyn was trying to frighten her, she was failing. Alicia's determination only became more solidified. "Understood. I'll only pirate small prey to the north and stay out of his way."

"Good." Jocelyn took a deep breath and pulled the wooden box in front of her. "Now, this was given to Ric, but I believe if he were here…well, if he were here, we would not be having this insane discussion, no?" Her hands fluttered before covering her eyes as a wave of emotion tugged her under.

Alicia was quick to shift her chair around the table and sit closer to her. "We'll find them. I swear. Whatever we must do, we shall do." She rubbed Jocelyn's shoulder.

Dabbing at her eyes, Jocelyn gave a quick shake of her head as she recovered her composure. "As I am more convinced by the moment that we are both equally daft, I think it's fitting you have this."

Opening the box, Jocelyn pulled out something wrapped in a protective cloth. "It is old, but Ric has lovingly kept it in good working order. It was a gift from your father."

Jocelyn revealed a long pistol. Ornate in its fittings, the handle was inlaid with mother of pearl. The sharp smell of oil and powder met Alicia's nose.

"I was told this gun was owned by Samuel "Cookie" Burrows. Quite the character according to my Ric. In fact, he was the man who married your mother."

"I'm sorry?" Alicia raised her gaze.

Jocelyn nodded. "Oh, what is the proper word? Ah, proxy. He stood in place of your father, as the captain is the only one who can legally perform a marriage at sea, it was Cookie who stood proxy for your father the night your parents were wed."

"How did I not know this story? I thought it was a one-legged cook that married my parents."

"*Oui*, Cookie." Jocelyn nodded and pointed to the pistol. "In fact, the duke Tupper murdered was the same man who killed Cookie while he was protecting your mother. The duke stole this gun and held your mother captive."

Alicia sat back hard in her chair as if she'd been shoved. "Are you sure?"

Jocelyn lifted one shoulder. "That is the story Ric always told. Cookie was like family to your father. Trusted him to look after your mother while they all searched for the mad duke. It was quite a blow when he got the grisly word that Cookie was dead."

"Grisly?" Alicia's stomach gave an unexpected flip.

"You have heard all this before, no?"

Alicia leaned forward like a child listening to a ghoulish story. "No, never."

"The duke was a sick, evil man. Liked to send tokens from his victims. He tried to kill Tupper but left the task to a servant who could not do it, so I was told. He was obsessed with your mother, followed her to Jamaica and was furious when he found she had married your father. His plan was to capture Annalise, kill Jaxon, and take her for himself. He cut quite a bloody path to reach her. Cookie was part of that." Jocelyn rubbed at the barrel of the gun with its protective cloth. "After it was all over, your father gave Ric Cookie's pistol. Ric was just a young lad. Cookie liked to pull his leg, send him on fool's errands, tease him with wild stories about ghostly spirits aboard ship and sirens luring greenhorn sailors like Ric to their watery deaths. So, when Cookie was killed, your father figured he owed Ric for all the grief Cookie had put him through, and he gave him this."

Alicia's head spun. She could understand why her parents wouldn't tell such a tale to a young girl, but never in a thousand years could she have imagined such a story. "I'd heard mother stowed aboard father's ship to escape the duke. I was always told 'Aunt' Alice saved her, but I never knew the rest."

"It may be made up for all I know, but that is the way it was told to me. You need a proper pistol in any case, and this one just might bring you a bit of the pirate luck your father seemed to possess." Jocelyn handed Alicia the weapon.

Not expecting the weight of it, it dropped her hand to the table. "It's heavier than it looks."

"*Oui*, and your next lesson is to work up your strength to hold it steady and fire it with one hand." Jocelyn stood and gathered their empty glasses. "Be warned, Ric says it bucks like the devil himself when you pull that trigger."

Alicia held it away from her like it might bite. "Is it loaded?"

After a quick snort, Jocelyn shook her head. "One lesson at a time."

Alicia nodded and ran her fingers down the smooth grip. It was a beautiful pistol—if pistols could be considered beautiful. The pearl inlay shown in the fading light. The initials S.B. were scratched in the brass band at the bottom of the handle. Alicia rubbed the letters with her thumb.

Jocelyn smoothed her skirts. "I should go downstairs to hear what Raine needed to tell me."

Lifting her gaze away from her gift, Alicia reached out a hand and caught the cuff of Jocelyn's sleeve. "Thank you. For this, and for having faith in me. I won't let you down."

"You may be the image of your dear mother, but you carry the stubbornness of your father, Alicia. I pray we do not come to regret this. It is a great risk we are undertaking. If something happens to you, they will never forgive me. I will never forgive myself."

"The decision is not solely yours, Jocelyn. I'm stronger than you think. You'll see."

"Whatever happens, I do not feel like I'm facing it alone anymore." She squeezed Alicia's fingers. "If nothing else, I am grateful for that."

Releasing their bond, Jocelyn headed toward the staircase, and Alicia once more examined the pistol on the table. Curiosity still swirled in her mind surrounding the word Jocelyn used. *Grisly.*

"I have to ask," Alicia stopped her, "you said something about the duke sending tokens from his victims. When he stole this gun, what did he send to my father from Cookie?"

Jocelyn looked over her shoulder. "Why, his peg leg, of course."

Chapter 10

Alicia tested the weight of the weapon in her hands. She considered a smaller pistol, but the rush of power she felt when holding Cookie's gun overrode such thoughts. If only it could tell its story. Had it been stolen? Had Cookie been a dandy? A pirate in satin breeches with a pearl handled pistol. How many men had he killed with this gun? Did he fire at the duke before he was killed and stripped of his peg?

A shiver ran through Alicia at the images conjured in her mind. She struggled to raise the weapon with a straight arm and had to cradle it with both hands. Would she carry it in a baldric lashed to her chest, tucked into her waistband, or… held tight to her thigh… strapped to her leg? Certainly not in skirts. Especially pink ones.

The afternoon was growing late, and the small back room where she was staying was cloaked in the dim light of the fading day. Alicia brought the gun with her to stand before the mirror there, leaving the door ajar to let a weak shaft of light illuminate her image in the glass. She stepped back into that narrow beam, raised her skirts to bare one leg, and lifted her heel to bend a knee before placing the cold pistol barrel against her skin. Her thigh quivered at the sudden chill of the steel. Her image in the glass was reckless and yet somehow erotic. Alicia dipped her chin and gave a wicked smile. It felt good. Right. Powerful. Like she was finally in command. She felt invincible.

"At last." A low deep whisper caught her attention as a shadowy figure moved toward her from a dark corner. "I finally found y—"

Without hesitation, with her opposite hand, Alicia grabbed the pistol by its barrel and spun in the direction of the voice. Momentum and adrenaline propelled her arm into a high, wide sweep until the butt end of the gun connected with her attacker.

The pearl handle met flesh and bone with a sharp crack. Her attacker crashed into the washstand, sent the pitcher shattering to the floor, and landed in a pile of limbs. "Bloody, fucking hell! Are you trying to kill me?"

"Don't you dare move, or—" She fumbled to turn the gun around, "—or, I'll shoot."

"For the love of God, put the damn gun down!" The man on the floor shielded his head with his arms.

The door flew open to crash against the wall. Jocelyn and Raine filled the doorway. Light from Raine's candle flooded the room. "What on earth is going on?"

"Him." Raine pointed as if she were choosing a fish at market. "I recognize the coat."

"Him?" Alicia lowered the gun and looked from Raine to the man and back again. "You know him?"

"No." Raine replied coolly before handing Jocelyn the candle and walking away.

"Dammit, Alicia…" Lowering his arms, the man gingerly fingered the angry gash along his cheekbone. The flesh was already beginning to swell. Blood smeared his cheek.

A rush of unchecked emotions punched the air from her lungs. *"Ducky?"* She could only whisper. Dropping the gun on the bed, she rushed to help him. "Oh, God, Richard."

"I remember you," chimed Jocelyn. "Although the last time I saw you, you were not wearing a coat. Or anything else except a blindfold and a most disagreeable sneer."

The heel of his boot scraped across the water and porcelain shards littering the floor as Alicia helped him into a seated position. "Don't forget my bloody hat," he growled.

"Ah, *oui*, we did leave you your hat. It was a cool night if I recall. Did not want you to catch a chill."

A thousand thoughts chased through Alicia's mind. "Are you all right?"

"No, I am far from '*all right*,'" He barked, wiping at his cheek. "You tried to cleave my skull." One hand covered the side of his face.

Alicia attempted to move his hand away. "You scared the life out of me."

He pushed her fussing fingers away. "What the hell were you doing with that gun? Hoisting your skirts? Baring—"

"Never mind all that. What are you doing here?" She grabbed at his lapel then smoothed the rumpled fabric.

"Is it not obvious?" Jocelyn interjected from the doorway. "He has come to fetch you."

"Can you stand?" At his nod, Alicia helped him to his feet. "How did you know where to find me?"

"Lucky guess," he grumbled as pulled out a handkerchief and dabbed at the blood on his cheek before stuffing it back into his pocket. "There's a ship leaving on the next tide heading back to London. Gather your things, Alicia, I'm taking you home."

Jocelyn passed over the candle to Alicia, laughed, and turned to leave. "Good luck with that one."

"Insufferable woman," Richard grumbled under his breath. "The quicker I get you away from her the better."

Alicia raised the candle to inspect Richard's cheek. "I'm so sorry I hit you."

"Like a blasted bull." Crossing the room, he peered into the looking glass and prodded the swelling around his eye. "I'm going to look like I've been through a brawl come morning." He pulled his handkerchief once more and dabbed at the wound. "And lost. To a woman no less."

"I said I was sorry." She unsuccessfully stifled a grin. Still, she couldn't believe he was here.

"Yes, yes," he placated as he tried to smile, but flinched and laid his fingers against the wound on his cheek. Catching his breath, he moved to her and stroked her arm. "I promise I'll forgive you if you hurry with your packing. We haven't much time. We can pick up my things on the way. Where is your bag?" He gave a quick scan of the room.

"I'm not leaving." Not an ounce of hesitation marred her response. Even through the shock of seeing him, the jolting of emotions, her decision and resolve stood firm.

Richard closed his eyes and sighed. Planting his hands on his hips he tipped his head and gave her the most patronizing look. Alicia watched the muscle tick in his jaw.

"I'm sure you're having a wonderful time here in…in…Black Pocks or wherever the hell we are, but your parents are worried, your brother is beside himself, I've spent weeks chasing you across an entire ocean. Playtime is over. You've had your little adventure. It's time to go home."

Play time? Alicia crossed her arms over her chest and gave him a wooden smile. "I appreciate you coming all this way, but don't make me blacken your other eye. I didn't need 'finding,' and I'm not going anywhere. Certainly not home, and most certainly not with you. My parents and my brother will soon receive word that I am alive and well, so you can set your mind at ease." She pointed at him, indicating his body from top to bottom. "You've played the gallant rescuer brilliantly. You've really missed your calling, Richard. Perhaps there's still time for you to become one of those knights who like clanging and rattling about in brilliant bits of tin. Unfortunately for you it seems there is no dragon in need of slaying, and I do not need rescuing." She hitched her chin toward his face. "And as your eye is beginning to turn a lovely shade of purple, even you can trust that I'm quite capable of taking care of myself."

"Alicia…*dearest*…," he hissed the word. "I'm not here to argue. I've made a promise to your family that I would find you and bring you back into their loving embrace. While I admit I don't possess a fine reputation, or a dragon-killing set of gleaming armor, I am still a man of my word, and I've given my word to your family. Now, I've had enough nonsense for one day," his voice began to rise in anger. Richard brushed back his hair and tugged sharply on his coat hems. "Be a good little girl—"

Something in her brain snapped. "Get. Out."

He jerked as if she'd hit him again. "I beg your pardon?"

"You heard me. And we both know you're familiar with those two words. You used them against me when I *was* a 'good little girl,' but if you'd take a moment and look, I'm a grown woman now, and I'm feeling anything but *good.*" She turned to pick up the gun and lifted it with two hands. Struggling to keep it leveled at his heartless chest, the weight of the barrel forced her aim a wee bit lower. "The only one leaving is you." He was damn lucky she hadn't learned how to load the pistol yet.

Richard jerked, shielded his crotch with his hands and turned his hip, "Are you mad? What on earth has gotten into you?"

"Conviction. Independence. Determination. None of which are your concern." She gave him a nudge with the barrel of the gun toward the door. "I don't know what arrangement you made with my family to inspire this sudden concern for my wellbeing." She prodded him through the apartment. "But I've chosen to stay here in Black Point for as long as I see fit."

Richard kept looking over his shoulder at her as if at any moment the empty pistol in her hands would magically contain enough powder and ball to actually shoot. She sure as hell wasn't going to tell him any different.

"Alicia—"

"Keep moving." Alicia's anger built as she continued her assertion down the stairs and into the shop, past Jocelyn and a bemused Raine. "And furthermore, I neither want, nor need, your council, your sanctimonious comments, or...or...anything else from you, for that matter."

Having reached the front door to the shop, Alicia opened it and gave Richard a final push. "Goodbye, Mister Dunbar. Safe travels." She closed the door in his shocked, swollen face, threw the bolt to lock the door and turned the "Open" sign to "Closed."

Marching past Jocelyn and Raine again, she shifted a glance in their direction. "Lesson three. How to load this blasted pistol."

Back in her room, Alicia dropped the gun back in its oil-clothed nest and slid down the wall into a shaking heap of pink skirts. Anger clenched her fists. Tears threatened to breach the dam as she punched back at the plaster behind her.

Good little girl? Good little girl! Damn you to hell, Richard Dunbar! How did I ever have feelings for you—you horse's arse!

She knocked her head back against the wall with a solid thud. Jocelyn was right, he'd come to fetch her. *Fetch* her like one of father's hounds with a stick. Had her family sent him? Had they offered him money? No, Richard had plenty of coin. That would not have motivated him to sail all the way from England. And why not send James if they were so concerned? Why send someone like Richard? It was close to Samantha's birthing time, but Richard? James had about as much faith in Richard as Richard had in...in...in *her*.

And yet, here he was. Or at least until the night's tide. One stubborn question kept worming its way into her thoughts, however. *Why?*

She pushed off the floor and smoothed her skirts. It didn't matter why. She didn't care.

Alicia notched her chin. If anything, she'd stood her ground, defended herself and her decision. Her unleashed independence was a new experience. She liked it.

Then she spotted the bloodied handkerchief Richard had used to clean his cheek. He must have dropped it. She pulled in a shaky breath at the sight of it. Dammit, she hadn't meant to hurt him. It had been pure instinct to defend herself. Still, the man never saw it coming. If their paths ever crossed again—which was highly unlikely—he'd not make the same mistake again.

She fingered the fine embroidery in the corner. R.E.D. Richard Elliot Dunbar. Moving to her washbowl, she poured cold water over the stain and rubbed at it with her thumb. The wash water turned a sickly pink as she tried to sort through the jumble of thoughts and emotions colliding in her mind.

"So, that was quite the show." Jocelyn startled her, causing Alicia to slosh some of the wash water onto her skirts.

Alicia grabbed a clean cloth and dipped it into the pitcher. "I'm sorry. I had no idea he'd come, let alone how he got in here." She rubbed at the spot.

"Raine kept him from coming through the shop. Evidently, he stopped by earlier. The back is locked solid. He had to have climbed the oak tree near the east wall and come over the roof and through the window." Jocelyn leaned against the door frame and pointed to the front wall.

Alicia finished fussing at her skirts and glanced toward the tiny window. How had he managed to squeeze through? She went back to cleaning his handkerchief and poured a bit more water over the fine linen in her hand and smoothed it out over her palm. "I don't understand why he'd go to all that trouble. It's not as if I'm a fairytale maiden locked in a bloody tower."

"You never mentioned in your letters that you were involved with him."

"Him? Richard? No. We were never involved." She traced the elegant scroll of the initials with a fingertip.

"Perhaps he is the real reason you ran from Frederick on your wedding day, no?"

"What? No. That's absurd. What would ever give you that idea?"

"For one, you're stroking his handkerchief like it was a lover."

Alicia dropped the cloth back into the water and dried her hands. "You're wrong."

"Am I? There is something between the two of you or the man wouldn't have gone through so much struggle to reach you."

Alicia met Jocelyn's steady gaze and held it. "There is nothing between us. I may have had feelings for him. Once, when I was younger." She brushed the words from the air with a sweep of her hand. "An innocent crush. But I got over it. Years ago." Visions of a single kiss stirred in her memory. A tingle of emotions followed. Perhaps a few of those feelings hadn't completely vanished. Giving a slight shake of her head, she banished the thought.

"He saw me as nothing more than a foolish child back then. Still does." Alicia returned to the wash bowl and gave Richard's handkerchief another quick rinse and twisted it to wring out the excess water before laying it over the back of a chair to dry. "Maybe now, or at least for the next few days, every time he looks in the

glass, he'll be reminded how wrong he was to underestimate me."
She dried her hands once more. "At least until the swelling goes
down."

Chapter 11

What in blazes just happened? Richard stumbled away from the lace shop still holding his throbbing face in one hand. *Bloody hell!* That did not go the way he'd imagined. He stopped and looked back at the storefront as if it had been some sort of a joke, an illusion. His eye hurt too much to be dreaming.

He stood in the middle of the mucky road. Yesterday's rain stirred with today's travel and horse droppings made the fetid mire ankle deep. His boots would never recover. Had these people never heard of cobblestones?

Lifting a foot, he kicked off what he hoped was a clump of mud, slogged to a drier part of the lane, and started walking. His head pounded, and each blink of his eye warned him of the swelling building underneath. She could have killed him. Fool woman. What had gotten into her?

The image of Alicia hiking her skirts filled his mind. Her gown had slipped off one shoulder, her hair had fallen to two perfect pale curls at the nape of her neck. One bare creamy thigh caught the light…lifting her knee…even now the memory of such a sight seduced him. Stirred him.

Who was that siren? Certainly, she was not the Alicia he knew weeks ago. Not the innocent girl in the white wedding dress he'd left in a garden, that was for sure. Now she was toting a gun, bludgeoning strangers. Richard heard the colonies were wild, savage places, but dammit all, Alicia hadn't been here but a few days. What had they done to her?

He made his way in the growing darkness back along the docks, toward the public house called the Black Sheep. He'd gather his belongings and be on that ship heading back to Liverpool. Before the sun rose again, he'd forget this whole business. He'd return to Weatherington, report to the Steeles that their daughter had lost all the sense the good Lord gave her, and he could be done with it. Done with her.

Richard stopped mid stride and turned around. No. *Idiot.* What was he thinking? The blow to his head must have rattled his brain. He couldn't simply leave her here. He'd made a promise, damn him. He needed to try and speak with her again. Rationally. Calmly. No attempts to surprise her. And no bloody weapons. Alicia had a level head…or did before she left England's shores. Richard knew exactly how best to handle this. How best to handle *her*.

He turned back again and stared at the public house. Candlelight now shown in the wave of its window glass. His head continued to throb as if it was trying to beat some sense into his brain. *This is insanity.*

Richard glanced back in the direction of the Laced Ladies. There would be no rational discussions with Alicia. When had they *ever* had a rational discussion? The woman was as stubborn as a workhouse mule. If she'd made up her mind to stay, then there wasn't anything he could say or do to change her mind. Why waste his time? Hadn't he wasted enough already? He started back toward the docks.

Two strides later, it was his heart that had him turning around again. *Because you love her, you daft sot.* He couldn't get on that ship tonight without telling her how he'd come to feel for her, or he'd regret it for the rest of his life.

During the crossing, he'd imagined the scene a hundred times. He'd tell her he loved her and gather her in his arms while she tearfully confessed loving him in return. And then he'd kiss her. Tenderly at first, but the building passion between them would flash into something deeper. Primal. He'd pull her tight into his embrace, wrap her in the strength of his arms, and never let her go.

He imagined her donning another white gown. This one, she'd wear for him.

Now, given her reaction at seeing him again, he'd be lucky if she didn't shoot him when he professed his love. There was a good chance of that. And laughter. He could imagine her laughing in his face. All of them. The *Mistress* Robbins and the ice queen who worked for her. They'd all be quite entertained at his expense.

But the alternative was a lifetime without her filled with bitter regret. Hadn't he already suffered enough of that? If he walked away now, hell, he might as well ask Alicia to go ahead and shoot him.

His brain ached for it knew he had lost the battle with his heart. He looked about at the state of his rustic surroundings. God help him, he was staying.

Richard made a last slow turn. Chilled moisture seeped into his boots as he made the decision to see if the Black Sheep had a bed he could buy for the night. Given the warmth of Alicia's initial welcome, maybe two nights.

Pushing into the large common room with its thick round tables and a fireplace big enough to roast a hog, Richard slid onto a stool lining a raised bar. The odors of wood smoke and stale ale permeated the walls, a thin layer of hay covered the floor, but the rich smell of fresh baked bread made his stomach announce its hunger. Perhaps he'd get something hearty to warm his belly and roust his spirits.

A beefy man in an apron of dubious color stopped, dropped a glass in front of him, and poured him a healthy dram of something resembling scotch. "Ye look like ye could use this."

Richard stared at the pale amber liquid like a thirsty man looked longingly at the sea. If he drank it, it would surely be the end of him. The not-so-distant memory of those first agonizing days of sobriety flashed in his mind.

"Did ye get the name of the horse that run ye down?" The barkeep continued.

Richard pulled his rapt attention away from the golden glass of liquid temptation. "Horse?"

"Or did ye run full bore int'a another bloke's fist?"

"Oh…" Richard fingered the swollen skin beneath his eye. He sure as hell wasn't going to tell this stranger he'd been taken down by a woman. "Bastards came at me from nowhere. Three of them. They'll all be looking worse than me come morning, that's for sure." The lie turned to dust in his throat. Richard knew just what would quench that dryness. The drink before him whispered his name and beckoned him like an amber bathed lover.

Before he could reach for the glass, the barkeep pushed it closer. "Then the first one is on te house." He grabbed another glass, poured a drink for himself and raised it in a toast. "Te the victor."

Richard lifted his glass and tapped the rim with the fellow's and watched as the man tossed the drink down his gullet.

Turning the glass in his fingers, watching the play of firelight in its contents, he met the other man's gaze. "Could use a bit of a meal as well. What do you have to go with that bread I smell?"

"Oxtail stew. Fancy some?"

"Aye." Richard nodded as he brought the edge of the glass to his lips. The intoxicating aroma of the drink teased his nose.

When the man turned to bark the order to a passing serving wench, Richard gave a quick forward tip to the glass and spilled the contents to splash upon his boots. His mind released a strangled groan inside his skull as perfectly good liquor was wasted on perfectly ruined footwear.

He slammed the glass upside down on the bar and motioned as if wiping his lip when the man turned back, bottle raised.

"I'm good for now," Richard insisted as he placed a hand over his glass. "Food will be plenty. And I'm in mighty need of a bed for the night." He reached for his purse and pulled a few coins from the leather pouch and held them up.

The young serving woman approaching with a trencher of stew and bread, caught sight of his coins and exchanged a quick glance with the barkeep before setting the meal before Richard. She made an exaggerated show of her glorious cleavage in the process.

"Aye, we can manage a bed for ye." The man leaned forward, plucked the coins from Richard's fingers, and tipped his head closer. His cologne was a mixture of sweat, smoke, and scotch. With subtle undertones of filth. "For an extra quid, I can see te some company in yer bed as well." He jerked his head toward the serving wench.

She was a pretty one—once you looked past the dirt. Gentle brown eyes, a dimpled cheek, soft wide curves. A pair of which were currently threatening to spill out into his stew. In days past, he'd relish a tumble between her fleshy thighs, but the prospect surprisingly held little appeal to him now.

Richard lifted a hand to fondle the freely offered swell of her breast. A scattering of freckles like glittered sand upon the beach skipped across each rounded hill. But he couldn't bring himself to touch her. And not because she wasn't fresh from a bath, and not because she bore an odd resemblance to the bartender. *Would the bastard proposition his own sister? Or worse yet, his daughter?*

Had it been three months? Nay, had it been closer to six months since he laid with a woman? He couldn't remember. The last time might have been the week he'd heard of Alicia's engagement when he'd fallen into a vat of cheap brandy and woken up three days later with one of father's cooks in his bed. Estelle. Kind woman. Married to the estate's stable master, Roger. Old enough to be his mother, a bit like a depraved hellcat in bed—but a kind woman, nonetheless. She'd swatted his naked ass and called him a *"naughty, naughty boy"* before jiggling out of the sheets and back into her apron.

Richard grimaced at the memory. Not his proudest moment, but then there had been so many of late. It was surprising he could keep track.

"Ain't she good enough for ye, Mista High an' Mighty?" growled the barkeep.

Jerked back from his mind's wanderings, Richard frantically searched for the right words. "No…I mean, yes… What I mean is, she's lovely." He looked at the girl. "You're lovely. It's just I'm…I'm…" His brain shouted, *I'm in love with another woman and she has thrown my entire life into chaos*. How did he explain that without sounding like a complete idiot? "I'm suffering from a wee bout of…of…"

"Root rot?" Offered the bartender.

The serving wench covered her chest with her hands, and with wide eyes backed away as if he'd said, "Plague." Her employer/brother/father flipped a hand at her, and she hurried away. "Lousy bit of luck, that. Bloke I know got it so bad, screams takin' a piss. Can drive a bugger mad, ye know." He raised the bottle he still held. "Sure ye'd not care to drown yer sorrows?"

"There's not enough liquor in the world," Richard grumbled as he shook his head. "I'm sure, thank you." He looked down and watched a fat, iridescent fly struggling in the layer of congealed grease topping his bowl of stew.

Richard closed his eyes and convinced himself that food was overrated. Was he really hungry? His belly protested. Pushing the stew to one side, he reminded himself, for what seemed like the hundredth time, why he was there. If he didn't convince Alicia to return to England with him soon, he'd surely starve to death.

"Perhaps you could just point me in the direction of my bed."

The barkeep jerked his thumb over his shoulder. "Upstairs. On the left, end of the hall. Near full up t'night but lucky you, being new te town, ye get the 'King's Suite.'" He and several other patrons within earshot laughed and jostled each other.

Reaching his room, he came to understand their joke. Prisoners in a brig had more space. The door wouldn't open to its fullest as it hit the side of the narrow bed. Richard had to squeeze into the room sideways. He popped up the collar of his coat and shivered. A broken window at the foot of the bed allowed for a lovely breath of fresh air. Fresh, frigid, damp air. No curtains. No lamp. No washbowl. No sheets. A questionable blanket the size of a handkerchief covered a mattress as thick as a sheet of parchment. Walls so thin he swore he just heard someone break wind in an adjoining room.

He didn't even bother to take off his fouled boots before he flopped onto the bed. It leaned oddly to starboard. Someone next door did break wind—with grunted gusto. Had he truly missed that ship leaving for Liverpool and civilization? His teeth chattered as he tried to cover himself with the meager blanket, wondering why it smelled oddly of cheese.

Richard closed his eyes and prayed sleep would come quickly and save him from this nightmare. His neighbor farted again.

In the room to the right, a couple began rutting with such enthusiasm their headboard—Richard assumed it was the headboard—began rhythmically banging against the wall as a woman—again, an assumption—squealed, "Yes, Gerald, yes!" with a repeating crescendo of exhilaration.

Hands over his ears trying to shut out the symphony of sounds surrounding him, Richard shivered. *I never imagined hell would be quite so cold?* He moaned as he turned his back on Gerald, Geraldine, and the trumpeter on the left.

Curling into himself, his stomach growled, his head throbbed, and his spirit struggled like a fly drowning in grease.

Chapter 12

Next morning Richard was hungry enough to fight that fly and cold enough to welcome all the fires of hell, but first things first.

Alicia.

He was determined the sun would not set on another day without her listening to him, knowing his heart, and agreeing to come back with him to blasted civilization. Then, dear God, he would lift a glass of the finest brandy ever to come in a cut crystal decanter and wash the taste of this entire experience out of his mouth. Repeatedly. And continue to do so until last night at the Black Sheep—the longest night in the history of nights—had been forever washed from his memory.

Speaking of washed…he so wished he could do so before professing his love to Alicia, but alas, no. Still in his rumpled clothing and ruined boots, unshaven, unkempt, face beaten and bruised, he was on a mission.

He'd realized his mistake during the long dark hours of last night. Both of them had been caught off guard yesterday. The blow to his face had been an accident. They'd each reacted poorly out of shock. Said things that could have been said differently. Tempers were lost. Frustration and impatience only served to fan the flames.

But in the light of this new day, with calmer heads, softer words,

Alicia would come to see the error in her thinking.

This was not the world for her. Her world was with him. In England. With her family. Where the two of them could build a life together, however she wished. They could travel. He would show her Paris, Rome. He'd love and spoil her. Lavish her with expensive gifts. Give whatever her heart desired. Go wherever she wanted to go.

And then the children would arrive in good time and tame all thoughts of travel and adventure. He and Alicia would settle down into a blissful domestic haze of home and hearth and live in quiet contentment into their golden years surrounded by their family and friends.

As Richard stepped out into the sun, the bright day lifted his mood. Its brilliance chipped through the chill and warmed his back. He straightened his stock and attempted to tame the waywardness of his hair. His mind was clear. His course set. Yes, he could almost see their future. It began in this very moment.

With a renewed spring to his stride, he headed off toward the Laced Ladies and stepped perfectly into the middle of a fresh deposit of horse droppings.

Closing his eyes, he notched his chin, clenched his jaw against the string of profanity threatening to explode from his mouth, and refused to take it as an omen of things to come. *Onward.*

His short trip to the shop resembled an odd drunken dance. Two steps, wipe his foot, one step, two steps, drag his toe.

He entered the shop in no temper to debate, defend, or discuss. The Ice Queen at the counter scanned him from head to fouled boots and greeted him with a bemused expression.

"Did you lose your way? I believe England is in *that* direction." She pointed a slender finger past him before she gave a gentle sniff. "Perhaps you missed your ship and had to spend the night in a stable?"

Richard marched past her toward the back curtain. "I've no time for your impertinence. I'm going upstairs to speak to Alicia, and there's nothing you can do or say to stop me. Feel free to plant your hidden blade in my back. I cease to care."

"She is not here."

He glared at her. "Ha! I don't believe you."

"I speak the truth. Alicia and Jocelyn have gone to Wakefield's Cove." She pointed again. "If you follow the main road, and take a right at the fork, it is less than a mile beyond the north beach before you reach the bay. They'll be there for some time, I imagine. You're sure to catch them." She gave him a small, smug smile.

Richard narrowed his one eye that wasn't already swollen to a slit. "You're being most helpful today. Why?"

The Queen lifted one elegant shoulder. "You look and smell as if you've been dragged behind a mule. Maybe I feel sorry for you. Or, could be I simply want you and your equine cologne out of the shop."

He didn't buy any of it. Not for a bloody second. His boot wasn't the only thing full of shit. "Or...?"

Richard caught a glimpse of utter amusement in the glint of her eyes before she dropped her gaze and returned to her work. "Or...could be that Alicia spent all of last night learning how to load her new pistol."

* * * * *

Following her directions, Richard cautiously headed toward Wakefield's cove. The deeper he walked into the thick woodlands surrounding Black Point the more nervous he became. Richard feared he'd been sent straight into the hands of the wild indigenous people known to this part of the new world.

Tales of the conflicts between colonizers and the native tribes here were well known. Ambushes were common as the Indians fought to reclaim what they continued to lose through the spread of the established British rule. Battles could be ruthless from all accounts. Savage. On both sides.

Richard strained his ear to hear anything over his own steps. Giving a cursory glance over his shoulder regularly, he continued on, and was relieved to discover the Ice Queen's directions to be clear and accurate. Around another bend the woods parted as the path opened to reveal the promised Wakefield's cove. A crude sign tacked to a tree trunk confirmed it.

The view was foreign, yet stunning. Was this land covered with trees? The narrow cove appeared surrounded by tall evergreens that reached straight and tall into the clear blue of the sky and whispered the secrets of the wind. The water caught the kiss of the sun as it danced in bright sparks across its surface. Richard had to admit, this was beautiful country.

The cove was also the quiet home to a handful of ships, most small, oared boats. A bark-clad canoe lay keel up in the brush near the water's edge. Makeshift slips fingered out into the water. One longer than the rest sat closest to what must be the waterway toward

Admiral's Bay. At its end sat a sorry looking merchant schooner listed at her berth. It, like his bed last night, tipped at a sharp angle to starboard. Fair sized. One mast was cracked and splintered several feet from the tip as if it had tried to sail under a bridge too low. Narrow hull, shallow draft. She was in need of a good careening with tar and tallow before the mollusks claimed her. One sail hung unsecured. Rigging could use a tarring as well. She was a wreck.

A right shame, too, she had good lines. Fair guns that he could see. Equal share of fixed to swivel guns. Eight at least, perhaps more. Unusual for a ship her size, but he supposed merchants along these waters needed a fair amount of protection. What was she…sixty feet, stem to stern? Whoever laid claim to her hadn't seen right by her.

Richard removed his jacket, unwound the stock from his neck, and went to the water's edge. He bathed his face and neck and used the water to tame his hair into place. The damp linen of his shirt clung to his shoulders and chest, but in the strong, warm light of the sun, he'd be dry in no time. Lifting the cooling cloth to sooth his eye, he looked about.

Maybe he was wrong. Maybe the Ice Queen sent him on a fool's errand, after all. He couldn't see Alicia or Jocelyn anywhere. Had they taken one of the boats for a sail around the cove? Perhaps this wasn't the right place, after all. He glanced back toward the path. The sign did say Wakefield's.

Richard waded into the water to rinse the dried, caked filth from his boots when he heard them.

"I told you not to get your hopes up."

"It's not…horrible."

"No, it is worse."

Alicia shielded her eyes and looked up at the broken mast as she struggled to navigate the pitched deck. "It definitely needs a new mast."

"And perhaps a nice big fireplace…right about here." Jocelyn pointed to a spot mid ship. "We can use the old mast for kindling."

"Where is your optimism?" Alicia tugged at the loose rigging.

"*Finie*. It drowned below deck in that vile bilge."

"The pump is rotted. We'll need to bail."

"We?" Jocelyn shook her head and climbed off the ship onto the slip. "No, I say, it is a lost cause. You would do better to steal a whole new sh—" She saw him and stopped. Brushing her skirts, she waited in silence for Alicia to join her.

"Steal a whole new what? Pump?" Hopping down to the slip, Alicia wiped at a smudge on her sleeve. When she didn't receive a reply, she reached out a hand to her. "Jocelyn? Are you ill? What is it?" Giving Jocelyn a frown, Alicia followed her gaze. Surprise flitted across her face before what could have been anger. Her pale brows knit together.

Richard didn't see a weapon, but he wasn't taking any chances. He held up his hands in surrender. "I'm unarmed."

Alicia's heels tapped along the boards of the slip. "What are you still doing here? I thought you left?"

Holding his arms out from his sides, his wet shirt still clung to his shoulders. "Evidence would suggest otherwise." Richard waded back to shore.

Alicia met him at the end of the slip. "My God, your eye."

He fingered it gingerly. "I haven't had the pleasure of a looking glass, but if your expression is any indication, I must look a sight." Alicia on the other hand looked more beautiful each time he saw her. The sweep of her honey hair caught the sun. Errant strands blew like golden silk strands across the gentle pink of her lips. How the taste of those lips continued to haunt him. In a gown of soft blue, she stole his breath away. It captured the exact shade of her eyes.

Those same eyes scanned his face in concern. "I'm so sorry."

"Must be our day for sorry sights." Jocelyn muttered and moved past them. She raised her parasol. "I, for one, have seen my fill. I have a business to run." She turned toward Alicia. "I suggest you clean up one mess before you begin another, no? Although I'm fairly certain you will not be successful with either. I shall meet you back at the shop."

"You warned me it's unwise to venture through this area alone. We should have brought a carriage. I'll come with you."

"I am perfectly safe here in Black Point. Ric saw to that before he left. Besides, I could use the walk to clear my head. Sort some things out in my mind." She looked at Richard. "You will see her back to the shop before you leave? *Oui*?"

He gave a small nod. "Of course."

"I don't need an escort," argued Alicia.

"Yes, you do." Richard and Jocelyn said in unison before Jocelyn walked away. It did not escape Richard's notice that at least where Alicia's protection was concerned, the insufferable Mistress Robbins and he could agree.

Expecting more of an argument from Alicia, he was again surprised to find her staring back at the leaning hulk of the doomed schooner.

"Speaking of unsafe. I pity the poor fool who owns that tub. What were you two doing out there?"

"I'm the fool," Alicia brushed at her sleeve again. "The *Ruby Mist* is mine."

Chapter 13

"Yours?"

Alicia's heart tripped at the sight of him. She'd never seen Richard quite so undone. Somehow, he'd gone from a slightly disheveled tippler to something much more rakish. A touch of scruff caught the morning light and emphasized the strong line of his jaw. Water dripped from the ends of his darkened hair. Without his stock, his shirt lay open at the neck. A hint of darker hair flirted at the parting. The wet linen clung to the broadness of his chest and the definition of strong arms.

Her mouth went dry. "For now."

"Did *she* sell you this pile of driftwood?" He pointed down the lane. "If you paid more than a shilling, you were cheated."

While his handsome looks had temporarily distracted her, his accusing tone was all too familiar. "No one cheated me. Jocelyn has given me the *Ruby Mist*. For the time being."

"Whatever for?"

Now was not the occasion to enlighten Richard as to her arrangement with Jocelyn. With any luck he'd not miss the next ship heading back to England, and she'd be free to continue with her plan. While he could insist she needed him to get her back to town, in this matter he was an obstacle she could ill afford.

Alicia simplified her answer to its barest essence. "She's helping me, and in return, I'm helping her."

Richard narrowed his gaze. "Seems everyone is being overly helpful today. Why then do I have an uneasy feeling in the pit of my stomach?" He slapped a hand to his midriff.

"Because you're a cynic." Alicia fired.

"And you're too trusting," he volleyed back.

Alicia brushed aside his remark. "I have no reason to mistrust Jocelyn."

Richard ran a hand over his hair and mumbled, "I could give you a list."

She shot him a look before glancing back at the ship. True, it wasn't all she'd hoped, but given some proper attention, the ship would be perfect. Not too big, not too small. It wouldn't need much of a crew. Alicia bet once she was bailed and buffed, the *Ruby Mist* would skip across the tips of the waves like a gull. She needed to make a list of supplies to "acquire." Where the hell did one steal a mast and a pump?

"What are you going to do with a broken-down schooner, Alicia?"

She planted her hands on her hips and gave the ship an assessing look. "The first thing I'm going to do is get her seaworthy. Don't you think she'll be beautiful?"

"With a lot of work, perhaps, but it would take quite a bit of capital. New mast, full careening. I'll bet coin on a good amount of rot along the water line."

"I didn't say it was going to be easy, but it will be worth it in the end."

"And what end is that?" Richard caught and held her gaze.

Alicia avoided the question. She couldn't tell him. He'd think she'd lost her mind. She'd had a difficult enough time convincing Jocelyn her proposal, while unorthodox, had merit. Richard would not understand no matter how sound her arguments.

He persisted. "Do you intend to sail this ship alone? It will take five crewmen, at least. Are you becoming a merchant? Is that how you plan to help Jocelyn? The lace business is that lucrative? Or does this tightening in my gut tell me something else?"

Alicia met his penetrating stare. "You're mocking me again."

"No, I'm trying to understand your sudden interest in ships? You grew up days from the sea. Did you ever learn to swim? Fish? Had you even sailed before coming here?"

His gaze pinned her to the spot. She felt like an insect under a magnifying glass. Alicia broke the connection and stepped away. "My brother was in the Navy. He was raised the same distance from the sea as I. Did he know how to swim and fish and sail? Did you dare question him?"

"Of course, not. He was trained as an officer. It was his duty."

"Perhaps you would call it his destiny?" Alicia headed down the path.

Richard fell in step with her. "Perhaps."

Alicia kept her gaze lowered. "Then possibly it is my destiny as well to learn what I can about a life at sea. My father *was* a pirate."

His hand reached out to grasp her arm, stopping her. She had no choice but to meet his inquisitive stare. "Your father was a privateer, back when the crown condoned such things. Now, it's a sure path to the end of a hangman's noose. But what does any of that have to do with you? Thinking of sporting an eyepatch and hitting the high seas?" He teased as he covered his bruised eye with a hand and winced.

When she hesitated in answering, Richard lowered his hand and gave her a curious look. "That would explain the sudden interest in fast ships and loaded pistols. What are you up to?"

Alicia pulled out of his grasp. Her heart threatened to beat its way out of her chest. Dammit. He could read her too easily. It was one of the things she hated about him. If he learned what was truly going on, he'd never leave. She needed to distract him. But how?

"You never answered my question." She flicked a small glance back at him.

"Which question?"

"You were leaving Black Point last night. What are you still doing here?"

The muscle in his jaw pulsed, and there was a long pause before he answered. "There's a matter I wanted to discuss with you. Something I wish to ask you. Could we sit?" He swept his hand back toward the slip.

Sitting with the sun warming their backs, he was quiet again for a time, as if he were struggling to find the right words. Alicia took that opportunity to study him.

He was unkempt and unshaven. Of course, she'd seen him in

worse states over the past year, but there was something different about his appearance. His eyes were clear—at least the one she hadn't blackened. His skin had a healthy pallor. He didn't smell like a garden of her mother's roses, but he didn't reek of brandy either.

"About yesterday," he began. His voice low and hushed. He reached out to take her hand.

Warm fingers entwined with her own, sending a delicious tingle up her arm. "I truly am sorry I struck you. You startled me coming out of the shadows."

"I understand. It was my fault. I should have announced myself immediately. And afterward..." He turned his face to look at her. "Things were said in the heat of the moment without thinking. I apologize."

Her eyebrows reached for her hairline. When had Richard Dunbar ever apologized for anything? Never to her, surely.

His gaze captured and held hers. She could count the flecks of silver in the gray of his eyes. A bit of her defenses melted away. "I should be furious with you, but I forgive you. Why can't I stay angry at you?"

His fingers gave a gentle squeeze. "Because you still care for me."

Alicia's heart hitched. "What?" she whispered.

"You asked me why I was here. I had to come. To bring you home. When you disappeared, your family was beside themselves with worry. I promised them I'd find you."

"I tried to explain last night. I've written them. They'll soon know I'm here and that I'm safe. You found me. You've fulfilled your promise."

He nodded. "Aye, part of it."

"I'm not going back."

Richard made a slow sweep of his thumb along the side of her finger as he continued to hold her gaze. "Not even for me?"

All the air left her lungs in a rush. "What are you trying to say?"

"When you left, something in here…" He laid his free hand over the center of his chest. "Stopped." Richard released her and stood up. He kept his back to her and seemed to study the toes of his boots. "I believed the final blow to my heart came when I learned you were getting married, but then when I thought I'd never see you again…it felt as if there was a hole in my chest where my heart used to be." He turned to face her and shook his head. "I put all the pieces together and figured out where you'd gone. I had to follow and bring you home with me. *To* me." He sat back down and took her by the shoulders. "I made an utter mess of things, but the truth is…I love you, Alicia. I'm *in love* with you. Seems I've been in love with you for a very long time."

"Oh, Ducky," she whispered.

Alicia blinked, and he was on his feet again. "My life is a disaster. I know." He paced. "I've been stripped of it all. My career. My standing. My honor. I've tried to drown myself in brandy for months. But everything's changed. I'm a new man." He held his arms out from his sides. "Because of you. I didn't think I had a chance after I pushed you away that night in my father's study. I should have come after you then and begged forgiveness, but my damn pride had taken such a lashing. I couldn't see past my own disgrace. I'm a bloody idiot. Then there was Frederick. I thought I'd

truly lost you to him. But that ridiculous note? Talk about an idiot."
He threw up a hand.

Alicia's head spun. He loved her? How long had she waited to
hear those words from him? And he waited until now to tell her?
Now? After the reckless weeks of humiliation, and shame that
dogged her steps after that fateful night. Trying to run away from the
heartbreak and move on with her life. Finally facing her future, and
now he tells her this? All this time he'd been too—wait...

"Note? What note?"

Richard stopped his pacing. "Damn." He put a hand over his
lips.

Now, she was on *her* feet. "Damn, what?"

He grimaced and shook his head. "My mouth got away from
me. You weren't supposed to hear about that, least of not from me."

"Well, you're the only one here, so tell me."

Richard dragged in a deep breath. "Frederick. He wrote you a
letter. James found it the morning of the wedding. Although, without
a bride or a groom, is it technically a wedding? Let's just say if you
were concerned about his reaction to you leaving him at the altar,
you needn't have worried."

"He didn't show up either?" Alicia couldn't decide if she was
outraged or relieved.

Richard threw his hands wide. "See, you didn't need to sail
across an entire ocean to get away from him."

"I wasn't running away from Frederick. What did his note say?"

He rubbed at the space between his eyebrows. "It was a fuzzy day. I don't remember exactly." Richard swept at the air with his hand. "What does it matter?" He took her hand and brought them both back to sit. "It means your wake is clear. You've left no obstacles behind and are free to go home. You and I, we can go back and start fresh. Together."

Alicia gave a slow shake to her head. "Richard—"

He held her gaze and lowered his voice. "I know I hurt you and lost your trust. Your family's as well. But by finding you and bringing you home, I'll prove to them, and to you that I've mended my ways. You can trust me now. Trust that I finally know my own heart." He rubbed his thumb in gentle sweeps across her knuckles before lifting them to his lips. "We can start a glorious life together, Alicia. I lo—"

"Stop." Alicia pulled her hand from his, covered her ears, and stood. She couldn't listen to anymore. A year ago, his profession of love and redemption would have been everything she wanted. How many nights had she imagined a scene like this? It had been a fantasy playing over and over in her mind. Him, realizing he loved her, coming to her to beg her forgiveness, sweeping her up in his arms and kissing her. He'd carry her off to a faraway land to live their magical life together. She'd clung to that image like a drowning man clinging to a bit of driftwood.

And now, here it was. When Alicia turned back, Richard was on his feet again watching her. Waiting for an answer. Still there was a small corner of her heart that wanted to race back into his arms. Live the fantasy. Be with him. Lay with him. Love him. But…

"You're too late."

Chapter 14

A chill of dread splashed over Richard. "Don't say that. It's never too late."

Alicia's stare fell to her feet. "I'm afraid it is." After a long agonizing pause, she lifted her gaze. "What did you expect me to do after all this time? Pine for you?" Alicia pressed a hand to her heart as if rubbing away an ache. "Lay in hope that one day you'd come to realize how wonderful I am and come claim me?"

Richard took a step toward her needing to close the gapping crevasse that was opening between them. "You *are* wonderful. I was so consumed by frustration and anger I couldn't see it. But you have to know even then I did have feelings for you."

A short breath escaped her. "You've an odd way of showing them."

"I was trying to shield you."

Alicia's brows furrowed. "From what? You?"

"Yes. Especially from me. I was a bigger wreck than that ship." Richard flung a hand toward the *Ruby Mist*. "No amount of tar and scraping could have saved me."

Her eyes got wide. "And you didn't think I could, what? Care for you when you had fallen so far from grace? Do you think I'm that shallow?" She crossed her arms and glared.

Richard sighed his frustration. "I had nothing, Alicia."

"I wasn't asking for anything."

"Yes, you were," he snapped. "You were asking me to look past my association with your brother and trust me to hold your tender, innocent heart. You wanted me to love you, and I couldn't, not then. I was too caught up in watching my life go to absolute shite. I was too busy drowning my misery and hating myself."

"But you're ready now?" Anger laced her words.

Richard closed the distance between them and stroked her sleeve. The sun through the leaves on the trees dappled her in shifting light. She was so beautiful. He'd been wrong about a great many things. She wasn't fragile. Alicia had forged Steele within her. The very thing that at this moment he found so infuriating, also made him love her all the more. His mind searched to find the right words to keep her from walking away from him forever.

Her arms were still crossed. Trying to break through her barrier, Richard swept the bare skin below the lace ruffle at her elbow with his thumb. "I wouldn't be here if I wasn't."

"I'm sorry, but you had your chance." She stepped away from him. "You say you've changed, well, take a look." she flung her arms wide. "I've changed as well. I've moved on. A new life. I can't—" Her voice caught. Richard watched her throat work. Watched some of that Steele armor fall away before she notched her chin. "I can't afford to look back. Once upon a time, I would have given anything for you to love me. But it was a fairy tale. Nothing more." Tears brightened her eyes. One threatened to breach the edge of her lashes. The sight was nearly his undoing.

"Look at me, Alicia. Here I am. Loving you."

She gave her tears an angry swipe. "It's not enough. Not now."

"Is there someone else? Another man?"

"No, there's no one else." A frown marred her lovely face. "I'm past searching for a suitable match. Pretending I'm someone I'm not, pinning my future on the fickle heart of any man and feeling like a bit of chattel to be bargained for, auctioned off to the highest bidder." She met his gaze. "I want more. My independence to start with." Alicia looked toward the ship. "Frankly, the only man I'm interested in today is a man who isn't afraid to get waist deep in bilge water and knows how to bail."

Richard followed her line of sight but saw nothing past the racing of his mind. If he didn't think of something, he was going to lose her. Hell, according to her, he'd already lost. Alicia didn't trust him anymore, and he didn't blame her. He'd been an utter fool and hurt her. Made a mess of both their lives. Did he imagine she'd suddenly forgive it all and fall blindly into his arms? What could he say to get her to give him another chance? No, it was going to take more than words to win her back, but Richard refused to surrender. He was prepared to fight for her and do whatever he needed to gain her trust and earn her respect. Get her to love him again.

Think, dammit!

Richard pulled in a deep breath and released it slowly. He needed a new plan of attack. "Fine. If you say you don't have feelings for me anymore, I must believe you. And you're right, you have changed. You set out on your own. Propriety be damned. Traveled unaccompanied across an entire ocean. Remarkable. I've always known you to be headstrong and determined, but this exceeds my expectations. Frankly, I admire your courage. I'm curious to hear your plans. Tell me about this new grand adventure. I want to hear it all."

"I'd rather not." Alicia shook her head. "You'll make a mockery of it. Or worse, try to dissuade me."

"I swear, I won't." He stroked her arm again. "It is obviously very important to you. Perhaps I can help in some way. Lend a hand? Offer advice?" He lowered his voice. "Don't you see? If I can't have you in my life, at the very least, I need to know you'll be happy in yours."

"I am happy." Alicia met his gaze and held it. He watched the tug of emotions in the deep ocean blue of her eyes. "All my life, I've lived inside a beautiful bubble. A safe, lovely, world where each of my days was ruled by the clock, and by whichever gown was laid out upon my bed. But somehow it never felt right. I was always waiting for something bigger and more exciting to happen. Each time I was tied into my corset, a bit more of me felt reined in. Suffocated. Extinguished." She rolled her eyes. "Oh, you wouldn't understand."

She turned to walk away, but he reached out a hand to stop her. Coming to stand close to her, Richard dipped his head. "But I do understand. I was raised under the thumb of a heartless man. I escaped by entering the King's service and lived a life taking orders. I know how it feels to be controlled straight down to the polish on my boots." He ran a hand down her arm. "What are you searching for, Alicia? Tell me." His voice was no more than a whisper. "Please."

She trembled beneath his touch and turned to face him. Taking a slow breath, she notched her chin and met his gaze. "Me. I'm searching for me. My life. My place. My purpose. I've made the decision to claim my destiny."

At the utter determined look in her eye, the queasy feeling returned to his gut. "What destiny?"

"I am Alicia Gabriella Steele. Daughter of Pirate Captain, Jaxon Steele. It is only right that like my brother, I follow in his esteemed footsteps." Alicia pointed a slender finger. "I'm taking charge of the *Ruby Mist*, making her seaworthy by whatever means I can. I'm signing on a few crewmembers, under my control as Captain, and setting out to pirate these local waters."

Did she just say pirate? He must have heard her wrong. Richard tipped his ear closer and started to say, *"Excuse me?"* but she held up a hand to stop the question before it was asked.

"It will be a small operation. I'll be able to hide my identity behind my station, not only as a woman, but as a member of the local gentry. With Jocelyn's help, I can continue to make those connections, and keep up the charade during the day. But at night, my crew and I will plunder certain desirable items."

Plunder? His mind spun. There was nothing wrong with his ears. *She wants to be a bloody pirate?* Richard opened his mouth to object. Words failed him.

Alicia continued, "Jocelyn will, in turn, profiteer those items out to buyers further north. She'll get a share of the take to…" She lifted a hand. "To do with as she sees fit. And I'll gain what I've only recently come to crave most in this world. My freedom."

Richard's brain and mouth finally connected. "You're to be a *p…p…pirate*?" he sputtered.

"I've thought long and hard—"

"Long? How long? A month?" His voice rose.

"I knew you wouldn't understand," Alice snapped back and pointed a finger at his nose.

Richard gaped at her. "I understand you've gone mad. Do you have any notion of what you're proposing?"

Alicia set her jaw and raised her hands in surrender. "I've already had this argument with Jocelyn."

"Jocelyn agrees that this is madness?" Richard wasn't sure which surprised him more. The fact that the woman he loved was standing before him professing her desire to become a bloody pirate, or that the woman he loathed with every fiber of his being actually agreed with him.

"At first. I've convinced her that I am neither simple nor a lunatic."

Richard jerked as if he'd been struck. "And she believed you?"

"It's a hard existence. I'm going to require weeks if not months of training. The danger is great. Men will be difficult to hire. I'm unlucky. I'm a skirt. I'm the lessor sex. Yes, I've heard it all, and." She threw her arms wide. "I don't care." Alicia looked toward the ship. "I want to know that danger. I want to stand on those decks and fly across the waves. Feel the rush of battle, the blood pumping through my veins. I want to carve my own way. Make a name for myself. Carry on the tradition of the Steele name. Honor my namesake."

Namesake? Namesake! "Are you talking about Captain Quinn? Now I know you've lost your mind? Alice Tupper Quinn is a hunted criminal of the Crown. She's a traitor, a thief, and a murderer."

"I know the story. She was forced to kill that duke to defend my parents," Alicia countered.

"Yes. And no. I've heard a different version of what happened in Jamaica. From the blasted woman herself." Richard's voice rose a full octave. "How exactly do you plan to honor her? In addition to becoming a thief, do you truly intend to learn what it's like to take another person's life?"

She crossed her arms over her chest and set her jaw. "If I need to defend myself, it may come to that."

Richard closed his eyes and groaned. "Alicia…"

"If I were a simple shop clerk, and I was walking through the streets at night and assaulted by an attacker, wouldn't I be within my right to guard my life even if it meant ending another's?"

"Yes, in self-defense, but—"

"Then why would it be any different with a fathom of water under me?"

Never had he come so close to shaking another human being. The strength in Alicia he'd admired mere moments ago had become the stubborn, single-minded, unreasonable, infuriating creature standing before him debating the right to kill a man? "Because a simple shop clerk doesn't go trolling the streets, picking pockets for the thrill of it, flushing out her attackers, and provoking them. A fathom? More like twenty fathoms. That is how deep you can sink when you're washed overboard in a storm, or your attacker is bigger and has more firepower and blows that floating bit of driftwood into flotsam." He jerked a finger toward the *Ruby Mist*.

Richard slapped a hand to his forehead in disbelief, fighting in vain to rein in his fear and anger. "And let's say, for argument's sake, you survive all that. Hell let's say you're a bloody success. Jocelyn's happy, your crew is happy, and you've stuffed your pockets and had your fill of wild adventure. You'll *forever* be a pirate, Alicia. You're talking about stepping into a life you can never leave except by dancing at the end of a rope or being slipped into a watery grave. Do you care nothing about your future?" He planted his fists on his hips.

"No one can predict the future, Richard. Not even you."

"Do you never plan to marry? Settle in a home of your own? Have children?"

"There is nothing to stop me from having all those things someday. My father—"

Richard shook his head and held up a hand to stop her. "Your father is the exception. He married into the title to protect your mother. Not the same thing at all. You're a woman, for God's sake. Pursue this, and it will follow you for the rest of your days. It will ruin you and any chance at a normal life."

Alicia set her jaw. "I'm already ruined."

"Don't be ridiculous. So, you ran away from a potentially disastrous marriage. Bineau was an idiot. No one will blame you for that. But this? You're talking about signing on to be a wanted criminal. You'd be committing social suicide. Talk about ruined? What decent man would have you?"

"The right one, hopefully," Alicia snapped back. "A man who actually listens and can appreciate a strong woman with her own mind and her own opinions. Who isn't timid or afraid to live her own life, make her own decisions, who can… can…"

"Fire a cannon ball across his bow?" Richard bellowed.

"Maybe I don't need a bloody man at all!"

Richard covered his face with his hands. His rational mind was screaming. This was insane. He'd fought in many a battle. Seen the horrors of war. A series of gruesome images flashed in his mind's eye of every way Alicia could be maimed or killed in her quest to fulfill her so-called destiny.

What had addled Alicia's thinking? Someone had to have put this mad idea into her head. Was it Robbins? Was there more to their sudden partnership than Alicia was saying? That had to be it. Jocelyn was as cunning as they came. There was more to this. He could feel it, and he was going to put an end to it.

Lowering his hands, he locked angry gazes with her. Either way, he had to stop Alicia, but how? Taking a breath, he forced himself to gain control of his temper. He'd known her long enough to know if they continued to cross swords and argue the point, it would only serve to solidify her resolve. No, he wasn't going to let this happen. He had to think of another way to convince her that choosing such a dangerous lifestyle would only lead to suffering, or worse.

One thing was certain, Richard wasn't leaving Black Point any time soon. He'd figure out a way to safeguard Alicia, and he wasn't giving up on winning her heart, either. She said he was too late, but she never said she'd stopped loving him. He'd hurt her enough for her to deny ever loving him, but that night, in his father's study, he'd seen it in her eyes. Tasted it on her lips. Why else would he have pushed her away? He wasn't about to make the same mistake again.

No, he wasn't going anywhere, not without the woman he loved.

He'd do whatever it took to get Alicia to trust him again. Remind her of her feelings for him. Convince her that her destiny wasn't on some leaky schooner eating hardtack and rats and fighting for her very survival. Alicia's destiny was with him. Richard just needed enough time to convince her.

With his initial anger and fear subdued, he ran his hand through his hair. "I suppose it's futile to try and talk any sense into you."

Alicia headed toward the path. "I'm done talking. It may look as if I'm racing toward this blindly, but I'm not. I've got things to do, things I need to learn. A ship to repair. Supplies to obtain. A crew to secure."

"Say no more. Where do I sign?"

Alicia looked back over her shoulder with an impatient smirk. "I knew you'd make a joke of this."

"I'm serious. You need a crew. I'm a social outcast, years of sailing experience, know how to fire a cannon, been known to drink. I'm the perfect pirate." He held his arms wide.

"Richard..." She shook her head and kept walking.

He caught up to her in a few strides. "You said it yourself, you need training. Who better to train you? I can teach you anything you need to know. You need a crew. I'm volunteering. I'll even help finance the repair of the *Ruby Mist*. Call it an investment." He straightened and saluted, "What be me first duty, Capt'n?"

Alicia stopped. "Ha. Now I know you're being flippant. You'd never take orders from a woman."

He gave her his most winning smile. "I might. If it was the right woman."

She folded her arms across her chest. "What are you playing at?" Suspicion laced her words.

"I'm not playing, Alicia. It's obvious you're determined, but you're wise enough to realize you need help. I have my reservations. I can't help but be concerned, but I'll feel a whole lot better if I'm the one training you. I can teach you how to defend yourself. How best to handle a crew. And my pockets are deep. By the look of that ship." He jerked a thumb over his shoulder. "You're going to need some working capital before you can start plundering unsuspecting merchant ships."

"And what do *you* get out of this arrangement?"

Seeing your face every day. Getting you to trust me again. Love me again. "Knowing you're safe." He tugged at the lace trim of her sleeve.

"I don't need you to protect me."

"Not after I've trained you, you won't. I can teach you how to take on men twice your size. I can also show you how to maneuver the *Ruby Mist* so you can't be caught. A ship like that is capable of changing directions in minutes and darting away like a silver minnow in the shallows. I'll show you how. Once she's sitting at the proper angle, of course," he teased.

Alicia gave him a begrudged grin as she looked back at the ship. Hesitating, she murmured, "I must admit, I'm tempted."

A tiny breath of relief gave him hope. It was a start. Richard pressed on. "You're the Captain. If I fail in my duties, you can put me off ship. Adrift in a skiff if you wish. Maroon me on an island with no water and one round in my pistol."

Alicia frowned at him. "Why leave you a pistol at all? What good is one round?"

"Because you're to be a fierce, yet merciful pirate like your father, and you'll leave me with the option of determining my own fate. Starve to death, die of thirst, or put my own sorry arse out of my misery."

He captured her arm, hooked it through his own, and started to walk her back toward town. "Speaking of starving to death, I haven't eaten a proper meal in more than a day, and if I'm staying in Black Point, I need to find accommodations that don't include fleas in my bed. And we can begin to build a list of supplies you'll need and discuss my first duties."

Richard tugged Alicia to a sudden stop. When she looked at him in question, he held her in his gaze. "That is…if we've reached an accord. What say you? Am I staying?" He took a step back and gave her a sharp salute. "Captain Steele, permission to come aboard?"

Chapter 15

Alicia pushed into the Laced Ladies. Her mind was a chaos of thoughts all vying for attention. Jocelyn and Raine held court behind the counter.

"*Finalement*. Where have you been?" Jocelyn planted her hands on her hips. "I left you hours ago."

"Setting our plan in motion."

Jocelyn's eyes narrowed. "Meaning what?"

"Meaning, I've secured us a benefactor, a Quartermaster for the *Ruby Mist*, and…" Alicia pulled a folded square of parchment from her reticule and held it aloft, "a proper list of supplies, tools, and whatever else we're going to need to get started."

"My, we have been busy, and here we thought you'd been sweet-talked by the smelly man and run back to London." Raine scoffed.

"*Silence*, Raine." Jocelyn came around the corner of the counter to pluck the parchment from Alicia's hand. "She *has* been sweet-talked by the good lieutenant, but into bringing him into *my* business." She unfolded the page and began reading.

"I wasn't 'sweet-talked' into anything. My negotiations with

Richard have nothing to do with your business or anything we've discussed. He knows nothing of our arrangement, and I can't see any reason why he should." Alicia snatched the list from Jocelyn's fingers.

Jocelyn gave her a hard look. "It is nearly dark. You've been with him all this time?"

Alicia lifted a shoulder. "We had much to discuss."

As it so often was with Richard, it had been a day of contrasts. Alicia had traveled from wanting to strangle the man to wanting to kiss him senseless. He could be infuriating and utterly charming within the span of a single breath. She liked their verbal sparring, liked the fact that she could be equally infuriating to him and raise his temper. They were a volatile mix at the best of times. Too bad she'd never know where a shared desire could have led them. She imagined they would have been like black powder and flame. An explosion of passion. Just the thought made her tingle.

"She bedded him."

Alicia spun on Raine. Had the woman read her thoughts? "I did no such thing." A rush of indignation pushed heat to her cheeks.

Raine pointed a finger at her accusingly, "But you wanted to."

"Don't be ridiculous." Alicia looked back and forth between the two.

"She may not have wanted to, but he certainly did. *Oui*?" Jocelyn raised her eyebrows. "I give him credit. Seems he will go to all kinds of lengths to get you into his bed."

The heat increased to her face and ears. Alicia imagined she resembled something akin to a ripe raspberry. "Just because a man and a woman spend a few hours together talking business, does not mean either of them wants to have sexual intimacies with the other."

Jocelyn moved back behind the counter. "It does when one of them is in love."

Raine nodded. "And the other is too dim to notice."

Alicia glared at the women. "So, he's in love with me."

"I knew it," Raine crowed.

Jocelyn held up a hand to stop Raine's enthusiasm. "Did he say he was?"

"Yes, but—" Alicia huffed.

Raine smirked, "Ha." Jocelyn reached into a pocket in her skirts and handed her a coin.

Alicia's jaw dropped. "You made a wager on me?"

Raine buffed the coin on her sleeve. "Not on you. On him."

"*Incroyable*. I did not think he would have the nerve to tell you," huffed Jocelyn.

Alicia sputtered. "Richard has plenty of nerve, of course not as much as the two of you. Whether he has feelings for me, did not influence my decision to take up his offer of assistance. Nor did it influence bringing him on as a member of my crew. If anything, it caused me great pause. But we've talked it through. He knows I do not share his affections—"

Raine snorted.

"I don't," Alicia insisted.

Jocelyn pointed an accusing finger at her. "Ah, but you did."

"Once, perhaps," she confessed.

"Ha!" Jocelyn put out her hand to Raine.

Raine stomped her foot and gave Jocelyn back the coin before disappearing into the storeroom.

Alicia snapped, "Now see here. I'll not be gambled on like some prize steed. What may or may not be between Richard and I is none of your concern."

"You are far too naïve. Do you not see what he is doing?"

"I am fully aware of what he's doing. As he is fully aware of my position. Had it crossed your mind that perhaps I'm far more savvy than you give me credit?"

"So, you are playing with his affections to get a new mast?" accused Jocelyn.

"Certainly not. I'm not playing with anything."

Raine returned with a basket of silk ribbon and gave Alicia another smirk as she passed, the exotic scent of her perfume trailing in her wake. "What must you think of me? The two of you acting like a couple of fish monger's wives. Gossiping and weaving tales. Taking bets on my life. Yes, the man has feelings for me, but I've been completely honest with him about my own. Any tenderness I carried for him was displaced long ago. His offer of aid comes from loyalty to my family and a concern for my safety. Nothing more. And frankly, I welcome his help. He has the knowledge and skills I need, not to mention the ready money to repair the *Ruby Mist*. That is all."

"Have you forgotten he was once a member of the British Navy? You know, the ones who like to hang pirates?" Jocelyn flipped a finger between her and Alicia.

"He has no loyalty to the Crown."

"Are you sure?"

Alicia notched her chin and turned a glare upon Raine, daring her to make another rude remark. "I'd bet my life on it."

Entering the apartment above, Jocelyn was tight on Alicia's heels. "Do you think it wise to let this man so close to you?"

Alicia rubbed at her temples. It had been a long day, and she was tired of defending every decision she'd made. "I told you he is not involved in our dealings. I'll make sure of that."

"But what of your heart?"

Alicia ran a hand over her hair and sighed. "He's not involved in my heart, either."

"I hear your words. But I do not believe them."

"I'm too weary for this, Jocelyn, and I have much to think about. There is a great deal of work to be done if the *Ruby Mist* is to sail again, and frankly, I'm not happy you and Raine have used me for your entertainment today."

Jocelyn folded her arms over her chest. "What did you mean when you said 'displaced?'"

Alicia held her forehead. "What are we talking about now?"

"Downstairs. You said your tenderness for this man was 'displaced' long ago."

"I don't know. My feelings faded. I got over him." She avoided

Jocelyn's gaze.

"That is not what you said."

Alicia flicked a hand. "What difference does it make? It means the same thing."

"No, *chèri*, it does not." Jocelyn laid a gentle touch on her arm.

Some of Alicia's well-constructed armor slipped at the kindness of the gesture. Jocelyn led her to sit at the table and pulled another chair to sit close. "Do you want to tell me about the two of you?"

"There's nothing to tell."

"Again, your words do not match your eyes."

"Why do you want to know? How much did you wager on this?" Bitterness tinged Alicia's response.

"No, no, whatever you wish to tell me stays only with me." Jocelyn made the motion of turning a lock on her lips and tossing the imaginary key over her shoulder.

"Nothing happened with Richard and me. A single kiss. Long ago. That is all."

"But you loved him."

There was a long pause before Alicia answered. "Yes. I loved him."

"*Beaucoup?*"

"*Oui, beaucoup*. A lot."

"It is obvious the man loves you. What happened to change your heart? Was he cruel? Did he strike you?"

"No, he never struck me." *Get. Out.* Alicia could argue those two words had hit her like closed fists, but what she had done in the days following had been worse. Could you lash out at a person, do things to punish them and never let them know?

Looking back, she often wondered who she was trying to punish. Richard for rejecting her, or herself for losing her heart to the wrong man, only to turn around and lose her innocence to another. In the end the only one left hurting and full of guilt and regret had been her.

"If he loves you and you love him, I do not see—"

Alicia held up a hand to end this. "Loved. Past tense. I thought you were interested in doing whatever is necessary to find your son and husband."

Jocelyn gave her a long hard look. "Very well. If you do not wish to discuss it."

"There's nothing to discuss."

"Ah, but there is another lie." Jocelyn stood and smoothed the front of her gown. Reaching down she tipped Alicia's chin, so she had no choice but to look at her. "You may lie to yourself all you wish, *chèri*, but it is not something you will do with me. *Comprendre*?

"Yes, I understand."

"Good."

Chapter 16

By noon the following day, Richard arrived at Laced Ladies to announce he had secured a place to room that, according to him, didn't have flies in the stew or gas-passing neighbors. He'd begun gathering the necessary supplies and services for the *Ruby Mist* and had started the task of pumping the water to the proper side of her hull. The pump was worn, decaying, and it worked twice as hard for half the progress, but it beat hauling endless buckets of bilge water.

"The careening will begin once we can get her seated again and towed into the shallows. We'll be able to see where the damage lies as soon as she's stable. I only hope it doesn't lay along the chine. That could be the death of her. That side will need to dry out, the rotten boards replaced and rechinked either way, but good news, I found a source for the new mast. It arrives next week. Once that's secured, and rigged, we'll set about the tarring."

Richard had shown up at the lace shop and gathered Alicia and her pistol in a rented carriage for what he promised was a day full of surprises.

"All of that in less than a day? Did you sleep last night?" He certainly looked rested. In the bright light of the day, he looked every bit the proper English officer Alicia remembered. Clean. Shaven. He smelled wonderful. He was sharply dressed. His boots looked new. Even the bruise around his eye had begun to fade.

"Best sleep I've had in months. The good Widow Harper and her daughters run a tight ship. I'm one of three they rent to. My room is immaculate, and if breakfast was any indication, the lunch they packed for us will be delicious, as well." He indicated the basket at his feet.

Richard explained on their way to Wakefield's Cove that he'd found two men to do some of the "heavy lifting" where the *Ruby Mist* was concerned. He pointed them out when they arrived.

"Liam and Shrug. Liam's the big one. Not a great conversationalist. Bit of a dim flame, but he's strong. Shrug appears to be the negotiator for the two. Weasel-like, but they were available and cheaper by the pair. All they know now is they've been hired on for a few days to bail the ship. So far, so good. I'll keep an eye on them. May work well as crewmen, but that's up to the captain to decide." He gave her a small side grin that, despite the warning shot from her rational brain, heated various parts of her anatomy.

Alicia had spent much of the time Richard had put to good use, tossing and turning in a futile attempt to sleep. Her conversation with Jocelyn looped in her mind. How many times did she need to scrutinize, analyze and defend every minute of her time with Richard?

Jocelyn's concern was valid. Alicia didn't believe it extended to her tender maiden's heart, however. She was toying with a loaded cannon by keeping Richard close, but she needed him. Although every time that thought justified his presence and his involvement, it brought with it images of another deeper, more dangerous need.

The wisest, safest thing would be to admit she'd made a

mistake. Put a halt to this now. Promise to return the money he'd already spent and put him on the next ship back to London. But it was futile to deny she wanted him. Alicia studied his profile as they moved closer to the ship, and the way the sunlight ignited the gold in his hair. The handsome set to his jaw. Then he turned and smiled at her.

Loaded cannon… *Fire, starboard*!

Alicia forced her gaze away and focused on the men working aboard the *Ruby Mist*. "I'll talk to them. Introduce myself. See how they react to the idea of a woman captain, and then make my decision." She started to rise as the carriage slowed.

Richard stopped her with a quick hand. "Perhaps, for now, the fewer people associating you with the *Ruby Mist* might be safer. Unless you decide to bring those two on permanently, it's probably best they believe they're working for me. Just for now." He maneuvered the carriage into a turn to follow the cove south along the narrow lane that ran along toward the west end. "I think the pump is fighting its final foe, but we'll know better after today." He clicked his tongue to urge the horse back into a trot.

Alicia turned to watch a cloud of dust billowing behind the wheels and obscuring the view of the *Mist*. Where was he taking her?

"The one snag I've run into is securing the cloth for the new sail." Richard continued, "The vendor wants to charge three times what it's worth and won't budge on the price even though he's sitting on a pile of merchandise. He'd barely miss the amount we need but refuses to negotiate. I'll check on other vendors. We may need to look further north for a supplier."

Richard graced her with another smile. This time, however, it wasn't warmth she experienced. Suspicion crept up her spine. "You've been busy." Perhaps *too* busy? She wasn't so beguiled as to make her suddenly ignorant to his nature. He could be very charming when he deemed to be and was quite adept at using that charisma to his advantage.

Especially with me.

Last night's musings returned. The familiar remembrance of their kiss, and wondering what would have happened had he not pushed her away. What if he had desired her then and passion had taken over? Yet there her mind had taken the wheel, swapping her fantasy for reality. Changing faces, mingling emotions. She longed for it to be *him* making love to her. Taking her for the first time there in his father's study. Naked bodies and firelight, glistening skin, fevered touches building toward what, she couldn't know.

It was over before it began. And then the wave of reality washed over her. The truth of the lovers in the firelight. It wasn't Richard after all. She'd awoken in the night in quite a state. Drenched in sweat. A tender, aching frustration pulsing between her thighs.

Richard's voice drew her back to the present. "Are you well? You're quite flushed."

Alicia startled. "The sun. It's very warm today." She fanned her cheeks with a hand and looked back toward the cove. Part of her wanted to leap from the carriage. Put some distance between her and Richard. Race back to quench her rising heat in the cool of the water.

Stop it!

This wasn't the time to let her heart drag her into something she had already wasted too much time and tears getting over. She'd been so naïve. No more. Richard may claim to have changed, but he was still Richard. The small nagging voice in the back of her mind kept telling her to be cautious.

She turned back and readjusted her body another inch away from him. Any further and she'd be tasting the dust of the wheels. Alicia closed her eyes and caged her scattered emotions. *Focus.*

Alicia cleared her throat as well as her erratic thoughts. "Yes, the sailcloth. We'll need an alternative. You've managed quite well in a few short hours."

"I can't believe I'm about to quote the bastard, but my father always said, 'A man should wake every day with a purpose.' After sitting on my dead arse for months, it feels good."

"Don't forget our deal." Her words sounded cold to her ear. "I'm taking nothing freely. I won't be beholden to you."

"I haven't forgotten. I'm keeping a tally of every farthing."

"Good."

Richard gave her another side glance, then frowned. "Is something wrong?" He laid a warm hand on her knee.

"No." *Yes.* The slight pressure of his fingers sent a tingle up her thigh.

"Your high color is returning, are you feeling ill?"

"No. I'm quite fine." Alicia pushed his hand away.

"Have I overstepped? When we talked yesterday, you thought it wise to keep away from these initial dealings to protect your identity. I should have checked before hiring the men."

"No. You've done well."

"Then what is it? You were bursting with determination yesterday. I would have thought you'd be more excited by the progress." He looked her way again. "Did something happen last night to change your mind? Perhaps a good night's rest has you reevaluating your decision? Are you *reconsidering*?"

The tone of his question set off another warning shot in her brain. *Reconsidering?* Damn her foolish heart and traitorous body. Her intuition was right all along. Richard pledged his love one minute and signed on to her crew the next. He'd said all the right words, done the right things, but it had given her pause. To think she had chided herself for being so suspicious. Yet there it was. His "purpose." He was placating her. Hoping she'd come to her senses.

Why did she suddenly feel as if she'd made a deal with the devil? She swallowed the sudden lump in her throat and shot a glare at his profile. Before his own glance could sweep back to her, she turned away, bit back the stream of anger fueled words building on her tongue and lifted her chin a scant bit. "Oh, I'm reconsidering many things," she murmured.

"Pardon?"

She smiled back, longing to push his smug handsome face from the carriage. While satisfying, shoving him from a moving carriage would not be advantageous. Regardless of the fact he was lying in wait for her to "give up this insanity," she still required his assistance. His knowledge. His expertise. More importantly, his money.

Call it her first act of piracy, but dammit, she'd get every last farthing from him if need be. Her father always told her to be cunning and wise when it came to dealing with people. She'd be damned if she was going to lose her head to some ridiculous fantasy and useless desire and be bested by Richard "*Ducky*" Dunbar.

"I said I'm not reconsidering a thing." She adjusted the brim of her hat to keep the sun off her face. "In fact, it's quite the opposite. The more time I spend with you, the more confident and determined I become." The carriage jostled as one of the tall wheels encountered a stone. Alicia clutched at the seat to keep upright as Richard returned his hand to her knee. She looked at it as if it were a spider in need of squashing.

The lane narrowed, and the forest thickened around them. The warm smell of pine and woods did nothing to soothe her. "Where are you taking me?"

"I thought we should start your training by teaching you how to shoot."

Alicia's jaw tightened as she patted his hand. "What a perfect idea."

Chapter 17

The wind whispered through the pine boughs as Richard continued to guide the carriage down the path. The gentle breeze and the soft clod of the horse's hooves were the only sounds. All conversation had stopped.

He glanced in Alicia's direction. Her mood seemed to shift with that same wind, and somewhere along the way, the mood had turned decidedly chilly. Richard may have revealed too much by asking her if she'd changed her mind. He needed to stay the course. Sailcloth be damned. All he truly wanted to do with the *Ruby Mist* was anchor her on the bottom of the cove. *Patience.* If he attempted to thwart her outright, she'd never forgive him. It was worth the expense of a few repairs to give her the impression he'd resigned himself to her ridiculous plans.

He gave her another side look. She made such a serene picture in her lovely gown and bonnet. The flush of a cheek. Her sweet lips. His beautiful Alicia. What could she be thinking under that bonnet? Lord help him, he'd never understood the workings of a woman's mind. They were a complete mystery. He shot another glance in Alicia's direction and frowned. A muscle ticked along the tender sweep of her jaw. While he may be ignorant in most things about the fairer sex, he'd learned one important thing. Silence never bodes well.

Richard broke the icy quiet, "I found a small clearing not too far from here. Seems safe enough. I've already set up targets."

"Busy, busy, busy," Alicia murmured. A decided frost hung on her words.

Richard forged ahead. "There's a stream at the west side that curves around and runs back into the cove. I thought we could have lunch along the bank." At her stony silence, he added, "If you'd like to, of course."

"Fine."

Was there ever a more frightening word from a woman? "Are you sure you're feeling well? I could take you back to the shop."

"No. I'm quite well." The tick was back in her jaw. "I'm most eager to fire my pistol and get on with the rest of my training."

"Good. Yes." Richard nodded in forced agreement. "The training. I've brought along two swords to practice with and a throwing knife for you as well. When close-handed fighting starts, having a sword and a knife is critical when you don't have precious time to reload your pistol."

Alicia checked her supply of powder and shot stowed at her feet along with her treasured pistol. "How quickly should it take to reload?"

Richard lifted a shoulder. "I've had a bit more experience, of course, but a good man can get off four to five shots a minute."

Alicia nodded then frowned. "I'll need to be faster."

The sun warmed through some of the chill in the carriage when they pulled to a stop in an open clearing. Alicia was out of her seat before the horse settled and began to unpack her pistol.

"Whoa." Richard wasn't sure which he was talking to. The horse was the only one who obeyed. He reached Alicia's side just as she pushed the wadding and ball down the barrel. "Hold on. What's the rush?"

"I've been dying to shoot this pistol."

Richard grimaced. "Please don't say dying and shoot in the same sentence. It's bad luck." He reached for the gun, but she turned a shoulder blocking him and continued to load the piece. "Rule number one, a weapon is a serious tool. If you load it, you better be prepared to fire, and if you fire it, you better be prepared to kill whatever you're aiming at. Including whatever is directly behind what you're aiming at."

"Rest assured, I'm very serious and quite prepared." Alicia poured a small amount of powder into the priming pan. So far, she was following the loading procedure exactly. Jocelyn taught her well, blast her.

"I can see that. Just take your time. Don't overfill the pan." Richard watched over her shoulder as she cocked the weapon. "Easy does it." He pointed to a spot approximately twenty yards away. "I've set a wash pail, and a few jugs as targets and balanced an apple atop each. Now raise the pistol, cock the hammer back a second time, hold it in both hands—"

"Jocelyn said I should practice shooting with one hand." Alicia attempted to hold one arm straight in front of her but fought against the weight of the weapon. Her arm trembled with the effort.

Richard reached past her with two fingers and raised the barrel, then lifted her left hand to join her right. "I say, once you get the feel for how this pistol fires, and determine if your aim is straight and true, then we can work on firing one handed." He moved behind her and wrapped his arms around hers, placing his hands over her own.

The warmth of his body against hers seemed to dispel the chill of her mood. Perhaps he had misjudged some of the advantages of teaching Alicia to shoot. He tipped his head to see past the frill of her bonnet. Another few inches and he could press his lips to the tender column of her neck. Her hair tickled his cheek. He whispered into her ear. "Now bring the weapon high enough to look down the barrel and line the top center with one of the targets."

Alicia stiffened in his arms, lowered the gun and pulled out of his embrace. "Are you planning to stand behind me in battle and hold my gun for me?"

"Certainly not."

"Is this how you'd teach a man to shoot?"

"No, but—"

"Then, please allow me to do this on my own." The chill had returned.

Richard stood back and away, held up his hands in surrender, and gave her a sloppy salute. "Aye, aye, Captain."

Alicia shot him a glare and turned back to focus on the target. She took her stance and raised the pistol. With both hands.

"You want to squeeze the trigger not pull—"

The explosion of black powder knocked his last word from the air. The gun flew from her hand and tossed her lovely ass in the dirt.

"Bloody hell!" He was at her side before the smoke cleared.

"Are you hurt?"

"I…I don't think so." She looked at him with wide eyes and blinked while waving away the lingering smoke. "Jocelyn said Cookie's pistol kicked like a mule. Felt like a whole team." Richard helped her to her feet while she rubbed her battered backside. "Did I hit anything?"

"Oh, I'm sure you hit something, but it wasn't anywhere near what you were aiming at."

"Let me try again." Alicia picked up the pistol and started to reload. "Is your ear ringing," she shouted as she tugged at her own.

"Are you sure about this, Alicia?"

"Am I sure about what?" She poured a small amount of black powder into the barrel of the gun.

"It's not too late."

"Too late for what?"

"Too late to admit you might have made a mistake. No one would blame you. Your motives were honorable. You gave it a proper effort. Let's stop all this before you hurt yourself."

She glared at him while adding wadding and another round ball of lead, then tamping it down the shaft. "There's been no mistake. No reconsideration. I've only just begun, and I'm not even close to giving up, Richard. Now, if you will please stand back." She poured powder into the pan.

"That's too much powder, Alicia."

"Nonsense, it's the same amount I used before." She raised the pistol, took aim, and closed her eyes before pulling the trigger and ended up in a smoky heap on her ass once more. This time the powder burns to her sleeves and bodice, and the soot covering her face and bonnet only added a blackened exclamation point to his argument. But to her credit, unlike her last shot, she'd held tight to the pistol. It lay smoking in her lap. The hot barrel charred its shape into the delicate fabric of her skirt.

Again, rushing to her side, Richard pulled out a handkerchief to wipe at her face. "Alicia…"

She swiped at angry tears before shoving his hand away. "Bollocks!"

The look of utter frustration on her face gave him hope. A few more times with her bottom in the dust, and he stood a much better chance of talking her out of this absurd notion of a pirate's life. Richard sat in the dirt next to her.

"Are you all right?"

"My arms feel like pudding. And… the ringing has become more of … a buzzing." Alicia blinked sooty eyelashes at him. "Do you hear a buzzing?"

Richard took the gun from her and set it aside. "I think that's enough shooting practice for one day." She looked done in after just two shots. This all might be easier than he anticipated. "I brought along a few blades for you to try, but maybe we can save sword training for another day as well. Perhaps this would be a good time to teach you to swim? No? Never mind all of it, I brought lunch—"

"No. Stop. I'm *fine*." She pushed to her feet and shook out her hands. "Our picnic will wait. Give me the sword. What do I need to know?"

From the back of the carriage, Richard pulled two blades. He'd chosen both because they were far too large for Alicia's stature. Handing her one, he stifled a grin as the heavy tip hit the ground. He held up his sword and struck a pose. "Given your size, any opponent would surely outpower you, but that doesn't mean you can't defend yourself, or deliver a fatal blow." He slashed his blade through the air with ease. "Any hits to a man's arms, especially his fighting arm, would be good. It won't stop him, merely slow him down. Most seasoned warriors have learned how to fight equally well with both hands." Richard proved his point by tossing his sword up, catching it in his other hand and making a dramatic sweep of the steel as Alicia still struggled to lift her blade out of the dirt.

"Now, a powerful slash across his midsection, here." He drew his hand sideways along his waist. "Would be a fatal blow. Once the guts are compromised, your enemy is done. It won't be a fast death, and it is a gruesome sight—a man's entrails aren't pretty—but the result is effective." Richard swiped his blade to the right and spun on his heel. "Dodging a downward attack, you can use the momentum to circle behind. Swing low. Aim for the backs of his knees. Not a killing blow, but he'll go down like a sack, and then you can finish him off. Either a straight plunge into his belly—" Richard raised his sword and thrust it straight down into the ground and caught the grimace on Alicia's face. "I'd suggest a sharp thrust through the heart, but the breastbone might prove an obstacle given your lack of strength—or." He took his side knife and made a slicing motion at the base of his throat. "A carving blow here, and he'll bleed out in a matter of minutes."

Alicia paled. Richard sheathed his knife and continued. "It's always a bit of a shock at first, how hot a man's blood can be. Did you know, on a cold day, it literally steams as it leaves the body.

And how far the beating of his heart can spurt that steaming gush. It seems gallons, but in the bloodiest of battles it's hard to tell one man's blood from the next. It all simply becomes a slippery mess."

Richard noted the slight green cast to Alicia's ashen complexion. By the look, her legs were joining her arms in the pudding description. He pressed on. "I once had a man's blood fill my boot." Richard lifted his foot and shook it. "Ruined a perfectly good pair of wool stockings. Damn stains will soak anything you're wearing straight through to your smalls. And the smell…repugnant. Like hot, rusty nails." He gave a shudder, for effect.

Alicia dropped the sword and rushed toward the stream. She just made it into the tall grass before she dropped to her knees and proceeded to lose the contents of her stomach.

His success should have brought elation, but there was no joy in this. He was a cad. Richard's only solace was that he was doing this for her own good. She had to face the harsh reality of what she was proposing. Battling on the high seas was not the life for her. One way or another he'd convince her.

Reaching her side, Richard helped her into the shade and sat her at the cool edge of the stream. He used his handkerchief and bathed her face and the back of her neck. Alicia scooped handfuls of water to rinse her mouth and drink. She snatched the linen from his hand, dipped it into the water and held it dripping to her face and chest, soaking the front of her ruined gown in the process.

Alicia ripped her bonnet off and sat back along the bank with a thud, still holding the handkerchief over her mouth. Richard folded his legs and sat alongside her, running a comforting hand down her back. "My first battle twisted my belly for more than a week." He leaned close to confess. "Man next to me had his leg blown clean off. Gruesome. Had me retching over the rails more times than I can tell you. I blamed seasickness, of course, but every time I closed my eyes…"

"Stop. I beg you." Alicia clutched the handkerchief to her chest as she pulled great gulps of air.

Richard slipped an arm around her shoulders and welcomed her to lean against him. The weight of her felt right along his side. She smelled faintly of black powder with a hint of gun oil. Two of his favorite scents, but not on a woman. No, the scent she usually carried smelled faintly of citrus and warm spice. He rested his cheek upon the top of her head and tightened his hold. Richard turned his face and kissed her hair. "I'm sorry I've upset you. The truth can be a brutal master. I realized you must be disappointed that plans have come to such a disheartening and bitter end, but I think in time, you'll be happy—"

Alicia pulled out of his grasp and met his gaze. "My plans have not changed."

"Alicia," he chided. "You can't be serious. Look at yourself. When are you going to admit this is more than you can handle?"

She pushed away from him and struggled to stand. "I'll admit, I need more practice with that damnable pistol. I should consider a smaller weapon, but it was Cookie's and it's sentimental. I'll just have to build my strength. A smaller sword as well. As for the rest." She straightened her spine and clutched a hand to her stomach. "Experience will toughen me. I'm grateful you were so honest in your horrific descriptions. Now I'll know fully what to expect." Alicia brushed the dirt from her backside.

Who the hell is Cookie? Richard sat looking up at her,

dumfounded. "I can't believe what I'm hearing. After all of that." His arm swept behind them. "You're still considering this foolishness?"

"Foolishness?" Alicia threw his ruined handkerchief into his lap. "You said yourself that you were sick for a week after witnessing your first battle. How is this any different?" She planted her hands on her hips.

"I was in His Majesty's Navy. I didn't have a bloody choice. You do." Richard scrambled to stand. "Please, you must listen to reason, Alicia."

"We've been over this. You said you admired my determination."

"I do. I just don't want to see you killed."

"I've fired a weapon twice. Were you an expert marksman the moment you picked up a pistol? Did you know how to fight the moment you held a sword?"

"No, dammit." The woman could argue better than any solicitor he'd ever met. Frustration, anger, and fear washed over him. "I merely hoped getting dropped on your arse enough times would knock some sense into that brain of yours!"

Her jaw dropped a mere second before she turned on her heel and stormed back toward the carriage.

Richard cursed himself. "*Bugger!*" Why was it when he was around her, it was as if his brain and his bloody mouth weren't connected. He heaved a sigh and headed after her. "Alicia, I'm sorry. I apologize. I didn't mean that."

She didn't stop. "Oh, you meant it. You were just daft enough to say it." When he caught up to her and took hold of her arm, she spun on him. "I knew better than to trust that you wanted to help me. Admit it. You've only been humoring me, waiting for me to 'reconsider,' delighting in watching me struggle, just waiting for me to fail, so you can sit back on your superior high horse and say, 'I told you so.'"

"Oh, yes, of course," he shouted back, "I always humor women by spending good money on a bloody mast for a bloody ship that I should just leave to bloody well sink."

"I can buy my own bloody mast!"

"Like hell you can!" His jaw was as hard as granite. The woman was the most infuriating— "I can't decide which of us is the bigger fool. You for thinking you can trade your skirts for swashbuckling, or me for hoping you'd come to your own conclusions and see how ridiculous this is. I always knew you were stubborn, Alicia, but this goes beyond being pigheaded, it—"

Alicia's fists balled at her sides, and she took a step toward him. Anger burned in her eyes. Bright color stained her cheeks. "Y-you insufferable man!"

"Unreasonable shrew!"

"Bloody bast—"

Richard grabbed her by the shoulders and kissed her shocked mouth. What was meant to end the futility of their argument and cease the cascade of angry words pouring from her lips, shifted as his world tipped off its axis. The heated passion of their fight set the kiss to white hot like a lick of flame hitting black powder.

Alicia pounded on his chest before gripping his shirt in each fist and jerking him closer. He crushed her to him, slanting his mouth to plunder hers. She pushed back just enough to break the kiss and glare at him with a darkening desire in her eyes.

"I hate you," she panted, but made no attempt to remove herself from his embrace.

"Good." His voice low and graveled. Temper danced with lust.

She leaned in to kiss him again yet took his lower lip between her teeth and bit. Hard. Before plunging her tongue into his mouth. A shaft of pure blinding heat surged through him straight to his hardening cock.

Rage and passion, pleasure and pain, if she were trying to kill him, she'd chosen the perfect weapon. God, he wanted her. Now. Here.

He made a low growl in his throat and returned each aggressive kiss as he tugged at her hips silently cursing the fullness of her skirts and the barrier of her corset. He needed to rid her of her clothes. Feel her skin next to his. Test the wetness he was sure to find between her legs. Stroke her. Spread her. He imagined her opening her pale thighs to him. Burying himself to the hilt in her heat. Each thrust plunging deeper. Stronger. Pushing them both to a climax to rival the sun.

What the hell am I doing? Richard reined in every ounce of control he could muster. This was Alicia, not some whore to rut with like some beast in the grass. She was untouched. An innocent. He didn't want to take her virginity in some blind, mad rush. When he took her, it would not be in a fit of lust spurned anger. Never in anger. He needed to wait, make her his wife before he made love to her. Lie her in a bed of satins and silks. Worship each inch of tender skin he exposed. Gentle kisses. Slow strokes of his fingers until she cried out his name in a wave of ecstasy.

Panting, he pulled away from her. Alicia's breath matched his. Her eyes dark with passion, her lips rouged as evidence of their heated kisses. The very image of a ravished woman. It took all his resolve to release the clutching grasp he had upon her skirts and step away. He struggled to catch his breath and hang on to that thin thread of restraint as he wiped a hand over his mouth trying to erase the feel of her lips. *Bloody hell.*

"You lied," he rasped, his voice still thick with longing. Richard tugged at his hems to cover the raging wood in his breeches and ran a shaky hand through his hair. He retrieved her bonnet from the ground and handed it back to her. "Never have I been kissed quite so soundly by a woman who claims to hate me."

Chapter 18

"You lied."

Richard's words repeated in a maddening circle in her mind. Alicia tossed onto her back to stare at the ceiling. Sleep was futile. Her brain refused to still. Anger lurked along the edges as frustration and a fierce wanting ached through her body. She fluttered fingertips over her swollen lips. When he kissed her, she'd been so angry. How had it all turned into a desperate need to ravish him? What had possessed her? She could still taste him. Feel the power of her own kiss and the effect it had on him. Alicia ran a hand along her belly, remembering the hard length of him pressed against her. The memory made her body writhe and flush with a wet heat.

She covered her eyes with a hand and moaned. *I did lie.* The feelings she told herself were dead and buried, were alive and as raw as ever. She loved him, dammit. Wanted him. Had she ever truly stopped? Alicia pounded the mattress with a fist. *No!* He was infuriating. Exasperating. Insufferable. But when his mouth claimed hers... "Ahh."

Whipping off the covers, she bound out of bed and began to pace. Her nightdress clung to damp skin. How could a single man unhinge her so?

Because it was Richard.

And because she was in love with him and near mad with want and need. How else could she explain her current state of anger, burning desire and unfathomable shame? She tugged at her neckline.

Alicia dropped to the side of the bed and balled a hand over her heart. What had she done? Why did kissing Richard always leave her in a whirling storm of emotions? Their first kiss ended in a complete disaster. It nearly destroyed her. Afterward the hurt and anger had consumed her.

Fury fed on that pain like carrion. It spurred her toward a single-minded rush to prove him wrong. To convince herself she was worthy of everything Richard had cruelly cast aside. So, when another handsome man came along and showed her the least bit of attention, she rushed in like a headstrong fool.

Parker Lanford. Two days after Richard's first devastating kiss, Parker had appeared at a dinner party. Father was entertaining a business acquaintance, Parker's uncle, Eugene.

They were up from London. Apparently, according to rumor, Parker had gotten into financial trouble, and his father had shipped him off to learn more about responsibility and the family business under the strict watchful eye of his uncle.

Alicia pasted on a smile and played the dutiful daughter through dinner even though her heart lay shattered and bleeding in her chest. Parker was charming. Tall, dark, incredibly handsome, quite spoiled, and terribly bored. This wasn't London with its host of social clubs and parties. This was Weatherington where parties were long over before midnight and the majority of eligible partners were a bit long in the tooth. Alicia had no misconceptions about his attentions. He was a self-made rogue, and she was nothing but an amusing distraction. After Richard's rejection, she welcomed Parker's flirtations. Needed them.

At first Parker seemed surprised by her gregarious nature, but soon she had him hanging on her every word. She made him laugh at her insipid stories and call her "simply delightful," all the while his wolfish gaze rarely left her cleavage. And afterward, when he whispered an offer to escort her on a private, moon-lit walk through the gardens, she wasted no time in being coy. Instead, she adjusted the set of her necklace, skimming her fingertips over the laced edge of her low-cut gown. He practically drooled on his boots. Alicia took his hand in her own and led him outside.

In her inexperienced thinking, she simply wanted a kiss from a man who wanted her kiss in return. Proof she was desirable. Capable of stirring heated emotions in a man. Proving to herself that Richard Dunbar was the arse he claimed to be, and his rejection had nothing to do with her, her identity as a woman, or her ability to entice a man.

Parker left little question that not only was he enticed, but he was also more than willing to participate. In a dark corner of the garden, he showered her with compliments as his touches became bold. He told her it was all he could do to sit passively beside her at dinner and not touch her, kiss her.

Alicia quickly realized her mistake. She didn't know how to reply or possess the experience to evade his advances. But the honeyed words he whispered to her in the dark were a needed balm to her broken heart. Then his touches became more insistent. His lips met hers briefly before his mouth moved to suck upon her neck and her bared shoulder, while his relentless hands tore at her lacings and pushed her corset askew.

He moaned against her skin, turned her back to front, and

wound an arm about her waist. He pressed himself along the length of her and continued to complain as he kissed and nuzzled her nape that these past weeks away from suitable companionship was killing him. How long could a man in his prime be expected to be celibate? Especially when presented with such a tasty dinner companion. From behind, his hand snaked around and pushed once more inside the bodice of her gown to caress her breast. He continued to kiss her neck and describe the painful unhealthy state of the engorged cock trapped within his pants. He tugged her hand back to feel the truth of his words and forced her hand to stroke his length.

Alicia should have stopped him. She should have wrenched herself from his hold, turned around, slapped his face, and fled back to the safety of the house. She should have said no. But she didn't do any of those things. She had encouraged him. Wanted this. And while his kisses ignited a certain need within her body, they never reached the wounded heart within her chest. There was only one man who could do that, and for a moment, she closed her eyes and pretended Parker's insistent mouth, roving hands and hard cock belonged to someone else.

Sitting on the side of the bed, Alicia moaned at the memory. *Richard.* She wanted him to be Richard. And in that garden, imagining the hands kneading her breasts and the warm breath on her skin was his, she'd fallen under the spell of desire until it was too late to turn back.

Parker took her soft moans of pleasure as consent. Before Alicia could comprehend what was happening, cool air chilled the backs of her legs and buttocks moments before he bent her over a garden bench, pushed between her thighs, and took her from behind.

Pain ripped through her as he plunged his penis into her. Parker must have confused her cries for ones of pleasure. The pressure of the bench's back beneath her ribcage forced the air from her lungs and had her gasping for breath as he continued to grunt and rut. Each thrust felt like he was tearing her in two. His hands on her hips held her pinned against the solid stone of the bench, bruising her, crushing her, until at last, pulling out, he shot his semen into the grass with a great satisfied groan.

And then it was over. Parker gave her behind a rough grab and a quick slap before righting her skirts. When she could gain enough breath back into her lungs, she straightened and turned, Alicia found him buttoning the front of his breeches with a pleased grin spread across his lips.

"I knew you'd have a tight little cunny."

Alicia let out a sob and brutally slapped the insipid leer off his face.

Shock widened his eyes. "What on earth?"

"You... you..."

"What the hell is wrong with you?" He rubbed at his cheek.

Alicia still struggled to pull in a decent breath. "I've n-never..."

"Never what?" he bit. It took less than a heartbeat for him to realize what she was trying to say. "Bloody hell..." Parker made a sound like air being let out of a set of bellows. He pointed a finger at her. "I didn't force you. You were enjoying yourself just as much as I. How was I to know you were a damn *virgin*?" He spit the word as if it were bitter in his mouth.

Alicia reached behind her and held tight to the back of the bench. Her knees felt incapable of holding her upright.

Parker jerked his clothing back into place. "You should have told me. Stopped me. I'd never have…" Shock turned to indignation on his face. "Is this some ploy? A trap to get me to marry you? I've ruined you, so now I must wed you? Have you and your father conjured up some plot to join our two families, because I'm telling you right now, I have no intention of falling for that old trick—"

Alicia fought to keep from slapping him again. She wiped the tears from her cheeks and did her best to re-adjust the bodice of her gown. "No plot. No ploy. Profound lack of sanity. A huge mistake. You need to leave." Her breath came in pants. She was going to be ill.

"My pleasure."

Alicia grabbed his sleeve. "I warn you. If you spread one word of this." She gulped back the bile rising in her throat. "I will find you and force you to make amends for my honor—unless, of course, my father hears of it first and shoots you."

Parker visibly blanched. "I may be something of a debauchee, but I do have my standards. The breeding of a gentleman at the very least. No one will hear anything about this…this…" he waved his hand toward her. Parker straightened his vest. "Not from me. I assure you. I won't utter your name again. Hell, I'll swear we've never even met."

And then he was gone. Next morning over breakfast, Father pondered the reason for the Lanford's hasty, late-night departure, but their business dealings were concluded. Favorably for both parties, so Father assumed they were simply anxious to be on their way.

"Darling, are you feeling well, you're looking quite pale this morning?" Her mother asked.

Alicia sat in her shame and disgrace alone. "I'm fine."

She learned later why Parker had pulled out of her so abruptly. Weeks after, when she had her monthlies, Alicia gave a silent prayer of gratitude. Thank goodness no babe grew in her. If there was one blessing from her irresponsible behavior, it was that.

Until Frederick's proposal, only two people knew about what happened that night.

"Frederick, before I agree to marry you, there is something I must confess." Starting that conversation had been difficult, but something had happened to her in the time since Richard's rejection and Parker's seduction. A new hardness encased her heart. She wasn't the innocent maid she once was. Alicia had carelessly given away the only two things she had absolute governance over. Her heart and her body. She swore she'd never do so again.

Alicia stood, went to the window, and pulled back the curtain. The lightning of the sky announced the dawn of a clear new day. Hours of pacing had done nothing to clear her chaotic mind or ease the yearnings of her traitorous body. Kissing Richard at Wakefield's Cove had stirred up every memory, every emotion, and a longing so deep her body pulsed with a fiery desire to finish what they started. That was where her heart and her body continued to battle with her mind.

So much was at risk now. It was a dangerous future she was embarking upon. The most perilous aspect of all, was trust. Did she trust Richard? Did she trust herself? She could be strong when needed, but her heart.... Could she quell the love she was hopeless to deny? Could she satisfy the longings of her body and keep an emotional distance? Was that even possible where he was concerned?

Alicia yanked the curtain back into place and reminded herself to hold fast to the plan. Her gaze moved to Cookie's pistol. Yesterday's disgrace still hung about her. She had no illusions that the training was to be easy but being knocked in the dirt repeatedly was enough to make any sane person question their commitment.

It would be easy to give up. They all expected it. Not just Richard, Jocelyn and Raine as well. After seeing her condition as she stormed back into the lace shop yesterday afternoon, Jocelyn, too, asked Alicia if it wasn't time to give up her insane quest. Raine had insisted on it after seeing her ruined gown. Alicia had to bargain with her to loan her yet another gown. She had to promise Raine the first choice of stolen silks *if* Alicia ever managed to steal any.

Self-doubt chipped at the edges of her confidence. She rubbed her bruised bottom through the thin linen of her chemise. Lifting the braid of her hair, she sniffed. It still smelled of black powder. The curls about her face were singed. She was lucky to still have eyebrows.

Cookie's gun mocked her as if its previous owner were somehow conspiring against her, as well. Lifting the weapon, Alicia ran a finger down the barrel. It would be simple to call an end to all this frustration. She could give up the notion of becoming an outlaw of the sea. Confess her undying love to Richard. Return to England. Wed him. Bed him. Bear his children. And quietly die into a life of obscurity and ordinary. Or…

A small flicker of a flame still burned in her belly. Or, she could turn her jumbled feelings around and use it as kindling to stoke the fire of determination that brought her here in the first place. Yes, she was stubborn, but there was something to be said for fortitude. Steadfastness. Resolution. If she were a man, she'd be commended for such resolve. None would question her commitment or her passions. To hell with them. She'd show them all.

Alicia rubbed Cookie's gun with its oiled rag. She was not going to let her emotions, or a pistol with pearled handles best her. She would practice until her arms ached, build her strength, hold this damn weapon, and fire it one-handed, straight, and true.

As for the rest, perhaps it was futile to battle against her heart and body. It wasn't as if she could ruin her reputation any more than it was already ruined. Society's rules no longer applied, and Richard would love her as she truly was or not at all. It was his choice. Her heart had already been broken by him. She'd survived it once, if need be, she'd survive again. Best to know sooner rather than later.

Alice stared at her reflection in the standing mirror. *Lord, help me, I will not be beaten by the ghost of a one-legged cook...or by the kiss of a bloody Duck!*

Chapter 19

Abandoning any hope of sleep, Alicia left her room, and was startled to find she wasn't the only one up greeting the dawn.

"Raine?" At first, Alicia wasn't sure it was truly her.

Gone was the elegance of a fashionable gown and jewelry. Gone was the sophisticated coif. Raine's hair was loose, bone straight, and hung past her waist in a shimmering fall of black. The clothing she wore was the color of fresh butter, with a trim of red stitched pattern work and fringe running across her chest and down the sides of her breeches. In one hand she held the corpses of two fat hares. A sheathed knife hugged her thigh. A similar pattern and fringe decorated the scabbard.

"What are you doing?"

"None of your business." Raine set a long bow and a decorated quiver to lean against the wall.

Alicia was captivated. Raine was stunning. She couldn't help but stare. "You look…"

Raine glared and waited, "I look like what?"

"A native." Alicia swept her attire with the sweep of a hand.

Raine crossed the room and dropped the hares on the table. "Congratulations. You win."

Alicia frowned. A night of no sleep was making her brain fuzzy. "I don't understand."

"It's not hard." Raine moved past her.

"But I thought you were Spanish. Jocelyn told me—"

Raine stopped and faced her. "A lie. Jocelyn's life is full of illusions and untruths. Haven't you figured that out by now?"

It was true. Jocelyn's business, the shop, the stories she tells customers, or anyone who makes inquiries about Ric or Beau, all fictitious. The falsehoods slipped from Jocelyn's smiling lips with no hesitation. Alicia, herself, would need the protection of Jocelyn's fabrications. It made her wonder what Raine's truth could be. "But why would *you* lie?"

The question was met with a cool stare. "That's my story to tell."

It was futile to press Raine. Alicia raised a hand in surrender. "And it's none of my business."

"You win again."

"Maybe as my reward, you could help me." Alicia suggested. Raine braced her hands on her hips and remained silent. "I need proper clothing," she continued. "Not another dress. Breeches, similar to those." She indicated Raine's clothing. "And boots. Something I can move freely wearing. And a shorter sword. Maybe a knife like that one you have there?"

"Why should I help you? I've already lost two gowns with nothing but an empty promise of stolen silk to replace them."

"Perhaps we could work together. Become friends."

"I need no friends."

Alicia lifted her palms. "Then what do you need? A barter. I'll give you whatever you want in exchange."

Raine raised a sharp black eyebrow, was silent for a span of a breath, then turned to retrieve her bow and quiver. "Fine."

"I'll need them soon," Alicia rushed to add.

"I said, 'Fine.'"

"What is your price? What do you want?"

A small smile lifted the corner of Raine's lips. "I'll tell you as soon as I decide." With that she slipped out on silent feet, leaving Alicia with far more questions than answers.

Jocelyn was no help answering them a short time later. When Alicia questioned her about Raine's true identity, Jocelyn's response was a near repeat of Raine's words.

"Raine's business is Raine's. But circumstances are similar, hers and yours, no? One woman by day, another by night. I am not Raine's keeper. She is not one to be kept. She is her own guardian, but I give her a safe place to hide in plain view."

"By introducing her to everyone as European?"

Jocelyn gave a short nod. "Like I will continue to present you as gentry, when you've become nothing but a scallywag and a thief."

Alicia cocked her chin. Jocelyn was an expert at shifting the subject when she didn't want to reveal too much. Illusion and lies, Raine had said. Seemed Jocelyn was an expert on a great many things.

By later that morning, Alicia's body was too tired to crave anything to do with Richard Dunbar and his tempting kisses. Her arms and shoulders were screaming with fatigue. Through the early hours of the day, she had staked out a spot behind the shop where she could practice dry firing her pistol. As she'd experienced the barnyard recoil of the weapon, when she set her stance to fire, she braced her body for the anticipated impact and squeezed the trigger snapping the flint into a closed frisson as to not damage the firing mechanism—one of Richard's helpful do's and don'ts. No sense wasting balls and powder on Jocelyn's wooded back garden.

Practicing, she could hear Richard's voice in her head, giving her instructions, and then replaying the angry words they both fired at one another before they'd kissed each other senseless. Alicia had been primed and braced for him to show up, as well, but the morning had passed without so much as a word from him. Perhaps he was the one reconsidering things.

It was then she saw Raine again, the Raine she recognized. Gorgeous gown, hair piled high on her head, a touch of rogue on her cheeks and lips. Pearl fobs dripping from her earlobes. Nothing like the Indian maiden she appeared earlier, but now that Alicia had seen the real Raine, it was easy to see past her "Spanish" disguise. Alicia supposed it was true what Jocelyn said, "People will see what you tell them to see." She had told the world that Raine was a visiting beauty from Spain, and the residence of Black Point and the customers at the Laced Lady saw nothing else.

Raine glided up carrying wrapped bundles in her hands and dropped several at Alicia's feet. On top lay a light tan baldric with a short boarding sword in its scabbard along with another sheathed blade.

"These will do for you. If you want, I can teach you how to throw a knife, so your enemy won't ever get near enough to need a sword."

Alicia fingered the intricate weave on the knife's sheath before looking at Raine in surprise. "You'd do that?"

"For a price." Raine toyed with a ring gracing her long narrow fingers.

She gave a small laugh. "Another price? I'll end up owing you all I possess."

"You possess nothing." Raine started to walk away.

Alicia called after her. "But I'll soon change that."

"That is what I'm counting on."

Carrying her supplies and cache of weapons to her rooms, Alicia unwrapped her new garments. Pale gray suede breeches looked as if they would barely fit a boy. Slipping them on, the buttery fabric fit her like the brushed skin on a peach. Worn black boots were a size too large and with the bucket tops raised came to mid-thigh, but they'd do. She opened another parcel to find a wide sleeved shirt. Two of them to be exact. One, homespun, dyed the color of fine claret with a small three-corner tear that had been repaired at the hem, and a ruffle of fabric decorating the front. The other a creamy white linen with wide lace trim on the cuffs and collar, with black-dyed, hide lacings closing the neck. Unlike the trousers, the shirts looked large enough for a good-sized man. Each fell past her hips, but the addition of a wide tanned belt cinched it high and tight at the waist.

Alicia appraised her new attire in the looking glass. Her legs looked odd encased in the suede. Walking unhindered by skirts was a new experience, as well. Breathing without the cage of a corset felt freeing and slightly indecent with her breasts free to move with the ease of her steps. She liked feeling the rush of strength, as if the clothing were somehow woven with threads of courage and power.

She turned and appraised her backside. The way the soft suede hugged the curves of her and caressed between her thighs and tight along her yearn-swelled sex felt carnal and sensual. Smoothing her hands down the swell of her hips, Alicia spoke to her reflection. "I've heard tell that the measure of a man's authority is found in his breeches. Perhaps it's not his cock they're talking about, perhaps it is, in fact, the pants."

* * * * *

Back in yet another borrowed gown, bound and restrained in her corset and stays, Alicia returned to Wakefield's Cove. Things continue to look promising as the *Ruby Mist* sat higher and straighter at her berth. Carrying a basket of persuasion, Alicia boarded.

"Hello?"

The larger of the two men hired to bail the ship poked his head up from below, but simply stared at her.

"Good day. You're Liam, are you not?"

The man's eyebrows shot toward his hairline. "Aye." He stepped up onto the deck and scrambled to neaten himself. Raked down his hair, brushed the front of his filthy, stained shirt.

"Is Mister Shrugs with you?"

Liam snorted, "Mister? None calls him Mister."

"Who te hell ya talkin' to, idiot?" *Mister* Shrugs was quick to join them.

"Her." Liam pointed and leaned over to Shrugs and added, "Ain't she purty?"

"Ya, ya." Shrugs pushed Liam back. "What'd ya want?"

Alicia held up the basket. "I thought you two might be hungry. You've been working so hard bailing my ship, I—"

"Ye be Dunbar's Misses?" asked Shrugs. Liam eyed the basket and rubbed a dirty rag over his lips.

"No. Mister Dunbar works for me. The *Ruby Mist* is my ship."

Shrugs gave her a suspicious gaze. Liam's eyebrows took another leap. Alicia continued. "I'm Captain of this vessel, Captain Alicia Steele. I've come to offer you both a business proposition."

"We ain't got time for no propositions from no skirts." Shrugs grabbed the front of Liam's shirt and jerked him back toward the galleyway. "We's got a job te finish."

Alicia set the basket on top of a rotting coil of rope and opened the lid. "Surely you have time to fill your bellies. You must be famished."

Liam pulled out of Shrug's grip. "I be *famished,* Shrug. Couldn't we be takin' a wee break?"

"Ye don't ken what *famished* means, ye great clod." But Liam was already tearing into a loaf of fresh bread he'd snatched from Alicia's hands. She unwrapped the cloth covering a thick wedge of cheese and began cutting wide slices. Liam stuffed his mouth.

Alicia held out a piece of cheese to Shrug. He crossed his arms over his chest. When he didn't take it, Liam looked between him and the offered cheese and back again before stealing it himself and popping it into his mouth. Alicia brushed off her hands and held Shrug's disapproving glare.

"I don't blame you for not trusting me, but I'm here in good faith. I need men like the two of you. Strong. Hardworking. And whether you believe it or not, I am the Captain of the *Ruby Mist*, and I'm looking to secure a crew. Sign on, and I can make you very rich men.

Shrug snorted, "Wit this leaky tub?"

"The leaks will be fixed, the mast replaced, all will be made right, and then our operation will commence in earnest. Small raids. In and out under the cover of dark. Easy targets. Surprise attacks, no fighting. I already have someone waiting for the goods, which means fast money." Alicia pulled out a roll of parchment. "I've drawn up a set of Ships Articles for the *Ruby Mist*. The most important one being that if you agree to sign, you must keep my identity a secret. Mister Dunbar has agreed to be Quartermaster." *As long has he concedes to a few more demanding conditions,* she mused. "By day, you'd report directly to him, but by night, I'm the one in charge."

Alicia laid the parchment open. "If you two decided to be the first to join my crew, I'll give you both an extra share."

"A share o' nothin' is still nothin,'" Shrug argued.

"Yes, but a share of what I'm proposing, what's out there ripe for the taking." She pointed past the *Ruby Mist*. "It's bigger than his appetite." Alicia jerked her head toward Liam. "And." Pushing past Liam's hands, she pulled out two bottles and set them on top of the

Articles before offering up a quill and ink. "All the rum you can drink."

Liam wasted no time in wiping greasy fingers across his pants before grabbing the quill and making his mark. He gave her a grin and hoisted one of the bottles and pulled the cork with his teeth—the few that remained in his mouth.

Shrug gave her a hard stare. "Two extra shares. Each."

Alicia laughed and shook her head, never breaking eye contact. "One's the offer. And the deal's over the second Liam reaches the bottom of that bottle."

Shooting a quick glance at the big man gulping rum like water, Shrug grimaced and grabbed for the quill.

As soon as both were signed, Alicia lifted the parchment, blew lightly on the ink to dry before rolling it into a tight scroll. "Good. Our first raid will be tonight. I'll meet you both here just after dark."

"I told ya, ye ain't fit for no raid."

"Don't worry, we won't need the *Mist* for this one. A horse and cart will do. We're just after a wee bit of cloth."

Chapter 20

It had been three days. Three interminable days of traveling dust filled roads negotiating for a bloody scrap of sail cloth. Richard glanced over his shoulder at the cache of supplies he'd gathered to continue the repairs on the *Ruby Mist*.

Three days of debating with himself. Or was that berating? The anger of his argument with Alicia still simmered in his mind. The kiss still seared his lips. He couldn't get her out of his mind.

Love was maddening. Why on earth would any sane man choose to fall in love? So far it had caused him nothing but frustration, aggravation, sleepless nights, distracted days, and a discomfort of a most personal nature. Richard adjusted the positioning of his over-eager cock.

Thousands of miles from home, covered in dirt, sober as a bloody Puritan, becoming poorer by the hour, chaste to the point of pain, all so he can save a woman from herself. And for what?

He knew for what. Their kiss by the cove had given him a heated taste of *what*. It had shaken him to his very core. Ignited his desire. The anger and passion fusing into a single meeting of their lips. Pure combustion, and God help him, he wanted nothing more than to be consumed by those flames, consumed by her, adding his heart and soul to the pyre.

He readjusted his seat. When had he wanted a woman more? Richard had spent three days thinking of nothing else but winning Alicia over. That is, if he could get her to speak to him again. Perhaps she'd soften her anger toward him when she saw the new sail cloth and bilge pump he'd purchased.

Pulling his cart into Wakefield's Cove, several sights welcomed Richard. First of which was the *Ruby Mist*. She sat true at her berth. A small stack of hull planks lay close to shore. By what he could see, she'd already had several replaced. He couldn't tell from this distance, but it looked as though the repair to the cotton chinking had started. The broken mast was gone and was at this moment roasting what appeared to be potatoes on sticks.

Halting the cart, he jumped down next to the cook. "What the hell goes on here?"

"Lunch." Liam grinned. "We be *famished.*"

"And you're using the mast for kindling?"

"Capt'n Steele said it weren't good for much else wit a new one comin.' Got us a nice fire, too. Says it's a might nippy today, may as well keep toasty."

"Wait? Captain Steele said? Bloody hell is that the old pump?"

"Yep, told us to burn the lot." He stuck his potato with the tip of his knife before putting it back over the flames. "Said t'was 'unnecessary' being as we pinched a new one."

"Who pinched?"

"We pinched." He held up a bottle. "Rum?"

"No, thank you." Richard needed a map to follow this conversation "Who's we?"

"Ain't no more crew 'cept Shrug an' me. An' you, I sup'ose." Liam lifted another stick and held it out to Richard. "Sausage?"

"No, I don't want a damn sausage." Richard scratched his head. "So, you're telling me that you and Shrug stole a new pump?"

Liam lifted a shoulder and shook his head before he took a large bite of the sizzling meat, yelped and began moving the bite back and forth from one side of his open mouth to the other, breathing cool air over what had to be blistering his tongue. "Shrug was—look out, bein' as—I can haul the—heavy stuff." He spoke around his grimaced chewing. "Capt'n ken where everything be. Like she owned the place. Walked in, pointed out what we needed and we was gone. In, out, just like she promised." He swallowed. "Shrug's callin' her Iron Ali, not to 'er face, mind ya. Says she's got some brass 'tween 'er legs." Liam blew on the remaining half of sausage before biting it off the stick. Grease dripped into his whiskers.

"Where's Shrug?"

"On the *Mist*." Liam jerked his head in the direction of the ship before washing down his lunch with more rum.

Boarding, Richard was shocked to see most of the items he'd scoured three days to purchase, and more. The much-coveted sail cloth, two new brass gypsies for the anchor windlass, coils of new rope, more gleaming brass fittings, block and tackles, tar barrels. *What the hell?* He'd hoped giving her three days would have slowed down her resolve, by the look, it had only served in pushing her deeper. Or maybe Alicia found another to help her.

Shrug emerged from below wiping his hands on a rag.

"What the hell?"

"There ye be. We be wonderin' where'd ya run off te."

"I was off gathering supplies." He swept his hand over the lot on deck. "Seems I wasted my time."

"Seems ya did." Shrug stuffed the filthy bit of cloth into a back pocket.

"Where did all this come from?"

Shrug shrugged. "Here and there."

Richard's patience was wearing thinner by the second. "How?"

"Best be askin' Capt'n Steele."

"Excellent suggestion. Do you know where—" The report of pistol fire echoed across the cove. "Never mind, I know where."

Richard was out of his cart again before the horse heard the words "Whoa. Halt." It was the day for surprises, evidently. And one of the biggest was Alicia. In breeches and boots. Air left his lungs in a rush. *Oh, bollocks.* His own set tightened at the sight of her. A fist of heat pushed into his cock. *Bloody hell.*

Her hair fell in a straight pale braid down the center of her back. Over breeches that left no curve of backside to his imagination. She wore a loose sleeved top in a deep shade of red. A wide leather belt pulled it tight to the slim span of her waist. Its tails skirted her hips directing his gaze again to the shape and length of each slender leg ending in tall, polished boots. *Dear God.* The effect left him dumbstruck.

She'd temporarily abandoned the pistol in favor of a short boarding sword, with which she battled a sickly tree. Hacking high, followed by a slashing spin. Bark flying. Her boots kicking up dust as her braid swung. Stray hair clung to her pinked cheeks as she lunged and buried the tip of her sword into the soft wood.

"Never stood a chance." Neither the tree, nor him.

Alicia spun in surprise. Her sword at the ready, but she drew back when she saw it was him. "Richard." Her chest rose and fell sharply. She lowered her blade. "You startled me. Again. You need to take caution. Last time I blackened your eye." She leaned forward, "which is looking much better, I must say." She took a moment to catch her breath. Her face and neck shown with perspiration. "It's been days. Thought you'd caught that ship back to England, after all." She sheathed her sword and pressed the back of one hand to her cheek.

The front of her shirt laced loosely and dipped far too low. The pale curves of her breasts clearly visible through the damp fabric. "No. I...I..." When she bent to retrieve a baldric from the ground, he could see bare skin clear to her waist. His cock pulsed. *Kill me.* Richard shifted his stance and began again, "I've been off gathering supplies which you clearly don't need." He pointed back in the direction of the *Mist*.

Alicia pulled a lace-edge handkerchief from a pocket and dabbed at her forehead. "Oh, I'm sorry. I had no idea what you were planning. Our last conversation ended...rather abruptly."

"Ah, yes." The kiss had haunted him for the past three heated days. And sleepless nights. Richard had to look away, before he was tempted to end their current conversation in a similar yet equal manner. How could one woman continue to make him feel as if the earth was shifting beneath his feet? Richard wrestled his thoughts back to the conversation at hand. "Where did it come from?"

"It?" Alicia pulled a cork from a bottle and lifted it for a drink. Richard followed the enticing curve of her neck and watched her throat work. *Lord, help me…*

Frustration flooded him from every side. His cock gave another painful pulse as his reserve snapped. "The supplies, Alicia. The sailcloth, ropes, the bloody pump. Where did you get it all?"

Wiping the moisture from her lip with the sweep of a thumb, she lifted her chin as she set the bottle aside and crossed her arms over her chest. "I can't answer that question."

"Why the hell not?"

"I don't know where we stand. You and I. I want to trust you, but frankly I don't seem to think rationally when I'm near you."

"I'm having the same problem." Richard held her gaze.

"And I'm no longer in a position to make rash assumptions. Especially where you're concerned." Alicia unfolded her arms to wipe a hand over the alluring curve of her hip before continuing. "I need to know some things before we can continue."

Richard cocked an eyebrow and planted his fists on his own hips, "Like what, pray tell?"

"To begin with, were you indeed serious about being my Quartermaster? If so, you must sign the Ship's Articles *before* we discuss any business concerning the *Ruby Mist*." She pulled the parchment out of her sack and unrolled it. "As you can read, Article three deals with discretion and confidentiality." Alicia pointed to the section in question. "Liam and Shrug have already signed on as you can also see, and if you still want to, there is a place for you on my crew." Alicia pulled out a small bottle of ink and a quill. She held out the quill but pulled it back before he could even consider taking it. "But, the position comes with certain conditions."

He frowned, "What kind of conditions?"

"I want complete honesty from you, Richard." At the slack of his jaw, Alicia held up a hand. "I'm not ungrateful. You've done so much already." She swept a hand toward the cove. "Hiring on men, securing a new mast. I'm in your debt."

"But."

"But I have to know, do you believe in me or don't you? Yes, or no? You are either totally with me, or you are against me, and we can end this relationship between us before it goes any further. I don't have time to waste convincing you. Nor do I care to have you lying in wait hoping to watch me fail. Or…or…" She flung a hand. "Patronizing me while you bide your time waiting for me to come to my senses. I will succeed with or without you. I want you." She paused to take a breath and held his gaze. "I want you to be more than a part of my crew. I want you to be part of my life, but I need the truth." Alicia set the ink and quill atop the Articles. "Are you with me, or aren't you?"

A myriad of thoughts raced and collided in Richard's mind. Frustration and anger volleyed for top position. "With you? Do you have *any* notion of what I've been through, endured, and sacrificed to be *with you*?" He threw his arms wide. "Forgive me if I don't cheer at the prospect of the woman I love strapping on a pistol and risking her bloody life every minute of every day for reasons she still has not fully explained."

He raked his hands through his hair. "*With you*? I've thought of nothing else *but* you for months. You are my first thought on waking and my last as I close my eyes at night. Even in my dreams, I'm bloody well *with* you, Alicia." Richard lowered his voice and held her in his gaze. "I love you. How many times do you need me to say it? I hurt you and trust me I'll spend the rest of my life making amends for that. But I love you. I want you, and the way you kissed me the other day, here on this very spot." He pointed at his feet. "You owe me the truth, as well. You love me, too."

Alicia looked away. "And what if I do? It changes nothing."

Suspecting it and hearing it were two separate things. *Dear God.* Richard's heart took a leap. "It changes everything." He reached for her, grasping her arm.

She focused on his hand before lifting her gaze to his. "But it doesn't answer my question. I'm bound and determined to live my life by my rules. I do want you, but if you can't—"

"If you love me, I can do anything?"

"Including watching me strap on a pistol and risk my bloody life every minute of every day?" She cocked her head.

He was lost and conceded victory to her without even begging quarter. The choice before him was clear. Live in constant fear of her losing her life. Or live without her for the rest of his. He huffed at the ridiculousness of the thought. There was no choice, not where Alicia was concerned. Not when he was so deeply in love with her. "At least I'll be by your side to help protect you."

"And if I don't need your protection?"

"I'll protect you anyway."

Richard pulled her into his arms then and kissed her. This time it was not in anger or gratitude or despair. This time it was with the knowing that she loved him, even if she hadn't said those exact words. She said she wanted him. That was enough for now.

Alicia sighed against his mouth as he slipped his tongue between her lips. When her arms curved about his neck, his heart soared. He tightened his hold on her, crushing her body tight to his. Alicia returned his kiss. Following his lead, she slipped a tongue between his teeth. Heat continued to rush through him. His erection threatened to burst through his trousers.

When Richard slipped a hand down the curve of her back, he could feel the seductive channel of her spine beneath her shirt. She wore no corset. No barrier, save a thin bit of linen and laces between them. He reached lower to grab a handful of her skirts and ended up grasping a breeches-clad behind instead.

Richard pulled back panting. "These new garments of yours, I feel as if I'm kissing a man."

Alicia lifted his hand and moved it up and forward to cup her breast. "Is this better?"

He groaned against her mouth and kneaded the soft, round flesh to tease the hardened tip beneath the fabric. "Bloody hell. I want you so much, I can barely think."

She arched her back, sighed into his caress, and placed an encouraging press to his hand. "At least I'll be the first woman in trousers you've ever had in your bed." Alicia boldly straddled one of his legs.

"And I'll be the first man without trousers you've had in yours." Richard teased between heated kisses. "Just promise me you'll be in skirts when we wed."

Alicia pulled away. "Wed? When did we say anything about marriage?"

Having all the blood from his brain currently residing elsewhere, it took him a moment to recover from yet another shifting of the sands. "What are you saying? Of course, we'll be wed. That is generally how it's done. Two people fall in love, they want to lie together, share their lives, share a bed." He ground his hips to hers to accentuate his point. "They get married."

"And you've married every woman you've bedded?" Wide eyes blinked at him.

Wait. *What?* He shook his head to clear his thoughts. "Of course not, this is different."

Alicia raised her eyebrows. "How?"

Richard gave another quick shake of his head. How had they gone from caressing hands and heated kisses to this? He was incredulous that he needed to explain. "For one you're a virgin, and I'll not dishonor you, or your family." He slid a hand down over her hip. "Regardless of your current state of dress, you are a lady of good breeding and an innocent."

Alicia dropped her gaze, pushed away, stepping out of his embrace. "Does any of that truly matter?" She challenged. "My family is an entire ocean away. Breeding? You make me sound like some prize mare. What if I don't care about my so-called honor? What if I simply want to be with you?" She stepped closer and ran a hand over his chest. "Bed you?"

Richard stopped her hand. Was she trying to kill him? "Of course, it matters. Perhaps you don't care in the passion of the moment, but it does matter."

Alicia stared at their joined hands resting on his chest. "And would it still be so important that we were married if I told you I wasn't a virgin?"

Richard huffed in amusement. "Don't be ridiculous. Why even ask the question?"

She lifted her eyes and held his. "Because I'm not."

It took a moment for her words to make any sense in his brain. Richard started to accuse her of lying, but looking into the clear blue of her eyes, she was telling the truth. Air rushed from his lungs, and he took a step back and turned away from her. *When? Who?* Lurid images flitted across his mind's eye. *Stop. You don't want to know. It could only have been that sop.* Richard turned back to her. "Frederick? He took you before the wedding?"

Alicia gave a quick shake of her head. "No. Frederick would barely touch my gloved hand. We never even kissed. He knew, of course. I confessed everything to him before I accepted his proposal." Alicia gave a small laugh. "I expected anger, but the poor man appeared honestly relieved. I'll never forget the look of delight that crossed his face. Frederick almost seemed pleased by my admission. Something about loathing virgin blood and such. He actually shivered in disgust when he spoke of it. Said the whole act of intercourse was slightly abhorrent. Vulgar. All so uncivilized. I do believe had we gone through with our wedding, our marriage may never have been consummated."

"Maybe if he saw you in your breeches," Richard mumbled as he scrambled to search his memory. *Weatherington was hardly London. If not Frederick, who?* A horrifying thought crept in. Rage filled him. "Did someone *force* you? Tell me who. I'll kill the bast—"

"No." She held up her hands "No, nothing like that."

"Then how? Who?"

"I'd rather not say." Alicia turned her gaze from him. "I take full responsibility. I made a mistake. It's not something I'm proud of, but it was just one night, and what's done cannot be undone." She studied the toes of his boots before raising her eyes back to his. "So, you see, the question of my honor no longer exists."

A myriad of emotions skittered across her face before she turned her back to him. It had taken a lot for her to confess. The shame of it still rested heavy on her shoulders. Richard remembered something Alicia had said earlier. Her words flittered back through his mind. "This is what you meant when you said you were already ruined."

She faced him again but kept her gaze averted. "Yes."

"Is that why you've decided to flee England and embark on this life?"

"No. One has nothing to do with the other." Alicia frowned before notching her chin and meeting his eye. "I don't want any lies between us. You needed the truth."

"I don't know what to say."

"You don't have to say anything. I understand if this changes your feelings for me. Some men wouldn't be able to accept—"

Richard grasped both her arms to stop her from turning away. "No. Nothing's changed. I haven't lived the life of a saint either. The only difference is you already know about my indiscretions, or at least most of them." He tipped the corner of his mouth. Cupping her cheek, he traced the edge of her bottom lip with the pad of his thumb. "I love you, Alicia. If you can forgive my past, I can surely forgive yours. Nothing you could do would change how I feel for you. I still want you as my wife."

"Richard," she whispered. Dipping his head to kiss her again, he angled his mouth to capture hers. "I won't marry you."

He reared back as if he'd been slapped. "Why the hell not?"

"I *can't* marry you. Not now. It wouldn't be right to make vows to you I cannot pledge to keep." Alicia stroked his chest. "My father always said pirates couldn't afford to make promises. They have no guaranteed tomorrows. I cannot promise you anything beyond who I am right now. I want you. In every other way, save that. I offer myself to you freely. But all I can honestly give you is today."

Alicia took a step back and held out her arms, "If you want to be with me—believe in me, fight with me, lie with me? After all we've been through and knowing the truth about me. With no declaration of anything more? Here I am."

Richard took in the woman standing before him offering him everything and nothing at all. No future, no forever. Just her. Now. The ground beneath his feet shifted once again. Alicia wasn't like any woman he'd ever known. How had he missed seeing her all this time? Was it arrogance that had cast his own expectation on who she was? He was a blind fool not to have seen this extraordinary woman. It was so obvious to him now.

Alicia Steele was exactly who she claimed to be. She was a pirate. In every sense of the word. She was bold, brash, outrageous, impetuous, and bloody glorious. She wasn't offering him a future, she was offering him what he'd been trying to drown in brandy for more than a year. Something he realized he'd lost somewhere along the way. She was offering him a life. Whether he lived twenty more years, or twenty more hours. A life of daring, purpose, adventure. A life with her.

Richard picked up the Ship's Articles and scanned the parchment before holding it up in a fist, "Does it say anywhere on this document that I'm prohibited from making love to the captain for as long as we both shall live?"

Alicia pulled in a quick breath as the corners of her lips tipped into a suggestive smile. "Why, no, Mister Dunbar, it does not."

Richard picked up the quill, scribbled his name, and pulled her into his arms. He spoke low, emotion turned his voice to gravel, "I'm bloody well *with you*, now, Alicia Steele. Always." The last word came out as a whisper against her lips before he crushed his mouth to hers.

Chapter 21

The setting sun painted the sky in golden pinks and lavenders by the time Alicia and Richard returned hand in hand to the cove, Shrug and Liam had gone back to wherever Shrug and Liam returned to at the end of each day. The charred ends of the broken mast still smoldered in the sand.

Alicia boarded the *Ruby Mist*. The slow but steady progress on the ship continued to thrill her. The fruits of her first raid lay at her feet. Aye, she was dusty and sore, but Alicia was renewed. Everything she longed for was right here, within her reach. Including Richard. All the time and miles and heartache had not been in vain. Without the struggle she wouldn't be filled with such fierce emotion. If only she could steal time as easily as a coil of rope. She never wanted this feeling to stop. She never wanted this day to end.

Richard inspected each item and graced her with an incredulous smile. "Will I ever cease to be dumbstruck by you, Captain Steele?

Captain Steele… She trembled as his gaze took on a more heated quality. His kisses in the woods still tingled on her lips. He'd filled her with a longing she couldn't begin to understand. In her hand, she held the parchment that said he finally understood and accepted her decisions and was more than willing to join her in fulfilling her destiny.

"I still have to know how you came by all of these supplies." A measure of respect laced his words as he pulled her into his arms.

Alicia placed her hand on the broad span of his chest. "Perhaps I've inherited more of my father's bravado than I believed. It was one of the most terrifying and exhilarating things I've ever done."

But not the only. Standing before Richard earlier, confessing her truth and offering herself to him had been far more terrifying than stealing sail cloth in the middle of the night. He loved her, and even though she couldn't give him everything he wanted, he'd agreed to take all she was able to give. What a relief to push their tangled past and heated arguments behind them and be free to simply be together without all the expectations, without all the stifling constraints of proper society. She was heady with the scope of new-found independence. And yet, the idea of having him…all of him, in her life and in her bed, filled her with a fair share of trepidation. Like the midnight raid, she was feeling her way blindly through the dark. She knew the treasure she sought. The end goal was clear. But getting there?

A shiver skipped over her skin. In his arms, all she could think about was how to entice Richard into bed and finally know what loving a man was truly like. Not just any man…him. Alicia pulled a shaky breath at the erotic images setting her heart racing. Talk about necessary training. Her last attempt at seduction had ended with her bent over a garden bench with her skirts bunched to her shoulders. If it was anything like learning to shoot… *dammit.* It was fair to say this was where her boldness faltered.

Richard moved to kiss her, but Alicia pushed away. "I'll tell you the whole tale…later. I have a surprise for you." She turned and headed aft.

"More? I've had nothing but *fascinating* surprises all day." His voice held a low seductive tone.

Alicia glanced back over her shoulder to find his gaze a good deal lower than she expected. Heat rose in her as his appreciation made a slow move up her body. Turning, Alicia closed the distance between them and ran a fingertip down the center of his chest. "You shouldn't look at me that way."

"What way is that?"

"Like you want to have me for dinner."

Richard slipped an arm about her waist and pulled her tight. "Then you shouldn't wear clothing that leaves so little to the imagination." The words whispered against her lips as he dipped his head to kiss her.

"Perhaps it would help if you imagined what I'd look like without them?"

"God help me, I am." He kissed her then. All the tumble of emotions she'd felt over the last few days fell into the pastel glow of the sunset. He loved her and she loved him, even if she hadn't said the words yet. They were together. The past was where it belonged. The truth was told. Well, most of the truth. Alicia would tell Richard everything in time, but right now with his lips playing with hers, their breath dancing, the heat of their bodies building as they pressed against one another, she wanted to revel in it all. And more.

She broke the kiss and took his hand. "Come along."

"Where are you taking me?"

"To my quarters."

"The last I saw the captain's cabin, it was thick with mold and crawling with spiders."

Alicia tipped an eyebrow. "Are you afraid of a few spiders?"

Richard shook his head. "No, but *you* are."

She gave him a coy smile. "True, but Liam isn't."

Opening the door, Alicia was pleased by the catch of astonishment in Richard's breath. Being one of the few cabins above deck, much of the room had been spared the heavy water damage found below. "I set Liam to task to scrub down every inch with pine soap and kill anything that moved."

Three small, rectangular windows ran along the back bow of the ship and illuminated the room in the peached glow of the sky. Alicia opened them to ease the afternoon's stuffiness from the room and dispel her sudden rush of nerves. She moved to lift the flame on two affixed lanterns filling the shadowed corners.

"It's tiny." Reaching high, she could touch the low ceiling with her fingertips. "But how much room do I need? I imagine I'll be on deck much of the time. Most of our raids will be short. A few hours at best. I doubt I'll need a place to sleep, but." Alicia sat on the edge of a set-in bunk and leaned back against a new feather mattress, rolled and bound in twine which waited to be set into place. She fingered the edge of a new woolen blanket. "I'm now seeing some of the benefits of a private resting place."

Richard didn't move. Should she pat the space next to her? Crook her finger to beckon him to her bed? How exactly was this done? Alicia doubted there was a lesson for this. The heat and tension in the room continued to rise.

Unable to keep still, she moved to the small desk built into the side of the room. Richard hadn't said a word, hadn't moved an inch, but he also hadn't taken his eyes from her. Her breath began to race. She lifted a handful of scrolls. "I've maps and charts. In case we need to make a hasty escape up the coast. I've had a chance to study the coastline. There are a dozen caves and coves that we can tuck into if need be. I'm thinking we should have several chosen to lay anchor and wait out the Watch. If we switch places regularly, even if they search for the ship, we will never be where they expect us to be."

Richard's silence was starting to unnerve her. She was talking too much.

Alicia pulled open two drawers in the desk. They were empty thus far. "I wonder what to keep in here?" She straightened and ran damp hands down her thighs before placing her hands on her hips and scanning the bare room. There wasn't anything else to show him. Her rambling had only increased the beating of her heart. "I can't help wondering if my father's quarters looked anything like this."

Richard frowned. Damn she shouldn't have brought up the *Scarlet Night*. What was wrong with her? He shook his head. "No. His quarters looked nothing like this. Your father's cabin was twice as large. A large span of windows across the stern. And the biggest, most elaborately carved desk I've ever seen. And the bed." He took a step toward her. The flutters in her stomach turned from butterflies to sea gulls. "The bed was longer, wider. Built into an alcove of sorts. Built for a king."

The tightness of the quarters gave her little room to maneuver. The pounding in her chest gave her little room to feign disinterest. A whisper of an evening breeze brushed over her heated skin. "Maybe we shouldn't be talking about my father."

"Maybe we should be talking at all." Richard closed the remaining distance between them. "Although there is one thing, I am anxious to hear."

"Oh, yes, the supplies," Alicia gushed through another wave of nerves. "Two nights past, Liam, Shrug and I—"

"No, not that." He held her gaze and teased the lacings of her shirt. "Tell me you love me." The husky whisper of his voice hit her broadside.

"W-what?" Her throat tightened to a whisper.

"Say it." He moved to kiss her. "I need to hear the words." His mouth hovered over hers.

Alicia swallowed. "Is it that important to you?" She blinked. She felt pinned to the spot. Held motionless, helpless against his charms. Fearing if she moved even a fraction of an inch, the spell would be broken, the dream would end, and she'd awaken.

"At this very moment, there is nothing more important."

She forced a boldness she had no right to claim and ran her hand up his arm. "Wouldn't you rather I show you?"

The muscle in his jaw pulsed. "Aye." The word came in a rush of his breath. "Right after you say it."

It was a simple request. Three words. They screamed in her mind. *I love you. I love you. I love you!* But the distance between her mind, her heart and her lips tangled and fought with uncertainty. This was one lesson she'd already learned. The past was a strong teacher. "The last time I tried, things did not end well," she whispered before stepping back dousing the white-hot heat growing between them.

Richard released a breath in a rush. "Because I was a selfish idiot."

Alicia created more space between them by turning her back on him to stare out at the rising of the moon. She'd spent so much time denying her feelings, so much time soothing past hurts, accepting a future without him. She was finding it challenging to convince herself otherwise.

"I'm not that man anymore. I just signed away my life to you." Richard came to stand behind her. The warmth of his body heated her back.

Alicia closed her eyes and nodded. "True."

He rested his hands on her shoulders, kneading at the soreness of her muscles. "And I've pledged my heart and offered marriage." The low whisper of his voice washed over her.

"Also, true."

Richard gave her a slow turn to face him. "Do you trust me?"

"I do."

"You claim to want me." He watched her mouth.

"Oh, I do." Her body trembled with that want.

"Then, say it." He insisted.

When she tried to distract him with a kiss he pulled away.

"Duck—"

"No," he growled, "my real name."

"Who's in charge here?" She ran her fingers down his chest.

He caught her hand. "You are. But every man has his price. This is mine."

"Fine. Richard."

"Yes?" he cajoled.

Alicia blew out a frustrated breath and pulled her hand from his grasp. "I've brought you to my cabin to be with you. Isn't that enough?" She held her arms wide.

"No." He studied her. "Unless you're stalling."

"I don't know what you mean." Once more Alicia turned from him and tried to create some distance between them in the tight quarters. Blood rushed in her ears. Again, Richard closed the gap.

"You are. You're stalling. All this bravado is nothing but a show. You're nervous." He turned her back to face him and began to tease the lacings of her shirt again, slipping a finger beneath to stroke the valley between her breasts. "Because you know as soon as you say those three little words, I'll not be able to contain myself. I'll ravage your mouth, run my kisses down your neck." He traced a finger down the front of her throat and across the line of Alicia's shoulder. "Trailing them across here." Richard's touch slipped the opening neckline of her shirt wider to dip off her upper arm. "Then I'll strip these enticing clothes from you, strip you bare, lay you down, spread your—"

Pure heat flooded her sex. "Stop." She pushed his hand away.

"Stop?" Richard held his hands wide.

Alicia shoved at his chest, but he didn't move. "Damn you. Why do you always have to be so…so…"

"Irresistible?" he grinned.

"Infuriating." She glared before closing her eyes in surrender. "So, I'm nervous."

"But this isn't your first time?"

"It's the first time it's meant anything," she insisted. Alicia lifted her eyes to his. "It's the first time with you." There was no use fighting to protect her heart. It wasn't hers anymore. It belonged to him. In truth, it always had. "I've spent so much time wanting you and pushing away my feelings, but everything has changed between us now." Alicia pulled in a full breath. "I can't deny my heart still yearns for you." She swallowed her trepidation. "I love you, Richard. Even when I was sure I hated you, it was because I couldn't have you. I've always loved you. From the first time I saw you. I don't think I ever stopped."

Richard cupped her face in his hands as his mouth claimed hers. Alicia grabbed fistfuls of his linen shirt and held tight as the world spun out of control. They continued to hold one another captive as their kisses became more desperate, more heated.

Breath pounding, heart pumping, Richard steered her back toward her bunk, only breaking the connection with her long enough to pull a knife from his belt and slice through the twine holding the mattress together. He sheathed his blade and the two of them stood dazed, each struggling to breathe.

And then he reached for her belt. And she reached for his. Buckles were wrenched apart and cast aside in their haste. Laces untied. She pulled the tails of his shirt from his trousers. He tugged it off and then pushed her backward to land upon the bed and pulled first her left boot off, followed quickly by her right.

Alicia unbuttoned her breeches in a maddening rush before lifting her shirt over her head and tossing it among the growing pile of garments littering the floor.

Richard stopped. His gaze lowered to admire her breasts. She could almost feel his stare caressing them. Her nipples tightened. A quick flash of modesty had her covering herself, but Richard wasn't having any of it. He shook his head slowly and held out a hand to her. When she took it, he pulled her gently to her feet.

He was beautiful in the soft haze of light. A sprinkling of fair hair across his chest caught the lantern's glow and turned golden. He was leaner than she expected. The plane of his abdomen reminded her of the ribbed sand on the beach after the tide.

Brushing her braid back over her shoulder, Richard trailed a single fingertip along her collarbone and down the valley between her breasts to hook into the waistband of her breeches.

"You're beautiful."

"I was thinking the same thing about you." She smoothed her hand over his chest. The crisp hair tickled her palm.

His gaze never left hers as he gave her waistband a playful tug. "Take off these damnable trousers."

Alicia mimicked his action, yanking at the waist of his breeches in response. "You first."

And he did.

Having never seen Parker naked before he took her in the dark garden, she had nothing to compare, but Richard was far larger than the Greek statues she'd seen drawn in her mother's art books. Of course, those depicted in stone were obviously flaccid, and Richard standing before her in flesh and bone was so obviously not.

"Are you going to take them off, or shall I tear them off myself?"

Alicia fumbled with the twin row of buttons holding the front flap before pushing the waistband down. The fabric hugged the swell of her thighs and buttocks so tightly and the day had been close and warm. Unlike Richard's, it took a bit of time and maneuvering to shed them. At one point, she turned her back to shimmy them down over her legs only to hear a strangled moan from Richard behind her.

"Skirts are so much quicker," she teased over her shoulder.

Kicking them away, Alicia straightened, took a steading breath, and turned around. Richard's gaze swept her from top to toe and back. The only sound in the room was the rising cadence of their breathing and the pulsing of her heartbeat in her ears. Surely, he could hear her heart trying to beat its way from beneath her ribs.

Alicia teased the leathered tie on the end of her hair before removing it and unplaiting her unruly braid. Running her fingers along her scalp, she gave her hair a quick shake.

Richard groaned again. "God help me, Alicia. Are you trying to kill me?"

He looked pained. His eyes burned dark with desire. Lips parted, he dragged air into his lungs as if he'd been saved from drowning.

It was a powerful thing to realize how just the sight of her affected him. Had she ever felt so beautiful? And it was contagious.

The image of him standing before her, gloriously naked, the lantern light casting shadows over every muscled curve and plane, sent a mirrored rush of longing flooding her limbs and taking refuge as a pleasant aching pulse between her damp thighs.

Was this how it was supposed to be? This feeling of rampant desire? This was all new to her, and there were no charts to navigate this. In all but one way, she truly was a virgin, yet one errant encounter over a garden bench could hardly be called experience.

Alicia stepped over discarded boots and clothing to close the space between them. She was near enough to feel the heat of his skin bathing hers. Smell his scent of spice and sweat and male. Unable to meet the heat of his gaze, she watched the pulse of his heart in the dip at the base of his throat and longed to kiss him there.

Richard didn't move save the rapid rise and fall of his chest as his breathing raced. He didn't reach for her. What was he waiting for? Was there a proper way to begin? Was she supposed to touch him first? Her gaze flicked over the beautiful length of him. Where? Trail her fingers over his shoulders? Down his chest? Maybe she should take his hand and place it on her. Grasp his erection and simply tug him to the bed?

Locking her gaze with his, she knew only one thing to do. "I love you."

Chapter 22

Alicia stood before him more stunning than he ever imagined. Richard watched the words tumble from her lips. Their effect was like a jolt to his chest. "I—I love you, as well." Dammit, he stammered like a green buck. What was wrong with him? He wanted to pull her into his arms, but as he reached for her, he hesitated. As if touching her would shatter the illusion like glass. Was he trapped within a dream? She was close enough to smell the sweetness of her skin. See the flecks of gold in her eyes.

God, what was wrong with him? He was a confirmed rake. A rogue. He'd had dozens of women, why did the sight of this one make him feel like a fumbling novice?

Because it was her. Alicia. Because she was offering him everything he wanted. Everything he desired. Because he had allowed himself to believe he'd never have her and had purposely blocked this possibility from his mind.

But never from his heart.

And here she was. Naked. Glorious. Presenting herself to him, proclaiming her love for him, and all he had to do was reach out and take her.

"Are you unwell?"

"No. It's just that…"

Alicia bent and retrieved her shirt and covered herself. Pink flooded her face and chest. "I thought you wanted m—"

Richard grabbed for her wrist to stop her. "I do." He closed the space between them. "I do," he rasped again. "You're just... so... beautiful."

"You've seen beautiful women before."

"None were you." Richard released the shirt from her hands and returned it to the floor. "And none ever claimed to love me."

Sweeping his arms about Alicia's waist, he drew her to him. The sensual feeling of skin upon skin stirred his passion. His pulsing cock lay tight against her belly.

"I was afraid once you'd seen me, you'd changed your mind."

"Never." He stroked her back and urged her hips forward, pressing her even closer. His mouth found hers as a soft purr sounded from her throat. He ran his kisses down the side of her neck to nuzzle the apex of her shoulder.

Alicia swept her hands up his arms until she wrapped hers about his neck and slowly rocked her hips. "Mmmm. You feel so good. Warm. Hard."

He reached for the swell of her breast. "And you're so very soft," he breathed against her skin. When he brushed his thumb over the firm tip. Alicia gave a little gasp and arched into his touch.

"Oh…." She breathed and writhed with pleasure.

Richard moved them to the bed. It was cramped, bare, and smelled of pine soap, but he didn't care. The only thing that mattered was her. Laying Alicia on her back he maneuvered into the shadowed quarters and dipped his head to pull a tight nipple into his mouth. He swirled the tip with his tongue.

"Ah...."

He raised his head and hovered over her. "And so very sweet." His fingers continued to tease her. They held one another's gaze as Richard moved his hand over the bowed edge of her rib cage, sweeping over the soft swell of her belly until his fingers parted the soft curls between her thighs. Alicia's eyes widened. Her lips parted in a gasp, and when he began to trace tiny circles on the slick flesh of her sex, she let out a whimpered sigh and opened her legs wider.

Heat pumped through him. Even the slightest touch brought a delicious response from her, and they'd only just begun. *Dear, Lord...*

She raked her fingers into his hair and tugged his mouth to hers. "Oh, that feels so...mmmm..."

When she began to trace fiery paths across his chest and reached lower to brush the sensitive tip of his cock with her fingertips, he froze. "No. Not yet. I'll never last." He moved her hand away and pinned it to the mattress before returning to his teasing between her thighs.

"Not fair. I need to touch you," Alicia protested until he slipped two fingers into her. She was hot and wet, and Richard wanted nothing more than to move between her thighs and bury himself deep within her, but this wasn't about him. He wouldn't last. It had been too long since he laid with anyone, and he wasn't interested in a hasty, mindless rut. He wanted to love her. Bring her to climax until she cried out with pleasure. Dipping his head, he suckled at her breast as he continued to make her squirm beneath his touch and buck against his fingers. He quickened the pace and moved his attention to her other breast.

"Oh, God." She writhed against him. Alicia lost herself to her passion. She tugged at his hair and held him to her breast. The muscles of her sheath clenched about his fingers as she opened her legs even wider for him. She was magnificent. Each touch met with a heated reply. A sigh, or a moan, or an arching of her back, a roll of her hips, an upward press against his penetrating presses.

"Please…" She panted and tried to move him into position.

Richard raised above her and relished the beauty of her face in the throes of passion. His slick fingers withdrew to swirl over her swollen flesh, faster, and faster still until her climax was upon her. Then in one swift move, he settled between her quivering thighs and pushed into the tightness of her. She gasped as he drove himself as deep as he could.

Alicia's nails raked at his back and clutched at his buttocks as he withdrew and plunged into her again and again and again. Richard could feel the building of his own release. He cursed himself, wanting to make it last. Wanting to lose himself in her body and in this moment forever.

But when Alicia bucked beneath him, crying out his name, the walls of her vagina clutching at his cock, he lost the last thread of his control. He pumped into her again, stronger, thrusting his hips forward, driving into her deeper and harder until at last, his body poured his hot seed into her in pulsed release as his world ignited in a flash of color and spark.

Richard dropped his head to her shoulder, still joined with her, his body reverberated with the aftershocks of his release. His arms trembled with the effort of holding his body over hers.

"Dear God…" Alicia's hand released her grasp upon his hip and dropped to the mattress. "I just…I didn't know…"

Lifting his head, he met her gaze, kissed her before pulling out and collapsing into the tight space beside her. "What didn't you know?"

"That it…it could be like that," she sighed and closed her eyes. The warm musk of sex surrounded them. Sweat glistened on their skin. Her cum shimmered on his cock.

He wanted her to explain. He wanted to ask about the man who had taken her first. What it had been like. Had he pleasured her, as well? But as the questions burned in his brain, he didn't want to know. *Don't ask.*

"It isn't always so…explosive." He let his head fall back. "Or so bloody fast."

"I've had faster," she murmured.

Don't ask.

"This was…you were…" She rolled onto her side and ran a hand across his chest. "…perfect."

Richard stopped her hand with his own before lifting her fingers and kissing her palm. "You continue to surprise me."

"Good surprises?"

"For the most part." He smiled and curved toward her. The day had faded into night around them. The twin lanterns cast her in a soft golden light and got caught in the strands of her mussed hair. He tucked it behind her ear before tracing the line of her jaw. "You're so much more than I ever dreamed."

"More?"

"Yes. How you've set out on your own. Headstrong. Stubborn."

"Foolish?"

He gave a slight shake of his head. "Determined. Courageous." He ran a fingertip along the edge of her collarbone. "More passionate than I could have imagined."

"Too bold?"

"Not for me." He traced the curve of her breast.

Alicia held his gaze and smiled. "I'm glad. There's no turning back now, I'm afraid." She teased the flat of his nipple sending ribbons of pleasure to his reawakening cock.

"I wouldn't think of going back. Not now that I've had you."

She brushed the backs of her fingers down the front of him. "You could have me again."

"You are trying to kill me." Everywhere she touched seemed to stoke the fire beginning to build once more within him.

Alicia shook her head before kissing him. "Just tempting you."

"Shall I add seductress to your growing list of attributes?" He murmured against her lips.

"Yes." Curious fingertips skipped over the head of his penis causing it to jerk. "Will you let me touch you now?"

He was growing hard again. "Do I have a choice?"

"No." Her hand encircled him. "How can you be so firm and so soft at the same time?"

Richard let out the breath he'd been holding. "Tis the nature of a cock." He took her hand and showed her how he liked to be touched in long slow sweeps from tip to base and back again.

"I like yours."

With a firm grasp upon him she followed his instruction. She was making it difficult for him to think. "Umm...Thank you?"

Alicia continued to fondle him to distraction. "It seems bigger than most. Wouldn't you say?"

Richard groaned softly and rolled his hips in smooth opposition to her strokes. "Why are we talking about my cock?"

"Just another thing I'm learning about." She kept up her torture as she kissed the side of his neck. The tips of her breasts brushed his chest.

"But I'm not your first." Alicia swept a thumb across the cleaved tip. "Oh, *God...*"

She rested her head on his shoulder. "The first one I've seen in the flesh, as it were. First I've held. Caressed."

He pulled back enough to look down into her face. "What? How is that possible?" Richard gave a quick shake of his head and shut his eyes. "No. Pray don't tell me. I don't want to know."

"My only time before tonight was one blind fumble in the dark. It was fast, painful. Nothing like what we just shared."

Richard couldn't stop the vile images from his mind's imagination. He relaxed his position and pulled her back into his embrace. "Promise me you'll never tell me who it was."

Alicia laid a kiss upon his chest. "I promise."

He rested his chin on the top of her hair. "Because it would ruin me. Crush my heart. I'd be forced to hunt him down and kill him."

"I promise." Alicia rolled him onto his back and lifted her head to gaze at him. "I wished he had been you."

God, he loved her. "I wish that, as well." Richard cupped her cheek. "It's me now."

A smile graced her lips. "Thank goodness."

He kissed her then, pulling her closer. Pressing the fullness of her breasts against him. The strokes of her fingers making him think of little else other than ending this sweet torment. Richard ran a hand down her back to grasp at her hip. "Come here," he rasped against her mouth.

"What are we doing?"

"Time for another lesson."

"Oh? Will I end up like our last lesson with my ass in the dust?"

"Hell, no." He ran a reassuring hand over that ass before grabbing her thigh and pulling her knee across his body until she straddled him.

Chapter 23

Alicia pulled tight to the laces of her corset, before slipping the fullness of her skirts over her head. Trousers were so much easier, and she would happily give up corsets forever. Love-worn places of her body still hummed with a pleasant ache. Her nipples, teased pink and tender to the touch, complained as they were laced into their female prison. Running her fingers through the unruly tangle of her hair, she looked back over her shoulder toward the bed.

Richard lay splayed across her mattress, his face turned away from her. She took her time admiring the strong plane of his back, the tight curve of his behind, the length of his legs with their soft covering of pale hair hanging well past the edge of the bed.

They had made love once more after he'd shown her how to mount him like a wanton woman rides a horse. She'd loved being on top, and the sense of control it gave her. She'd loved, too, the expression on Richard's face as she lowered herself over the stiffness of his cock. The angle of such a position brought another new understanding. The pace was frantic, as if they couldn't get enough of one another. She'd lost herself in the fever of their passion.

But the last time…if she hadn't already been in love with Richard, she would have fallen for him in those tender, sultry moments. He made love to her. Every inch of her. Slowly. Tenderly.

With his fingers, his mouth, his body. Alicia never imagined she could experience such pleasures. No one had told her such a thing was possible.

And then, in the dove gray light of pre-dawn, he had held her in the encircled warmth of his arms in the lingering haze of sexual satisfaction and pledged his undying love to her. Opened his heart. Vowed to be hers and hers alone regardless of a marriage contract, regardless of any promises she couldn't make. As far as he was concerned, she was all he'd ever want for the remainder of his days. And whether she liked it or not, in his mind, this had been their wedding night and she was his bride.

A small smile tugged at her lips.

"You look like the cat who stole the King's cream." Richard's voice startled her out of her musings. He'd turned onto his side to watch her. His hand held his erection. Her sex pulsed in response.

"Was she a pirate too?"

"Aye. Stole the cream, his crown, and sharpened her claws on his scepter."

Alicia laughed. "All that from a single grin?"

"Aye." Richard stood and donned his breeches before crossing to her and giving a playful tug at her skirts. "I never thought I'd say this." His voice still thick and husky with sleep. "But I believe I prefer you in trousers."

"Why is that?" She swirled her fingertips through the crisp hair on his chest.

The muscle in his jaw pulsed as he gathered fistfuls of fabric at her hips and drew her closer. "In trousers, you are Captain Steele, pirate woman, extraordinaire. Sword swinging, pistol firing." He pulled her roughly into his arms and kissed her. "The most passionate of lovers, procurer of stolen goods, my heart included."

"And in skirts?" she asked between kisses.

Richard lessened his hold and traced a thumb across her lip and sighed. "In skirts, you are our Alicia. Daughter of Jaxon and Annalise. The woman I have cherished from afar. Stubborn. Infuriating. Another man's bride. My best friend's sister. Forbidden. Unattainable. Innocent."

"Boring." She pulled out of his grasp.

He gave a small laugh before tugging her back. "Nay, never that."

Alicia wrapped her arms about his neck and pressed into the warmth of him. "I may refuse to wear skirts again." She brushed a teasing kiss across his lips.

"How is it that you are the same woman?" he growled.

"Easy, it was never about the clothing. It was about the happiness of the woman in them."

He searched her face before capturing her gaze. "And you're happy now?"

"I am."

"With me?"

"Yes, with you." Alicia cradled his cheek feeling the prick of his morning's beard against her palm. She laid a gentle kiss upon his lips. "And without you."

Richard frowned. "You want me to leave?"

"No. Of course, not. Don't be daft." Alicia took a step back and held her arms wide. "Whether I'm in your arms or alone, in breeches or in skirts, or bare as the day I was born, I'm happy with who I am now. Standing in this cabin on this ship, I finally feel whole. I've found my purpose and a happiness in my own skin that doesn't depend on anyone else's expectations or limitations." At his frown, she stroked his arm and continued, "I love you, and last night with you, it was wonderful. More than perfect. But so was sneaking along the dark shoreline with Liam and Shrug and the pounding of my heart when we came upon the Watch. The danger, the risk, all of it." Remembering her first raid sent a shudder through her. She hugged herself.

"Wait? The Watch?" The horrified look upon Richard's face was priceless.

Alicia grabbed his shoulders. "It was exciting and invigorating. I've wasted too much of my life cocooned in an existence that never inspired me to be more." She moved closer and wound her arms about his neck and pressed her length along his. "I love that you see the woman I am now in trousers just as much as who I once was. I love that you're here, and I get to have this mad adventure with you. I love the way I feel in your arms, how our bodies fit together so seamlessly."

"Alicia…" Richard's voice rumbled low in his chest.

She ran her fingers into his hair and lowered her voice, brushing her words over his lips. "I love how it feels when I spread my legs and you push into me, how we're able to bring each other such pleasures." She kissed him then, their bodies pressed tight to each other just as she described. Alicia broke the kiss and held Richard's heated gaze. "Don't you see?" she whispered. "It's all destiny. Mine and yours. All is coming to pass. Our future is cast out before us ripe for the taking. It's all I've ever wanted."

Had it not been for the sound of boots hitting the deck boards beyond the door signaling the arrival of her "crew," she would have happily taken Richard back to bed, skirts and all.

"I'm afraid, duty calls, and they mustn't find you in just your breeches." She reluctantly left his embrace to allow him to finish getting dress. Crossing to the desk, Alicia opened a drawer, pulled out a small cache, and tossed Richard the leathered pouch. "I almost forgot. This is for you."

She caught him mid donning of his shirt. At the sound of coins hitting his palm, he looked at her with raised eyebrows and shrugged his shoulders into the garment. "Is this your way of making me feel like a whore?"

"No, foolish man, it's your share of the profits."

He peered into the pouch seemingly counting the contents before raising his eyebrows in a look of surprise. "Perhaps now would be a good time to tell me about those supplies." Richard tucked the tails of his shirt into his pants and slipped into his waistcoat. "And what the Watch had to do with it."

"I'll be happy to tell you on our way back to town."

A short time later with everyone in their proper attire, and Liam and Shrug set to task, Alicia and Richard headed down the road, leading his horse with the cart rumbling behind.

"So?" Richard prompted.

"Well, it's as you'd imagine, we stole the sail cloth from the same sail merchant you told me wouldn't sell to you. The new pump as well. The ropes and pulleys we found in a vaguely concealed storehouse Shrug stumbled upon along with some other choice items we couldn't use for the *Ruby Mist* but could sell. Jocelyn saw to that. It's part of our deal." Alicia tipped her head toward the back of the cart. "We can give her this load, as well, and hopefully recoup the money you've spent. She may even make you a few extra quid on the deal."

Richard frowned at her. "And what is that deal exactly?"

"I bring her certain items. She handles distribution."

"She's profiteering." It wasn't a question.

Alicia answered him anyway, "Yes."

"For an extra share."

"It's what she does, and I'm happy to help her. She allows me use of the *Ruby Mist*, and I give her an additional share of the profit."

"Help her with what?"

"That's a longer story."

"How about the part of the story that involves the Watch."

"Oh, that. We were almost bloody caught." Alicia smiled at the horrified look on his face. Teasing, she shrugged it off as if it were a trifle, but she would never forget what took place that night, or how scared she'd been when they'd seen the patrolling soldiers.

Their entire raid had almost been too easy. The unreasonable sail cloth merchant was lax in the security of his shop. Liam was as strong as an ox, and Shrug's expertise seemed to be in keeping them well hidden and an instinctive knowledge of back trails and unguarded stores. That was until they tarried too long congratulating each other on their luck and were in danger of losing the night's cover.

Heading back, they suddenly found their escape path blocked by several crisply uniformed members of the King's men. With the telling flash of red, Shrug began cursing under his breath. If they were caught with a cart full of stolen wares, the three of them would soon find themselves dancing at the end of a rope.

"If we could skirt 'em, I ken a back way." Their horse began to dance with agitation. Liam jumped out and soothed the beast to keep it quiet.

Alicia's heart pumped fit to bursting, and her mind raced in fear. *Skirt 'em, skirt 'em.* There didn't seem a way to do that, and it was only a matter of time before they were discovered.

"I have an idea." Alicia was quick to pull back the protective oil skin hiding their night's findings and wrestled two bolts of fine linen they'd found. "Shrug, give me your cloak."

"What are ye about?"

"You'll see. Give me your cloak and be quick about it." Taking a knife, she cut off a length of cloth and dropped it into the muck beneath the cart, grimacing at the ruination of such lovely fabric. She gathered another bit of fabric and rolled and tied it into a small bundle.

It took short work to put her plan into action. Alicia loosened her hair from its braid, dirtied it's ends and pulled the gritty hood of Shrug's cloak low over her face. "Give me two minutes to distract those fine gentlemen, then make your way past. Take the back trail.

I'll meet you at Laced Ladies.

Liam's eyebrows touched his cap, and Shrug snorted, "Yer a cunnin' one, there Capt'n."

"Only if it works. Remember. Two minutes."

"Aye. Be careful."

"Don't worry about me. If it goes awry, flee. Leave it all and hide yourselves in the woods. Understand?"

"Aye." Both men nodded.

With that, Alicia headed toward the four officers holding the wrapped bundle tight to her belly, under the makeshift skirt she'd fashioned from the soiled linen. Her heart pounded. Shrug's cloak smelled like someone had died within its folds. Died of some rotting disease after being wrapped in fish and dipped in manure. Twice she faltered and considered turning around and abandoning this folly, but she forced one foot in front of the other and forged ahead.

Closing in on the men of the Watch she raised an arm and called out. "Albert? I beg you, please. I must speak to you! I told them. I had to, I canna hide it anymore."

The four men turned to her in unison and raised their weapons. She chose the youngest of the group and rushed toward him. "I didn't want to tell them it was you, but father threatened to beat me again if I didn't confess."

Pushing aside the barrel of his rifle, she grasped at the man's sleeve.

The officer jumped back and wiped the dirt from his uniform. "Get off me woman. What goes on here?"

"I had to tell them you were the father, Albert. That we were in love. I told them everything. But Father is beside himself with anger. You must come with me now."

The man's lip curled with disgust. "I don't know what you're talkin' about."

"Albert?" She moved to touch him.

"I am not Albert, madam," he insisted.

"Don't be silly, of course you are." She looked at the others. "I certainly know the father of my own child." Alicia rubbed a telling hand over the swell. "My belly grows riper by the day. Your son will be a brawny lad." She grabbed his hand, "He kicks me now, ye canna feel it for yourself."

The officer ripped his hand from her grasp. "Stop spouting such foolishness. I'm not the father of your babe I don't even know you."

"Albert." Alicia feigned a gasp. "Stop it this minute. It has been a long, trying night. He's waiting for me to bring you to him. To discuss the marriage."

"What marriage?" The man's compatriots, having relaxed after the initial shock of her arrival, lowered their guns and began nudging one another and smirking at their friend's predicament. He looked to them in shocked disbelief. "I swear, I don't know this woman."

Alicia grabbed at his arm again. "Why would you say such a hateful thing? How can you be so cruel? You told me you loved me." She began to cry arid tears. "You said…you said you wanted to wed me. That you'd take care of us. The babe and me. Make a home for us."

"Unhand me." He jerked out of her hold.

She covered her face and pretended to wail.

"Y-you've obviously confused me with s-someone else," the young soldier stammered. "My name is not Albert. I did not lie with you. T-that." He pointed toward her stomach. "Is not my child."

Alicia wailed louder. "You promised. You said you loved me. What about our wee babe? Do ye want yer son to be born a bastard? You promised! You gave me your solemn word…as…as an officer and a gentleman."

"You're mad. I never said any such thing." He turned and emphatically plead his case to his comrades. "I've never laid eyes on this vile creature before, and I never wish to again."

"Oh, Albert!" Alicia bent and wracked her body in theatrical sobs. She clutched at the top of his boot.

He kicked her off. "Go back to wherever you've come. Be gone. Go home. Or I'll be forced to arrest you for harassing an Officer of the Crown."

"Oh, Albert." She dramatically sank in defeat to the ground.

Alicia shrugged as she relayed the story to Richard. "The four headed off in the opposite direction. I swore I heard one of them mocking the officer, calling him Albert, laughing at him. I sat in the road for a minute to make sure they wouldn't turn back and then I headed off to meet up with Liam and Shrug.

The look on Richard's face was incredulous. They walked in silence for several minutes.

"Nothing to say? No thoughts?"

"'Tis not often, I'm at a loss for words."

A familiar irritation flared. Alicia folded her arms across her chest and waited. "I suppose you're preparing to admonish me for being foolishly daring. For risking my life. What if I'd been found out? What would I have done then?" She shot him a pointed stare, daring him to begin his worn lecture.

"Nay." He frowned. "What I'm thinking is…" he paused to look at her, giving a small shake to his head. "You're astounding. In fact, you continue to amaze me more and more with each passing hour." He gave a smirk and turned his attention back to the road. "I almost pity that poor man. The bugger didn't know what to make of you. I can picture the entire scene in my head. I bet the other three were just thanking their luck it wasn't them." Richard threw back his head in laughter. "Bloody brilliant!"

Chapter 24

Jocelyn looked over the items in Richard's cart before brushing imaginary dust from her fingertips. Her gaze rested on each of them in turn. "I hear from the village there is a reward for information concerning the recent theft at the Ship's Loc. I do not recall the exact figure." She raised an eyebrow. "This is perfect, no? I shall return this to the shop owner—how will he recognize one bit of cloth from the next? I collect the reward, I will say someone, I did not know brought the goods to me to sell, and in good conscience, I knew they had been stolen from one of our own merchants. It will cast me in a fine light, no? And dispel the curious attention the authorities have started to have toward new ships in the area."

"The reward would then go back to Richard." Alicia moved to his side, and Richard placed his hand on the small of her back.

Jocelyn caught sight of Richard's touch and gave a cool smile in his direction. "After my cut of course, after all, it is I who am taking all the risk."

Richard narrowed his eyes at her. Jocelyn Robbins was no amateur. She was as cunning as they came. He didn't trust her as far as he could throw a cannon.

When he and Alicia entered the shop a short time ago, they had interrupted some sort of dealing between Robbins and her icy clerk, Raine. Without Alicia's notice, he witnessed a substantial stack of bills being passed between the two, which was now hastily and unceremoniously shoved deep into the older woman's cleavage. He would bet his last quid it had nothing to do with a profitable day selling bits of lace.

Raine skillfully deflected the moment by acknowledging their arrival. "There she is. And she's brought us a guest."

Jocelyn adjusted the set of her bodice and covered her concealment by fussing with the lace at her neckline before coming from behind the counter. "Should I inquire as to where you spent the night?"

Raine gave a short laugh. "No need to ask. Look at her."

Alicia ignored the woman's jibe. "I didn't mean to worry you. Jocelyn, I spent the night on the *Ruby Mist.*" At the mention of the *Mist,* Jocelyn's eyes shot to him. "I promise to be more forthcoming with my plans in future." Alicia continued smoothing her skirts. She gave Richard a warm smile. "Last night was unexpected."

"Did you make another raid?" Jocelyn shot a look in Richard's direction before returning her attention to Alicia.

"In a manner of speaking," Raine mumbled.

Alicia once more chose to ignore the crudeness of Raine's remarks. "There is a cart out back, but the goods were legally obtained. Just unneeded. We were hoping you could sell them."

Not long after, Richard left the cart and the lace shop to return to his rooms at the boarding house. A myriad of thoughts jostled for his attention. His body's satisfied fatigue brought the more pleasant of those foremost in his mind.

Alicia lying naked, glorious, and well sated in his arms, whispering words of love in the darkness.

Last night had been one he had dreamed of for months, but like all dreams, the reality had proved to be vastly different than anything he could have imagined. It exceeded his most wanton of musings. Tenfold. The passion he found in Alicia had been yet another revelation. Would he ever stop underestimating her?

Alicia may not have been a virgin in the truest sense, but she was in most every way, or so he surmised. She never told him any of the details, thank goodness, save the fact that it was rather fumbling. However blundering, it hadn't turned her away from wanting and believing there could be more. It was as if the taking of her innocence had been a necessary chore, and now done, she was free to explore and enjoy all the pleasures to be found between a woman and a man. Richard lifted more gratitude to the heavens that man had been him.

He saw a few signs of her inexperience, but she never hesitated. Not timid or shy, but when had those ever been words to describe her. Neither was she brazen or crude. Alicia was passionate. Fervent. Anxious to learn everything all at once, whether it was firing a pistol or finding pleasure. Her voracious desires drove her.

And she loved him. Hearing the words filled his heart to overflowing. Even if she hadn't agreed to be his wife, it hadn't tarnished the glow in the least. Her reasons were just and true, and he respected them, but in his mind, they were already wed. He whispered the truth of it in her ear as they both fell into an exhausted sleep. Last night had been their wedding night. A honeymoon without the pretense of a wedding. As long as he had her in his life, he could live with the absence of a formal ceremony. Alicia was his.

Whether surrounded by yards of white satin or glorious and naked within the circle of his arms, she was his bride.

And now there was a sheet of parchment and ink that said he was hers. First mate of the *Ruby Mist*. Quartermaster of a motley crew of two. A far contrast from when he'd served under her brother and managed five hundred and two. But it wasn't about the size of the ship or the crew. The sole reason he'd signed those Articles was to stay with her, by her side, to keep Alicia safe. Nothing else mattered.

Richard reached the boarding house at midmorning. Mistress Harper and her two daughters were busy in the kitchen well into their daily chores.

"Mister Dunbar, we were ready to notify te Watch of yer disappearance. Ye missed yer dinner last night, and breakfast agin this mornin.'"

"I'm sorry to have caused you worry, Mistress. I was conferring with an acquaintance about procuring a new, exciting position." Richard's mind flashed the sultry image of Alicia in a new, exciting position, on her knees, poised over him moments before she lowered her heat over the swollen head of... His cock thrummed at the memory.

One of the daughters was busy with a large bowl of apples. A pile of peelings grew before her. The juicy tang of the fruit made his mouth water. An image of Alicia as Eve in the garden, joined with the scent of the apples. "And were ye successful?" the daughter asked.

Richard shifted his stance at the sudden discomfort in his trousers. "Oh, aye. Very successful. I'm imagining many late nights of hard, physical work to come, but I am the man for the job."

The second daughter worked at rolling pale disks of pastry. "Are ye sure yer up to the task?"

Richard stood tall and tugged on his hems to conceal his growing erection. "Oh, aye," he coughed, "I am up to it, I assure you."

Mistress Harper wiped flour from her hands. "Ye must be ravenous. Ken we fix ye a plate?"

"No, thank you." He helped himself to a leftover heel of bread and an apple. "I should just like a few quiet hours to refresh myself, and then I'll be off again."

One of the daughters left her chore to push a few bits of cheese into his hands. She gave him a coy grin before moving close and brushing his arm with her bodice. She had lovely eyes, and there was no question as to her motive.

Her mother shoved her away from him. "Certainly, Mister Dunbar, we'll see to it you're not *disturbed*." She gave her daughter a scolding look.

"Thank you, Mistress." He held up the food. "Thank you, all."

Reaching the stairwell, Richard stopped just out of sight to readjust himself, and heard their conversation begin again.

"What's wrong with ye?"

"He's verra handsome, ken ya blame me?"

"Don't we have enough worries without ye pressing yer tits agin the man?"

"It's not yer tits 'es interested."

"How do you know?"

"Had the smell of whore 'bout 'im."

"Well perhaps he'd rather a whore closer te home."

"Hush the two of ya," Mistress Harper's voice snapped. "My head is splittin' with yer caterwaulin.' We've more important things te concern ourselves than warmin' that man's bed. Ye spoke te her, aye? What'd she say?"

"Mistress Robbins told me she knew just how te help us."

At the mention of Jocelyn's name, Richard halted his ascent and tipped his head to listen.

He heard Mistress Harper snort, "Thief doesn't take a piss without a price. How much is her *help* gonna cost?"

"More than we have, for certain, but she says she be wantin' somethin' other than coin from us."

"Ken we trust her?"

"Do we have another option?"

"I suppose not. "

"Shame her bonny son isn't still around. He was lovely."

"Is that all ye think about? Lifting yer skirts for a pretty face and a stinkin' cock?"

"Shut yer mouth, or I swear—"

"What? What will ye do?" A scuffle sounded.

"Girls! Enough. *You*, go lay the fire in te front room. *You*, tend to te bread."

Richard bolted up the remaining steps before he was caught eavesdropping. Once in his rooms, he set down his food. He'd lost his erection as well as his appetite. The muscle in his jaw tensed and a growing unease worked its way up his spine.

Seems Jocelyn Robbins was everyone's patron these days. So helpful. So bloody scheming. Always for a price. The woman would sell her own skin for a good wage. Plus a little extra on the side '*for her trouble.*' Alicia, Raine, now the Harpers? What the bugger was Robbins up to? And why? And how the hell could he get Alicia to see the woman was going to get her killed?

Richard dropped to the side of the bed. The ropes strung beneath the mattress moaned as they pulled taught against the wood. He pulled off his boots. Each movement made the bed creak and the headboard bump against the wall.

On his feet again, Richard began to pace. The wide boards beneath his feet squeaked with every step. One thing he could say about Widow Harper's house, it kept no secrets. Beds creaked. Voices carried. Movements announced. Comings and goings were known by all.

He stopped to brace his hands on the windowsill. His view looked back toward the center of Black Point. There had to be someone in this town that, like this house, knew of Robbins' activities. Fortunately, his father's name still carried a fair amount of power—*the bastard.* Perhaps he could use that to his advantage. Seek out some more influential company. Ask a few casual questions. Keep his ears and his eyes open.

He'd not dissuade Alicia, either way, of course. She was

working too hard forging ahead with her plans, but at least with solid proof she'd know the full extent of Jocelyn's web. See the truth. Lord knows, he'd spend far too much of the last year being blind— blind drunk. So unseeing, he'd come far too close to never noticing the truth about Alicia and the incredible woman she had been all along. All those wasted nights numbing his mind against what his heart clearly knew.

Richard ended his pacing at the bed and once more sat. He rubbed at his chest after pulling his shirt over his head. No more. His eyes were open. His mind clear, and for once in full council with his heart. He loved Alicia with every corner of his being.

Chapter 25

Alicia slid deeper in the large copper tub Jocelyn had moved before the stove. Curled fingers of steam rose from the water. Soaking her well-loved body made her languid and pleasantly weary. She closed her eyes and drifted back to relive every moment of last night. Each touch. Each new glorious sensation. Richard had been amazing. Guiding her when she needed guiding. Helping her discover what most pleased her and showing her how to please him in return.

In the fragrant water of her bath, her fingers slid through the soft curls at her apex and along the petals of her sex as she recalled his fingers tracing there. She raised one knee and slipped a touch between the folds. The slick flesh, still sensitive from their night of sensual discoveries, sent a delicious flush though her limbs. Alicia caressed herself with gentle sweeps as she recalled the feel of his mouth upon her, spreading her legs, sucking gently until she felt as if she'd burst into a million stars. And then, having him drive into her with one powerful thrust. His cock filling her. Over and over...

Even Richard's goodbye had left her breathless. Before heading back to his room at the widow Harper's, he led her into the shadows on the far side of the wagon, out of sight of Jocelyn and Raine, and kissed her. Deeply. Soundly. And without another word, left her trembling with want.

Her body ached for him again. She needed more. Alicia slid a slippery hand across her abdomen and up to cup her swollen breast. A soft moan hummed from her throat as she kneaded the silky flesh.

An abrupt thought stilled her hand. Opening her eyes, she sat up straight. Water sloshed over the lip of the tub as Alicia searched her memory. Since he arrived in Black Point, Alicia had noted a difference in Richard that she couldn't lay a finger on, but it suddenly dawned on her.

She hadn't seen him with a bottle in his hand, or smelled brandy upon his breath, or seen any evidence of his drinking whatsoever. Not since that day he found her in the garden waging a losing battle with her unrelenting wedding gown. Stepping from the tub, water sluiced down Alicia's body. The chilled air peaked her nipples.

Richard was sober. He had been for a while if his healthy good looks were any indication. His eyes were bright, the dark circles beneath were gone. His color was more robust, and he didn't reek of alcohol. He wasn't sleeping until noon. It was surprising she'd hadn't noticed before.

Alicia wrapped herself in a drying robe and pulled a comb through her tangled hair. Perhaps she hadn't been paying attention, or perhaps he was getting better at hiding his addiction. No. She raked the teeth of her comb over her scalp. He had reformed.

The realization made her smile. Yet, curiosity nibbled at her. What had changed? Back in Weatherington, he was determined to drown his life away. What had caused his dramatic turn? Whatever the reason, Richard was once again the man she fell in love with all those years ago. Was it any wonder that she found herself in love with him once more?

Raine startled her out of her musings. She was so quiet when she moved about, Alicia hadn't heard her come into the room. "Here." Raine thrust a small bag into her hands.

"What's this?"

"Herbs. For tea."

Alicia opened the cloth bag and lifted it to her nose. The acrid smell made her retch and hand it back. "No, thank you."

Raine pushed it back. "You'll thank me when you find yourself with child."

"With child?"

"You and him. He's putting his cock in you. Cocks bring babes. Tea brings your flux, so no babies grow. Two small pinches, no more. More brings sickness and death."

Alicia opened the bag and sniffed again. "What the hell is in here?"

"This and that. Drink one cup. Tastes like the shite only bitter." Raine tapped Alicia's wrist. "Two small pinches. Remember."

Alicia nodded. "I'll remember." In all the reckless passion of last night, the possibility that she and Richard had created a child hadn't occurred to her. Certainly, if they continued to lay with each other, a pregnancy was sure to occur. She should talk to him about precautions. Wasn't there something that sheathed men's cocks? French? Perhaps she should ask Jocelyn. Alicia sniffed the tea again.

A child was indeed a blessing, but not for her. Not now. If she couldn't make a promise of a future to its father, she certainly couldn't bring an innocent babe into the same uncertainty. Alicia always felt a bit odd not joining her peers in their maternal desires. She slid her hand over her belly and frowned. Her own mother had always said her children were her heart and her life. But did that make Alicia wrong for wanting something different?

And what about Richard? Maybe he wanted an heir. Being an only son, wasn't he bound to carry on his family's name? Perhaps he dreamed of a dozen towheaded children racing through the halls of his estate? As anxious as she was to share her bed with him again, and soon, she couldn't lead him into any misconceptions. Alicia smirked, *pun unintended.*

"You're not dressed. We are due for tea in an hour." Jocelyn smoothed the back of her hair as it swept up into a dark nest of curls.

Alicia stood. "I'll be ready."

Jocelyn stopped at the door, her hand on the knob. She paused before looking back at Alicia. "I hope you know what you are doing."

"Dressing? I think I can manage it." Alicia gathered up her combs along with the sack of tea.

Jocelyn spun on her. "Do not be flippant. I am talking about tossing all caution into the air and lying with that man."

Alicia headed toward her room. "I appreciate the concern, but I'm a grown wom—"

"Barely," Jocelyn snapped as she followed.

"*A grown woman,*" Alicia continued prickling at the insinuation before spinning back to face Jocelyn, "who knows my own heart and mind." She held up a hand to stop Jocelyn's inevitable objection. It was exhausting having to constantly defend herself and her decisions. She was done with explanations. "Don't worry, I've not shared any confidences with him."

Jocelyn flipped a hand at her. "Just your body, then?"

Alicia dropped the items she carried and stripped out of her drying robe showing said body. Modesty be damned. "Yes." She held her arms wide before grabbing at her shift and slipping it over her head.

Jocelyn failed to be shocked at Alicia's brazen display and continued to nag. "It is a dangerous game. Business and pleasure in the same arrangement. I am worried he is deceiving you. He could get you killed."

"Amusing. He says the same thing about you." Alicia sat on the edge of the bed to don her stockings.

"*Ridicule!*" Jocelyn huffed and tossed up a hand.

"You're both being ridiculous." Alicia slipped into her corsets. "You, two, behave as if I'm being led around like some daft farmyard beast." She yanked at the lacings.

Jocelyn moved to help her, pushing her hands out of the way. "A handsome man has ways of seducing you into all sorts of things, can he not?" She gave a vicious pull before tying the boned prison of Alicia's breasts tight as she pinned her with a stare.

Alicia returned a stare of her own. "Richard hasn't seduced me." Moving to the bed she grabbed her skirts by the waist and gave them a sharp shake to ease some of the wrinkles.

"Do not try to fool me. I watch the way he touches you." Jocelyn pointed to the back window. "How you gaze at each other. You stayed away last night. There is a sparkle to the eye. A bright blush to the cheek. Lips full." Jocelyn waved her finger toward Alicia's face. "I know what has happened between you." Jocelyn tapped the side of her nose and narrowed her eyes. "I know. You cannot hide it from me."

"I'm hiding nothing." Alicia continued dressing. "Richard didn't seduce me. I was the seductress. I wanted him in my bed, and *I* took him there." She finished hooking her bodice and pushed past a gapping Jocelyn to retrieve her combs once more. "You'll call me a whore now, I suppose?"

Jocelyn grabbed her arm to stop her. "Do you love him?"

"Yes." There was no hesitation in Alicia's reply.

"And he loves you?"

"Yes." Alicia pulled out of her grasp and moved to the vanity to arrange her hair. "He's asked me to marry him."

Jocelyn blew out a huge sigh of relief and threw her hands wide. "*Magnifique!* We will celebrate."

"There's nothing to celebrate." Alicia shoved pins into her hair. "I said, no."

In the mirror's reflection, she saw Jocelyn's jaw go slack once more. "You are the most exasperating child. Why would you do such a thing? You love him. He loves you. Do you imagine proposals of marriage fall from the sky like rain? First Frederick, now him?"

Alicia spun in her chair. Her impatience reached its peak. "I'm not going to try to explain it to you," she snapped. "I cannot be a pirate *and* a wife, and right now, I'd think you'd be happy that I chose the one that best benefits *you*."

Some of the bluster faded from Jocelyn. She gave a small sigh, "Not at the sake of your happiness, *Cheri*."

"I am happy. Blissful. I have everything I've ever wanted. I have purpose. Passion. Love. It is more than most can ever claim. And I've only just begun. You mustn't worry so much. Least not about me." Alicia stood and began urging Jocelyn out of her room. "Now, if you don't let me finish getting ready, we're sure to be late, and Mistress Wilson is not a patient sort."

"No, she is not." As she walked past, Jocelyn reached out to lift the bag Alicia set next to the washbowl. "What is this?"

Alicia stopped fussing at her hair to look. "Special tea. A gift from Raine."

"Raine gave you a gift?" Surprise raised Jocelyn's eyebrows. "Raine never gives gifts."

Alicia smoothed the front of her skirts. "She's afraid I'll ruin yet another of her gowns by having to let out the seams to accommodate a swelling belly." She puffed the material and gestured a hand over the rounded shape.

Jocelyn's eyebrows pushed higher. "Ah...*la grossesse*."

Alicia straightened her gown. Moving back to the mirror, she pinched at her cheeks. "For the same reason I cannot make vows to be a wife, I cannot be a mother. I'm not saying I never want a child." Alicia shook her head. "Just not now."

Silence greeted her. In the mirror, Alicia watched a sadness pass over Jocelyn's face before she set the tea back upon the washstand. She brushed a hand over her own abdomen. "There is no greater love than looking into your child's eyes for the first time. It never leaves your memory. Like holding a miracle in your arms. You have met them before the rest of the world meets them. Fallen in love with them as soon as you feel them begin to move within you." Jocelyn gave a quick shake of her head as she straightened. "And yet, there is no bigger heartache when they leave you, which of course, they must. It is a life you create only to give away." Unshed tears wet her eyes. "Perhaps you are indeed the wise one, no? Without a child, you will never have to experience the anguish of losing one."

Alicia moved to lay a hand on Jocelyn's sleeve. "All this talk of children, I'm so sorry." She pulled Jocelyn into her arms. "We'll find Ric, and you'll be reunited with your Beau. I promise."

"You will not promise yourself to your man, or a child, but this promise you can make?"

"Aye. I made this one before all the rest. I'll keep my word to you. Or I'll die trying."

Chapter 26

The following morning, Alicia poured over the maps before her. Liam and Shrug were already working. The soft rapping of chinking repairs thudded beyond her quarters on the starboard side of the *Ruby Mist*. At this rate, they wouldn't hit open water for months. Releasing the parchment, the map sprang back into its tight roll. Alicia blew out a frustrated breath as she moved to the windows lining the stern and looked toward the open mouth of the cove. She was beginning to share Mistress Wilson's impatience.

A knock at the door jarred her from her thoughts. "Come."

"Good morning, Captain." Richard ducked to come through the low bulkhead.

"Richard."

"I see the crew is hard at it."

The sight of him polished and pressed caused the breath to catch in her throat. He still reminded her of a bright day. And now he brought the reminder of a fiery night, as well. Was it too early in the day to tempt him back into bed? Impatience, it seemed, came at her from all sides.

"How much longer before we can set sail?"

"We'd have to have sails to set before that," he joked. When she refused to see the levity, he sobered. "Well, installing the new mast will take a few days, at least, re-rigging, setting the new cloth. That's after the chinking is complete. Careening. Then there's the tarring, painting. Six to eight weeks should do."

"That's much too long. We need more hands. Sign on more crew. Three or four more men. Maybe five." Alicia planted her hands on her hips. "Whatever it takes to be ready to sail in nine days."

Richard gave a snort of amusement. "Nine days? What's the rush?"

"We're missing out on some profitable goods moving up the coast. Shipping has increased by twelve percent in the last six weeks alone. It's all slipping through our fingers."

"How do you know about shipping figures?"

"The same way I know there's to be a ship loaded to the gunnels with very lucrative plunder sailing right past the inlet to this cove in nine days."

There was a certain advantage to her position at Mistress Wilson's tea parties. Near invisibility. The other woman had disregarded her almost from the beginning. And because *Governor* Wilson preferred to chat with his contemporaries outside of Jocelyn's hearing, Alicia's covert positioning and keen listening skills had paid off.

Yesterday's tea had been most informative. Governor Wilson's mood shifted rapidly and in distinct opposition to that of his wife's.

He'd bragged about the increase in shipping at the same time Gladys bemoaned losing a beautiful Dutch writing desk to a storm offshore. But when she beamed about the arrival of new silks, silver, and china, all due to arrive in time for her dressmaker to create the latest fashions for their adopted, much anticipated "social season," the governor's disposition had soured like old wine before he muttered as he passed Alicia's notice, *"Not if I stop it first."*

"I want that ship." Alicia slapped a hand on the table. A rush of adrenaline raised heat to her cheeks. The sharp blow pricked at her palm.

She'd often wondered what spurred some people to action. This was it. The thrill was intoxicating. She turned to face Richard. Her entire being flooded with a heady mix of anticipation, impatience, and a certain lust—for life, for adventure. For him.

Alicia blew out another breath and eased the sting of her hand against the crisp white of his shirtfront before teasing the ties of his stock. "I want it, and I want you as well," she whispered, slipping her arm about his neck. "Must you be so terribly handsome? You need to kiss me."

A coy smile teased his lips as Richard ran a smoothing hand over the roundness of her behind. "Aye, aye, Capt'n." He pulled her roughly against him. "I never defy a direct order."

"That wasn't an order." She brushed her lips past his. "Just a yearning. A heated desire." Another sweep of her lips had his parting and his breath quickening. "I can't seem to get enough of you."

"I've thought of little else since I left you yesterday. Every time I close my eyes, I see you, can hear your soft moans. Feel you move beneath me." His words brushed over her lips as he urged her closer. "I swear I still can taste you on my tongue." Reaching behind her, Richard cleared the table with a wide swipe of his arm. Rolls of maps and notes scattered to the floor as he lifted her to sit upon its edge. Alicia gasped as he spread her knees apart and stood between her thighs. He wrapped her tight in his arms.

"Was it just yesterday?" Alicia teased, "It feels longer."

"Longer and harder," he growled against her mouth and ground his hips against her heat.

When Alicia laughed, he took advantage and laid hot kisses against the sensitive side of her neck. He kneaded her breast as he nipped at the line of her collar bone.

"Richard…" Insistent fingers worked at her lacings. "We shouldn't."

"I heartily disagree." He slipped the top of her blouse off her shoulder and slid a warm hand inside to palm the tightened tip of her nipple.

"There are things we need to discuss." Heat spread through her limbs as he lowered his head to take the sensitive peak into his mouth. "W-we can't fall into bed at every chance."

"We're a good two feet from the bed." Her belt hit the floor.

Alicia caught his hand as he worked the buttons on her trousers out of their holes. "I'm serious."

"Oh, so am I." He moved her hand to cup the hard length of him straining against his own buttons. "We can talk later." Impatient fingers pushed into the front of her pants to tease the slickness he found there.

Alicia gasped. His touch brought another rush of wetness. She was having trouble forming thoughts, let alone words. "You m-may change your mind later."

"I'm trying my best to change yours now." He moaned against her lips. "My God, you are so bloody wet." He pushed two fingers into her.

Conversation stopped as Richard's mouth captured hers in a searing kiss and his swirling, probing touches drove her to orgasm.

Panting with her release, Alicia freed the hard length of him from the confines of his trousers at the same time he raised each of her legs in turn to rid her of her boots and the final barrier of clothing between them. He tossed her breeches, inside out, to the floor before laying her back across the cool hard surface of the table and spreading her legs once more.

When Richard dropped to his knees, Alicia cried out at the ecstasy of his mouth upon her sex. She clutched at his hair, pulling it out of the neat queue as he pitched her to yet another climax. Then he rose and continued to take command. He entered her in a single fiery thrust that made her gasp with the sweet welcoming pain of his cock filling her. Richard ground out her name as he set a vicious, reveling pace she had no hope of matching. Alicia surrendered to it all until he unleashed the tense coil of his body into hers in deep glorious thrusts.

What clothes failed to make it to the floor, clung to heated skin. Still joined, their breathing labored to return to normal. Alicia dropped the hand that clenched at Richard's hip and untangled one trembling leg from about his waist.

"Bloody hell," she gasped, pulling air into her lungs.

Richard's damp forehead rested on hers. He couldn't yet speak. His hands continue to grip to the edge of the desk. His heart matched the pounding of her own.

Slipping from her, he rose, cupped her cheek, brushed her lips with a feathered sweep of his thumb. "I-I'm sorry. I lost my head. Did I hurt you?"

"No." She gave him a small reassuring smile. "You didn't hurt me." Alicia slid from beneath him and off the table. Gathering her clothing along the way, she opened a back window to cool the overheated room. Dark sodden clouds were building off to the west. A shift in the wind lifted her hair.

Worry nibbled at the back of her mind as she dressed. Her body continued to thrum with the aftershocks of her release. It was all she could do to not turn back for more. She and Richard were insatiable. The two of them couldn't be within an arm's length of each other without clothing scattering like leaves in the wind. At this rate she'd be carrying his child before the next full moon. Alicia gripped the windowsill.

"I did hurt you." Richard came up behind her and slipped his arms about her. Concern laced his words. "I'm such a b—"

"No, you didn't. I swear." She turned in his arms and gave him a reassuring kiss.

"One moment we were discussing ships, and shipments in nine days, and the next, I—"

Alicia gave a small shake of her head. "We."

"I've never been with a woman who I've wanted more than I want you. You've completely bewitched me." He ran his hand over her hair. His gaze sweeping her face as if it were the first time he truly saw her.

She met his gaze and held it. "And being with you is more amazing than I ever imagined."

A frown creased his brow. "But?"

Alicia stepped out of his embrace and smoothed a hand over her forehead. "But we need to remember what we're doing here and why. We can't lose sight of our goals. Not when we're so close."

Richard gave her a sultry smile. "So, we steal an hour to indulge in another passion along the way. We love one another. We bring each other so much pleasure. There's no harm in that." He reached for her again.

"There is if I end up carrying your child."

Richard jerked as if he'd been slapped. "Oh, of course. I hadn't considered that possibility."

"My future doesn't have a place for an innocent child, Richard." Alicia braced her hands on her hips. "There are ways to prevent such things, but it would be wrong to mislead you." She swept a hand to indicate the desk. "If we continue at this pace, letting our lust run away with us, without an understanding or a single thought to the consequences, it wouldn't be fair to you. I do love you. I've already disappointed you once by refusing your proposal of marriage. But to reject your child as well? That may be more than you're willing to concede. You're an only son with responsibilities to your family to carry on the Dunbar name. You'll need an heir sooner or later, won't you?"

"Are you saying you never want children?"

"No. Maybe?" Alicia lifted a shoulder. "I don't know. Certainly, not now." She stooped and gathered the rolls of parchment from the floor and held the ship's articles aloft. "You signed away your life to me in the heat of the moment. It's only right I give you the chance to reconsider. You're free to X out your name."

Her next words tripped in her throat. "It's not too late. You can leave. Go back to England and live the life you planned. Find a proper wife to fill your estate with a dozen blond babes. No harm will be done. Your hands are clean. You can still walk away an innocent man. After tonight, you won't be able to say that. I'm planning another raid."

Richard's gaze held hers. "Do you want me to leave?"

"No, I don't, but then I'm selfish and bull-headed."

He plucked the Articles from Alicia's hand and retrieved an inkpot and quill from the drawer. Richard took a moment to pull his hair back into the neat queue before he unrolled the parchment and added a flourish under his name. He held it up to show her before blowing the ink dry and setting the Articles aside.

"So where is this raid you're planning?" He opened a map of the coastline. "Will it just be the four of us, then? I think I can secure the additional men you're after at the Black Sheep. I saw a few brawny types that look the part. I'll wait until they're fully in their cups to make the offer, however." Richard looked back at her with raised eyebrows.

He hadn't missed a beat. He was behaving as if they'd been talking about what fine weather they'd been having. Thunder rumbled off in the distance. "Richard…"

Closing the space between them, he grasped her arms and captured her once again with his beautiful eyes. "I heard all that you said. I'm not going anywhere. I don't care about a child that may or may not ever exist. I certainly don't care about any obligations to my family. I'm sure by now Father has disowned me, anyway," he quipped, then cupped her cheek. "I care about you. I love *you*. You are my future. Whatever that brings. I realize I've given you more than just cause to doubt my word and my intentions in the past, but these last few days have left me a changed man. I am totally and completely in love with you, Alicia Steele. I would walk into fire for you."

"And sheath your cock?" She raised an eyebrow.

"I'll sheath anything you wish."

Chapter 27

The small raiding party huddled in the shadows. The storehouse due to hold tonight's plunder stood cavernously empty.

Shrug wiped his nose with the back of his hand. "I thought ye said te goods be 'ere?"

Alicia's brow knitted in concern. "I believed they were. Perhaps I got the day wrong? No, my information is true, I'm sure of it. It's supposed to be here."

A million questions swirled in Richard's mind. Like whom was providing this "true" information. The damp night closed in around them. "Could we be too late?"

"Just the opposite, I fear. The transfer hasn't been made." Alicia waved a hand low toward the building. "Look at the ground. No mire by the doors. The rainstorm that blew through like a gale this afternoon must have held things up."

"Either way, it ain't here." Shrug complained. "No sense standin' about holdin' our dicks." He slapped Liam's shoulder. "We'r outta 'ere."

"No wait." Alicia grabbed at his sleeve. "I'm not giving up."

Richard narrowed his gaze. "So, what do you propose?"

"We ken come back. When tey move the goods." Liam nodded.

Alicia gave a quick shake of her head. "Or."

Richard braced himself. The look on Alicia's face was not a look he was fond of. Determination set her jaw and notched her chin. No, that was not a look that ever brought him comfort or pleasure. He was almost afraid to ask, "Or what?"

"Or we help out the good hands of the *Gull Wing* and take it straight from the ship ourselves."

"Past te guards? Like we be comin' fer tea?" Shrug threw a hand toward their transportation. "How you want te handle our arses danglin' in te breeze wit this 'ere cart sittin' on the dock."

"There are other carts about," Alicia countered.

"Not at this time a night, and none wit a horse still attached."

"Be easier with te *Ruby*," suggested Liam

"Not wit no mast, ye dumb clod." Shrug gave Liam a shove.

"Quiet," hissed Alicia, "Let me think." She gave a look about while she worried her lip. Richard was all for calling it a night. The air was turning damp and raw. Fingers of fog crept across the water of the harbor. Visions of warmer, more pleasurable pursuits filled Richard's mind.

He and Alicia could go back to the ship, snuggle up together, have a late supper. He could start getting used to wearing a silk stocking on his cock.

"We'd need a distraction," she continued. "Something to hold the attention of those guards away from the ship."

A finger of that frigid fog slithered down Richard's spine. He didn't like it. He hadn't even heard it yet, but he would bet he wasn't going to like it. "What do you have in mind?"

Alicia turned to Liam and Shrug. "You, two, know what we're after, right?"

Shrug crossed his arms over his chest. "How'd we even ken 'tis on that there ship?"

"If that's the *Gull Wing*, it's there. They won't be expecting an attack, not at dock." She pointed a finger at the other men's faces. "Bow trunks, and crates. As many has you can haul in ten minutes. That's it. Forget the barrels. We're not after supplies this time. No rope, no canvas, no equipment. Trunks and crates. Got that?" When they nodded, she patted Shrug's shoulder in satisfaction. Lifting her baldric over her head she placed it at her feet.

Richard's brows knit. "What are you and I going to be doing while they're snatching trunks and crates?"

Alicia untied the sheath holding her knife. "I'm going for a swim."

I knew I wouldn't like it. "You don't know how to swim."

"Exactly." Alicia flashed him a smile, dropped to the ground and started to pull off her boots. "That's where you'll come in handy."

"Wait, so you're planning on drowning?" He swept his arms out from his sides.

"No, I'm planning on being saved by the guards of the *Gull Wing*." She stripped off her stockings.

"And if you're *not*?"

Back on her feet, she patted his chest. "Then *you'll* be the one doing the saving." She added her boarding sword to the growing pile.

Richard's unease reached a new level. "I don't like this plan." He laid a hand on her arm to stop her.

Alicia gave him an impatient look. "Do you have a better one?"

"I'll go for the swim," he offered.

She jerked her head in the direction of the *Gull Wing*. "Those guards aren't going to risk a plunge for a man. They'd just throw you a rope. They'll jump in for a woman."

"You're sure about that?"

"Aye." She nodded before turning back to Liam and Shrug. "Wait until you hear me hit the water, then move. In and out. Quick as you can, then you're off."

Richard grabbed at her wrist. "Alicia."

"I'll be fine."

His brain scrambled for something—anything to get her to reconsider this foolish plan she was hatching. "And when they pull you out of the water and find you in breeches. How are you going to explain that?"

Alicia gave him a sly smile. "I won't be in breeches." She unbuckled the thick belt about her waist and handed it to Liam. "Bundle all our things and stow them out of sight fifty feet north of that grove of trees."

"Hold on. You're not—" *She was.* Richard choked as she slipped out of her pants. The hems of her shirt barely reached to her knees. She was practically naked, and he had an instant image of what was going to happen when the white linen of her shirt got wet.

"That th're be one hell o'a distraction," snorted Shrug. Liam's eyes went round, and his jaw went slack. He practically drooled.

"See?" Alicia jerked her head in their direction.

"Yes, I see, and then the whole bloody fleet ken see, Alicia." He shook his head. "I can't let you—"

"I'm the captain. You're not *letting* me do anything. Discussion is over." She turned to Liam and Shrug. "You clear with what you're to do? Soon as I hit the water." Alicia bundled her breeches with the rest and pushed it all at Liam.

"Aye, aye." Both men nodded.

"We'll meet back at the *Mist*. Good luck. Don't take any foolish chances."

Worry gripped Richard's gut. "Right, the only one taking foolish chances here is you," he hissed.

Alicia flashed him a grin. "And possibly you. Add your things to mine and follow me.

A few minutes later, as they picked their way along the deserted dock, Alicia whispered. "My name is Gwendolyn, and I sleepwalk."

The chilled breeze blowing up his shirt tails distracted him as he followed her in the dark. "What?"

She pulled them into a shadowed niche. "That's what you'll tell them if you're questioned or stopped. I'm Gwendolyn, your sleepwalking wife. Your name is… Nevil?" She lifted a shoulder. "We're a poor married couple making our way north to my aunt and uncle's homestead for work. We had no coin to sleep in town at the inn, so we stayed aboard that passenger vessel a dock over. I sleepwalk. When I go over, I'll scream, you race down the dock and yell for help. That's our story." She pulled her hair from its braid.

This was madness, but short of knocking Alicia unconscious, he couldn't think of a way to stop her. When she made to move, he grabbed for her and blurted, "Kick your feet."

She shot a look over her shoulder. "What?"

He clutched at her arm. "When you're in the water, don't panic. If you lose your head and thrash about, you'll sink. Wave your arms back and forth along the top of the water and kick your bloody feet as fast as you bloody can." Richard looked out over the dark ripples of the water. "It will keep you near the surface."

Alicia faced him and gave him a quick kiss. "That's just what I'll do, *Nevil*. Shout your head off, we want all eyes on the port side of the ship. If no one comes in to drag me out, you'll have to. Otherwise, stick to the story. Make as much noise as you can, and I'll see you back on shore."

With that Alicia slipped from his grasp and ran on silent feet before she leapt from the end of the slip, "Aaahh!" Richard watched in horror as the dark water silenced her cry and closed over her head.

"Ali—*Gwendolyn*!" He yelled at the top of his lungs as he sprinted down the dock. "Help, someone *help*!"

Alicia came up sputtering and flailing her arms. "Hel—" The water pulled her down again.

A quick glance over Richard's shoulder showed him that her plan had succeeded in garnering the attention she thought it would, but no hero was diving off the rail to save poor drowning

Gwendolyn. "Gwen!" He screamed again.

Alicia broke the surface of the water, fighting for all she was worth. Her shirt clung to the roundness of her breasts and left nothing to the imagination as to what lay beneath.

"Help! Nev--!" The water sucked her below, shortening her cry.

Richard waited what seemed like hours for her to surface. There was no splashing, no flailing. There was no sign of her. Pure panic drove Richard to dive into the frigid water. Breaking the surface, he still didn't see her. "Bugger." He kicked toward where he'd last seen her, dove, and groped blindly into the dark depths until his lungs burned. And then he felt the brush of the tips of her hair.

"Alicia!" His scream sounded thick and garbled beneath the water. He'd been under too long. He needed air, but there was no time. He'd lose her.

Kicking, his arms pulled him deeper until his fingers grasped the thin linen of her shirt and caught her limp form. He pulled her body against his and wrapped one arm under her arms and around her chest while the other clawed and grabbed at the water, pulling them both back to the surface.

Please, just one more stroke. How much farther? Where the hell is the top? The cold of the water sapped his strength. Alicia hung motionless in his arms. His lungs were fit to burst when he finally pushed into the air. Richard sucked a great breath into his lungs before the weight of Alicia pulled them both back down.

He fought to keep them at the surface. Above him shots fired, and alarm bells rang out from the *Gull Wing*. Had Liam and Shrug been caught? Clearly, none were paying any attention to the drowning couple any longer.

Tucking Alicia under one arm to keep her face to the night air, Richard pulled and kicked toward shore. "Alicia, dammit, don't you dare die on me." It wasn't long before his knees scraped against stones, and he was able to haul them both onto dry land.

"Alicia, can you hear me?" Richard dragged her beyond the slope of the shore and rolled her onto her stomach while positioning her arm to keep her face clear of the stones. He wasted no time in straddling her hips and began pushing up under her rib cage to force the water from her lungs.

"Dammit, dammit," he panted. A sob caught in his throat. "Alicia, please…don't…don't you dare leave me… Please… bloody hell, woman, breathe!"

Richard struggled to keep the panic from causing him to break her ribs as he continued to work. "Come on, come on…Breathe, Alicia…breath, damn you!"

Beneath him, Alicia's body jerked, retched, and expelled a gush of water before coughing and sputtering back into the world of the living.

Richard rolled her on her side as she continued to cough. Utter relief bloomed in his heart. *Thank you, God, thank you!* He crushed her to him, pulled her into his lap and curled his body over hers while she continued to gasp for her next breath. Her body shook from cold and shock. "Oh, God, I thought I lost you. Dammit, I thought…" Richard pushed the hair away from her ashen face and kissed her temple. Her fists clutched his sodden shirt. "It's all right. You're all right," he soothed as she began to cry between coughs. "Shhh, it's over. You're safe. I've got you." Richard rocked her. "Shhh."

It was a few minutes before Alicia was able to gather herself. She sat straighter and turned to look back toward the docks. More lanterns had been lit on the *Gull Wing* and neighboring ships. Men milled about the decks. "D-did they... W-what happened? D-did Liam and S-sh..."

"I don't know. I was too busy saving poor Gwendoline." He cupped her cheek. Alicia's teeth started to chatter. "We need to get out of here and find our clothing. I have to get you warm." Richard rubbed at her arms.

"H-h-ow do we get b-back to the *M-mist*?"

"Clothes first." His gaze swept her. She might as well be naked for all the modesty of her transparent shirt. "Can you stand?" Getting to his feet, he reached down to help her up, but when her knees refused to hold her, Richard scooped her into his arms and made his way over the course rocks into the cover of the trees.

Lowering her to lean against the trunk of a wide pine, Richard stood and pulled the clinging fabric of his own shirt off his body. Crouching in nothing but his smalls, he wrapped her in the sodden cloth. "It isn't much, but it's better than nothing."

"Y-you'll freeze to death."

"Then I've great motivation to keep moving, don't I? Stay right here. I'll be back as quick as I ken."

Chapter 28

Alicia's body wracked with the aftershock of nearly drowning and the added combination of cold water, cold night air, and no clothes. She pulled Richard's shirt tighter, curled into herself, and fought to still the tremors. Her teeth would surely shatter if they kept chattering together. "P-please, Richard, h-hurry."

She remembered thinking those same words when she realized in her panic that all the kicking and arm waving wouldn't help. The water was so cold. It made her limbs heavy and slow. Kicking felt as if she were in mud. She couldn't make it back to the surface of the water and she was sinking toward the blackness of death. Alicia was blind. Saltwater filled her mouth when she let out a final scream.

Strangely, for her the panic suddenly ebbed. There was something peaceful in the ebony silence that called to her to stop struggling and accept her fate. She stopped kicking. Stopped fighting. The water simply engulfed her in its dark, liquid embrace.

The next thing she remembered was Richard's voice calling to her from a great distance. Cursing her, begging her not to leave him. Then all at once the pain of her body pulled her back into consciousness. Rocks abraded her face and legs. Her head pounded as her lungs burned with great gulps of precious air. Her ribs ached and her stomach convulsed to relieve itself of a hog's head's worth of seawater.

Richard had saved her. In her impatience, she'd rushed into a situation thinking herself invincible, and nearly killed herself. Talk about in over her head! Alicia uncurled to sit back against the rough bark of the tree. She was so cold. And bull-headed. What the hell was she thinking? She pushed to her feet on shaky limbs. The heady rush at a handful of successful raids had made her overconfident. That was no way to captain.

"I'm smarter than this. I have to be smarter than this." She leaned against the tree until the strength of her legs returned and her head began to clear. What had become of Liam and Shrug? Had they gotten away clean? Had her plan even worked? Or had she put her whole damn crew in jeopardy? Yes, it was just three men, but they were the only crew she had, and the only crew she'd ever have if she continued to make the same mistake that she made tonight.

Alicia's body still trembled with the cold, but her anger at herself had started a fire low in her belly. She strained to hear any sounds in the night. Which way had Richard gone? She was turned around. They'd ended up a fair distance from where they'd begun, and he'd given her most of his clothing. He'd followed her practically to the bottom of the bay, saved her life and then given her the very shirt off his back. She'd never question his loyalty or his love for her ever again.

She heard the soft clod of horse's hooves coming through the underbrush. "Alicia?"

"Here." Her voice rasped. "I'm over here."

Richard moved into the faint light of the moon, secured the reins of his new-found horse, and rushed toward her with the bundle of her clothing. He wore his coat over a bare chest. With his night's growth of beard and hair unbound and hanging about his face in wet strands, he looked every bit a pirate.

He caught Alicia as she rushed into his arms and held her in a firm embrace. The heat of him set her body trembling again. "It's all right. Let's get you out of those clothes and be away. We're not safe here. They've sent a patrol into the woods. Can you ride?" Alicia nodded while he released her and tugged on the hems of her sodden shirt.

In no time, she was dressed, or at least covered. Richard wrapped the blanket about her shoulders and helped her mount the horse before handing her the rest of her things and swinging up behind her.

"Hang on to the mane." Richard wrapped a strong arm about her waist and pulled her tight to him. "We can't go by the road, so we'll have to circle south before we head north and feel our way through the trees for a bit."

"Where did the horse come from?"

"I stole him." He tightened his hold. "I figured you'd been through enough tonight without having to walk miles back to the cove."

"Thank you."

"You're welcome."

"I mean for everything. Not just the horse."

"You're welcome." She couldn't see his face in the shadows, but his tone was clipped.

Warmth from the animal below and the man behind began to thaw her as the trio continued to travel through the woods in strained silence.

"I'm sorry, Richard," Alicia whispered. "I was in such a hurry to succeed tonight I didn't think things through. I put my crew in danger, behaved impulsively, and could have killed us both. Had you not been there to—to pull me out of the water, I... You saved my life."

Stony silence was his response. Alicia wasn't surprised. She deserved his anger. There was no defense for what she'd done. No excuse except for being a stubborn, head-strong fool with more bravado than brains.

The only sounds for the rest of their ride came from the beast beneath her. The pull of air into its huge lungs and its footsteps through the forest. As for the man behind, his silence screamed louder with each mile.

When they finally reached the cove, Alicia was overjoyed to see Liam and Shrug were safe and had started a small fire. Relief filled her.

"There ye be! Look at ye." Shrug helped her off the horse. "Look like a drowned bilge rat, ye do."

Behind him Liam grinned at her despite a huge lump protruding from his forehead. "What happened to you?'

"Knocked his head on a low bulkhead in the rush," Shrug explained. "Te bang of 'is skull, and 'im crashin' te the floor is what alerted the guard. But we was gone 'fore they made us. In 'n out, just like ye told us. Once they saw they'd been pinched, they set up the alarm, but we was in the woods headin' off by then. Left them shiftin' 'bout the deck like water bugs."

"Did'n grab much." Liam gave her a sheepish shrug.

"Nae, but what we did is gold. Weel, not gold, but close."

Alicia looked back over her shoulder. Richard was busy tying off the horse. He'd been too quiet on the ride back, but she doubted he'd raise that anger in front of the others. She pulled the woolen blanket tighter about her and moved closer to the fire.

"Did ye want a look see?" Liam urged.

"Let me warm up a might." She looked beyond the flames to see a small cache of trunks and crates, just as she had instructed.

Richard moved closer to the fire himself. He reached out to warm his hands.

"Course. Ye must be chilled clear te yer innards." Shrug bumped Liam. "We pinched sometin' be helpin' ye warm yer very cockels." He dragged over a crate and pulled one of the boards from the top. From the straw packing, he pulled a shiny bottle. "When our clumsy friend took his tumble, he fell straight on a pile of fine French swill. Couldn't be leavin' such a thing behind, now could we?" He handed Alicia a bottle. "That there will cure ye."

She inspected the bottle. "You two did a great job. Help yourself. You've earned it."

Liam wasted no time in pulling the cork and pouring a goodly amount of the fine quality brandy down his throat.

When Shrug offered the brandy to Richard, he looked at the extended bottle for a long moment before shaking his head. "No, thank ye."

"Suit yerself. All the more fer us." Shrug turned away and began flipping open the lids of the trunks they'd stolen. "Packed tight with silks, these three." He pointed to two smaller chests. "Silver in those two. Knives, forks an' the like. An those." Shrug jerked his chin toward two crates with packing straw peeking out between their slats. "Those be full of verra fancy glasses. I dinna get a good see. 'Fraid we'd break the lot to look at it."

"Verra sparkly." Added Liam.

"Good work. All of it." Alicia praised them. "Before you get too deep in your cups, load it all safely in the cart. I'll take it back to Jocelyn at first light. It's sure to bring us a handsome profit."

Shrug yanked the cork of his brandy and took a pull before raising his bottle toward Alicia. "Gotta say, that was one hell of a plan ye pitched there te-nite, Capt'n. Brilliant it was. I thought muckin' with that there guard ta other nite had been a bit of genius, but what ye did te-nite. Bloody hell."

Richard turned away and walked beyond the reach of the fire's light into the darkness. Alicia waited for the other two to begin moving the goods back into the cart before following him.

She found him at the edge of the water, peering out at the smudge of moonlight trailing across the surface of the calm cove.

"I know you're angry. I said I was sorry."

"It's not anger I'm feeling, Alicia."

"Then what is it? You've not spoken a dozen words to me." She flung a hand back toward the fire. "And you just refused what I know to be a bottle of your favorite brandy. You've a right to be cross. I forced you to risk your life to save mine. That was wrong. The next time I choose to put myself in harm's way, I won't drag you there with me."

"Next time." The words came from him in a rush as if they'd been punched from his chest.

"I am sorry, don't be angry, you're trembling with cold, come back to the fire." She gave a small tug on his sleeve.

"I'm not angry." He turned to her. "And I'm not cold. The shaking in my limbs? That's the pure, unadulterated panic that's still racing through me. It won't cease." He grasped her upper arms. "Do you have any idea what it was like to watch you sink below the surface and watch the water grow calm over you? Do you know the terror of diving into that water and not being able to find you? Diving until my lungs were fit to burst and still not finding you?" He shook his head, his eyes wide. "Or worse, finding you. Lifeless. Holding your limp body and fighting to reach shore praying I was not too late. Praying I could get the water out of your lungs in time. Praying to God I wasn't holding your dead body in my arms."

"Richard…"

He released her, turning back to face the cove. "I swore to protect you and fight alongside you. I'm just trying to figure out how to do that and not have to watch you die."

"I'm not going to die."

"Aye, you are. We all are. But some are in more of a hurry to do so than most." He shook his head. "I've met many men that have sailed these seas with nothing left to lose. Tempting death at every turn. Willing it to take them. Cursing life. Wanting to leave this world."

"I'm not like that." She insisted.

"Nay, you're not, but with you, it's worse. You believe you're stronger than death. That you're beyond its reach. Immortal. Invincible. It makes you reckless. Alicia." He shot a glance back at her. Turning away, he continued, resolution tinged his words. "And I need to have a plan for that day. The day when death is going to win. Do I step in front of the cannon before you? Push you aside to take the shot? Do I keep you at my back, so I don't have to witness you fall?"

"Stop. I'm not going to die." Alicia turned him to face her. "I'm not. I promise."

"That's a promise you canna make, love."

"Then I promise not to behave recklessly from now on. I promise to be more cautious and not take any unnecessary chances." She laid a hand on his cheek. "I'm sorry about tonight. Truly. I realize what I did was incredibly foolish. I won't make that mistake again. You've every right to be panicked. If the positions were reversed, I can't imagine watching you almost drown." She kissed him tenderly. "But you saved me. I'm standing right here. Breath in my lungs, because of you. I'm alive." Alicia's lips brushed his again as she whispered against them. "Kissing you, wanting to hold you in my arms until all the worry and pain ebb. I owe my life to you. And when all this is over, I promise to spend what's left of it with you. Till we're old and gray and twisted with age." She kissed him once more. "And when I do die. I'll make sure it's one full minute after you. So you'd better wait for me and not rush off to heaven."

Richard wrapped her in his arms. The night cocooned them. "Just one minute?"

Alicia gave a small nod. "I swear. Just one."

He tightened his hold. "Then I promise, I'll wait."

Chapter 29

Richard hadn't slept. The nightmare of last night wouldn't let him close his eyes. Each time he did, the horrific scenes that would haunt him forever flashed through his mind. He'd been a decorated member of the King's Navy and fought in vicious battles that would have curdled the blood of a lesser man, but he had never been as scared as he had been last night at the fear of losing Alicia. It had completely undone him.

And then when he had her safely back to the *Ruby Mist*—the bloody brandy. An entire case of it. Begging him to ease his pain with the lure toward its numbing inebriated abyss.

Lord, if this is some sort of test.

They stayed with the *Mist* long after Liam and Shrug had stumbled happy and so drunk it was a wonder they could stand, let alone walk away.

At first light, he sent Alicia on her way back to Jocelyn with the small cache of goods from the raid while he returned a horse. He may be a pirate, but he sure as hell wasn't about to lower himself to the level of horse thief. Horse borrower, he could live with.

It was later that afternoon when Richard returned to the cove. Along the way he'd recruited three other men to help with finishing the work needed on the *Ruby Mist*. They went by the name Fitz, short for Fitzroy, Simms, and a man everyone called Tippy. Seems the fool accidently shot off three of his toes and now he tips slightly to starboard. But he's broad as an ox across his shoulders with arms thicker than trees and could heft Fitz and Simms and Liam combined. Two more were scheduled to join their motley crew within the next few days.

A very hungover Shrug was appointed Boatswain and given the task of supervising things. Richard hadn't broached the subject of being captained by a woman to these men. Not yet. Shrug and Liam were the best convincers of being a member of Captain Alicia Steele's crew he had. Time would tell if the others decided to stick around.

When he went to the far end of the bay to find Captain Steele, his heart took another jolt. She was several yards from shore thrashing in the blasted water.

Son of a bitch! Richard tossed aside his weapons, stripped off his boots and raced into the surf, but the tide was out, and he soon realized that she wasn't in deep water.

"Alicia! What in blazes are you doing?"

"It isn't working," she sputtered. "I'm waving and kicking, and I still bloody sink."

He reached her in shoulder deep water, pulled her into his arms and crushed her to him. "Why the hell are you back in the water?" His heart threatened to beat itself out of his body.

"I'm trying to learn how to swim, dammit." She panted.

Adrenaline surged through him. "After last night, I never thought to see you in the water again."

"If you fall off a horse, they make you get back on." Alicia blinked at him. Spiky eyelashes ringed her beautiful eyes. "I can't be afraid of the water. What kind of pirate captain would I be?"

He had her tight in his arms. That alone should have caused a small measure of relief to bloom in his chest. "Indeed."

"And unless you'd like to consider me the new anchor for the *Ruby Mist*, I need to stop dropping to the sea floor like a stone."

"Agreed." His breathing was beginning to return to normal when Alicia wrapped her arms about his neck, and her legs about his waist.

"I was going to ask you to teach me how to swim, but after what happened last night, knowing how you felt, I didn't think it a fair thing to ask."

Richard had walked them backwards into shallower water. The water was decidedly warmer or was that her? Alicia was buoyant in his arms, and as he slipped his hands lower to cradle her behind, the discovery of bare skin brought a different warmth to his body. "I'm in your service, Captain Steele. You can ask me anything."

"Good. Then kiss me."

"Aye, aye." Richard slanted his head and heated her chilled lips with his own. She tasted of salt and sea. His hands caressed the rounds of her bottom. When she slipped her tongue between his lips, a tortured moan slipped from his throat. "Alicia…" She tightened the grip of her thighs and pressed the fullness of her breasts against his chest.

"Will you?" She murmured against his mouth.

"Will I?"

"Teach me to swim?" Alicia blinked at him again. "I can't cling to you like driftwood every time we're in the water."

Richard ran teasing fingers along her clef, making her gasp. "I can think of no objections."

Alicia's back arched in response to his touch. "We can't make love in the water."

"Fish do it all the time."

"That's only because they're born knowing how to swim."

Richard ended his intimate caress and untwined her legs from him, setting her to stand chest deep before him. He gave her a quick kiss. "Fine. I will teach you, and then I will make love to you."

"Is that my incentive?"

"Nay, it's mine." With one smooth movement, he scooped her back into his arms. Alicia let out a gasp when he laid her back along the surface of the water. "First, you must learn to float."

Hours later, Richard and Alicia lay sated and sleepy in the grass. The hot afternoon sun warmed their bodies and dried the scattering of clothing set among the low bushes that surrounded them and created their own private oasis.

"I told you I was a fast learner."

"You were clearly motivated." Richard swirled a fingertip over the firm tip of her breast before lowering his mouth to pull it between his lips. He couldn't get enough of her. Couldn't stop touching her. As if he had to keep proving to his traumatized brain that she was indeed alive. Living, breathing, writhing beneath him, gasping his name.

He moved his kisses lower over the soft plane of her stomach. Alicia stroked his hair.

"Richard?"

"Mmmmm?" He circled her navel with his tongue.

"I'm curious about something."

"Mmmmm?" His fingers trailed lower. Alicia caught his hand and diverted his attention.

"Last night. At the fire."

With a frustrated sigh, he straightened his body to lie along her side. "What about the fire?"

"You didn't take the brandy."

Richard rose onto his elbow and lifted one shoulder as if to minimize the fierce cravings he was still fighting hours later. Thank goodness the bottles Liam and Shrug didn't claim were now safely in Jocelyn's possession. "So?"

Alicia rolled on her side to look at him. She held his gaze. "So, I've noticed you're not drinking."

He shook his head. "No."

"And you haven't for some time?" She pressed.

Feels like a bloody eternity. Richard pulled in a deep breath. "No. It's been a little while since I had anything stronger than tea to quench my thirst."

Alicia had already deduced the truth, but still looked at him with a small measure of surprise. "I suppose I should be relieved, given your…your…"

"Reputation as a drunkard?" he countered.

"I wasn't going to use those exact words."

Richard sat up, brushing bits of grass from his skin. There was no sense in defending what he once was. They both knew the truth only too well. "Perhaps I merely decided to change my ways."

"Something tells me it's not that simple."

He looked back over his shoulder at her. "I made a promise not to drink."

She frowned. "To whom?"

Richard turned away. "Saint James."

"My brother?" Alicia sat up and pulled her knees in to wrap her arms about them. The sun was beginning to pinken her skin and dry her hair into shining, pale waves. "What does he have to do with any of this?"

For a long moment, Richard considered brushing her question aside. Coming up with some glib remarks and changing the subject. Hell, she might as well know. "Because James had lost his confidence in me, and he wouldn't agree to allow me to come find you otherwise."

"What?"

Richard reached out and fingered the end of her hair. He lifted it and brushed the soft curl across his lips. "My last taste of brandy was on the day of your wedding."

Her eyes got wide. "That was months ago."

"Aye." He stood and tested the dryness of their clothing before tossing Alicia her shirt and donning his breeches.

When he turned back, she sat with her blouse clutched to her chest. A frown knit her pale eyebrows together. "James ordered you to stop drinking?"

Richard gave a short laugh. "No. I bloody well volunteered."

Alicia's frown deepened. "I don't understand."

He sat down again, folding his legs beneath him and faced her. "I had to find you, Alicia." Locking his gaze with hers, he continued. "James didn't trust me, that was obvious. None of them—James, Samantha, your parents—none of them trusted me to see myself home, let alone set off in search of you." He held up a hand. "I don't blame them. I wouldn't have trusted me either. But time was wasting. I had a sense as to where you were headed, and I could feel you moving further away with every tick of the clock."

Richard wrapped the curled end of her hair around his finger again. "I told you how I'd resigned myself to losing you to marriage, but the thought of never seeing you again? I would have made a bargain with the Devil himself. So, I gave your brother my word. Swore to him on our friendship that I wouldn't have a single drop until I found you and returned you safely to your family."

"Then you traveled all this way, and I refused to go back."

"Aye, you did." Richard gave a short huff of laughter before meeting her gaze. "But I gave my word, and I will keep my promise forever if need be. What matters to me most, is that I found you. That I could finally tell you how much I love you. What we have between us now is far more important to me than anything else on this earth. Certainly, more important than numbing my brain and rotting my belly."

"But you must have cravings?"

"Of course. I thought I was past the worst of it, but that case of brandy last night tested every fiber of my resolve. It would have been far too easy, given what we'd just been through, to drown myself and escape my worries. But it also made me realize I crave you far more than any drink." Richard gathered her in his arms and pulled her into his lap. "Even the finest of brandy cannot compare."

Alicia captured his gaze and gave a small shake to her head. "I've misjudged you. That you would go to such lengths. Give up so much for me."

"You've given me far more in return." He held her cheek in his palm and kissed her. "My head is clear, and my heart is full. My future is with the woman I love." He smiled. "And in the mornings, my head no longer pounds like someone's chinking my skull. And it doesn't feel as if something has died on my tongue."

He kissed her again, and when Alicia wrapped her arms about his neck and opened her lips to the deepening of that kiss, Richard was quick to toss her blouse aside and return her to her back. Looking down into the clear beauty of her eyes, his heart skidded in his chest. Had he ever loved another creature as much as he loved her? "I'd much rather wake to the sweet taste of you."

Chapter 30

Jocelyn held up a tall wineglass of cut lead crystal, so each shimmering edge caught the candlelight. "Lovely."

Raine, meanwhile, had begun rummaging through the trunk of silks.

Alicia brought each of them a cup of tea. "You've first choice. As promised," she assured Raine.

"These are all fine, fine goods, Alicia. I will be able to find buyers at once." Jocelyn polished a silver spoon on her sleeve.

Both Jocelyn and Alicia turned as Raine let out a small gasp before sliding a length of shimmering silk the color of claret from the growing nest of fabric. "This." And then Raine did something shocking. Clutching the silk to her chest, she smiled. Smiled? Other than a bitter smirk, Alicia had never seen her smile. She wasn't sure she was capable, but there it was. Brilliant and stunning. There was no denying Raine was beautiful, but a smiling Raine was breathtaking.

Even Jocelyn was slightly taken aback. Her eyebrows rose sharply as Raine gathered her prize and left without another word.

"I am impressed. You did well with this lot. Is there more?"

"No. It was a quick pinch. We ran into some trouble."

"Trouble?" Jocelyn frowned. "What kind of trouble? The Watch?"

Alicia had purposefully withheld the more harrowing aspects of last night's raid. The time spent with Richard in the cove this afternoon, the swimming, the lovemaking, and the honest, tender conversation had done much to ease last night's trauma. Accepting the dangers was part of the whole, was it not? Dwelling on the horrifying "what if's" would only cripple both of them. "No, not the Watch. We're all well," Alicia reassured Jocelyn. And at the same time, herself.

She was grateful to be alive, grateful to Richard for saving her and loving her. She was thankful for so much. His admittance regarding his drinking had truly touched her. Alicia remembered all too clearly the scene in the garden the morning of her doomed wedding. He was so deep in his brandy, he could barely stand. His fine clothing hung stained and wrinkled on his disheveled frame. His pompous words slurred on the ends. Richard was a mess, and he had been for more than a year. To learn it was because of his love for her all that changed. The revelation was overwhelming.

Alicia fingered a length of white silk. It slipped over her fingers like fresh cream. Jocelyn chose a deep sapphire silk from the lot and held it to her chest before looking in the mirror on the shop's worktable. "Our dressmaker will be busy, no?"

"We need to sell this, not wear it." Alicia pushed the silk back into the trunk.

"With the governor's ball coming up?" Jocelyn tugged the white fabric back out, "together with my lace? What better way to advertise the quality of our current wares, no?"

"I've no time for dressmakers and endless fittings. You said it yourself, we need more." Alicia lit a few extra candles in the fading light and covered a yawn. "I'm far more concerned with those six ships due to sail soon. The *Ruby Mist* is still unworthy. We've brought on more crew, but without a ship, the raids have to be small and fast. It's not enough. We're running out of time."

Jocelyn cupped Alicia's face and ran a thumb across her cheekbone. "You are exhausted, and the sun has reddened your beautiful skin." Jocelyn swept her hand across the crates and trunks. "This will bring us a fine bit of coin. The women of town have heard rumors about our particular form of trade and are clamoring for what we can bring them. I guarantee this lot will be sold before the sun rises tomorrow." She placed a hand on Alicia's shoulder. "You have done well. And you have worked hard. Harder than I ever believed. Learning to battle, building your strength, building a crew, never backing down from challenge. You are a tenacious woman. Far more ambitious and determined than I. You should be proud."

"I'll be proud when we've done what we sought out to do and bring your son and your husband home."

Jocelyn gave her a watery smile and laid a kiss on each cheek. "We will succeed. You have given me what I feared I had lost. Hope. You lift my spirit." She returned to the trunk and raised the white silk again. "And I shall show my appreciation by making you a stunning gown to wear at the ball. A gown to wrap you in the color of innocence and goodness, while you continue your acts of illegality and impropriety."

"I'll look like a bride."

"So, we will drive that man who is so besotted with you a bit mad as well, no?" She smirked. "Give him a glimpse of what awaits him, perhaps?"

"Richard won't be at the ball to see me. He loathes such things. Besides, I told you I wasn't marrying him." The sudden catch in her heart when she said the words gave her pause. She was falling deeper and deeper in love with the man with each passing day. She was too close to achieving what she'd set herself to do. She needed to keep her resolve.

"I know what you said, but I see what is happening between you. There will be a wedding."

Alicia shot her a glance. Jocelyn was giving her a smug, all-knowing stare. Could she read her mind as well as her heart? Alicia flipped a hand to distract Jocelyn's curiosity. "You'll believe what you wish no matter what I say. I'm too tired to listen to your romantic musings. Please stop."

"Fine." Jocelyn pulled a numbered tape from beneath the counter and dangled it in front of Alicia. "I will cease the minute you give me your measurements for your new gown."

* * * * *

The following week, Alicia met a grueling pace. Work on the *Mist* was moving at full speed. The new men were tireless, although Simms was none too pleased with the announcement that Alicia was to be his Captain. However, two more signed the Ship's Articles even after learning they'd be answering to a woman. Hewes and Copperfield. Or was it Kent?

"Nay, Kent's where's I be from," the man explained. His name was in truth Malcolm Copperfield, but he'd signed on to the ship as Alfred Kent. "Alfred be me mum's name 'fore she met me da."

"Is there a reason you're not Malcolm Copperfield?" Alicia inquired.

"Aye." The man lifted a meaty shoulder. "Be times when being Alfred Kent keeps them which be lookin' fer a Copperfield lookin' somewhere else."

Did she want to know why? "Then if you're looking to hide your identity, why tell me your name is Copperfield to begin with?"

"Figure someone sh'd know. 'Case I meet me end. Can't be roaming about after I'm dead cause they got the wrong name stitched to me nose."

Did he imagine a guest list at heaven's gate? Or hell's? "Kent it is then unless…"

"Unless ye be slippin' me cold arse inte the sea."

"If you're telling the truth about being an expert gunner, then that won't need to happen."

"Oh, ye 'ave me word. Fierce shot, I am. Fierce." He scowled for effect.

"Fine, Mister Malcolm Alfred Copperfield Kent, welcome aboard the *Ruby Mist.*

With considerable struggle and the strength of all, the mast had been hauled into its standing position with a slight tilt toward the stern, and a gold coin placed beneath for luck. The deadeyes were strung, and the new rigging was nearing completion. The *Mist* was finally looking like she could manage more than a three-foot swell without sinking.

After another successful land raid, the men were fine taking orders from a woman if it meant the easy coin they'd each made that night. Even Mister Simms gave her a begrudging huff of respect when he came to gather his share—and a goodly amount of rum.

It was planned the ship's maiden raid would be set for the day after next. All hands were making the necessary preparations. Richard had abandoned his coat and stock and rolled up his sleeves to man a tar brush or help run a line. His afternoons were spent with her.

Alicia was finishing her training with pistol and sword. She'd still not mastered firing Cookie's pistol with one hand. The heavy barrel continued to drop before she could fire, but the technique of using her left forearm to brace the gun had proven helpful in hitting her chosen mark six times out of seven. She and Richard would spar and swordplay until they fell dirty, hot, and exhausted into one another's arms.

They slept on the *Mist* these past nights and made love into the pearl-gray light of dawn most mornings. Alicia caught her reflection in the window glass as the sky began to lighten. Mused and sated, her lips kissed full, she no longer resembled the woman she once found in the looking glass. She was a woman in love. In love with a handsome man, in love with a beautiful ship, in love with daring adventure. In love with her life. A ripple of excitement raced through her at the thought of what was to come.

With the rush of anticipation, however, came the heavy weight of responsibility, and Alicia took that fully into her heart as well. She had a crew now. A bloody crew! True, they were rather the bottom scrapings of society's barrel, but they were hers. Her men. What they lacked in skill and finesse, they more than made up in a willingness and eagerness to succeed. It was as if each of these men had moved through their lives as lone figures. Scratching out their own solitary existence. Except for Liam and Shrug, of course, who seemed joined at hip in some odd codependent brotherhood. The *Ruby Mist* was for them a chance to be part of a whole. A clan of their own. For a few it was a second or third or fifth chance.

For Alicia, it was a first. A first chance to prove to herself she was indeed her father's daughter and bold audacity as well as sea water ran in her veins. If she failed, there wouldn't be another chance for her. She owed it to herself, and her men to make sure that didn't happen.

She owed it to Richard most of all. Watching him toil these last few days, his shirt open to the waist, sweat glistening on his broad chest with the play of strong muscles outlined in the tightness of his breeches and the cling of his shirt. He was handsome and clever. A born leader of men who could squeeze every bit of strength from them without resorting to bullying or intimidation. He showed them respect, and in return they gave him their all.

Alicia turned back to watch him sleep. She couldn't have done this without him. Not just his vast wealth of experience and knowledge, but his understanding and encouragement—albeit hard given, at first. Richard's hesitance came from a place of love and concern and not one of dominance or control.

Slipping back into their bed, she curled into his warmth. Richard stirred and woke enough to tuck her tight along the length of him. He breathed a contented sigh before laying a kiss at her temple and murmuring, "I love you."

The gentle pull and sway of the *Mist* against her tethers combined with the sound of the water lapping at the hull soothed

Alicia's soul. Soon her ship would awaken and begin flying over those waves. Clean sea air would fill her lungs and her sails. Canvas bowed and guns at the ready. The thought caused a thrilled rush to course through her.

Richard reached for her breast in a slow, sleepy sweep. The roughness of his palm pebbled the tip and sent a different sort of rush through her. She reached between them and found him rock hard and hot. He moaned as her fingers circled his morning erection and gave a slow sweep of her own.

"Alicia," he rasped.

She was desirous and insatiable, a dangerous combination. Her new life was dawning along with the new day, and each minute that passed made her stronger and eager for the next. She was ready. Her sex pulsed in anticipation as her strokes to his cock became bolder. His hips rolled as Alicia lured him from his sleep into his seduction.

"Oh, sweet God," he groaned. His hand joined hers as she increased the pace of her movements and laid a line of kisses down his neck and across his chest. "Alicia... Bloody hell."

She smiled against his skin before licking and teasing the flat of his nipple. Richard pushed his hand into her hair and moved in waves beneath her. Alicia slipped over him like water over the shore, harboring his hips between her thighs before lowering herself upon his wooden cock. She cast a moan of pleasure on her own.

It was a heady business being in control. Alicia reveled in the feeling. There was power in being on top. She positioned Richard's hands at her breasts. Her gaze locked with his in the growing light as she moved over him in small torturous circles. Alicia braced one hand above her head on the low ceiling and took charge. Setting the pace, taking command.

Richard clutched at her hips, her ass, urging her to move faster and end his torment, bucking beneath her, but his insistence only caused her to slow her ride, making him wait, prolonging both their pleasure.

"Are ye trying to kill me?" he gasped.

Alicia gave him a slow smile and stopped moving completely. "No," she panted, "not kill you, seize you. Capture you."

Richard's breath quickened as his head dropped back against the pillow. His fingers dug into her thighs. He growled her name through gritted teeth while his cock pulsed impatiently within her.

Alicia arched her back and ground him deeper inside her. "What say you, Mister Dunbar, do you surrender?"

Chapter 31

"Release the bow line!" Richard called out the order. The anchor was raised, the foresail set. It was time to test the main mast.

Alicia stood midship and peered up into the freshly tarred rigging at their new flag. A winged skull on a red field, bordered with black banding. Shrug and Liam's contribution. Above that flew a single black pennant. Alicia shielded her eyes.

Richard's gaze followed the line of her braid, past the hem of her shirt to the curve of her behind. He wondered if his fingers had bruised her when he gripped those two rounds of soft flesh this morning. She'd been an unbelievable seductress, climbing astride, and the sweet agony of her torturing him as she took total command of their lovemaking. Where had she learned to do something like that? He'd been at her complete mercy. Her body giving and taking pleasure, both his and hers. She'd bring him to the very brink of his release and stop. His balls still ached at the punishing thought.

Alicia had laid siege to him, and he'd gladly surrendered. The resulting release equaled a full-scale broadside attack at close range. But never let it be said Richard Dunbar didn't return fire with equal intensity.

It was fair certain that after this morning, Alicia Steele had ruined him for any other woman.

At the helm of the *Ruby Mist*, Richard made a slow, measured turn to point the stem toward open sea. With the foresails and jibs catching the breeze, he motioned for Alicia to join him at the wheel.

"By right, you need to be the one to take us out."

"How does she feel?"

"Solid." He shook his head in amazement. "We'll see how the mast performs with the load at full sail, but other than that she's handling well. She rides high, and the deeper blade of the hull should make for quick maneuvers."

Alicia took the wheel and Richard got behind her. "Watch." He swept the boat in a tight wave from port to starboard with little turn of the wheel.

"And that's unusual?"

"For a ship this size, probably not. I don't want her to be top heavy. More ballast might be needed."

Around them the ship creaked and popped as the *Ruby Mist* rose and stretched from her long-neglected slumber. The sharp smell of new tar and freshly varnished spars mixed with the first breath of open sea.

"Head for the deep blue." Richard pointed over Alicia's shoulder. "Now, Captain Steele," he spoke into her ear. "Let's see how fast she be. I think it's time to give the men the order to set the mainsails."

Alicia looked at him with the same passion-filled glint in her eye as when she'd gained his surrender earlier. A slow smile tipped the corners of her lips. "Drop the topsail and the main, Mister Dunbar," she almost sang the words. With a passing call, Alicia's first official order at sea as Captain of the *Ruby Mist* was carried out.

Richard joined the men to help. He wanted to be close should the mast prove incompetent, but when the wind caught the cloth and bowed the brilliant width of sail, the rigging held. The mast stood, and the *Ruby Mist* began to fly.

Looking back, Alicia stood with splayed legs to ride the pitch of the deck. The white of her blouse shown brilliant in the sunlight. Somewhere along the way, she'd begun wearing a smart tri-corner hat of thick dove grey leather with a plume of snowy ostrich feather decorating one side. She held the ship's wheel as if she'd done so all her life.

At this speed, her jaunty feather danced behind from where it was secured, and her shirt clung to every curved inch of her chest. She was a sight to behold.

So, too, was the *Ruby Mist*. Remembering what the ship had looked like a few months ago, Richard couldn't help but marvel at how they'd pulled her back from the brink of decay and ruin. He could feel it in the ship's renewed spirit as well as it leapt over the waves like a new colt. The rigging began to sing.

Soon every inch of sail flew, and the ship followed. Richard had the men on the lookout for any hint of problem. Any issue. Staying within sight of land should a hasty landing be needed, they pushed the *Ruby Mist* to its limit, and then some. Everything held tight. The new mast sat solid. The keel, having been scraped and cleaned, sliced through the water at more than eighteen knots.

Richard walked the length of the ship and back a dozen times before returning to the helm. "She's sound. And fast," he shouted into Alicia's ear.

"She's bloody magnificent," Alicia shouted back. The wind whipped at her hair, rouged her cheeks and plucked at her words.

"You're bloody magnificent." He slipped his arms around her waist and pressed himself against her back. The power of the ship passed through the wheel in her hands and the hum of the deck beneath their feet, through her, into him. All his sailing experience had been on huge war ships, with hundreds of men and miles of sail. A floating army. As a young lieutenant, he'd been in awe of the scale and fighting strength of those vessels. He'd not been aware of such an intimate, personal connection with a ship this size, however. The ship seduced him almost as much as its captain.

"So, we're ready?" Said captain asked over her shoulder.

"Aye, I think we're ready." At his response, Alicia shivered in his arms. Her excitement was contagious. "We should add some ballast," he continued, "but aye, we're ready. Let's head back to the cove."

"Not just yet." She shot him a smile.

Richard tightened his hold. "Take all the time you wish, Captain."

* * * * *

Fitz and Hewes rolled two barrels onto the deck of the *Ruby Mist*.

"Midship, starboard." Richard ordered the freshwater ballast moved below. "And lash it tight."

Liam and Tippy loaded a crate of shot for the cannons with Shrug overseeing the storage of powder.

Alicia studied a map spread out over the deck. "We'll set off at eight bells. The moon will be with us tonight. If we tuck into this cove, here." She pointed at a spot further up the coast. "We'll lay in wait and be in place to strike just before dawn."

She turned toward the man closest. "Mr. Kent, in my cabin, there is a trunk, bring it on deck, if you please?"

"Aye, Capt'n."

"*Capt'n*," she repeated with a smug grin and turned toward Richard. "I do like hearing that."

Back at the map, Alicia continued. "Beyond the line of outer banks, we'll use the morning's mist to conceal us until we can approach on their starboard flank. If we time it properly, the rising sun will hamper their aim should they decide to fight. And we can tuck in here, she pointed to another inlet due south, should they decide to give chase. Or here." She pointed again. "Or here. If we make a habit of no habit, there'll be less chance of the authorities knowing where we are from one day to the next. And, here." Alicia circled a section with her finger. "Brighton Bay, when we take on the six, we'll be close enough to land to off load the goods to waiting carts and get them back to Jocelyn."

"Here ye be, Capt'n." Kent dropped the trunk at Alicia's feet.

Opening the lid, she crouched and began pulling long lengths of what looked to be loose woven linen. Richard lifted a strip of the fabric. It looked more suited to wrapping cheese than anything useful to them. "What on earth is all this for?"

"If we drape the ship, hide the hard lines and dark rigging. Cover the guns. Keep the men hidden. Then use the mist as I said, they'll not see us until we're practically on their gunnels and it will be too late. We'll have them at a disadvantage. We may never need to fire on them."

"Clever." He fingered the cloth. "What if we choose to run silent?" Richard suggested.

Alicia looked at him and frowned. "I'm not sure I know what you mean."

"Teach the men to watch for signals. None will be shouting orders. No drums or ruckus to try and intimidate. We're too small an operation for that. I say slip in quietly. Use of stealth will conceal our identity, yours specifically. You might consider a mask, as well."

She nodded and smiled. "Clever," she returned the compliment. Alicia stood and looked down the deck. "Yes. I like that plan." She turned back to him. "You've used such tactics before?"

Richard shook his head. "Nay, the ships I've served on used their size and might to win the day. We wanted our prey to know we were coming for them. Your brother's ship, HMS Lion, had the biggest, brightest golden lion as its maidenhead. We wanted everyone to know who we were. At the sight of that beast and our forward guns, most crews gave up the battle before we ever reached them. It's a fine deterrent to be the biggest, fastest dog in the fight."

At the mention of her brother's last adventure as sea, Alicia had to ask. "Is that how you captured the *Scarlet Night*?"

Richard's reaction to the mention of that particular ship still stung. He gave a bitter huff. "Of course not. Didn't matter that they were out manned, out gunned, out of options. They couldn't begin to outrun us or out fight us, and yet they stood their ground, screeching like a band of banshees, and were prepared to battle to the very last man. Or woman, if necessary."

"I've only heard stories of Captain Tupper Quinn. Alice. I can't help standing on this deck today, thinking of her. And of my father."

"It's true. You're a descendant of a tenacious group. By blood and by name."

"Do you suppose Tupper still sails?"

"Last I heard they were spotted off the African coast, but that was years past now."

"I'd love to meet her."

A begrudging respect crept into Richard's memory. "You share more than a name with Alice Tupper Quinn. If memory serves, she was stubborn as an old mule, too."

At Alicia's indignant gasp, he pulled her into his arms. "She was also savvy, brave, and loyal. Honest, for a thief." He frowned in remembrance. "You know, to give her her due, she never tried to talk her way out of her crimes. Admitted them fully. Never once begged for leniency because she was a woman. Never asked your brother to grant her any favors given their connection. In fact, she was adamant that he not."

"And yet, she still got away. Who knows, you may still cross paths with her."

"Please, no. Once was more than enough."

"Still, I can't help but wonder what she and father would think about all this." Her hand swept the length of the *Ruby Mist*.

"They'd probably have a few choice words to say. None you'd listen to," he teased. This time, Richard took advantage of her indignant gasp to give her a searing kiss.

Late afternoon shadows stretched long on the deck. All was ready as the lines were cast, and the anchor raised. Excitement and a good deal of rum ran through the crew. Everyone had their orders, and all had been instructed to watch for those orders rather than listen for them.

It was still dark when they left their cove and sailed far enough east to lay their trap in the outer edge of the morning's mists hugging the land. The crew draped the ship and they waited.

At the first glimpse of the sun's peek over the horizon, Alicia caught sight of a merchant ship. It flew the flag of England and rode low and slow in the water. Donning a white mask to hide her identity, she alerted the crew, then the *Ruby Mist* did everything possible to disappear.

Pushing to port, Richard maneuvered the *Mist* to intercept the merchant ship close to the stern. A boarding ladder was moved across and the crew slipped over to the deck of the other ship in relative silence. Alicia drew her pistol, braced it on her left forearm, and led the raid without uttering a sound. She startled the first man, and with Liam's knife laid quickly to his throat they easily subdued the few men in these wee hours to be found on deck. With the tapping of Alicia's wrists and a quick fist, Hewes and Simms knew to tie and gag those men to the center mast while the rest of them ducked below deck to help themselves to the goods to be found there.

They paid no attention to the cache of guns, or black powder, although Shrug traded his pistol for a larger one and pocketed several pouches of shot. Chests of spices were grabbed. More trunks of silks. Barrels of china. Crates of wine. Rum. Sacks of sugar.

Like their land raids, this one was swift. Remarkably easy. They were back aboard the *Mist*, the ladder retracted, and the merchant ship sailing away to the shock of them all. In fact, the men stood on deck with wide eyes watching their prey sail serenely away, almost waiting for the alarm to be sounded and the guns to be run out.

And just as quietly, Alicia simply said, "Hard to port, away with our veils, and full sail, gentlemen. Time we were away."

Had Richard not witnessed it with his own eyes, he would never have believed it. They'd done it. Exactly as planned. Not one hitch. Not a single shot fired, nor a single drop of blood spilled. Relief flooded him.

When they were finally out of sight of the slightly plucked merchant ship, a cry of celebration erupted from the men. They couldn't believe their luck. Liam and Shrug sat like two smug toads passing the rum around. "Dinna we tell ye…"

In fact, there was only one aboard the *Ruby Mist* who wasn't happy about the success of the day. The captain.

Richard broke away from the reveling men with their rum and joined Alicia at the helm.

"Ye've a very happy crew."

"So, it seems." Her response was clipped.

"Why aren't you rejoicing with the rest?"

"That was hardly a test of our metal. I've had more dangerous raids on tiptoe stealing jam biscuits from the kitchen when I was but six." She slapped her hand against the wheel and tore off her mask.

Richard placed a hand over his heart. "I, for one, am relieved."

"Aren't you afraid it will give us all a false pride?" Alicia swept a hand toward the dancing crew.

"Those men aren't stupid. They realize how extraordinary that was. I'm a bit astonished, myself."

The muscle in her jaw twitched.

"What has you so upset? Everything went perfectly. The ship and crew performed beautifully. You've a fine stash of goods. Your crew is crowing your praises. No one's body is being stitched into a shroud to be lowered into the sea. Yet you look ready to shoot someone."

"Exactly my point. I've been training for weeks, and never even got the chance to reload." She shook her head. "I'm glad Tupper Quinn wasn't a witness to this. I'm a piss poor excuse for a pirate."

Chapter 32

Piss poor or not, Alicia and her crew struck a Spanish galleon with much the same success. Liam had to knock a few skulls together to keep the morning's watch from sounding the alarm, and some blood was spilled. Hewes bloodied a Spanish nose with a sharp blow from his elbow. But like the last, they crept in in silence and backed out with a profitable store of goods. This time actual gold flatware and a tea service in ornate silver with enough pieces to serve twenty. No silks this time, but cotton calicos coming from the Caribbean. And more rum. Lots more rum.

At Gladys Wilson's tea that week, Alicia recognized a certain tea service and smiled at the huge trays of sweets. Gladys was a happy woman who'd spent that morning with her dressmaker. Her gown for the ball would be the perfect shade of plum.

The governor was livid. Alicia overheard him telling his male colleagues about a new threat. A schooner draped like a ghost ship attacking ships at dawn, coming out of the mist like a specter. The captain was a masked white shadow that didn't speak. The crew barely made a noise.

One of the governor's companions huffed in disbelief, "How does a Captain give an order without speaking?"

"Bloody hand gestures," explained the governor, flipping his hands about like sick birds. "All the man need do is clap his hands or tap his wrists, and the crew scrambles to do his bidding. They can strip a ship of all its goods in no time. Their captain has no scruples. No shame. Loses have been in the tens of thousands. And then they simply turn tail and vanish back into the mist from whence they came. I've had search ships combing the coast with no sign of any ship meeting their description."

"Such losses," fussed one.

"Whole shipments, gone." The governor flipped a lace-trimmed wrist.

"Surely the owners of these merchants carry insurance," remarked another man.

"Of course," insisted Governor Wilson. "One would be foolish in these uncertain times with these barbarians just off our shores not to protect all of our interests. Shall we retreat ourselves, gentlemen, for a fine cigar?"

Alicia fumed. She had scruples. The *Ruby Mist* was too small to strip any ship of their entire cargo. They hardly took enough worth tens of thousands. Sounded to her that once again the governor was protecting a bit more than just his interests. He continued playing all the angles and was now using her attacks to cover his own thievery and put even more money in his pockets. Short of setting fire to what remained on the ships after she and her crew were done picking their *choice plunder*, Alicia couldn't figure a way to stop him. The bastard should be thanking her.

She turned back to the women in time to see Gladys stuff another glazed sweet into her mouth. At least there was one member of the Wilson household who was grateful. Jocelyn said Gladys had nearly wept with joy over the availability of sugar and spices for her kitchens and didn't hesitate to pay full market price. Perhaps tonight's raid would prove equally profitable.

Once again, the *Ruby Mist* hit open water in the still of the night, during the witching hour between three and four in the morning to be in place as the sun began its rise. Today, however, the sun was hidden within blankets of sodden clouds.

Alicia scanned the southern horizon and spotted their prey. A frigate. Dutch by the flag. She gave the order to lower the flags and conceal the *Ruby Mist*. Without the dense morning fog due to the rain, they'd have to be quicker with their attack, but with any luck there would be fewer men on deck in this weather.

As in the past raids, Richard maneuvered the *Mist* to nose in close to the other ship's wake. Due to the rough seas, the boarding ladder was dismissed in favor of hooks and swing lines. Alicia's arrival to the deck of the Dutch ship was less than graceful. Swinging out over open water had terrified her and the rope was slick in the wet dawn. With her mask on, it was difficult to properly judge the distance to the ship below. Her legs hadn't expected the force of such a drop and her heels slipped on the deck. She came down hard on a hip and scrambled to recover.

The ship was loaded to the gunnels with all manner of cargo. Huge crates covered in oil skin were tied down tight in the rising seas. Alicia skidded to place her back against one of those crates to pull her pistol and gather her bearings. Richard was at her side in an instant. They could see where some of the other men had chosen similar hiding places.

Alicia rose and peered over the top of the crate. The deck was so cluttered it was hard to see in the dim light of the shrouded day where the members of the Dutch crew were stationed. Sound was difficult to gauge in this weather, but she thought she could hear several men midship to starboard. Was there also a small group in the stern?

Using hand signals, she conveyed that information to her men, and with a jerk of her head, they struck.

A silent attack was not meant to be, however, as a member of the Dutch crew saw them ahead of the rest and was too far away to stop him from raising the alarm. A pistol fired, then another. Shouts carried before the sound of blades connecting rang out. More gunfire sounded. The deck erupted with the fight. Shouts and screams and pistol shots surrounded them.

Alicia turned in time to find a man leveling a gun in her direction. Instinct had her twisting away and covering her face. She heard the shot hiss by her ear and shatter the corner of a crate behind her. An explosion of splinters tore through her sleeve. Raising her own pistol in haste, Alicia turned back toward the man. A rush of adrenaline raced through her as she squeezed the trigger. She hadn't had time or the sense to brace the pistol on her forearm, and the weight of the barrel pulled the shot low. An anguished cry of pain from the other man pierced through the cloud of smoke from the flash of black power. When she could finally see, the man lay on the deck. Her shot had hit him just above the knee. He writhed in agony. Bright blood pulsed from the wound to stain the deck boards beneath him.

Alicia's hand shook as she pushed the hot barrel of her pistol back into her baldric and pulled her sword. The acrid smell of black powder stung her nose. The clashing of blades and shouts of the others added to the chaos swirling around her. They were more than outnumbered.

Then as quickly as it began, the fighting ceased. Richard emerged from the ship's stern and had a captive by the back of his hair pulling his head at a painful angle with the barrel of his pistol shoved tight beneath the man's jaw. Richard must have caught the man at his breakfast. He still wore a napkin tucked into his neckline. The man was shorter by a head, and twice as round. His jacket marked him as the captain. He was shiny with sweat. His eyes wild. Richard gave a sharp jerk to his hair and shoved the pistol harder into the man's jowls before the man pulled the white napkin from his neckband and waved it like a flag of surrender. He called out to his crew to lay down their weapons and begged Richard to spare him.

Alicia's heart pounded. Blood rushed in her ears. She was quick to tap her wrists together and her men made short work of liberating the Dutch crew of their pistols and blades and tying everyone to the masts. Then she and her men swept the ship of what they could carry back to the *Mist*.

Once they were away, Alicia's legs turned to something akin to steamed pudding. Her men congratulated her on a fine shot and pounded Richard on the back in admiration for securing the captain like he did. Tippy was holding a wounded arm. His sleeve was bright with blood, but he brushed off any concern. "A scratch," he huffed.

Hewes was sporting a new hat and a black eye, and Fitz had lost one boot. Other than that, they were safe and whole and singing each other's praises once more. They'd stolen a pile of goods along with the poor crew's breakfast. Loaves of fresh bread and cheese were passed around along with some fine ale. Liam wore a string of cooked sausages about his neck like a minister's stole.

"Are you all right?" Richard pulled up alongside her and wrapped an arm about her waist.

"Yes." She nodded.

Richard stroked her back and frowned. "You're shaking."

"I know."

He gave her a comforting squeeze. "It's perfectly normal to have this kind of reaction to your first battle experience. You should expect a bit of shock to linger. Regret. Guilt. Some men have nightmares."

Alicia shook her head. "I'm not in any kind of trauma. I'm fine. I have no guilt. He fired on me first."

"Still, it's jarring to the system when you witness your first hit. The sight of so much blood can make you lightheaded."

Alicia couldn't tell him that what she was feeling was far from remorse. She wasn't lightheaded. In fact, she'd never been so energized in her life. The whole scene, while frightening, was at the same time invigorating. Her blood still rushed through her veins. Yes, she would most likely remember the man's screams. Better that than if he'd been silent. "I didn't kill the man."

"No, but there's a good chance he'll be dancing on a tree for the rest of his days."

Alicia laid a hand over top of her pistol. "Cookie's gun." She lifted a shoulder. "Only fitting, don't you think that the pistol of a pirate with a peg leg, passes his peg on to another?"

Richard shot her an odd look. "You sound as if you believe the weapon is haunted by a spirit."

"Haunted? No. But it definitely has a mind of its own."

Chapter 33

"Maybe you should lay low for a few days, no?"

"No. I heard there is a particularly plump French ship preparing to set sail. We've another raid planned for tonight." Alicia hefted the leathered pouch of gold coins she'd received from Jocelyn. She wanted to get back to the *Ruby Mist* and split the money amongst her men. It always made them eager for their next share. So far what they'd captured was quickly sold at a good price. And she was keeping her men much too busy to squander their money and raise suspicions in town. "I would think you'd be happy with our success."

Jocelyn lifted her own leather pouch. "Oh, I am, but I am trying to warn you. You are causing quite a stir. Governor Wilson is looking high and low for the elusive White Pirate." Alicia gave her a wicked smile in response.

Jocelyn continued, "Seems their last raid was one of the governor's own ships and after taking what they wanted, the White Pirate had her crew toss the rest of the cargo overboard to bob and float in the water."

"He does like his tall tales." Alicia shook her head.

Jocelyn feigned a frown. "Thank goodness for insurance, no? Wilson is seething. He is increased patrols all up and down the coast.

He searches for the ship that flies the winged skull. He's obsessed. There have also been rumors that behind the mask, the White Pirate may actually be a woman."

Alicia feigned a gasp, "No, not a woman? Heavens. What has become of the world? Imagine, a woman, sailing about, pirating of all things." Alicia stood. She rubbed a weary hand over her eyes. When was the last time she had more than an hour's sleep?

"Could be worse, the poor woman could have gone into a much more suitable occupation for her fair sex—like whoring."

"You are in a sour mood." Jocelyn tucked her gold away.

"I'm tired. And frustrated. Richard brought news last night that the big transfer has been pushed up to the night of the ball." Alicia gave her an exasperated look. "How am I supposed to be ready for our biggest raid so far after a night of being stuffed into a corset and suffocating in an over-crowded ballroom? There are preparations to make. Details to see to. I can't be in two places at once."

"Exactly. Do not even think about missing the ball," warned Jocelyn. "It is part of his plan. Wilson will be watching very closely to see who is there and who is not. Besides, you will be stunning. I wish you would take a moment and try on your gown. It is *exquise*." Jocelyn kissed her fingertips.

"And white. Don't you think that might draw Wilson's attention and suspicions even more."

"Not if you're in attendance as you should be." She emphasized. "You will be a vision of an English maiden, all purity and innocence. Besides, one would have to be mad to be the White Pirate and be seen in a gown of the same color, no? It would be *la folie*. Pure lunacy." Jocelyn smoothed the back of her hair. "Plus, you will accompany Raine and I. There will be safety in a group. And our combined beauty will blind them to all else."

"Fine, fine. I will be back before midday tomorrow, and you can use your magic to make me gorgeous in time to attend the bloody ball." Alicia raised her hands in surrender. "Then I will strap a pistol to my chest, join my crew, and sail off to dance at a much bigger party."

"You will take off the gown first, Alicia." Jocelyn threatened.

Alicia shot Jocelyn a rebellious look. "If there's time."

Back in the cove, Alicia was grateful as there was no more talk of gowns and balls, unless you were talking about those of the male physique, which, according to her crew, Alicia had a mighty pair. Made of brass. Dumping the governor's shipment in the drink earned her high praise indeed. And obviously earned the governor's ire in return.

Only Simms grumbled about it being a bloody waste, but after receiving his share of the profits, he soon curbed his tongue before Tippy and Fitz offered to curb it for him.

"Where's Mister Dunbar?" Alicia hadn't seen him since she returned.

"Ain't seen 'im, Capt'n," Shrug offered. "No since this morn'n."

"When he shows up, tell him I'm in my cabin."

"Yes, ma'am, Capt'n."

"Get some rest, all of you. Easy on the rum. After tomorrow you can drink as much as you can hold and spend your days lying about in the sun, but I need you to be sharp tonight. We're needing to say, '*Bon Jour*' to a plump French fish."

"Mayhap we be findin' some of that there fancy French swill?" Liam added.

"Possibly. Then when we get back here tomorrow. I want the *Mist* primed and ready. I need every man at his best. If what I've heard coming our way is true, we'll all have full pockets when it's over. Enough to buy your own fancy French swill if you like."

Hours later they were preparing to leave. Still there was no sign of Richard.

"Ready to shove off, Capt'n." Shrug reported.

Concern crept along Alicia's spine. Where was he? "Let's give Mister Dunbar another few minutes. If he's not here by eight bells, we'll have to leave without him."

"There he be, miss." Liam pointed.

Richard pulled his carriage up short, leapt down, and tied off his horse in the tall grass. He hurried toward the Mist, raking a hand through his unbound hair. The tails of his coat looked like wings. Relief filled her.

With long booted strides, he bound down the dock and dropped onto the deck.

"You almost missed your ride, Mister Dunbar. Would be a shame to have you needing to swim to our next battle," Alicia teased.

"I was unavoidably detained. Forgive me." Richard straightened his stock and pushed his hair back once more.

"Prepare to depart." Alicia nodded to Shrug.

"Aye."

As Shrug moved off and the others attended to their duties, Alicia turned back to Richard. His cheeks were flushed as he looked down the length of the ship. Catching his breath, the muscle in his jaw pulsed.

"Is all well with you? I was concerned."

"I'm fine."

"You don't seem fine. Where have you been?"

"Nowhere important." He glanced back at her and gave her arm a reassuring rub before looking out to sea one more. "You're sweet to be concerned, but I'm fine. Truly."

Alicia gave the order to set the mainsail. Richard passed it along to the men and soon they were hitting the open sea. But soon, the air changed. The crisp wind from the north no longer smelled of salt air and sea. The chilled breeze gave Alicia a small shiver.

Richard made his inspection of the ship as was his habit each sail, but tonight he didn't return to stand with her at the helm to help guide her through the necklace of islands making up the outer banks. Something was amiss regardless of his reassurance. She could sense it. He scrubbed at his jaw and kept his gaze firmly out past the stem.

The cold night closed in and wrapped them in stars and the ship sang her song to them. Alicia took a long moment to enjoy the sights and sounds and breath in the night.

Richard finally joined her. "Beautiful night." He slipped an arm about her waist.

"I was just thinking the same." She tucked into his warmth.

Richard spoke into her hair. "Why don't we take the *Ruby Mist* further north. Run by the stars, enjoy the sail. Greet the dawn, and sail home again."

Alicia gave a small shake of her head. "We've plans to raid the French ship *Monique* at dawn. We'll anchor just north of the cut and wait."

"Surely we can let one sail past." He tightened his hold and nuzzled her ear.

"Not this one."

Richard pulled back. "Haven't the good ladies of Black Point had their fill of silks and silver?"

"Evidently not. Jocelyn can't keep up with demand." She shot him a side glance. "Besides, there is something I want to check. Something interesting I learned about the *Monique*."

"What was that?"

Alicia slipped from his embrace. "The *Monique* sailed the same day the *Wind Rider* sailed for Brest."

Richard frowned in confusion. "The *Wind Rider*?"

"Yes, the ship that Ric Robbins, Jocelyn's husband, was supposed to board for France. That same morning, the *Monique* set sail for the gulf coast of Louisiana." Alicia leaned closer and continued. "I may be chasing a shadow, but when Albert Kent signed on to the *Ruby Mist*, he gave me the idea. What if Ric never got on the *Wind Rider*. What if he boarded the *Monique* instead and gave them the wrong name to add to the passenger list?"

"Whatever for?" Richard grimaced. "There's nothing in Louisiana save swamp."

"And a growing population of French settlers."

"Aye. It's where the French are sending their prisoners and prostitutes, from what I've heard. Whatever would be his reason for sailing there?"

She gave a quick shrug. "I have no answers for that. But it's worth a look, don't you think? There has been no word still, and Jocelyn is near her rope's end. I haven't mentioned my idea to her, I don't wish to give her false hope, but when I learned that the *Monique* was our prey tonight, I thought this could be an opportunity to find a clue."

"Why do you care so much about Jocelyn's husband all of a sudden?"

Alicia bit her lip. She'd let the excitement of possibly discovering some information about Ric loosen her tongue. Alicia swore to Jocelyn she would keep Richard out of her personal business. Promised her. *Dammit*. Richard was still convinced Jocelyn had pushed her onto this unholy path, and she'd just given him a key piece to that puzzle.

"Jocelyn is my friend." Alicia tried to brush it all away with the flip of a hand.

But Richard was too clever and not so quick to dismiss their discussion. "Why would a man head south when his own wife believed he was heading east? You said Ric was originally bound for Brest. What business did he have there?"

"I couldn't begin to guess. Forget I mentioned it. It's not important." She flipped her hand again. "A mystery."

Richard gave her a hard look before turning his gaze back toward the ship's bow. "I doubt raiding the *Monique* will give you any answers."

"Perhaps not, but her full hold will more than make up for any disappointment."

Hours later, with the *Mist* in position, they waited. The sun was already on its rise, and the morning mist had all but burned away.

"Where the hell is she?" Alicia kept a glass on the southern horizon, scanning it in continuous sweeps. There had been no sight of the *Monique* or any ship for that matter.

Richard had begun to pace the deck, and the men, too, were growing increasingly impatient. They were ready, had been for hours. Ill temper spread quickly.

"How long we gonna sit 'ere, Capt'n?"

"As long as I say we sit." Alicia's own impatience gave an edge to her voice.

"Men be gettin' a bit antsy. Could be she ain't comin.'"

"I say we wait."

"Aye, aye."

Alicia closed the long brass spyglass with a series of sharp snaps. Richard was at her side again. "Perhaps the men are right. The *Monique* could have altered her plans."

"I don't believe that."

"You've lost your cover, Alicia. The sun is up. The mist is gone."

"And you've done nothing since boarding this ship tonight but try to get me to abandon this raid. Why is that?"

Richard moved behind her and slipped his arms about her waist before whispering in her ear. "It's been a long night. I'm tired. You're clearly exhausted. Let's head back to the cove, dismiss the crew, and you can take me to your cabin, and we'll use the last of our strength to make love to one another."

Alicia opened her glass once more. "You'll not seduce me."

He ran his tongue along the curve of her ear. "Is that a challenge? Shall I make you surrender?" He sucked the lobe into his mouth.

"There she is!" Alicia lowered the glass and pointed to a distant speck on the horizon.

Richard took her spy glass from her and had a look for himself. "From a mast tip you can see that it's the *Monique*?" As soon as the words left his mouth, he caught the colors of the French flag and cursed softly under his breath.

"Prepare the men. Prime the guns." Alicia hastily tied on her mask and pushed her hat down tight upon her head. "She's running full. We'll not have the advantage, but she's riding low and slow even hanging all her cloth. If we can bring down some of that sail, we'll be able to come about and board." Alicia headed toward the helm.

"If they don't decide to fire on us first." Richard continued to watch the *Monique* close the distance between them.

"I'm willing to take that chance." Alicia turned back toward the crew. "Mister Kent, time to see if you're as good a shot as you claim."

The *Monique* drew closer, and Alicia had the men hang back until the very last moment when she gave the signal for full sail and the attack was on.

Kent was loaded and stationed at the swivel gun in the stern. The other three starboard guns would deliver the first hit, however. Without the crew to reload those guns, the *Mist* had to keep moving. The plan was to strike midship forward, overtake, and have Kent take down the front mast as they passed.

If needed, they could drop back and use the port cannon, but they'd never recover their speed that way and the other ship would be in the perfect position to return fire and end them.

"Pull her as close as you dare." Richard joined her at the wheel. "On my signal, straighten her. As soon as we hit, swing the ship wide to port then hard to starboard. If Kent misses, we'll end up sliced in half."

"He won't miss."

"So much for going in quiet." Richard shot her a glance before looking over his shoulder and manning his position.

"Fire when ready, Mister Dunbar!"

Alicia's blood ran high as she manned the wheel and waited. Richard knew the timing of this maneuver better than anyone. She looked back at Kent. "He won't miss," she repeated. "He won't miss."

Chapter 34

"Bloody hell!" Richard hung on to the rigging as the recoil from Kent's shot gave a kick to Alicia's hard starboard turn.

Kent hadn't missed. His shot shattered the main spar and crippled the forward mast. On the deck of the *Monique*, men fought the collapse of heavy canvas and the tangle of rope. The *Ruby Mist* had struck so fast, they hadn't had a chance to get to their guns, let alone fire them.

The ship pulled beneath him, cutting through the water crossing in front of the injured ship so close, he could almost kiss the maidenhead. The men scrambled to slow the *Mist*. At this rate they'd over run her. The *Monique* had time to man their starboard guns and returned fire. Their first shot flew wide, but the second crippled the windlass and blew a hole in the starboard rail.

The men began firing into the smoke. Tippy caught the third gunner with a shot to the thigh and Hewes took down another man.

Alicia held the turn too long and the *Mist* scraped along the hull of the *Monique* with a hideous grating sound. The men hung on through the jarring impact but wasted no time in throwing the boarding ladder across the tight span and jumping into the battle. Richard and Alicia soon joined them.

The crew of the *Monique* fought back, however. Richard took down one man only to turn to find another ready to fire a blunderbuss in his face. "Fuck…"

A shot came from behind him. So close, the blast set his ear ringing, but the man before him took the hit to his shoulder, was thrown back onto the deck, screaming, and wouldn't be hoisting the heavy blunderbuss any time soon. Richard spun to find Alicia at the end of a smoking pistol braced on her forearm.

"Fuck…" Richard bit out again at the quick flash of her grin before she shoved her gun into her baldric and pulled her sword.

Richard did the same and yanked Alicia behind him, so they were positioned back-to-back.

Ahead of them, Liam knocked out the captain of the *Monique* with the hilt of his cutlass. The fight quickly went out of those members of the *Monique* crew still standing. The battle had been won. Tippy grabbed a man by his shoulder and punched him in the face, to emphasize the fact.

Alicia leapt from behind Richard, tapped her wrists, and with sword raised, left the crew of the *Ruby Mist* to secure the deck. Richard followed her and caught up with her in the captain's quarters where she was having a standoff with a young cabin boy wielding a small blade.

"I won't hurt you, but I will if I have to." She placated the boy. She repeated herself in French.

Richard wasted no time and grabbed the boy's wrist and plucked the knife from his fingers. He pointed the blade at the wide-eyed boy and simply shook his head when the boy made to bolt.

Alicia frowned, "Don't hurt him, he's just a child."

"A child that would stab you in the heart if you gave him half a chance."

She began rummaging through the captain's desk and pulled a leathered log from a drawer. Opening a small cache on the desk, she gasped, closed it, and tucked it under an arm.

"What?" He shot a glance back and forth between her and the boy.

"Later." Adding an ornate boxed sexton to the items in her arms, she pushed past him. "I've got what I came for, and then some. Let's go."

Richard backed out, grabbing another small chest on his way. He closed the door and took the boy's knife and wedged it firmly into the lock.

On deck, the crew of the *Ruby Mist* hauled boxes and crates over the ladder to their own decks. In no time, they were saying, "*Merci beaucoup*" to the *Monique* and were away.

Shrug inspected the battle damage done to the ship while the rest were busy celebrating their good fortune once again.

Richard was at the helm. The ship was wounded but not critically.

"Two cracked ribs, and a break in te plankin' on the starboard afta comin' in hard. We be bracin' te ribs now, and bailin.' Got the sea to keep te her side of the hull fer the time bein.' Starboard rail be a right bloody mess. Took out te cathead an' te windlass be done. What I ken tell, te anchor fell 'alf way wit te blast. Lost the devil's claw. Gonna have te haul it by hand most like."

"And the men?" asked Alicia.

"Nary a scratch. A stitch here 'n there."

"See what you can do about shoring up that rail. I don't want anyone falling overboard. As for the anchor, Is the windlass beyond fixing?

"Aye."

"But once we've raised anchor, we can secure it without the cathead?" ask Alicia.

"Oh, Aye, Capt'n. Just be takin' a bit more muscle."

With so much at stake on tonight's raid, Alicia was almost afraid to ask. "So, there's no reason why we can't sail later tonight?"

"Don't see why not. Bit of patch 'n spit. She be bruised, but she still be floatin.'"

"Before we make the cut, we'll have to get the anchor raised and set, or we'll never get through the sound." Richard added.

Shrug nodded, "Take a bit o' time once we drop sail."

"Fine," decided Alicia. "Mister Dunbar, set course to take us back to the cut, we'll stop there and secure the anchor."

Richard scrubbed at his chin and frowned.

Alicia raised a palm at his hesitation. "Did you have another suggestion?"

His frown increased. "No."

She smiled. "Then it's settled."

Between congratulatory toasts of rum, the crew did its best with what was on hand to "patch n' spit" the *Mist*. The men's mood was high and contagious. Once they had the matter of the anchor settled, and the ship back at her dock, Alicia could hang up her captain hat and spend the afternoon turning herself from pirate to pampered socialite. But as soon as she was able, she'd be back, checking her weapons and setting out once again.

Less than a league from the inlet that would give them access through the barrier islands of the Outer Banks and bring them into the sound, Alicia gave the order to drop all sails, and bring the *Ruby Mist* to a slow stop so the men could wrestle the crippled windlass and secure the anchor.

While the others heaved at the load, Liam struggled with a bent gypsy. Hewes hand fed the gathering warp inch by inch past the gears. The sun beat down strong, sweat glistened on straining muscles. It was slow work without the windlass. Alicia joined in the pull.

The sound of cannon fire erupted off their port bow. Followed by another, and another.

Tippy called out. "The bloody patrol!"

"Who invited those bastards?" spit Hewes.

The warning shots fell short, but it was only a matter of time before the galleon barreling toward them aimed true and blew the ship to splinters. They were dead in the water.

"Sails! Now!" cried Alicia.

"Can ye hold it?" Shrug yelled at Liam. The big man nodded, wide-eyed as the others raced to raise all the canvas they could. The deck turned chaotic. Men shouting. Richard ran to man the helm. If anyone could get them past the governor's patrol it was him. Alicia threw all her weight into hauling on a bunt line when she saw Hewes trip.

His foot caught in the warp near the end where it secured to the heavy anchor chain. Reaching out to catch himself, he stumbled against Liam. The jolt caused him to lose his grip. The rope wrapped tight around Hewes' ankle and yanked him overboard after the falling anchor. He was there one second and gone the next.

Liam cried out and tried to reach into the windlass to stop the anchor's plunge. The gears caught his arm and pulled it into the mechanism. His screams pieced the air.

Shrug rushed to shove a belay pin between the teeth to keep the gears from crushing Liam's arm. "Cut the warp! Cut it!"

Liam shook his head in panic. "No! Hewes!"

"Man's done! Ye'll lose yer bloody arm!" screamed Shrug. "Cut it!"

Cannon fire erupted again. Tippy drew his blade and hacked at the anchor warp. With a snap, the rope cut clean, and its end flew over the edge. Liam slumped against Shrug holding his battered, bloodied arm against his chest and wailed.

A shot fell less than a meter from their hull. Alicia pushed Shrug aside and gathered Liam in her arms as she barked, "Go! Full Sails. Now! Richard, get us the hell out of here!"

Spinning the wheel, Richard pointed the *Mist* straight for the galleon. The wind caught the rising canvas, and the ship began to leap through the water. Still there was no chance to run hard to starboard. The barrier islands of the banks were notorious for catching unsuspecting ships along the underwater shoals there. But to run wide to port, would be suicide. The galleon's guns would blow them out of the water.

In her arms, Liam shook as shock took hold of his body. He was losing so much blood. The coppery smell stung her nose. It soaked through her clothing. Even if they managed to get past the imminent annihilation from the galleon and made it in one piece back to Wakefield's Cove, Liam would be dead before they got there. Alicia laid him on the deck, tore the sleeve from her shirt and used the length to staunch some of the flow by tying it tight as she could around his upper arm. Shrug was back by his side. "Stay with him," she ordered.

The forward guns of the warship exploded once more, but with the *Mist* at full speed, and dead straight on their path, the shots went wide and long.

"Take cover!" Richard cried from the helm.

Alicia ran back to join him. "What the bloody hell are you doing?"

"If I can thread her in fast and close, past those port guns, they'll overshoot. We can make it to the cut before they can come about."

"What about the shoals, they'll rip the bloody keel off the ship."

"It's the risk we have to take. We don't have a chance in hell of making it otherwise. It's the only way." Concern etched his face. Richard gave her a sharp look. "Your decision, Captain."

Alicia set her jaw. She watched the patrol's warship growing larger by the second and looked back at Richard. She ground her teeth and nodded. "Do it."

Richard dropped his chin and tightened his grip on the wheel. "Get below."

"Hell, no."

"Coming in close, they will be shooting at us from the railings. Get below."

Alicia shook her head. "I'm not leaving you."

Richard jerked his head. "Then, at least get below the rail."

"What about you?"

"Someone has to keep us off the shoals." Richard shot her a grin.

Alicia ran a hand down his arm. The muscles were tense and hard beneath the fabric of his shirt. "If we get through this—"

He gave her a shove with his shoulder. "Tell me later. Go."

Alicia hesitated, gripping a fistful of his sleeve.

"Go," he barked.

From where she crouched, hidden below the rail, she did something she hadn't done since she was a child. She prayed.

Chapter 35

Richard gripped the pegs of the wheel so tight he feared they would snap off in his hands. He had to get them out of this. He'd been afraid they'd cross paths with the governor's patrol since they set sail but voicing those concerns would have put them all in greater danger.

Just don't let me lose her on the shoals.

The *Mist* flew as each of the sails caught every bit of power. The rigging screamed. The wind whistled past his ears. His heart threatened to beat its way out of his throat.

As he had feared the maneuver to thread the *Mist* between the banks and the war ship made them vulnerable to drawing fire from the deck. Shots erupted as they began their pass. Balls splintered railings, pins and barrel rims. Punched holes in their sails. One shattered a peg on the wheel. It was like running a deadly gauntlet. Richard ducked and bobbed as all hell broke loose around him. Tippy, Simms, and Fitz popped their heads above the rails to return fire. Alicia motioned for Kent to man the swivel gun in the stern and soon the *Ruby Mist* wasn't the only one to sustain damage.

And then they were past. With their speed combined with the speed of the galleon heading in the opposite direction, they flew by the great ship and were soon out of range. Richard swung to port and into safer water and was able to reach the cut through and into the sound before the patrol could begin to turn their massive ship about and continue its chase.

Alicia was quick to set the men to task with assessing damages and what was needed to make quick repairs. "When we reach the cove, I'll take Liam to Jocelyn's. She'll know a doctor to see to him."

Richard fingered a slice in his jacket sleeve caused, no doubt by flying debris. "I'll go with you."

Shrug still held Liam. He was unconscious. His arm still bled. "I be goin,' too."

"No, I need you both here." Alicia laid a hand on Liam's forehead. "I promise I'll take good care of him." She handed Shrug a bottle of rum. "Get as much of this into him as you can."

"Aye." As he took the bottle from her hand he frowned and looked down at his friend. "Bit of bad luck that patrol bein' where it be. Can't rid te naggin' on me head that 'em damn bastards ken we was comin.'"

Alicia returned his frown. "An unfortunate coincidence."

Coincidence? Richard hoped to hell it was. He was playing a dangerous game by digging deeper into Jocelyn's shady dealings. If someone had linked him to the *Ruby Mist* or gotten suspicious about his questions. Did they still link the ship to Jocelyn and her husband Ric? Link it to the White Pirate? Nay, he'd been careful. He would bet his life on it. There was no chance he'd led the patrol to them. No chance. He'd never put Alicia in that kind of jeopardy. Never.

Alicia's added interest in the *Monique* had spurred even more questions, however. How deep was she involved with Jocelyn, and did she have any idea of how far reaching and serious this could be? But even more, after what happened today, did he dare attempt to discover the answers and possibly stir up more curiosity and attention?

"We owe Mister Dunbar a debt of gratitude," added Alicia.

Gratitude?

"Aye." Several of the men agreed with their captain. "Fine bit of sailin' getting' us past them guns." "And them shoals." "Aye, saved our arse." "Woulda all ben joinin' Hewes, poor bastid."

At the mention of Hewes' name, hats and scarves were removed and heads bowed.

"After we set sail tonight, I'll be saying a few words for Mister Hewes." Alicia looked back at Liam. "A terrible accident. Let's get docked and tied down tight. Without our anchor, run line fore and aft. Then help me move Liam as quickly as we can to the cart. He's lost a lot of blood, and I don't plan to be grieving two men tonight."

The men made short work of docking and following Alicia's orders.

"Are you certain you don't want me to come with you?" Richard ran a hand over her shoulders.

"No. I'll be fine. As I said, I need you here more. None of our damage is critical, but I need the *Mist* shored up tight. We can't risk any more accidents. I'll be back just before we set sail. After I see to him." She tipped her chin toward Liam. "Jocelyn insists I accompany her and Raine to a social gathering. After everything, it feels superficial and ridiculous, but it will benefit us in the long run." She dropped a quick kiss upon his lips. "I'll be back as soon as I can get away."

"Bones not broken. Flesh torn. Maybe muscle." Raine examined Liam's arm.

The big man had faded in and out of consciousness on the way back to town. It took all three of them, Alicia, Jocelyn, and Raine, to help him out of the cart and up into Jocelyn's apartment before he collapsed on the sofa.

"Can you mend him?" Alicia's stomach roiled at the sight of Liam's wound.

Raine gave her a look of pure annoyance. "Do I have to?"

"Yes." Alicia snapped, then softened, "Please."

"I'm not sitting with this ox all night waiting on the fever. I have a new gown and a ball to attend."

"You do not have to play the nurse," injected Jocelyn. "I shall have one of the Harper girls stay with him. They owe me a favor."

Raine sighed. "Fine. I'll need yarrow and willow bark."

Relief washed over Alicia. "Whatever you need."

"Yarrow and willow bark." Raine's dark eyes flashed their impatience.

Jocelyn and Alicia gathered the needed herbs and supplies that Raine demanded and gave her room to do her work. Alicia moved to the table and dropped into a chair. She'd retrieved the logbook and cache she'd secured from the *Monique* and laid them on the table. Jocelyn added more water to the kettle and stirred up the embers of the fire.

She looked over her shoulder at Alicia and waved a finger at her. "Is any of that blood yours?"

Alicia looked down at the gruesome condition of her once white blouse and pale trousers. Dark bloody patches soaked the cloth and feathered to a sickly pink where she'd held Liam in her lap. "No, it's all his." She looked back at Liam as Raine laid compresses into his wound. "I lost a man today." Her voice sounded small. The scene of Hewes being pulled overboard played over and over in her mind.

"It happens quite often in your business," assured Jocelyn.

"I know." Alicia nodded, resigned. "It was just that it happened so quickly. He was there, I blinked, and he was gone." She snapped her fingers.

"I think sometimes it is better that way. Quick. No pain, no anguish." Jocelyn straightened. "What is all of that?" She swept her hand toward the table.

"This is the log from the *Monique*.' Alicia patted the thick leather-bound book. Silver mountings adorned its corners. "I stole it from the captain's quarters."

"Not much to sell. The silver could possibly be melted down. Why would you steal something so worthless?"

"I didn't steal it to sell. I'm following a hunch." Alicia opened the hasp and flipped through several page of parchment. She used her finger to sweep the pages although what she was looking for, she didn't know.

"A man signed on to the *Ruby Mist* and gave me a long story about signing the ship's articles with a false name. It started me thinking. I checked the shipping schedule for the day Ric left. The *Monique* sailed the same day as the *Wind Rider*, but she sailed south where the *Wind Rider* sailed toward Brest. I'm wondering if Ric could have boarded the *Monique* instead."

"I have already questioned the harbor master. You should not have wasted your time. Ric's name was on the passenger list for the *Wind Rider*."

"That doesn't mean he got on. Or stayed on." Alicia insisted. "What if he was trying to disappear? What if he thought he was being watched or followed?"

Jocelyn brushed her questions aside with the flip of a hand. "Then why has he not contacted me?"

"To protect you. Perhaps he's afraid to send word should whoever it is still be watching?"

"And why would he go south when our Beau is in danger in France?"

Alicia looked up at Jocelyn and shook her head. "I don't know. I can't begin to guess. Perhaps it is foolish to even ponder, but when one of my men, Kent, came aboard, his situation put the thought into my head, and I had to check. Even if it comes to naught." Alicia hated seeing the pain in Jocelyn's eyes. "We've had no leads. No word. We should follow any possibility, shouldn't we?"

"*Oui.*" Jocelyn looked at the logbook and chewed the edge of her thumbnail. "Look for the name *Henri*."

"Henry?"

"*Oui,* it is Ric's real name. Ric is short for Ricochet. A nickname he earned on the *Scarlet Night*. His given name is *Henri*.

Alicia scanned the pages again, looking for an entry with the first or last name of Henry. "We may be wasting our time."

"Look anyway. Is there no…"

"*Henri!*" Alicia heart leapt until she saw the last name. "No this isn't him. This is a *Henri Beauchamp.*"

Jocelyn gasped and fell into the chair next to Alicia. She pulled the book from Alicia's grasp. "Where?"

Alicia pointed to the signature. Jocelyn's breath caught. "*Tu l'as trouvé!* You found him…dear God, you found him." She ran shaky fingertips over the signature. "This is in his hand. *Beauchamp* was my name. Before I married. It is where Beau got his name." She clutched the book to her chest and gave Alicia a watery smile. "You found him."

"We found where he was." Alicia reminded her. "There still has been no word from him, but at least we know where to start our search."

"It is more than I had a moment ago." She set the log back on the table and hugged her tight. "*Merci, mon ami dieu vous bénisse. Merci. Merci.*"

"Wait to thank me. Save it for the day I bring him home." Alicia patted her on the back.

Jocelyn dabbed a laced handkerchief at her eyes. She stroked the logbook like it was suddenly made of gold. "I have woefully underestimated you, *mon cheri.*"

Alicia dragged the wooden cache closer. "Aye, you have." She flipped open the lid to reveal a treasure of jewelry. Gold chains, pearls, precious gems set in silver and gold. Rings. Ear fobs.

Bracelets. "We've a ball to get ready for. I saw these and thought they might come in handy."

Chapter 36

Their hired carriage pulled up in front of the governor's estate. A footman was quick to open the door and help the three women disembark.

"I don't see why we needed to hire a carriage when we could have perfectly walked here." Alicia argued.

Raine scoffed, "In these shoes, I think not."

"Stop it, the two of you." Jocelyn smoothed a long lace cuff and gave a final pinch to her cheeks. Her sapphire gown was simple elegance of a woman befitting her age but was trimmed and adorned with the finest deep cream-colored lace money could buy. They all wore their hair swept up and styled upon their heads, but as unwed young ladies, Raine and Alicia wore few adornments in their hair, Jocelyn's crown of curls, however, flew feathers and matching lace and a large sapphire clip. Her ears were unadorned, but a necklace, courtesy of the captain of the *Monique*, dripped an untold wealth of diamonds and amethysts into the allure of her cleavage.

Raine was, in a word, stunning in her deep red gown. She looked almost regal. While her stomacher and underskirt bore little embellishments, her split over skirt had been embroidered with golden threads and ended in a fanned train that shimmered in her wake. Her beautiful warm skin glowed in the candlelight as her neckline dipped low. Tiny rubies, nestled in her dark shining hair, caught the light within the shimmer of twists and braids. Teardrops of gold mounted rubies dripped from her ears.

"You should be thanking me instead of complaining." Jocelyn smoothed a wayward strand of Alicia's hair. "Those skirts would not have survived two feet without being soiled."

"Now you sound like my mother." She held Jocelyn's quick gaze. "Soiled skirts were a great concern the last time we spoke."

"Ah, your wedding day." Jocelyn gave her a pitying smile.

"Yes, but my gown that day made me feel like a satined warship. This gown…" Alicia looked down and ran a hand along her stomacher, "is simply the most beautiful thing I've ever worn."

"*Oui*, my dressmaker outdid herself." Jocelyn flipped a bit of lace.

The white silk of Alicia's gown fairly glowed in the moonlight, but it was the lace overlay that made it truly unique. The bodice was plain, the sleeves a simple puff gathered beneath each elbow, but the neckline dipped off each shoulder and dripped with creamy lace pieces in the shape of leaves. Larger pieces of lace in the same shape ringed the top of her skirt and petaled the full length to form a soft train which fluttered past the hems. Each laced leaf lifted slightly in the breeze as she walked. The pale off-white of the leaves complimented and softened the brightness of the white silk beneath. Overall, the effect was lovely and light.

"You are a vision of purity."

Alicia wore combs in her hair decorated with pearls the size of spring peas. Long loose curls caught behind her right ear and trailed over one shoulder. A matching strand of pearls fell just past her collar bones.

"It is too bad your pirate lover cannot see you." Raine teased as they entered the crowded ballroom. "He'd think you were once again a virgin."

"Hush," Jocelyn hissed. "Comments like that could get us all hung."

Raine held up her hand in surrender and disappeared into the crowd.

Jocelyn arranged the fall of Alicia's curls. "Now, your only goal tonight is to make certain Wilson sees you."

"No." Alicia lowered her voice. "My only goal is to get out of here in time to get back to the cove. Do you think Liam will be all right with that Harper woman?"

"He will be fine. Do not worry. Raine did a fine job stitching his arm. The willow bark tea will keep the fever at bay. With any luck he will sleep like a babe until morning." Jocelyn clutched at her sleeve and whispered. "For the next few hours, you are not a captain. You are a lady of sophistication and breeding."

"But I feel naked without my pistol," Alicia teased and widened her eyes. "Cookie's pearl handles would match my gown beautifully, don't you think?"

Jocelyn glared at her. "You and Raine are determined to exasperate me this evening. Go. I need to find our hostess and compliment her on all the fine silver and china on display tonight."

"I imagine you'll find her very close to the puddings table. She bought enough sugar in the past week to ice six dozen cakes and the governor himself."

"She does have a fondness for sweets." Jocelyn patted her hand. "Find the governor and be sure to tell him how delicious the food looks. The pantry budget for this party must be turning his hair greyer than his wig."

Alicia scanned the room. There was quite a military presence here this evening. British wool must be stifling to wear at a ball, she mused. Her usual method of disappearing into the background and listening unobserved was hampered by her gown tonight. Alicia was attracting much more attention than usual. She prayed Jocelyn was right and that she resembled more purity than pirate in their eyes.

"We had her this very morning. Caught her bobbing along. Fell right into our snare." A young lieutenant boasted within her hearing.

His companion snorted. "But you lost her."

"Saw us, set sail and vanished. Not a bloody trace. Like the sea opened a hole and swallowed her," explained the lieutenant.

"So, the White Pirate is really a white witch? Is that what you're claiming?" ribbed another.

Alicia's jaw tightened. These were the men who attacked them. Fired on her ship. Caused Hewes to die and Liam to almost lose his arm. Fury raised her heat and had her reaching for her pistol, but her fingers met silk and lace instead. One of the men caught the gesture and looked in her direction. She quickly pressed her hand against her heart and feigned indignance. "Did you gentlemen just call me a white witch?"

Horrified shock marred each handsome face. "No, milady, certainly not. We were discussing something as far from you as night is to day. You are far too beautiful to ever be thought of as a witch. Nay, we were talking about the White Pirate."

"White Pirate? I've heard such incredible stories." She leaned close, giving the lieutenant a full glimpse of improper cleavage. "Is it true she's a woman?"

The lieutenant pulled his gaze away from her chest and cleared his throat. "That is the rumor."

"And you say you were bested by her this very day?" Alicia blinked up at him.

The man's companion laughed and quickly covered it with a cough. The lieutenant shot him a heated stare before returning his gaze to Alicia. "As I was telling my friends, she simply slipped past us. The ship is tiny, but fast. Like a slippery little minnow." He held his finger a small measure from his thumb. "But fear not, milady, she'll not be escaping again. We'll be using a much smaller net next time."

"Or setting her out as bait," joked another.

The lieutenant raised a hand. "This is certainly not the conversation we should be having when someone as lovely as you grace our company. May we offer to get you a drink? Or perhaps beg a dance?"

"No, thank you, gentlemen, I must defer. I see my cousin just there." Alicia flipped a finger toward a group of women. "I promised to bring her a bit of cake."

The Lieutenant also pointed to a point further down the hall. "The table groaning under its own weight has cake of every description, milady."

"Thank you." She smiled and gave a small tip of her head. "Gentlemen."

The men all gave her a proper bow before she left. As soon as her back was to them, she ground her teeth. *Tiny minnow! Use me as bait, will you? Is that smaller net what you use to carry your balls? We'll see who's laughing at whom come morning.*

Alicia reined in her temper as she made her way through the crowded room. Heat flushed her cheeks. There were too many people. The smell of so many bodies doused in far too much perfume was making her nauseous. Pirates smelled just as bad, but they rarely used some flowery stench to cover their scent.

Combine that with the smells of food. Table after table filled with everything imaginable to eat. Roasted meats and ripe cheeses. Breads and plates of spring vegetables. It was all utterly excessive. Trays of crystal held wines. This was costing the governor a bloody fortune.

It was then that she saw Governor Wilson. Wigged and ribboned, he resembled a peacock in his garish coat, with a wake of peachicks falling into step with him. More military men. Majors and Generals. And dignitaries. The town's own fathers. He was surrounded by only the highest-ranking men.

Alicia stopped before him and smiled. "Governor Wilson, how handsome you look this evening. The food, decorations, and flowers…everything is sublime. I must say, your lovely wife has outdone herself. It is all simply splendid."

"Gladys will be most happy to hear that. Mistress….Mistress…." He gave her a shrug when he couldn't conjure her name from his memory.

"Steele, milord. Alicia Steele." She gave a small dip.

"Ah, yes, you're a guest of Madam Robbins."

"Yes, milord."

"A recent visitor to our fair shores."

Alicia feigned a smile. "Indeed, milord. I'm honored you remember me."

"Of course, my dear. It is lovely to finally make your acquaintance. You should meet someone." He peered over his shoulder scanning his peachicks. "Another new visitor. Arrived not long after you, I believe. Gladys thought the two of you would have something in common. That perhaps you, two, should meet. I'm happy to make the introductions." Governor Wilson searched behind him. "He was just here a moment ago. Did he disappear for yet another drink? Oh, there you are. Richard, come here." He waved his hand, beckoning him closer. "There is someone I want you to meet."

Richard? Alicia's heart skipped at hearing the name. Surely there was more than one Richard in Black Point. Her Richard was at this moment aboard the *Ruby Mist* overseeing repairs of the cathead, preparing for tonight's raid. Her Richard loathed balls. *Her* Richard came through the clutch of peachicks laughing at something someone said and raised a glass to them as he passed. Raised a glass. *Raised a glass?*

Shock registered on his face upon seeing her, but he was quick to hide it along with the glass of amber liquid he held to his lips. Straightening his spine, he tucked his drink behind the hip of his fine wool breeches.

Time slowed. Through the blurred haze that edged Alicia's vision, the governor introduced them. "Richard, I want to introduce you to Mistress Alicia Steele. She's new to our shores as are you. Mistress Steele, may I present Lord Richard Dunbar."

Lord Dunbar? A buzzing sounded in her ears. Richard's gaze held tight to hers. It was the only thing keeping her feet nailed to the floor. He extended his hand, and she looked down to see that through no conscious action of her own, she extended her hand to meet his.

"Mistress Steele, did he say? It is a pleasure to make the acquaintance of such a beautiful lady. Might I say you are the loveliest woman in the room." He lifted her hand and kissed the back of her knuckles. She couldn't feel her fingers.

"Lord Dunbar," she mouthed. Did words come out?

The air around them stood still along with her heart. "Look at her. She's utterly besotted." The governor beamed. "Just as Gladys predicted." He looked back at his clutch. "Now there will be no living with the woman. She'll be matchmaking for every eligible man in town from now on." Laughter followed him as he pounded Richard on the back. "You're welcome, you lucky man." He moved his group past.

"Alicia?" Richard whispered.

At the hearing of her name, Alicia yanked her hand from his grasp, turned, and rushed out of the ballroom, pushing past people in her rush. *Air.* She needed air. The misty edges of her vision turned dark. She could hear her crumbling heart pumping in her ears.

"Al—Mistress Steele, a moment. Please." Richard called for her to stop.

She lifted her hems to run. Jocelyn reached out to stop her. "Alicia, what?"

Alicia never slowed. Back outside, she didn't pause to find Jocelyn's carriage but ran off on her own toward the lace shop.

Pressing a hand to her chest, she stifled a sob. *Lord Dunbar?* Lord Dunbar! Bloody bastard played her. Again! And she had fallen for his charms. Believed his lies. Handed him her heart. Had he lied about everything? Days of questions not answered, coincidences brushed aside. Richard disappearing for long lengths of time. It all made sense now. But why? What was he trying to gain? Her mind tangled with sorting one lie from another trying to make sense of it.

Alicia didn't stop. Circling the building, she hoped like hell the wagon was still waiting. She'd left the horse hitched so she could leave as soon as the ball was over, and the ball wasn't the only thing over for her. In her beautiful gown, she climbed aboard, flicked the reins and set the horses racing in the direction of Wakefield's Cove.

Only one thought broke through the chaos in her brain. *I'm a bloody, blind, naïve fool.* Alicia yelled her frustration into the night, startling the horse. She hung onto the reins like they were the last threads of her sanity as the beast tore through the night.

Chapter 37

Richard lost her. He searched the crowd. Alicia shouldn't be too hard to spot; she was the most stunning woman in the bloody room in her white gown. It wasn't the shock of seeing her that stole his breath. She was a vision. *Where the hell is she?*

He tugged at his cravat. The room was stifling. Why didn't she tell him she was coming to the governor's ball? They could have saved them both from a good measure of shock. Now he had to track her down and explain why he wasn't at the *Ruby Mist* like she expected and why he was suddenly so friendly with that arrogant bore, Wilson.

After the ambush of the patrol earlier, he wasn't about to risk all their lives again. He needed to find out what Wilson's plan was for the Watch that night so he wouldn't make the mistake of being in their line of fire again. What he found out, however, would not be good news to Alicia. She needed to give up the idea of tonight's raid. Regardless of the wealth on those ships, it was just too dangerous. Their usual plan of slipping in and slipping out was not going to work this time. There was too much at stake and too many after the prize.

By all accounts, the seas were going to be a very busy place tonight. The patrols had been increased three-fold, according to Wilson, and there were rumors spreading through the ranks that

Lucifer had been spotted further north than was his reign. The collective military might at the ball expressed their concern that news of the lucrative shipment had reached the *Devil's Breath*, and Lucifer was coming to take his due. "God help any patrol that tried to stop him."

Or any headstrong, gorgeous, vision-in-white pirates, either.

He raised on his toes and scanned the room once more. Where the hell had she gone?

"She left." Richard spun to find Raine at his side.

The deep red of her gown suited her. "Is that you, Raine? I almost didn't recognize you without your trusty blade or your usual sneer.

She lifted her chin and narrowed her gaze. "My blade is lashed to my thigh. Would you like me to show it to you?"

"Another time perhaps." He forced a smile. "Where did Alicia go?"

Raine lifted a shoulder. "I have no idea. I only know that she raced out of here as if the Devil himself was chasing her."

"Or she decided to give chase to him herself," Richard muttered.

"Excuse me?" She raised an eyebrow.

"Nothing." He flashed her another grin. "You know how much I adore our little chats, and as delightful as you are, I need to go find her."

Outside there was still no sign of her. How had she moved so quickly? The evening was humid, and Richard stripped out of his heavy jacquard coat and strangling neckcloth as he made his way back to the lace shop. The door was locked. No light shown in her rooms, but a quick check out back confirmed his worst fear. The cart was gone. She was on her way back to the cove.

The night closed in, fog crept in off the water, and the *Mist* was lit with various lanterns when Richard dismounted the horse he'd stolen from Jocelyn's neighbor. Try as he might, among his other faults, he was now a verified horse thief as well as a pirate. But the cart was there, so Alicia was here, and he still had time to talk her out of tonight's folly. He tossed his coat and baldric aside as he dropped onto the deck.

Around the ship, the crew continued to tighten up the minor repairs to her rails and ribs. Simms and Fritz were fashioning a temporary anchor out of stones and chain. Shrug pounded on the windlass with a hammer.

Richard never slowed. Spoke to no one.

Making his way aft, he gave a quick knock before twisting the wrought handle of the door. His shoulder rammed into the wood, stopping him mid stride. He tried the handle again. Had she locked him out? Richard pounded on the cabin door. "Alicia, it's me, open the door."

To his utter surprise, she did.

Standing in little but her corset, she turned her back on him to yank on her britches and began to pull the pearl combs and pins from her hair.

The air in the cabin fairly sparked with her anger. A muscle pulsed in her jaw. The delicate, lace-petalled gown was discarded on the bed. She'd ruined the hems. Her silence screamed at him.

"I'm sorry," Richard rushed to explain. "When you said you had a social engagement, I had no idea you were going to the ball tonight. I wish I'd known. You completely caught me by surprise. Stole my very breath. You were so gorgeous." He moved to the bed and fingered one of the lace leaves of her gown. "You're positively stunning in white, Alicia. Do you know I've dreamt about seeing you in a white gown since we spoke in the garden on your wedding day?"

"Don't you mean the day you quit drinking?" She'd unlaced her corset and tossed it aside. With her hair down and loose and her naked to the waist, she was yet another vision of stunning. The perfume of her soap filled his senses. Had she not been fit to strangle him he might have been tempted to sweep her into his arms.

"Yes." The word cracked. "The day I quit drinking."

"I don't believe you." She planted her hands on her hips. "That was hardly strawberry punch I saw in your glass tonight."

Richard gave a short laugh, "I was only dancing that brandy around the ballroom. It never touched my lips."

The look on her face said she didn't trust his explanation. "Wilson told me you'd gone to refresh your drink."

Richard flung a hand toward the door. "Alicia, I swear to you, the only one drinking from my glass tonight was Gladys' palm tree." He put his hand over his heart in pledge and gave her his most charming smile. "I may have killed it."

She was not charmed in the least and leveled him with a glare. "Like you killed Hewes."

"What?" he jerked as if she'd struck him. "No. I had nothing to do with Hewes's death."

"Oh, no?" Alicia yanked her shirt over her head and settled it on her shoulders and down over her hips. "You knew that patrol was waiting for us earlier today, didn't you?"

Richard sighed and held his arms away from his body. "I didn't know for certain, but I had my suspicions, yes." He raised his hands in surrender. Aye he was guilty on that count. He scrambled to add, "But I got you out of there, didn't I?"

"At the expense of one of my men's lives, and the maiming of another." Her voice rose.

"Wait just a minute," he countered. "You can't blame me for an accident, Alicia."

"I *do* blame you. And just what business do you have with the governor?"

For half a second, Richard thought to lie, but the game was over, he had to tell her the truth. He crossed his arms over his chest and met her heated gaze with his own. "I'm gathering information regarding Jocelyn and her business dealings." At Alicia's dark frown, he rushed to continue. "I used my father's legitimacy to get close to Wilson and his associates because I wanted to know the full extent of Jocelyn's operation."

Alicia's jaw dropped. "So not only have you betrayed me, betrayed my crew, but you're helping Wilson get to Jocelyn?"

He shook his head. "No. I haven't given him any information he didn't already have. Richard jabbed a finger back at the door. "This is so much bigger than you have any notion. I'm convinced Jocelyn is up to no good. She's using you, Alicia. And Raine, the Harpers, and who knows how many others." Before Alicia could utter a single syllable, he raised his hands in surrender again. "But *you* don't want to hear that because she's your friend. Jocelyn has her fingers in more shady business in this town than you have any idea, and Wilson has eyes all over this stretch of coast. He's been watching her ever since Ric disappeared." He mirrored her stance with her hands on her hips. "And just for the record I haven't betrayed you or this crew. I saved your necks earlier. In fact." His voice rose along with his temper. "If you hadn't noticed, I *keep* saving your bloody neck whether you realize it or not."

"How stupid and inept do you think I am?" Alicia ground the words through clenched teeth. "I know exactly what Jocelyn is doing and why. It was *my* idea to pirate for her, not hers." Alice worked on fastening the wide belt about her waist. "Any danger I've put myself in, is my own, and right now your dealings with Wilson make *you* a bigger danger to me and my crew than she is."

"I swear to you, Alicia, I'm no danger to you. Wilson isn't playing me, I'm the one playing him. I'm getting first-hand information that will benefit us in the long run."

"I don't believe you." She got closer and lowered her voice. Her eyes sparked. Icy words fell from her lips "Tell me, were you honest when you were making love to me, or was that a lie too?"

"Alicia…" The verbal slash cut him.

"I'm done listening to you." She slipped her baldric over her head and donned her sword. "My ship is ready to sail, and I have other business to attend to tonight."

"Hold on. Wait." How could he make her believe him? He couldn't let her leave. Not like this. Not with things unsettled between them.

"I said, I'm done. You're dismissed. We're leaving. Without you."

"You can't. That's one of the things I learned tonight. I need to warn you. Wilson has increased the patrol. Three times. You'll never get by them."

"We got past them before." Alicia turned her back on him.

"*I* got us past them before," he snapped. Richard's anger was quick to turn to fear. "I understand you're angry at me, but please you have to listen. Tonight, I also heard rumor that the *Devil's Breath* has expanded its reach. If it's true and if you're lucky enough to make it through the patrols, you'll never get past Lucifer."

Alicia spun on him. "Even if I believed you, which I don't, that's my choice to make, not yours. I'm not listening to rumor, and I no longer need or want your advice." She made to push past him and opened the door.

"Alicia." Richard caught her and held her by the tops of her arms. He fought the urge to shake some sense into her. "You can't go out there tonight. Didn't you hear me, the patrols have been tripled, and if Lucifer is out there, it's bloody suicide. He'll blow you out of the fucking water!"

"Enough!" She snapped. "It's nothing but rumor." Alicia wrenched out of his hold and pushed him away. "How many times do I have to remind you that I am Captain of this ship. *I* make the decisions." Alicia pulled her sword and pointed it at him. "And while I'm busy making those decisions, here's another one. I want you out of my cabin and off my ship. I'm relieving you of your position as my first mate for endangering the safety of this ship and the lives of my crew."

"Alicia…" The blade caught the light. He held his arms wide. "What do I have to say to get you to listen?

"There's nothing you can say that I'll trust. We're done. Move." She pushed the tip of the blade toward him and backed him out of the room. Richard didn't believe she would kill him, but it was obvious she wouldn't hear him no matter what he said. Turning so he wouldn't trip walking backwards, he led her back on deck. In front of the crew, he'd try another tactic.

Once on deck he spoke loud enough for all the men to hear. "You need me, Alicia, admit it. Even the crew knows I'm the only one who could have steered the *Mist* past that patrol today. If you dismiss me now, you don't stand a chance at what's waiting for you out there tonight." At her silence he turned back to her. The men had formed a small band behind her. Richard tossed a hand toward them. "Talk to them. Ask them. If you won't listen to me, perhaps you'll listen to your crew.

Alicia notched her chin. "There are some understandings my crew and I have without speaking."

Sheathing her sword, Alicia turned to the men, she tapped her wrists together, and they descended on him. Richard swung on them cursing, but with five of them and one of him, it was no fight at all. Before he knew it, he was face down on the deck with his arms wrenched behind him. Hauling him to his feet, they dragged him from the ship and off the end of the slip and pulled him into the water. The tide was low, but water still filled his boots.

Fitz now wore his coat and tossed his baldric into the sand. Kent held a rope between two fists.

Cold realization filled more than his boots. *No, not again. She wouldn't!* They were tying him to the bloody dock!

"Alicia," Richard shouted to her as he struggled against the men tying his wrists. The dock post pressed hard against his spine. The wet slip of algae seeped through his breeches to chill his arse. Richard's shoulders burned at the brutal angle in which he was tied. He remembered this burn. It brought him straight back to another dock years ago. Another scene just like this one that was the lowest point of his bloody life. He closed his eyes against the memory and knocked his head back against the post. At least this time he still had his pants.

"Alicia, stop this! Please. Dear God, I love you. I've never lied to you about that. If you trust nothing else, trust that."

Shrug grabbed him by the hair, pulled a knife from his belt and held it to Richard's neck silencing him. There was no question, Shrug would slit his throat if provoked. The blade bit into his skin. Shrug growled into his face. "Mayhap she be done listenin' te yer bullshite. Last crew I be on, Capt'n cut out te tongue of te fuckin' bastard who ratted on te crew."

Richard met the man's stare with his own. "I never ratted on anyone. You've got me all wrong. I'm sorry about Liam and Hewes, but I swear I didn't have anything to do with that patrol."

Alicia came and took the knife from Shrug and ordered the men away. "Back aboard. Make ready to shove off." Her gaze locked with his. The night's breeze caught her hair. The moon turned the golden strands to silver. When they were alone, he tried once more to convince her. "Alicia, you don't have to do this. Please. You must believe me. I would never betray you. I lov—"

She returned Shrug's knife to his throat stopping his words. He saw it then. There in the moonlight Richard saw the truth in her eyes. He whispered to her. "You're not going to cut me or take my tongue, are you? I've hurt you, and I'm sorry, but you love me, Alicia. You can't deny it. You've always loved me."

"I *have* always loved you." She nodded before lifting the knife from his throat and kissing him there. Alicia blazed a trail of slow, hot kisses down the side of his neck. "Since the very first time I saw you. I loved you." Opening the neck of his shirt, she kissed and nipped along his collarbone. A warmth flooded him. The sweet scent of her added to the seduction. His cock tightened the front of his breeches.

Their breath raced as Alicia pulled back to tug the tails of his shirt from his pants. Taking the knife, she slit down the front and slashing at the sleeves, cutting it from his body as she returned to trail a line of kisses over his chest. Her tongue teased the flat of his nipple. The night air was cold, but her mouth on him had his blood running like liquid fire.

They were both panting when Alicia stopped and held his gaze once more. She ran a bold hand over the ridge of his erection before removing his belt.

"Alicia—"

She began unfastening his breeches. "You know, when I first heard about what those pirates did to you that night when they stole back the *Scarlet Night*, I felt so badly for you. Leaving you out there. A proud Lieutenant in the King's Navy. You didn't deserve to be treated like that. Not that night." Alicia finished unfastening the last button and pushed his breeches over his hips and down to float around the tops of his boots. "This night, however, you do."

The cold chill of the night air snatched at his balls and stole the heat of his erection. "Not again, Alicia, for the love of—"

"Don't you *ever* say the word love to me again," she hissed. "You don't get to. Not to me. Not anymore. You don't even know the bloody meaning of the damn word."

"Fine. I'll not say it again. I don't care what you do to me. You can hate me if you must." His teeth started to chatter, and his balls pulled tight to his body to keep from snapping off. "Bloody hell, its fucking freezing." He swore a curse at the moon. "But dammit, Alicia, you have to listen to me about the raid."

"Wrong. I'll not hear one more lie come out of your mouth. I never should have believed you. I won't make that mistake again," she spit the words before walking away.

"Stop," he yelled at her back. "If the rumors are true, Lucifer will slaughter every last man to have the bounty for himself. You're no match for him. He'll blow the *Ruby Mist* out of the water." Chills shook his voice. "I-I admit, I was wrong to go to Wilson without telling you, but I was only trying to protect you. I promise you to be completely forthcoming from this moment on. Untie me. Let me come with you at least. You're going to need every man you can get out there. I swear to you. You can trust me."

Alicia turned back and gave a slow shake to her head. "But you can't trust me, Richard. Haven't you learned your lesson, yet. You should never trust a pirate."

Lifting his baldric from the sand, Alicia removed his pistol and tossed it nearby. "There's that one shot I promised you, however."

"Alicia…"

"Goodbye, Ducky."

Chapter 38

"Ah, *dé·jà vu,* does this scene not look *familiar?* All that is missing is your jaunty hat."

Richard opened his eyes and groaned. His body wracked with tremors. He was slowly freezing to death. The tide had made its turn and the frigid water was to his mid-thigh. His balls were trying to retract into his body, and his cock was in serious danger of frostbite. He'd rubbed his wrists raw trying to get free from the blasted dock post he'd been tied to. Now this.

"God must have a wicked sense of humor, no?" Jocelyn and her ice queen, Raine, stood at the edge of the water. Jocelyn held a lantern high.

Raine tipped her head and appraised his frozen appendages. "My, my," she mused. "It is true. They do shrink in the cold."

Richard jerked at his bindings. "Instead of gawking at me, bloody untie me!"

"I'm not soaking my skirts for you," Raine scoffed. She ran a hand down the front of her gown.

"Dammit." Jocelyn handed off the lantern, kicked off her shoes and stockings, hoisted her skirts, and waded in. "When did they leave?"

"Don't know. Less than an hour? I have to go after them. The patrol has been tripled. They'll never make it past the sound."

Jocelyn struggled with the wet ropes. "Do not worry. There is no patrol tonight."

Richard shot her a look as the ropes finally let go. His shoulders burned as he took a moment to rub at his wrists before reaching into the water to retrieve his breeches still floating around his knees. The shock of yanking the cold, dripping garment over his arse had him gasping. "I know for a fact Wilson increased the patrol tonight."

"That is not what I have heard. You are not the only one gathering information, *Lord Dunbar*." Jocelyn cocked an eyebrow at him. "Do not look so surprised. I have known what you were up to since you arrived."

Jocelyn stood back on dry land and began wringing the water out of her hems. "You might think you are so very clever and know how to use Governor Wilson's influence, but *Mistress* Wilson knows everything and has ten times the influence of her husband. She is privy to all her husband's business, all the business of his associates. What do you think the women at her weekly teas talk about? Plus, she knows every inch of this town and where to buy all the best things." Jocelyn pointed a finger at her chest. "And she knows the only way to get the best price is to bring me the best information. Wilson's playing you like he plays everyone. Except his loving wife Gladys."

"Well, there's one tidbit of information even Gladys doesn't have yet because I'm the only one who has put the pieces together. It concerns your husband Ric and his possible involvement with the Mississippi Company in Louisiana." At Jocelyn's gasp, Richard held up a hand. "I'm only concerned with Alicia right now and what she might be sailing into." He dropped into the sand and took off his boots to pour out the water before shoving them back on his feet. "Why would Wilson pull the patrol when the biggest shipment of the year is sailing tonight?"

"Because he is not going to risk his precious patrols against the likes of Lucifer. That is what I came to tell Alicia."

Richard shook his head. "That was just a rumor."

"Not a rumor if it is true, no? Lucifer has Wilson under his thumb. They are working together. How do you think Lucifer has avoided capture all these years? But this shipment is much too valuable for Wilson not to want his share. He is smart enough to know the White Pirate is out there, too. She's bested him twice now, and he is not about to give her another chance. He will not lose a prize this rich or have her make him look the fool again. If Alicia manages to get close to that shipment, the orders are to scuttle the *Ruby Mist*. No quarter given."

No quarter given meant they would leave none alive. Panic chilled him more than an hour freezing his balls off. "I have to get to her." He rubbed at his forehead. "Let me think. I know they'll position offshore before they attack. A bay up the coast. She's coordinating men and carts to transfer the goods back to you. What was the name of that cove?" He frowned, then remembered. "Brighton. Brighton Bay."

Jocelyn tugged at his shoulder. "Take my carriage. It's faster."

"If I hurry, I have a chance of reaching them in time and stopping them before they sail." Richard retrieved his baldric from the sand and grabbed for his pistol. "If not, and Lucifer sees them..." He couldn't finish the sentence, the thought made him want to retch.

"Alicia is impetuous, not stupid. I warned her about Lucifer. Described his ship." Regardless of the conviction of her words, worry lined Jocelyn's face. "She would not dare to cross swords with that bastard, would she?"

Richard called over his shoulder as he raced toward Jocelyn's carriage. "I think she might. She's angry and hurt. Thinks I've betrayed her. You know what she's like. Proud. Headstrong. Out to prove something. Tonight especially."

Jocelyn chased after him. "You must stop her! If Lucifer catches sight of the *Ruby Mist*, he will destroy her and kill them all."

* * * * *

"Have the men keep an eye out for any sign of another ship. Be ready at my order to raise those sails. The lead ship will be empty. As will the ship at the tail. It's the ones in the middle we want." Shrug nodded and left her standing at the helm.

Alicia used her glass to make slow repeated sweeps of the horizon to starboard. *"You love me. You've always loved me."* Richard whispered words wound about her chest like a chain and circled endlessly to tangle in her mind. Her anger still burned white hot, however. Seeing him at the ball tonight had stripped away everything that had happened between them over the last few weeks. It was only fitting that she stripped him as well.

Leaving him and setting sail, Alicia paced the deck from stem to stern and back. She'd been a fool. How many times did the man have to crush her heart before she learned her lesson? Well, she's bloody well learned it now. Fury waged battle with the pain in her shattered heart. Alicia rubbed the heel of her hand over the ache in her chest. But her rage, she was forced to admit, was more at herself.

Over the last few weeks, she had pushed herself to become the strongest she'd ever been. Forced her way headlong into a man's world. Toughened her resolve. Sharpened her edge. Taught her how to fight. But tonight, it felt like she was all at once back in that drawing room. A silly, daft girl. Powerless against a naïve heart that yearned for something she'd never have. Foolish enough to believe a man...ney, foolish enough to believe *Richard Dunbar* had changed. Reckless once again in giving him the power to captivate her. Seduce her into trusting him with her love again.

The muscle in her jaw threatened to crush her back teeth. Enough. Looking out across the black water tipped with moonlight, Alicia straightened her shoulders. It was a night for victory. They were ready for a fight. And come the first gray light of dawn, when the *Ruby Mist* anchors back here in Brighton Bay with its crudely fashioned anchor of stone, and its stores full of bounty, she'll talk to the crew about what lies ahead for them all.

If the *Monique's* logs are true and Ric headed south into the gulf, the *Mist* was more than capable of making that journey now. Jocelyn could come with them. They could begin the search for Ric together and Alicia could put the memory of Richard Dunbar firmly and completely out of her mind for good. She'd managed it once before. Almost. She'd manage it this time if it took the rest of her bloody life. Last time she'd buried her hurt in seducing Parker Lanford. Tonight, she'd bury it in a far more satisfying conquest.

"Light, Capt'n." Shrug pointed off their stern.

Alicia found the light in her glass. "That's her." To Shrug she added. "We'll sit here and let her sail past. At the back of her draft, we'll ease out of the bay on half sail to catch number two. I want you and the men to man the starboard guns when we decide to come in for the attack. Tell Kent to put one over their bow. No slipping through the mist tonight. No sneaking in like children stealing sweets. Tonight, we come in hard and fast. Let the stories of the White Pirate run wild and true. I'm done hiding behind my skirts." She threw her mask over the rail. "Black Point and the bloody world can know my name is Steele."

Shrug gave her a nod and a quick salute. "Aye, Capt'n. Steele." Shouting her orders to the rest of the crew, their eager rush of excitement washed over the deck. They were ready. Half the sails set. Now they wait.

Through her glass, Alicia watched as the first ship sailed past to disappear into the moonlit night quietly and undisturbed. The next ship in the line would not be so lucky.

Alicia checked her pistol as the now familiar wave of adrenaline surged through her. It was finally upon them. All the work and training, and she was in command. The time had come. This was her night. They'd all been building to this for weeks. Working day and night to get the ship ready. Function as a crew. They—They, the men, her… Richard.

A nagging thought wormed its way through her brain as Alicia set her glass aside and gripped tight to the wheel as the ship began a sluggish move out of the bay. If Richard truly wanted to betray them, why would he have gone to all the trouble to get the *Ruby Mist* and her ready for this raid?

Alicia jerked at the wheel and gave herself a mental shake. That didn't excuse his actions concerning the patrol, however. He knew they were waiting for them and said nothing. Was it his plan all along to save them and prove her incapable? Set her up to fail? Did he think she'd still reconsider if the battles got too intense? If the risk became too great?

But what if she was wrong? His words echoed in her memory.

"Why don't we take the Ruby Mist *further north. Run by the stars, enjoy the sail. Greet the dawn, and sail home again. Surely we can let one sail past."* He had tried to convince her not to raid the *Monique*, but she hadn't been swayed. She was too caught up in securing their logbook and looking for Ric. Had Richard been trying to protect them by getting them out of harm's way, and she hadn't listened?

"Capt'n, there she be." Shrug's call shook her from her memories.

"Mister Kent, make ready to announce us," Alicia ordered, pulling the ship's wheel again to starboard.

"She's moving fast, Capt'n."

At this speed they'd never catch her. "Full sail, Simms." The men scrambled to follow the order.

The ship still pulled with all her might to port. "Anchor secured, Tippy?"

"Aye, Capt'n."

"Why is the *Mist* handling like it's broken loose again?"

Tippy rushed to the newly repaired rail and peered over just as the sails caught and the *Ruby Mist* began her chase in earnest.

A sudden report of cannon fire split the night. "Are we being fired upon?"

"Nay, Capt'n. Seems we ain't the only one announcing

ourselves," called Kent.

More cannon fire erupted.

"Glass!" Alicia ordered.

Shrug raced aft and took the wheel while she peered into the night. What the bloody hell was going on?

The flash of cannon fire from the merchant ship's starboard side lit the scene as if it were day. There was a third ship. Three masts. The *Ruby Mist* was dwarfed by both ships, one was a frigate and the other, a huge brigandine and both were in a race for speed with every inch of canvas they had.

Alicia couldn't make out the flags of the other attacker. "Hard to starboard."

"We'll never catch 'em at this speed, Capt'n."

More explosions filled the air. "I'm not about to join their fight. It would be rude to cut in on their dance. I'm happy with waiting for the next." Alicia continued to watch the "dance" through the glass. If she could only make out the other ship's flags.

Another blast sounded from the merchant frigate. Seemed it wasn't pleased with its dancing partner. Alicia watched as it toppled the other's forward mast. The foresail of the brigandine was clear to see in the brightness of the cannon's blast. It was black.

A cold thread of unease wound about Alicia's chest. The frigate raced ahead of their wounded attacker and fired a final round from their rear cannon. It was then Alicia saw the flag. She only caught a glimpse. Icy panic raced down her spine. Red. Horns and a spade tail. The air rushed from her lung, "Dear God, it's the *Devil's Breath*." The words slipped between her lips.

"Did you just say *Devil's Breath*?"

Alicia looked back at Shrug and nodded. "Lucifer."

"Bloody hell, we be aimed straight at 'im."

"Then bloody hell, un-aim us. To port. Hard to port!"

It was too late. Both ships had been on a direct course to overtake the frigate, and when the merchant ship slipped through their fingers, the two were left headed straight at each other.

"We can't outrun 'em, even wit 'em runnin only two masts. They out gun us, out man us a good twenty te one."

"Don't tell me what we can't do. Tell me what we can." Alicia watched the *Devil's Breath* grow closer by the second.

"Jump ship?"

A shot over their bow ended the discussion. Lucifer was upon them. They'd run out of options. "No. We're not jumping ship. We're fighting for all we're worth."

"We ain't worth piss," Shrug spit. "Not agin' the Devil 'imself."

"Then it will be a short fight, won't it?" Alicia spit back.

The distance between the ships closed fast. *Devil's Breath* towered over them. Alicia called out to the crew, "Hold fire!" If they fired their few starboard guns, there wasn't time to reload. They'd be dead in the water. "We defend our decks and nothing else!"

Pistols, swords, and knives were drawn as the men positioned themselves for the fight. It could all be for nothing should Lucifer decide to unleash the *Devil's Breath* and deliver a broadside attack. There'd be nothing left to defend. Alicia held her breath waiting for the blast that didn't come. Instead, the thud of boarding ladders echoed over the water. The crew of the *Devil's Breath* began to scream like banshees. The sound was horrifying.

A fear greater than anything Alicia had ever experienced chilled her blood as she pulled her pistol and braced it on her forearm. Her knees threatened to abandon her. "Hold your positions! Wait for my order. God's speed, men!" Her voice shook.

Tippy panicked and shot wildly at the first man over their rails. The man behind stopped Tippy with a clean shot to his shoulder knocking his gun to the deck. Chaos erupted, and the battle was on. The crewmen from the other ship were few in number but massive in size. They laughed at the ease in which the *Mist's* crew was so quickly overpowered and subdued. Alicia watched in horror as her men were brought down by less than a dozen of Lucifer's men.

Before she could fire a single shot, a huge man swung from the *Devil's Breath* and landed mid ship. His shoulders made Tippy look like a half-starved street urchin. He wore a red topcoat over breeches the color of mud and scarred bucket top boots. A wide brimmed hat was pinned on one side revealing dark ginger hair and a long beard to match. His baldric carried three pistols. A knife was lashed to his thigh, and the blade of his unsheathed cutlass flashed in the lantern light.

"Lucifer." Alicia had her pistol braced and pointed at his chest.

The man took off his hat and dropped into a dramatic bow. "Milady."

"I-I'd welcome you aboard the *Ruby Mist* h-had you been invited." A shaking started in her knees. Alicia fought to keep her teeth from chattering.

He laughed and looked around. "I've been in bathtubs bigger than this bit of driftwood. Here I'd thought you'd be sailing something a bit grander. More suitable to your rank and standing. You are the White Pirate I've heard so much about, are you not? And tis true what they say about you being a woman, after all," he mocked.

Alicia narrowed her eyes at him. "The breasts give me away."

He laughed at her again. "Well, I've no fight with you or your sad ship of castoffs. You've had a nice little run, but I'm here now. Time for you to leave. The sea is mine."

"I don't think so. You've overstepped your boundary. Aren't you a fair deal further north than you're supposed to be? This part of the sea is mine." Alicia shook with false bravado. "But there's plenty to go around. As you say, I'm certainly no threat to you. Release me and my crew and we'll keep to our side of the shore. There are four more ships heading this way tonight. We'll take one and you can have the other three."

Lucifer chuckled but his face grew dark. "Do I look like a man who shares? Aye, there's plenty to be had tonight, and it's all mine. Take what belongs to me and I'll smash your little ship into splinters and serve you and your pathetic excuse for a crew to the sharks."

He moved closer. His gaze traveled the length of her as he gave her a cold sneer. "But maybe I'll keep you for myself, now that I've had a good look at you." He ran a hand over the swell in his breeches. "Might make a nice warmer for my bed."

Alicia cocked her pistol.

He cocked his eyebrow. "So you want to play, do you?" Lucifer turned to the man closest to him. The one holding a cutlass over a badly beaten Shrug. "Kill him."

The man raised his blade and in one motion Alicia reached into the top of her boot and threw her knife in his direction, hitting him in the thigh. The man screamed and all at once the deck erupted. The crew of the *Ruby Mist* was down, but they were by no means out. Shrug grabbed Alicia's knife and sliced the man's throat as Tippy used the commotion to snap the neck of the man holding him.

Lucifer launched at Alicia, and she fired. He laughed maniacally when she missed, pinning her brutally to the mast. His massive forearm threatened to crush her windpipe. He growled into her face, "You've played with the Devil, *little girl*. Now you're gonna feel the fires of hell." His eyes darkened to coals as he knocked the smoking pistol from her hand with the butt of his sword.

"I wouldn't call her *little girl* if I were you. She hates that." A voice came from behind her. "Step away."

Alicia twisted her head. *Richard?* He looked as if the ocean had spat him out. Seawater dripped off the blade of his cutlass. *How?*

Lucifer shoved her aside, knocking her to the deck and took a mighty backhanded swing at Richard, while he pulled a pistol from his baldrick. He pointed it at Alicia's face.

Richard rushed him and barreled his shoulder into the man's midsection. The pistol flew out of his hand, but Lucifer was quick to recover and shoved Richard back to swing on him again. This time, his blade connected.

Richard let out a scream as Lucifer delivered a deep slice across the top of Richard's arm. Blood bloomed from the wound. The sickly color raced down his sleeve. Alicia cried out to him as she scrambled to her feet to face Lucifer once more, sword drawn. With one sweep, the force of his blade ripped hers from her hands and knocked her back. He laughed at her again before he turned back to Richard. "Time te die."

Around her, men lay dead and injured. Alicia struggled to pull the pistol from the baldrick of a dead man. The smell of his blood made her retch. The pistol's grip was slick as she fought with two hands to cock the weapon. Turning back, she watched in horror as a laughing Lucifer raised his cutlass high over his head. Richard dove to one side and reached for Lucifer's pistol still laying on the decking.

Alicia aimed at Lucifer's chest and fired. Richard raised Lucifer's pistol and fired at the same moment. The twin blasts hit and lifted the big man off his feet and tossed him like a child's toy. His back snapped the rail when he landed hard against the side of the ship.

Alicia rushed to Richard and pressed her hand against his wound to staunch the flow of blood.

More cannon fire exploded around them. The third merchant frigate of the night was upon them and was seemingly prepared to blast their way past the *Devil's Breath* remaining crew with or without their infamous captain.

"We have to get out of here," Richard insisted, "before we're caught in their crossfire."

Tippy knocked the boarding ladders one handed into the waves along with their previous owners before sliding pale faced to the deck. Simms had a nasty wound to his head, and Kent had a shot lodged in his thigh. Shrug looked as if he cradled a broken arm, and Fitz lay unconscious in a heap in the stern.

"We'll never outrun them," argued Alicia.

"Of course, we will," insisted Richard. "Douse the lights and help me with the wheel."

Alicia helped him to his feet and slipped under his arm to hold him upright. Blood still seeped from his wound as he grasped the wheel and maneuvered the ship sharply to port.

"Hold it steady until I tell you to let up." He slumped against the rigging.

Alicia's hands shook on the wheel. Adrenaline, fear, and shock ricocheted through her. She clutched at the pegs to keep her legs from buckling. The edges of her vision hazed.

What the hell just happened? Was she dreaming? In her vision things seemed to move silently at half speed. Was she lost in some strange, twisted nightmare? Did she really just kill a man? Did she just kill bloody Lucifer?

In the flashes of cannon blasts behind them, Alicia jolted back into consciousness and looked out over the blood-stained deck of the *Mist* where every member of her crew lay injured or worse. Had Fritz moved? The ugly smell of blood still filled her senses. Each cannon blast behind them felt as if it echoed in her chest.

And Richard? Emerging from the sea like some sodden, sword-swinging tidal wave? She kept looking toward him, fearing her mind had simply conjured him. Perhaps none of this was real, and he was still lashed to a pier with his pants around his boots.

"H-how? How did you get here?" Her voice sounded strange to her ear.

"Holding on by my fingernails, no thanks to you. You bloody

well dragged me behind the ship for the last two miles. I've been hanging onto the aft tow line since you left the bay."

Alicia gaped at him. "Are you insane? Why didn't you call out?" Off the rear bow, the battle against the *Devil's Breath* continued to light the sky and shatter the air.

"Given how you left me tied to a damn dock, I figured you'd cut me adrift if you knew I was back there." He reached out and eased the sharp steer of the ship, closing his fingers over hers.

"Richard…" The warring of her emotions toward him mixed with the rest.

"You were sailing into trouble, Alicia." He left her side to slide down the ropes and sit against the hull. "I also know how you hate it when I try to protect you from getting yourself bloody well killed." He fingered the raw edges of his wound and winced. Dropping his head back, he closed his eyes.

Alicia lashed the wheel steady and went to kneel before him. Tearing a strip from the hem of her blouse, she tied it tight around his arm. The heat of his body penetrated through the cold shock of hers. She rested a hand on the crisp hair of his chest and felt the strong beating of his heart beneath.

He wasn't a figment. He was her Richard. Her stubborn, irritating, exasperating, maddening, magnificent Richard. He was her tether. Her anchor. Through all of this he'd been there. When she needed him most, and even when she didn't. Any anger she may have felt had been cast aside. "I do hate it when you try to protect me," she said softly, sending a silent prayer of gratitude that he did just that tonight. "Do you also know how I hate it when you're right?"

Richard opened one eye. "I was right?"

"When I saw you at the ball earlier, I saw the old Richard. *Lord Dunbar*. The wastrel, the drunk, the man who broke my heart all those years ago."

"Alicia, I—"

She put her fingertips over his lips to stop him. "Please, let me finish. I got so angry when I saw you. Blinded myself to the truth. But you aren't that man anymore. You haven't been him for a long time. All these weeks you've only wanted to help me, tried to shield me, teach me, fight by my side, and...and..."

"Love you." He held her gaze.

"Yes, love me." Alicia cupped his cheek. "I didn't trust it, didn't trust you. That was where I was wrong."

"What was the part where I was right? It's so rare I am, I'd really like to hear that part." He grinned.

"You didn't betray us. You tried to warn me off attacking the *Monique*. I didn't listen."

"I would never knowingly put you or this ship in any kind of danger, Alicia." He reached out to her with his good arm and stroked her shoulder.

"I know that now." Leaning forward, Alicia placed a kiss upon his lips. "I'm sorry."

"You tied me to a bloody dock."

"I am sorry about that, too." She kissed him again.

"Jocelyn and *Raine* found me."

"I'm *truly* sorry about that."

Chapter 39

It was the broken crew of the *Ruby Mist* and not carts overflowing with bounty that arrived at Jocelyn's backdoor in the middle of the night. Raine was set to the task of stitching wounds and setting bones. "You're paying me extra for this," she grumbled, but eased the pain of each man as best she could.

Alicia put willow bark on to boil and gathered whatever else Raine might need.

Jocelyn wrapped a blanket around Alicia's shoulders. "You're covered in blood. Is any of it yours?"

Alicia looked down. Jocelyn was right. She looked as if she'd walked through a massacre. "I don't think so." Alicia studied her stained hands and plucked at her ruined shirt.

"What the hell happened out there?" Jocelyn added wood and more water to the fire to boil. "I've been sick with worry."

"Lucifer." Saying the name aloud brought the whole scene into focus once again. Alicia pulled a deep breath to steady the renewed trembling in her legs.

Jocelyn's eyes grew round. "*Lucifer?* How is it you're standing here and not lying at the bottom of the ocean?"

Alicia rubbed a hand over her eyes and looked back at her men.

"By all rights we should be, but he underestimated us, underestimated me. He certainly didn't see us as any threat. Boarded us with less than a dozen men. Left the rest of his crew back on the *Devil's Breath*."

"Fool called her a little girl." Richard added and winced in pain as Raine took needle and thread to his shoulder. He growled at her. Raine growled back.

"And?" Jocelyn looked between the two.

Alicia saw the flash of powder in her mind's eye. Relived the buck of the pistol in her hand. "I shot him," Alicia admitted.

Richard fired her a look of disbelief. "No, *I* shot him."

Alicia rose and planted her hands on her hips. "Yes, after *I* shot him."

Jocelyn held up her hands in surrender. "What does it matter, who shot him?"

"It doesn't, I suppose." She frowned at Jocelyn, but pointed to herself and mouthed, *Me.* "After that, the merchants must have been prepared to run into the *Devil's Breath*, because they were more than ready to defend themselves against any attacks." Alicia watched as Raine applied herbs and a fresh bandage to Richard's arm. "We took a beating, but we fought hard, and by some miracle, we're still afloat." She turned back to Jocelyn. "We'll be back in business once everything, and everyone is patched up."

It was close to dawn before all the injured crew had been tended. Raine had been amazingly swift and efficient. Jocelyn made room and makeshift beds for all and insisted on helping Alicia wash away the evidence of the night's violence from her.

Alicia took Richard into her room where she laid him beneath her quilts and bid him some rest.

"Lie with me." He gripped her hand and refused to let go.

"You need to sleep." Alicia shook her head.

"I'll sleep better with you next to me." Richard gave her hand a small tug.

Alicia sat on the edge of the bed and removed her shoes before lying out alongside him. Exhaustion made her body hum. Richard pulled her close to his side and kissed the top of her head. Holding her tight, he whispered into her hair. "When I came over that rail tonight and saw Lucifer, I thought my whole life was over. My worst fear was coming true. I was going to have to watch that bastard kill you."

"I had the same fear. Something went cold in me. I thought he would kill you, and I wouldn't get the chance to make amends to you. Tell you how sorry I was not to trust you. Beg your forgiveness for what I'd done." Alicia rose up on an elbow and held his gaze. She slipped a hand over his chest. His heart beat strong beneath her palm. "If you had died without me telling you how much I love you one more time…"

Richard smoothed a hand over her hair. "You can tell me now."

"I love you and promise I'll tell you every day, should it be my last."

In the dim candlelight of the room, he held her gaze and brushed his thumb over the edge of her lip. "And no more doubts?" Richard asked.

"None," she whispered.

He gave her a scowl. "And no more tying my sorry arse to docks?"

She kissed him and shook her head. "No more. I swear."

"You have to leave. Now." Jocelyn rousted them both from a sound sleep. "Get up."

Alicia rubbed at her eyes. Richard groaned, "What time is it?"

"What does that matter?" Jocelyn tossed them their clothes. "There is not time to waste. You have to go." She gripped Alicia's arm and pulled her from the bed. "Widow Harper just left. Wilson knows it is you. He knows you are the White Pirate, and he is sending the Watch to arrest you." She looked back at Richard. "He knows you have played him for a fool as well, and the two of you are together. He means to hang you both. You must leave. Now."

Alicia struggled into her boots. "What about you?"

Jocelyn began stuffing things into a leather bag. "I am claiming *la méconnaissance,* ignorance. I had no idea who you were. Last I knew the *Ruby Mist* was listing to one side with a broken mast. Besides, he would not dare arrest me. I know too bloody much." Jocelyn raced around the room gathering Alicia's things. "Take the *Mist* and go. North. It is safer north."

"But Ric went south. We know that now."

Richard hissed a sharp breath against the pain as he sat up. "If what I learned is true, he may have gotten himself embroiled in some form of land fraud led by the French and a Scotsman named Law."

"My promise to you still stands, Jocelyn. If I go anywhere, it will be to find him." Alicia continued as she hurried to help Richard dress.

Jocelyn put her hands over her ears. "Do not tell me more. It is better if I do not know where you're headed." She pushed the hair back from her face. "But bless you." Jerking her chin toward the door, she urged them on. "Go. Raine is waiting out back. The main roads are crawling with the Watch. It's too dangerous, no? She'll bring you through the woods to Brighton Bay. Sail off. Go quickly. Do not tarry. Do not come back. Wilson has more men waiting at the cove for you." Jocelyn handed Alicia the bag and pushed them both out of the room.

By the time she and Richard got outside the others were already in the cart. Raine sat in the driver's seat wearing the native clothing Alicia had once seen her in. "Let's go." The other members of the crew looked at her with curiosity, but none seemed brave enough to question her appearance. "The Watch comes. We have to go."

Alicia turned back to Jocelyn. Sadness clutched at her heart. "There's so much I want to say to you."

"There is no time for sentiment, *mon cheri*." Jocelyn helped her into the cart and pulled a delicate lace handkerchief from her pocket. Raine clicked to the horses to move. Jocelyn followed the cart and reached out to Alicia, "Take a piece of me. If you find Ric, show him this. He will recognize my lace."

"I'll find him. I promise." Alicia was barely able to snatch the square of delicate cloth from Jocelyn's hand before the cart pulled her away. "We're not finished, you and I. This isn't the end."

Jocelyn put her fingertips to her lips and sent them into the growing light of the new day. *"Au revoir, mon cher."*

As Raine moved the cart along paths invisible to anyone but her, Alicia clutched the bit of lace to her chest. She looked back at Richard and the others and shook her head. "We are a motley crew, all broken and bruised. Stitched together. Sailing off on a ship held together with patch and spit and nothing but a stone anchor. Wherever are we going?"

"I hear the waters in the gulf are warm and the most amazing shade of blue. A man could rest his bruised body in that warmth." Tippy winced as the cart jostled over the uneven terrain.

"Maybe buy a new anchor?" Liam suggested.

Simms piped up, "Maybe steal one?"

"Try our hand at stealing something more than teacups and frills?" Shrug added, cradling his broken arm.

Alicia nodded, considering. "Perhaps."

Richard wound his good arm about her waist and pulled her to sit close to his side. The first rays of sun filtered through the trees and bathed his face in golden light. Alicia ran a hand over the scruff of his morning beard. The stress of pain showed on his face. "Or," he whispered low enough for the others not to hear. He rested his forehead against hers. "You and I could forget all of this, the whole lot. Send these men back to their lives. Abandon the *Mist* to her stone anchor and board the first ship we find sailing east. Go home to England. Get married. Make love every night in an actual bed that doesn't smell of pine tar soap and my feet don't hang over the edge. Fill an estate with raucous children and watch each other grow old."

"Perhaps." She kissed him and positioned him to rest against her. Her finger entwined with his. The only sound was the plod of the horse's hooves on the soft earth and the gentle squeak of the cart around them as they moved through the thick growth of trees. The men were quiet. Perhaps all were contemplating their futures like she and Richard. They were good men. Fine seamen, each one of them. They worked hard and fought harder.

Alicia considered releasing them from their bonds and abandoning the *Ruby Mist* to sail for home. To a life without danger. Without pistols that tried to kick their way out of her hand and guns that made her ears ring. A life without risking her life and the lives of others, just for the thrill of adventure and the exhilaration of each conquest. A life without wounds to stitch and blood-slick decks.

She pondered what a quiet, calm future with Richard would look like. Back in the lush green rolling hills of Weatherington. Living in a grand estate. Making love in their soft, wide bed.

No more ravishing each other on the hard desk in her quarters with the last heat of the day glistening on their skin. Or naked swims in the cool waves of the sea. Or together, side-by-side, at the wheel of the *Ruby Mist,* sailing through a clear, cloudless night, floating in an ocean of stars.

Alicia tightened her hold on Richard's hand and gave it a squeeze. Closing her eyes, she stretched out her breeches-clad legs and crossed one booted foot over the other. Alicia smiled to herself as she pushed away any thoughts of leaving her new life behind.

"Perhaps *not*."

Author Note and Acknowledgments

Once upon a time… How often do adventures begin with that phrase? Well, dear readers, I am thrilled to be starting out on this new adventure with you. Years ago, I began this journey and fell in love with my pirates and their stories. I didn't want them to end. I bonded with these characters and simply didn't want to close the book on them. But life happens and the world changes and there just didn't seem to be a home for my stories. No welcoming harbor for my ships. However, like "Alicia" in **THE PIRATE WORE WHITE**, it is time to strike out on my own and follow my destiny. It proves to be a wild ride and I feel blessed to have you come along with me as we head into another voyage with a new series,

THE LACED LADIES OF BLACK POINT

I have a favorite quote from Edward Teller that reads, "When you get to the end of all the light you know and it's time to step into the darkness of the unknown, faith is knowing that one of two things shall happen; either you will be given something solid to stand on, or you will be taught how to fly."
The "solid" is the love and support of my dedicated readers who wanted more stories, and the counsel and assistance of my guides. My mentors and partners, editors and contemporaries, who have cast light on the unknown and helped me take this epic first step into the world of Independent Publishing.

I want to thank Kathy, Peggy Nancy, Mary Ann, Theresa, Beth, and Leslie. And of course, the Bunnies, for their skill and talents. You lift me up, and I bow to your greatness!
As always, I thank my family, who is my strength.
I also want to thank Tim for my stunning cover. Your talent takes my breath away.
And I need to give special thanks to Claire C. Thank you for the gentle encouraging push. You reminded me that I have wings…

It's time to fly.
XOXO ~Lisa

About the Author

Lisa Olech loves art, pirates and a cranky curmudgeon she affectionately calls the Wizard of O. Currently the author of ten Romance novels in both the contemporary and historical genres with perhaps a touch of paranormal mixed in for flavor. A true hybrid author, Lisa uses witty dialog with a side order of sexy to bring to life multi-faceted, adventurous, smoldering characters you'll not soon forget.

A 2018 RITA Award nominee for her book, Within A Captain's Soul, the final book in her Captains of the Scarlet Night series, Lisa's won a variety of writing contests and achieved the ranks of Amazon Best Seller with her debut book in 2014.

Living on the shores of On Golden Pond, Lisa shares a drafty, old Victorian house with a wizard and two schizophrenic cats she brought into the house in an attempt to fill her empty nest and keep her from talking to herself in a British accent. As an author, artist, Justice of the Peace, and aspiring beekeeper, Lisa finds true inspiration in the beauty and love that surround her. And, she takes full credit that three homes on her quiet New England street now proudly fly a Jolly Roger from their flagpoles.

www.lisaolech.com
Facebook: https://www.facebook.com/Lisa.A.Olech.Writer
Twitter: https://twitter.com/LisaOlech
Goodreads: https://www.goodreads.com/author/show/7478599
Instagram: Lisaa.Olech
Pinterest: https://www.pinterest.com/lisaolech/

Other Titles by Lisa A. Olech

STODDARD SCHOOL OF ART SERIES, Published by The Wild Rose Press

Picture Me Naked
Rock Solid
Against The Wall

CAPTAINS OF THE SCARLET NIGHT SERIES, Published by Kensington, Lyrical Press

Within A Captain's Hold
Within A Captain's Treasure
Within A Captain's Fate
Within A Captain's Power
Within A Captain's Soul

GHOSTS OF NEW ENGLAND: SKULLERY BAY, Books From a Romantic's Heart Publishing

Widow's Walk / The Last Kiss